A Murderous Malady

ALSO AVAILABLE BY CHRISTINE TRENT

FLORENCE NIGHTINGALE MYSTERIES

No Cure for the Dead

LADY OF ASHES MYSTERIES

A Death on the Way to Portsmouth (A Lady of Ashes Short Story)

A Grave Celebration

Death at the Abbey

The Mourning Bells

A Virtuous Death

Stolen Remains

Lady of Ashes

A MURDEROUS MALADY

A FLORENCE NIGHTINGALE MYSTERY

Christine Trent

NEW YORK

Published in the United States by Crooked Lane Books, an imprint of The Quick Brown Fox & Company LLC.

Crooked Lane Books and its logo are trademarks of The Quick Brown Fox & Company LLC.

Library of Congress Catalog-in-Publication data available upon request.

ISBN (hardcover): 978-1-68331-929-0
ISBN (ePub): 978-1-68331-930-6
ISBN (ePDF): 978-1-68331-931-3

Cover design by Melanie Sun
Book design by Jennifer Canzone

Printed in the United States.

www.crookedlanebooks.com

Crooked Lane Books
34 West 27th St., 10th Floor
New York, NY 10001

First Edition: May 2019

10 9 8 7 6 5 4 3 2 1

For Lori Papadakis
Who entered my brother's life and
completely transformed him.

How very little can be done under the spirit of fear.

—Florence Nightingale, writing to "Aunt Hannah" Nicholson, May 1846

PROLOGUE

August 1854
Soho, London

Elizabeth Herbert was a firm believer that, to be respected, one must look and act respectable at all times. She was her most fashionable and respectable now as she settled back against the tufted burgundy leather of the Herbert landau.

The roofless carriage clattered roughly along the cobblestone streets, which after two centuries had become unconscionably uneven, broken, and—in her opinion—downright dangerous. The weather was bordering on stifling hot, but at least it was overcast, so there wasn't a merciless sun stewing them in the open air.

The carriage had made its way into a less desirable part of town on its way to its destination. Hadn't there been a rumor of cholera cases springing up around here lately?

Elizabeth heard the coachman shout, "General à Court and Mrs. Herbert coming through!" as he snapped his whip smartly in the air.

No doubt some young boy was chasing a dog into the road, or vice versa. Hopefully, whoever it was wouldn't stumble upon the street pavers as he scampered out of the way.

Elizabeth reflected that her life of wealth and privilege came with great power. It was readily evidenced by the command that was immediately obeyed, if the fact that their carriage hadn't ceased its forward movement for even an instant was an indicator.

But she had another firm belief, which was that any power must be accompanied by an equal measure of duty to others. Thank God her husband, Sidney, also believed this, and proved it every day as he toiled away in the Aberdeen ministry, reorganizing inefficiencies as he organized as humane a war as possible in the Crimea.

Elizabeth—Liz to her family and close friends—brushed away some errant blonde tendrils that had escaped her hat as she smiled wanly at her father sitting in the seat across from her.

General à Court did not catch his daughter's glance. He gripped the edge of the carriage, leather on one side and glossy black metal on the other. His calloused, work-hardened hand was incongruous against the luxury of the supple leather and newly painted exterior.

Her papa was an old war-horse, having joined the Army in 1801 and progressed through the ranks to lieutenant-general just three years ago. Even now he was advising Sidney on the conduct of the war in the Crimea.

Elizabeth didn't care to understand the intricacies of troop movements and casualty figures, all of which only served to make her think of the childless mothers and husbandless wives being created almost daily.

No, she much preferred to contemplate how she could be a help to her husband—and, by extension, her father—in bringing a quick and successful conclusion to the war.

Such work on her part would hopefully not only serve to limit the numbers of shot, stabbed, diseased, and disfigured British soldiers, but also bring glory to the Herbert name.

"Oomph," her father grunted as the carriage wheels managed to find a deep rut between the cobblestones. "Give me a horse's back any day to one of these bone-crushing torture devices." À Court huffed out another breath of disapproval.

This time, Elizabeth's smile was affectionate. "I'm sure we will arrive at the museum in a few minutes, Papa." Father and daughter had planned an excursion together to the British Museum, as Sidney was locked away in private meetings all day in which the General had no part.

"I was thinking we might have luncheon afterward at—" Elizabeth's proposal was obliterated by the sound of shouting between the coachman, Joss Pagg, and another man. The horses pulled up short and she pitched forward, inelegantly caught by her father, who gently pushed her back into her seat.

"What the deuce?" he demanded, using a favorite phrase of Lord Nelson, that great admiral who had been England's salvation from the French nearly forty years ago.

À Court turned stiffly to look over his shoulder, where he could see what Elizabeth now witnessed. The man had attempted to jump up with the coachman, but from his position on the seat, Pagg kicked at the man with his heavy boot.

The man, whose clothing did not suggest he was any sort of ruffian or vagrant, howled in outrage as he tumbled into the street, where he was nearly trampled by a taxi passing in the opposite direction.

As it was, the man quickly bounded to his feet, his pants soiled with straw and clods of horse dung. He shouted mostly gibberish at Elizabeth and her father, pointing wildly as his eyes rolled around. But not everything was gibberish. No, the man shouted something at her that was utterly terrifying in its accusation. Wherever had he come up with such a slur against her?

Now thoroughly frightened, Elizabeth's mind hardly registered the chaos happening before her eyes. The carriage halting in the middle of the road . . . her father rising from his seat and raising a menacing fist at the deranged man, who was now melting into the crowd . . . the driver cracking his whip overhead to scatter people away . . . the sound of the horses whinnying in fright . . .

She heard a faint buzzing in her ears, then felt an odd sensation of being detached from the events surrounding her, as though she were floating above them as casually as a puffy white cloud over Hyde Park. Everything was simply surreal—what sort of lunatic attacked such a fine carriage in broad daylight?—and she wasn't able to make sense from any of it.

The cloud evaporated as if releasing a torrent of rain and moving off, and then Elizabeth heard several loud cracks. At first, she was confused, for it seemed as though Pagg had developed unnatural skill with his whip.

But then she saw the look of horror on her father's face. Worse, she heard a strange hiss in her ear. It penetrated the buzzing, startling her out of her shock.

Elizabeth shook her head, and as a stray silk petal escaped her hatband and gently fluttered to the floor of the carriage, she saw Pagg crumple from the driver box down to the cobblestones with a sickening thud.

Then she, too, fell, her last thought being that the bit of silk flower was no cushion at all.

CHAPTER 1

Istill stood in the main hall of the Establishment, unable to make any sense of the letter in my hand. What did Sidney mean, there had been an attempted murder of his wife? Why would anyone wish to harm Liz?

Well, I wasn't about to waste time sending another letter back to him, even if there would be at least one more postal pickup for the day.

"Goose?" I called out, knowing that my faithful companion, Mary Clarke, would be somewhere nearby.

Sure enough, she materialized next to me in moments. "Yes, Miss Florence?" she said. "What may I do for you?"

She had once been the beloved wife of my old childhood tutor, Milo Clarke. He had unexpectedly died of a stomach obstruction, leaving behind a grieving widow with no means of support.

My mother had sent the stout and sturdy Mary to me, ostensibly as a companion, but without question as someone to watch my movements here at the hospital, a place Mother considered no better than a brothel.

Because of her sometimes silly and frightened manner, I had quickly dubbed Mary "Goose," which she didn't seem to mind.

"I need to go to Herbert House," I announced.

She immediately smoothed back one side of her graying hair and said, "I'll get my notebook." She turned on her heel to retrieve her writing implements, as she had quickly learned that I always had thoughts, ideas, or notes that needed to be committed to paper.

"No." I stopped her with a hand to her shoulder. "I will go alone."

Mary frowned. "Alone? The streets are always so much safer when we walk in pairs, aren't they? Even in the middle of the day."

She clasped her hands, and I knew she was resisting the urge to wring them together.

"I cannot have you there. I think it is too private a family matter." I held out Sidney's succinct note for her to read.

Herbert House
Belgravia

Flo, come quickly—Liz was attacked in her carriage—nearly murdered—do not want police involved.

—S

Mary handed it back wordlessly.

I took Sidney's letter back and in its place handed her the rest of the mail, which included an astonishing letter from Richard, to place in my study. Much as I wanted to scurry to my room and reread Richard's missive over and over to make sense of why he was reaching out to me *now* of all times, I had to put him resolutely from my mind. There would be time enough to dwell on him later.

Mary's skin had taken on the pallor of a rotten lime. She swallowed several times before asking tentatively, "But why would someone wish to harm a friend of yours?"

Until that moment, it hadn't occurred to me that an attack on Liz might have anything to do with *me*.

★   ★   ★

I was ushered into the Herberts' elegant double townhome by a servant. The minutes seemed to tick by endlessly until Sidney finally came to greet me with kisses to both cheeks.

The secretary at war was a handsome man—equally matched in looks by his pretty wife—and had a fiery drive and ambition that I greatly admired, even if I didn't always agree with some of his decisions. But what did I know about the conduct of a military conflict?

He ushered me up a wide staircase to his wife's suite of rooms two floors up, explaining the situation as we quickly climbed the steps. My one hand was safely tucked into the crook of his elbow for support while my other clutched my drab brown-and-black-checked work dress to keep me from tripping.

I regretted that I had not thought to change into a more elegant dress before dashing into a taxi.

"Liz and the General were headed through Soho on their way to the British Museum for a visit to their new Anglo-Saxon war weapons collection. I was none too happy about it, as there are rumors of cholera in that area, but Liz's father believes himself indestructible, and that, by extension, he can prevent any harm from ever coming to his daughter."

"He must have done so in this instance," I said, taking a glance sideways at Sidney as we reached the top of the walnut staircase.

Sidney's expression was inscrutable, except for a small tic at the outer corner of his right eye. There was a small mole there I had never noticed before, not that I made it my occupation to study the facial features of my dear friend's husband.

"Yes," Sidney said noncommittally. "As the open landau got caught up in traffic, a madman appeared and virtually jumped up onto the mounting step."

I halted in midstride as we approached Liz's private rooms. "Are you saying she was attacked inside the Herbert carriage? With the General right there?" My incredulity overshadowed my surprise.

I could hardly comprehend how anyone would do that, unless perhaps he was out of his mind with gin or opium.

"Actually, no, and that's what makes it so damnably frustrating." Sidney led me the remaining steps to Liz's rooms and paused with his hand on the polished brass knob. "The man seemed to vanish into the crowd when the General threatened him."

I waited, knowing there must be much more to this story.

"The actual attack came from a pistol somewhere in the crowd," Sidney told me.

"Heavens!" I exclaimed. "How do you know it wasn't from the same man who tried to jump into the carriage?"

"Both Liz and her father insist it wasn't. But I haven't told you the worst part." Sidney sighed heavily, and now I was terribly fearful that Liz had been bodily injured or disfigured.

"Enough shots were fired that one of them found my coachman. He's dead."

I instinctively put a hand to the lace collar at my throat. "Sidney, how terrible," was all I could manage. "Does he have a family? A wife and children?"

"Fortunately, no. And I confess I am relieved Liz was not the victim. I'll bury the man out of my own purse, of course. He was excellent with the horses and knew all the quickest routes throughout the city. He won't be easily replaced. But dear God, if it had been Liz . . ."

Sidney shook his head, unable to voice his thoughts on such an outcome. He twisted the knob as he lightly rapped on the darkly stained door.

"Come," barked a gruff male voice from inside the room, even as Sidney was opening the door and stepping aside to allow me in.

Liz and her father reminded me of an old masterpiece painting. Liz sat up in her carved tester bed, encased in freshly laundered and ironed snowy-white sheets. She wore an elegant burgundy dressing gown and lace cap with matching, dangling ribbons over perfectly coiffed hair.

At least I could thankfully see she had not been physically harmed.

In a chair at the left side of the bed was the General, leaning forward and fervently clasping his daughter's hand. It was sweet, yet a bit . . . dramatic.

I did have a vague remembrance of having met General Charles à Court before. He had struck me then as a proud military man, and that notion was not dispelled now.

Liz had told me years ago that he had gone to Parliament in 1820—the year I was born—to represent Heytesbury upon the death of his own father but had resigned the seat after only a few months. I suppose military men used to strict discipline do not fare well in the pell-mell bedlam of politics. I imagine they find war to be much more rational.

He had later gone to Afghanistan and served to quell an uprising against the East India Company rule in 1842. Later, the General had been given the colonelcy of the 41st Welsh Regiment of Foot in 1848, a post he still held. I wasn't quite sure what a regiment of foot was, although it sounded like infantry—men walking—to me.

Liz had referred to him as the General ever since his promotion to lieutenant general, and that was how I thought of him now. She spoke confidently of how he would one day be promoted to full general, and I had no doubt of it either, particularly with his current work at the War Office, assisting his son-in-law in various unofficial capacities.

He scowled darkly and sat ramrod straight in my presence, although he did not release Liz's hand.

"Flo!" Liz brightened visibly. "Sidney promised me that nothing would keep you away."

She gently disengaged her hand from her father's grasp and held both arms out to me in open invitation. I remained on the opposite side of the bed as I bent over to kiss her cheek and readily accepted her embrace.

"I came the moment I received his note. What happened?" I stepped back, and the moment she dropped her arms, the General picked up her right hand again.

"Didn't her husband tell you himself?" the General said accusingly before Liz had a chance to reply. I sensed Sidney bristling behind me.

"He did, but of course I wanted to hear it from dear Liz

herself." I sat on the edge of the bed, while Sidney moved over to the fireplace mantel along the wall nearest me. A heavily figured brass urn dominated the mantel, which was also littered with other bric-a-brac. He managed to surreptitiously move aside a couple of figurines to allow room for his elbow.

It was ironic to me that all the Herberts' public spaces were done in the old formal Georgian style, all pastels and light and exquisite plaster moldings, but up here in their private spaces everything was in the latest fashion of overstuffed heavy furniture, bold wallpaper patterns, and thick draperies in multiple layers across the windows.

"It's of no matter," the General said. "It is the police we need for this, not some skirted nurse."

Sidney sighed heavily. "Father," he began, offering a term of endearment to his father-in-law that was not reflected in his tone, "I told you that—"

"Yes, yes, we don't want notoriety brought upon the household." The General was repeating a notion with which he obviously didn't hold. "I'll say it again, then. We need to hire a private investigator."

"A private investigator is still not someone to be trusted," Sidney said patiently. "He would have no loyalty to us, and no doubt this event would make for juicy gossip. Imagine the bulging pouch of guineas one of the local rags would be willing to hand over for a lurid story about the secretary at war's wife. We cannot have such scandalous distractions while we are trying to prosecute a war."

Still holding Liz's hand, the General threw up his other hand. "So you are willing to permit the lunatic to come after my dear girl again because of your precious reputation?" Now the General's scowl was directed toward his son-in-law. "Uncon-scionable, my boy. Perhaps I should take matters into my own hands."

I sensed that Sidney was controlling himself with everything he had. He was an important man in Her Majesty's government and no doubt unused to being chastised for his decisions. The prime minister and Liz were probably the only people in the world who could challenge him, and neither would be so boor-ish about it.

Yet Sidney allowed it, and I knew it was a sacrifice he was willing to make for his adored Elizabeth.

"Father," he began again. "I have no intention of *permitting* a lunatic to come after Liz. However, I do intend to be cautious and intentional about my actions. I've called Miss Nightingale to us not only because she is Liz's friend but because she has already proven an investigative talent in a situation at her hospi-tal. We can trust her, and I believe she can help us."

"Papa," Liz jumped in, cajoling her father with a winsome smile that made it impossible to remember that she was already the thirty-one-year-old mother of three children, the most recent having just been born in May. "I'm sure Sidney knows best. Why don't we simply have tea with Florence and see if she can help us?"

Sidney left his place at the mantel and went to the hallway, where he entered into murmured conversation with a passing servant.

I sat on the bed next to Liz so that she was on my right side. Now I could more easily see both the General and Sidney. The two of them reminded me of caged tigers: wary, watching, and dangerous to cross.

"Tell me everything," I urged. "You know that I will do anything I can to be of service to you, dearest."

Liz quickly brushed away a sudden tear. The incident must have been horrifying, for my friend had never been anyone I considered to be of a nervous or hysterical nature. In fact, I couldn't recall ever having seen her weep, not even when her mother died.

"Papa and I were headed to the British Museum. They have a new collection of Anglo-Saxon weapons, you know. I was anxious to show it to Papa, what with his military leadership. We decided to go on Saturday, since he wasn't needed that day at the War Department. When we—"

"I told Sidney I should have gone down to study the War Department maps while he had his little henpecking party with the prime minister." The General was glowering again. "Those maps are riddled with errors. For instance, they never accurately reflect the distance between harbors and encampments."

"Yes, Papa." Liz smiled fondly at her father and addressed me again. "I finally had my father to myself and was quite happy that he had to put the maps away for a day."

That effectively silenced the General, although I suspected that he had been torn between his fatherly love for Liz and the need to rectify the War Department maps that might cost life and limb in a future battle.

Liz continued her tale. "As we traveled through Soho, the streets became so very crowded and narrow, much more so than they are here in Belgravia. It made it all so confusing, you see. Poor Pagg, he had to deal with something in the roadway and we came to a stop. He is typically so conscientious about ensuring that the carriage continues moving. That was when this deranged man came from nowhere and practically jumped into the carriage with us. He—" Liz halted her narration and shuddered delicately upon remembrance.

"He managed to perch himself atop the folding steps. I frustrated his attempt to enter the carriage," the General said, adding his own disquieting details to the account.

"Yes, Papa," Liz said again. "What was terrible was what he was shouting at me. It was so vile I can hardly repeat it."

The General interjected again. "I'll tell you what he—"

"Father, isn't it best if we let the women talk?" Sidney said, again employing a patient tone that I suspected was reaching its limit.

I wanted to take Liz's other hand in my own but refrained, lest she feel like a marionette being worked by two puppeteers. "Whatever he said to you was merely the ranting of a madman. You didn't recognize him, did you?"

"Of course she didn't!" the General said.

This time Liz didn't gently admonish her father but merely ignored him. "I have no idea who he was. I've been wondering to myself if perhaps I've met him before and caused some offense of which I was unaware, and he has now fallen upon hard times and is misguidedly seeking revenge upon people in his past."

Certainly her idea wasn't out of the question, but she still hadn't told me what it was the man had shouted at her. "Whatever he told you must have led you to believe this, I presume?"

Liz shuddered again. "It was terrible. He said—he said—" She took a deep, sustaining breath. "He pointed a finger at me and said that I was the British Bitch and the Babylonian Whore. That I knew it and would be made to pay for it. I apologize for my coarse language, but that was what he said. I confess I felt like Marie Antoinette riding to the guillotine."

Something registered in the General's eyes, but I didn't know him well enough to know what it meant. I could have sworn that it almost looked like guilt. Perhaps I would feel guilty, too, if I thought myself a towering figure of a man who had been unable to prevent his daughter from being insulted like this, not to mention from nearly being murdered.

"But that is positively ridiculous," I began, feeling greatly affronted for my dear friend. "You—"

It was as if the General couldn't help himself. "It most certainly is ridiculous! How dare he? When I find him, I will rip out his heart with my hands and feed it to him." General à Court closed a fist in the air as if he already had the man's heart in his hand and was readying to carve it into pieces.

I admit I was somewhat taken aback by the General's gruesome declaration, but I continued speaking, concluding that Liz's father might be best ignored. "You are the most faithful of women, in both your marriage and in your friendships. There has never been the slenderest wisp of scandal smoke associated with you. Or Sidney, for that matter."

Now it was Sidney's turn to shift uncomfortably. I wondered fleetingly what I had said to cause him sudden disquiet. Or was he merely vexed by the madman's accusation toward his wife? I had to remember that Liz had almost been killed. Any husband would be upset and uneasy.

Liz nodded. "I don't know why the man was so unpleasant. Worse, there was someone else so unhappy with me that he tried to kill me. Why, Flo?"

It baffled me also. Liz Herbert might be the wife of a famous man, but she herself was perfectly innocuous. "Who knew that you were going to the museum?" I asked.

"What business is it of anyone's where my daughter and I go?" the General demanded.

"Father, *please*," Sidney said through gritted teeth.

He said no more, for a maid arrived with a tea tray. She deposited it on a table without a word, offered a quick curtsy, and left. Since Liz was in bed, I took on the duties of hostess and poured fragrant hot cups of tea for everyone. The General refused to partake and instead dropped his daughter's hand and sat back, arms crossed on his chest in a belligerent stance.

"Well," Liz began, lips pursed in serious contemplation as she stirred a lump of sugar in her cup. "Of course Sidney knew. And my maid, Nichols. Poor Pagg knew, since he had to drive us. Why, I suppose all the servants were aware of it."

"Anyone else outside the house?" I probed, thinking that someone had to have known in advance that she would be in Soho at that exact moment.

She looked at me helplessly and shrugged. "I don't think so, but I suppose it's possible I mentioned it to someone somewhere."

I turned my gaze to Sidney, who had seemingly drained his tea in two gulps and was already setting the empty cup back onto its saucer. "Did anyone at the War Office know?" I asked.

Sidney shook his head confidently. "I don't discuss my wife's activities with anyone."

That left only the General. As I regarded him, he turned incredulous. "I am here as a lonely widower assisting my son-in-law while between assignments. Whom could I possibly tell?"

That was a bit of an overstatement. Liz's mother, for whom she had been named, had died just before the General was due to come back from Afghanistan. When he returned, he had simply never mentioned her again. Liz was positive her father made "certain trips to town," as she euphemistically referred to them, but he had never seemed to develop an attachment to another woman.

Nevertheless, someone associated with the killer—for that's what he was, even if he hadn't murdered his intended target—had known that Liz would be in Soho yesterday. All of a sudden, I had a thought.

I looked straight at the General. "Is it possible that Liz wasn't the intended target but that you, sir, were?"

I instantly knew that the General thought it not only possible but probable. It was only then that I noticed the sunken, haunted look around the man's eyes, which told the real story of his worry, pain, and again that tinge of guilt.

"Utter nonsense," the General muttered, but he avoided my gaze, and his protestation was unconvincing. I would have to find a time to talk with him privately.

Sidney, though, was thoughtfully nodding. "It would be easy enough for anyone to have seen the General and me walking in London together. If someone was angry at me, he might have actually tried to get at me by shooting my father-in-law."

Liz handed her cup and saucer to me as she shook her head. "My love, you are very romantic to think the shots were not intended for me, but it was obvious that I barely avoided being killed, whereas the bullets were wide of their mark where Papa was concerned."

There was no use in continuing this line of speculation, so I directed the conversation elsewhere. "What did the police have to say about it? Surely they were involved in the immediate aftermath of things?"

"Actually, no," Sidney admitted. "Our tiger riding on the back of the carriage reacted very quickly and bravely. He actually jumped down from the landau, ran forward, and hopped onto the driver box, then maneuvered the carriage out of there before matters could get any worse. I shall probably promote him to Pagg's position. In any case, I chose not to involve the police"— he flicked an inscrutable glance at his father-in-law—"and now I'm hoping that you can help us find out who did this, Flo."

All we knew was that a man had attacked the carriage, shouting obscenities, and then presumably a second man had fired shots at Liz, fortunately missing her but killing the Herberts' driver. There was no discernible motive for the act, and in all likelihood it had just been one of those random senseless acts that seemed to occur every day in London. I had no idea how I might be able to actually solve the mystery, but Sidney and Liz stared at me expectantly, so I didn't have the heart to admit that.

"Well, I shall certainly try," I said with more conviction than I felt. "I suppose I should get straight to work. Liz, I believe I would like to talk to your maid."

CHAPTER 2

Alice Nichols was fairly young for a lady's maid, in her late twenties by my estimation. She had nice quarters, directly above those of her mistress on the floor containing chambers for the Herberts' children as well as their guests. It surprised me that Nichols was not relegated to the servants' quarters in the attic. She was clearly one of Liz's favored servants.

In fact, I noticed a bell on one wall of her room attached to a cord that ran down the wall and into the floor, obviously providing Liz a way to directly summon her maid.

The room was furnished in secondhand pieces, but they were of high quality and better than the iron bedstead and pine chest that adorned most maids' rooms. Nichols also had an overstuffed feather pillow on her bed and several layers of bedcoverings, as well as an extra bucket of coal on her small brick hearth. She even had a recently applied floral wallpaper of pink and red-purple cabbage roses against a pale-green background.

The most interesting aspect of Alice Nichols's room, though, was a street scene painting on the wall over her oak headboard. It appeared to be of Windsor, judging by the familiar round turret shown in a background shadow. The tightly packed buildings, men and women walking about, and animals in the street were all portrayed very realistically inside the ornate gold frame. It had been done by an oil painter of some talent, and likely beyond the means of a lady's maid. It was also an unusual furnishing for the room of a servant such as this. Normally one would find a keepsake sketch of a family member, or a stitched sampler representing the servant's skills. Perhaps the painting had been a gift from the Herberts on some previous Boxing Day, but it struck me as extravagant.

However, it was none of my business and had nothing to do with the attempt on Liz's life.

Even more interesting than her room was Nichols herself. She was, frankly, striking and unusual, not at all a typical lady's maid. They were often more like Mary Clarke—older with faded beauty, frequently a poor or unmarriageable relation who found companionship with neither the family nor the staff. Alice Nichols, however, was . . . vibrant. That was the only word I could put to it.

She wore Liz's cast-off clothing, as I would have expected, and there was a lovely cameo at her throat. Her hair was long, spiraled, and the striking red of a sugar maple in full autumn color. She wore it tied back loosely with a ribbon so that it tumbled down her back like a blanket of fallen leaves on a river.

Nichols had large, expressive brown eyes framed with dark lashes and a tiny mole above her upper lip that only served to add to her exotic beauty. I confess I was surprised she wasn't married. I was also rather startled that Liz would allow her maid to outshine her this way.

"Welcome, Miss Nightingale, isn't it?" Nichols ushered me into her room as if she were a medieval estate's chatelaine. "Mrs. Herbert said you wished to see me? I didn't expect you to come to my room but thought I would meet you in one of the public rooms. Or perhaps in the basement."

Nichols tilted her head to one side, as if determining whether I was of Liz Herbert's station or more of her own, given my plain, workaday clothing.

"I saw no need to disturb anyone's routine belowstairs. I don't believe we've met on my previous visits. I am an old friend of Mrs. Herbert's."

I saw calculation in her expression now that she understood me to belong upstairs. "Of course, madam. She has been through a terrible time, as I am sure you well know." Her words seemed friendly enough, but she was definitely guarded against me.

I smiled to set her at ease. "I do indeed. Poor Liz, to have endured such a violation of her person." I figured that referring to my friend in familiar terms would make Nichols feel that I was bringing her into my confidence. "You can imagine that she is most anxious to see this lunatic removed from the streets."

Nichols exhaled on a long "Ohhhhh yes. What are the streets of London coming to that a woman of quality is unsafe even while out riding with her kin?" With a careless flourish, the maid put the back of her hand to her forehead. "It makes one despair of the future of mankind, doesn't it?"

A bit dramatically put, but an understandable sentiment.

"It truly does," I murmured. "I was wondering, though, if you can possibly help to shed light on the events of yesterday. You are, after all, closer to Mrs. Herbert than just about anyone else."

Nichols preened at the flattery. "I am. I know her moods and preferences and dislikes very well. For example, she adores the work of Hancocks Jewellers but does not care much for Mr. Robert Phillips's designs. She also prefers her silks to be bro-caded instead of taffeta—too noisy, she says. Mrs. Herbert also insists on gardenia scent for her bath, but lavender for her drawer sachets. I even know—"

"You certainly do have an excellent grasp of your mistress's preferences, Mrs. Nichols," I said, giving her the honorific of a married title even though I knew she was not.

She nodded at the compliment, tilting her head downward so graciously that I was almost willing to believe that she came from a more distinguished background than most women in her position.

"I was right, then," I continued, "to think that you were the appropriate person at Herbert House to help me."

She raised her head, and I saw spots of color flush her cheeks. "In any way possible, I would be happy to do so, but I don't know what I can offer you."

Ah, the sin of pride that courses through the veins of men and women alike. I liked to think myself impermeable to the scourge of that sin, but of course I was not. I had endured so much insult and scoffing at my ideas that how could I not help but preen when someone praised my efforts at cleaning up a hospital . . . or cleaning up a murder? This young woman in front of me had surely suffered her own slights in an unenviable position as lady's maid, so how could I blame her for puffing up now?

"I'm sure you can be most helpful," I said, continuing to encourage her. I noticed that she was not inviting me to sit, although with only one chair in the room, it would have made seated conversation awkward. "How long have you attended to Mrs. Herbert?"

Nichols tilted her head to one side and looked upward, as if in earnest thought. It was an exaggerated motion and made me uncomfortable for reasons I could not identify.

"She hired me when she and Mr. Herbert moved into the

house, so that would be three years ago." Her head came down and she smiled at me, as if pleased that she had provided the right answer.

"You answered a situations vacant column?" I asked.

This time her head bent toward the other shoulder. "Mmm, not exactly. Mrs. Herbert found me through Mrs. Birtles's servant agency. She wanted an entirely different staff here in London than what she had at Wilton."

Hmm. I could understand that, for staff such as parlor maids, cooks, and the like, as a family would have one set of servants continuing on at the family manor and another set tending to the family during the London Season. However, personal servants, such as the valet and the lady's maid, would frequently travel with the family, for they had no job to do within a household without the master and mistress there.

How Liz managed her household was none of my business. And perhaps her previous lady's maid—whom I recalled as having been of advanced age—had not wished to come to London, given that the Herberts were planted here for longer than just the Season each year.

I must have been quiet for too long, for Nichols said, "I came with excellent references, you know. I have a particular talent for dressing hair." At this, she pantomimed brushing and then braiding hair on an invisible head in front of her. Despite the fact that the maid was using only her hands, I understood exactly what she was demonstrating for me.

"I'm also skilled with a needle." Now it was no surprise to me that she portrayed the threading of a needle and making stitches on invisible fabric.

Alice Nichols was probably quite entertaining to Liz on long rainy days when Sidney was locked away in his office.

"And with a paintbrush?" I asked, nodding toward the oil painting on the wall.

She slowly turned to look at the painting, as if she wasn't aware of its presence. She turned back to face me and bit her lip. "That was, er, a gift to me from a dear friend." Nichols nodded, curls bouncing against her shoulders, and I had the distinct sense that she wanted me to nod as well, as if to indicate my agreement that the picture was, indeed, a gift. Why did she feel a need to do that?

Instead, I simply stared at her, then walked to the head of her bed to examine the painting more closely. It truly was well done. I felt I could almost walk onto the dusty street and peer into a shop window.

I glanced in the corners of the painting. In the lower left corner, it was signed "C.H.W. à Court." À Court? That was a family name of Liz's. It looked as though it really had been just a gift from the Herberts to a favored servant. I did have other questions for Nichols, though. She might have insight into what the other servants—

"Please, miss," Nichols entreated, putting the back of her hand to her forehead as if she might faint. "I haven't told the mistress that it didn't mean anything, but it truly doesn't. I shouldn't like there to be any trouble."

Now she clasped her hands in front of her and shook them together, as if pleading for her life. Whatever was she talking about?

"Pardon me?" I said, waving my hand so she would stop the dramatics. "What sort of trouble?"

"Oh." She bit her lip again. I think she suddenly realized ʼat I hadn't discovered any sort of wrongdoing of hers.

"Mrs. Nichols," I said gently. "Surely you didn't steal this painting from your mistress, did you?"

Her eyes widened. "No, never. It was truly a gift. I thought you had figured out—I thought you knew that—oh." Nichols sat down on her bed, both hands to her cheeks, which were flaming up almost in competition with her mass of hair.

Well, at least now I had an opportunity to sit down myself. I joined her on the bed.

"Are you hiding something from Mrs. Herbert?" I asked quietly.

Seconds ticked by. In the distance, I heard the wail of William Reginald, who was now all of three months old, followed by heavy steps and cooing noises. The crying ceased.

Nichols rose from the bed and crossed the small room, turning again to face me. She kept her arms clasped around her waist, as if she were holding a cracked marble statue together. "Not such that she would know it. Please, I would be dismissed without a character reference if she knew, and it would cause all sorts of bother with the family."

Was I already to be led astray from my burgeoning investigation? "Why don't you tell me the story of this painting?" I suggested kindly.

A single tear, impossibly large, rolled down her face and ended precisely at the corner of her lips. She brushed it away prettily and swallowed. "Not many people are aware, Miss Nightingale, that I have dreams of becoming a great actress."

I was fairly certain that anyone spending more than ten minutes with Alice Nichols and her antics would realize that. I said nothing.

"Mrs. Herbert's brother, Charles Henry, was rather fond of

me." She glanced at me tentatively, gauging my reaction to this news.

Charles Henry à Court was Liz's only sibling. I vaguely recalled having seen him from afar once, although Liz had mentioned him affectionately on numerous occasion. In fact, she had held a wedding breakfast for him in March. I had not been invited to the small affair but had been aware of it.

"Exactly how fond of you was he?" I asked evenly. "And did his fondness extend beyond his wedding day?"

Nichols blushed furiously. "No, of course not. It is a truth that all of the world's great love affairs must always end in disappointment. I, alas, am no different from all of the mortal women on this earth."

Now she spread her hands out in supplication to her audience of one.

"A woman's love goes where her heart leads her, whereas a man's love is led by his family's approval," she said in a loud stage whisper.

What twaddle.

"Men and women have always been guided by their families, Mrs. Nichols," I reminded her firmly. Certainly I had battled my own over the past few years and counted myself fortunate that I had managed to secure my own path in life. "And they have also always allowed their hearts to muck up their lives." Of this, too, I had nearly been a victim. "Did you . . . muck up Mr. à Court's life?"

I could hardly believe I was having such a conversation. I had barely started this investigation and already felt as if my skirts were mired in river mud.

"Quite the opposite, Miss Nightingale." She sighed and melodramatically put a slender hand over her heart. I was struck by how odd I found it that Liz would continue to keep Nichols on. Her entertainment worth had already plummeted in mere minutes for me. Surely Liz was far too astute to be taken in by this.

"Charles Henry—Mr. à Court, I mean—and I met at Wilton during the May Day celebrations last year. My poor mistress had just had little Sidney here at Herbert House and was not completely recovered, but she insisted on returning briefly to the family home to be present for May Day.

"I assisted her in handing out pennies to the girls carrying their garland sticks. It was a lovely time, so peaceful and informal, what with Mr. Herbert and the children remaining here in London. It was as if I were her companion, not just her lady's maid." Another sigh and a glance to the ceiling, from which dangled a modest iron gasolier. One of the jets didn't work, so only two of the three were sending flames up behind their glass globes.

"Mrs. Herbert contracted a mild cold, though, and was in no condition to attend Wilton Fair the following week. She bade me go on my own, and Charles Hen—Mr. à Court—offered to let me ride in his carriage."

I probably could have finished the tragic story for her at this point but let her continue.

"We spoke of so much on our trip back and forth. He was such a gentleman, and he asked me many questions about myself. He was so interested in what I had to say. I even worked up the nerve to tell him about my dreams of acting. He didn't mock me at all. He said I was a beauty and would have wonderful stage presence."

I had no doubt he had said all that.

"He confessed to me that he was an artist—and acting is an art too, you see—so that we were kindred spirits. He had painted a considerable number of works, some of which hang inside the family home. But his father doesn't think it a suitable pastime for the man who is intended to carry on the family name. There are no children other than Mrs. Herbert and her brother, you know."

I nodded impatiently. "Yes, Mrs. Herbert and I have been friends for many years, Mrs. Nichols."

She seemed unaware of my irritability and continued the story in her own dreamy state. "After Mrs. Herbert and I returned to London, Mr. à Court found reasons to come to town— meetings with the family banker, museum trips, and the like— and he always stayed at Herbert House so we might find some time together."

Another advantage of Nichols having quarters on the guest room floor. Surely Liz had had no idea what was happening above her head.

"He had started to talk of long-term plans with me. Finding our own lodgings together, maybe even running off to America. There is an important school of painters in upstate New York, and Manhattan has many theaters. We would have been so happy." Nichols smiled and stopped talking, caught up in her own reverie.

"But it was not to be . . . ?" I prompted.

She shook her head. "No. General à Court had already seen Mrs. Herbert married off in 1846, and Charles Henry was three years her senior. He needed to be married, and his father wanted the marriage to be as brilliant as his sister's."

"And a brilliant match was not to be had in his sister's lady's maid," I said flatly.

Nichols's eyes glimmered, but this time tears did not spill down her cheeks. "No. It's not as though the à Courts are aristocrats, are they? Did Charles Henry *have* to marry outside of his desires?"

"But your mistress married an up-and-comer, and the General has already made a name for himself. It wasn't unreasonable for the family to have expectations," I pointed out.

She sniffed and her eyes were clear again. "No, I suppose not. So the next thing I know, Mrs. Herbert is telling me in March of this year that her brother is engaged to a Miss Emily Currie."

"When did he marry?"

"Miss Currie had the nerve to plan her wedding right around the time Mrs. Herbert was due to deliver little William Reginald. Thoughtless little . . ." Nichols drifted off for a moment before coming around to finish her tale.

"Well, anyway, Mr. à Court was so kind and gentle about it all. He came to me before the wedding and explained about how he couldn't disappoint his father and, despite his great tenderness for me, he had to follow his father's wishes and marry Miss Currie, who came from a good background and had a yearly income. She isn't artistic at all, though."

It was such a typical story of a servant falling under the spell of someone upstairs, despite Nichols's fancy that it had only ever happened to her. I thought to tell her so, but why put her in more pain? Besides, I had my own tale of woe with Richard, even if he and I were social equals.

"The Herberts hosted a reception for Mr. à Court and his wife. You can't imagine what it took for me not to break down in hysterics."

Unfortunately, I could.

It would have been unthinkable for me to have had to endure Richard's wedding breakfast two floors below me. I repressed a shudder. Nevertheless, Alice Nichols was not as upstanding as Liz believed her to be. But I was not about to insert myself into it, for I had other work to do, and I had no idea how helpful Nichols might eventually be.

"As for the painting?" I asked, prompting her again.

Her face cleared at this remembrance, and her smile was genuine. "It was so clever of Mr. à Court. Mrs. Herbert admired her brother's abilities with a paintbrush, even if her father did not esteem them well. He told his sister that he would likely be giving up his art entirely once he married, and as such he wanted to give her two paintings: one for herself and one for her favorite servant, whoever that might be. He knew, you see, that I would be the recipient."

I shook my head. "And Mrs. Herbert didn't find this idea to be odd?"

"Oh no, Mrs. Herbert thought it a splendid idea. So it was his way of giving it to me without Mrs. Herbert questioning it hanging on my wall."

"I see," I said, thinking that perhaps I didn't wish to know any more.

"Mr. à Court left me a message in the painting," Nichols continued with a flippant toss of her red curls. "Do you see it?"

I rose to approach the painting once more, and she joined me on the other side of her bed. I could see no words in the picture other than his scrawled signature in the corner. "No," I said, continuing to study the picture in vain.

"Here," she directed, pointing to a portion of the street scene where a couple walked arm in arm, facing each other. "This represents Mr. à Court and me."

I squinted at the place she indicated. I had to admit, the two figures did resemble Liz's brother and Nichols. As sad and sordid as the maid's story was, though, I couldn't see that it had any relevance to my investigation, and it really only served to dredge up my own past hurts. And I was balancing on a very fine line between keeping the maid's confidence and having a responsibility to my friend. It was time to change the subject.

"Thank you for being forthright with me," I said to conclude our conversation. I was careful not to commit to keeping her secrets, something I wasn't sure I could do, depending on how things unfolded. "However, I am more interested in the conduct of other people in the household."

Now we stood facing each other across her bed. I felt a little foolish conversing with her across her mattress but hid my discomfort behind an encouraging smile.

Her expression was one of disappointment. "Oh, of course. About whom are you curious?"

Now I wished I had Mary Clarke at my side to take notes about this conversation. Why had I told her not to accompany me?

"Well, have you noticed anything odd among the servants in the household?" I said.

"What do you mean? Mrs. Herbert is a good mistress and keeps the staff in line."

"Yes, I'm sure she is," I said soothingly. "For example, is there anyone new on the staff? Have there been new delivery people at the rear entrance?"

She shrugged. "I wouldn't know, Miss Nightingale. Those are questions for the housekeeper. I take most of my meals alone up here and don't frequent the kitchens. In truth, I don't know the other staff very well. I have to make myself available for Mrs. Herbert, so there's no time for consorting with others."

But there had been plenty of time for Charles Henry à Court.

I kept that sharp retort bitten under my tongue and tried another tack.

"Perhaps a stranger has been in the house?" I suggested. "Someone you didn't recognize, who may have behaved abnormally in your estimation?" I was truly grasping for a short quill inside a plump feather pillow, but I was at a loss as to how to proceed on this investigation for Sidney.

Nichols formed another exaggerated expression on her face, this time one of great thought. I repressed a sigh of annoyance until finally she said, "I suppose you mean the General."

I stilled. "Mrs. Herbert's father? I know he has been staying here over the past few months while working with Mr. Herbert. Does he have peculiar visitors?"

Nichols considered this. "Not peculiar themselves, exactly. It's just that I can hear people coming and going at odd hours. Early in the morning before the staff arises, or late after everyone has gone to bed. His visitors don't ring the bell, of course. He must be on the watch for them, for it's as if it is quiet in the house one moment, and the next I hear whispering."

This was far more relevant information to me than her unrequited passion for the General's son. "Is the whispering that of a man or a woman?"

"I cannot say for certain. The noise floats up through the floor grate, but it is quite muffled by the time it reaches me."

I almost laughed aloud. I would have bet the Nightingale family fortune and home that Alice Nichols spent considerable hours on her knees with her ear to the grate, straining for gossip.

"What makes you certain that it is the General receiving guests, and not Mr. or Mrs. Herbert, or even one of the servants?"

Alice Nichols smiled again, this time condescendingly, and began ticking off the reasons on the fingers of one hand. "Because, my dear Miss Nightingale, there were never any mysterious visitors until my mistress's father came to stay. Not only that, the master and mistress never leave their rooms during the night, other than to visit each other. And we servants are far too tired to be traipsing about the house once we're done with our day's duties. A process of elimination, as they say."

What she said might or might not have been true. Servants were known to do plenty in the middle of the night while their employers lay slumbering. For the moment, though, I accepted her explanation.

"Is there anything else you can tell me about the goings-on here at Herbert House over the past few weeks?" I asked, ready to terminate the conversation as unfruitful.

"I'm sure I don't think so. All I could possibly know is what Mrs. Herbert knows, since I am with her almost round the clock. Is there a way to reach you should I remember something?"

I dug out a card from my reticule and handed it to her.

She read aloud: "Miss Florence Nightingale, Superintendent. The Establishment for the Temporary Illness of Gentlewomen. Number One Harley Street." She frowned. "Are you . . . a nurse, miss?"

"Yes, I run a small hospital in Marylebone."

I almost burst into laughter again at the look of distaste that openly passed across Nichols's face. Here was the actress lifting her nose at the nurse. I was used to dripping contempt from society members, but not from house staff. "You can see me there should you have anything more to add. Now, I should like to talk to the tiger who drove Mrs. Herbert's carriage to safety."

I could see that Nichols wasn't sure whether to keep my card or hand it back to me with two fingers. Manners finally prevailed, and she tucked it into her dress pocket. "You must mean Isaac Bent. He was the one on the carriage with Mr. Pagg."

I agreed that Mr. Bent was exactly whom I needed to see. I felt unsettled as I left the room with Nichols. Had I really learned anything from her, or had her interminable theatrical performance been a complete waste of my time?

I was fresh from solving a murder at the Establishment that had sprung from unrequited love. Based upon what Nichols had just told me, I hoped I wouldn't be facing the same situation again so soon.

★   ★   ★

After my odd meeting with Alice Nichols, I sought out the brave young Isaac Bent who had steered the Herbert carriage to safety. A servant offered to fetch him from the stables for me. I made my way down to the kitchens to meet him, as I didn't think Sidney would approve of my interviewing a servant with straw, dust, and the odor of dung clinging to him in the family parlor.

He was a bit old for a tiger—probably about fourteen, I surmised, given his small, wiry frame and coltish movements. However, he now wore a coachman's uniform of a white shirt beneath a black vest, with camel-colored breeches and black boots—not quite the typical striped livery of the tiger. Isaac was still in the throes of excitement over his brush with danger and his newly acquired fame at having rescued his mistress and her father from danger. His cheeks were flushed, and his gaze of radiant joy was barely able to focus on me, almost as if he were in the thrall of a deeply mystical experience. I introduced myself to him and invited him to sit with me at the large dining table in the servants' hall. I sat in the middle chair on one side of the table. Isaac placed himself at the far end of the table, making it impossible to have a normal conversation together. I realized that he was used to being seated at the opposite end from the butler or whoever was the highest-ranking servant in the Herbert household. Without a word, I got up and moved down until I was directly across from him.

"So, Isaac, I understand you were responsible for taking your mistress to safety yesterday," I began.

"People call me Ike, miss," he said with a grin, demonstrating an enormous gap between his two front teeth. "Rhymes with *like*, don't it? I'm pretty popular around here now." His narrow chest puffed out in pride, and I smiled. He gazed around the room as if hoping someone else would enter and notice his heroic presence.

"Then I shall call you Ike. I was wondering if you might answer some questions for me."

"Sure I will." Ike wasn't even curious as to who I was.

It was then that I noticed a delicious, spicy aroma in the air. Ike must have noticed it, too, for his nose was up in the air as he sniffed at it like a terrier who had caught the scent of a rabbit. Both our gazes locked on a loaf of walnut cake cooling at the other end of the table. However, neither of us had the authority to partake of it.

I tapped the table to bring Ike's attention back to me. "Can you tell me exactly what happened yesterday before you rescued your mistress and the General?" I asked.

"Oh yes. I were very brave. Mr. Pagg, he fell off the carriage, so I jumped down, ran to the driver box, and grabbed the reins. Yes, I did. I've not seen him since, have you? Everyone says he's gone to visit his mama in York, but that can't be right." He frowned, the first sign of clouds on his sunny face.

"Why is that?" I asked gently.

"Because, miss, she went to heaven last year." He glanced down the length of the table again at the cake stand.

This was not a conversation I wanted to have with him. Besides, if this was how Liz or the head coachman was handling relaying the troubling news to Ike, it was not my right to change the story. "I hope you don't miss him too much," I offered kindly.

He frowned as he brought his attention back to me, then in an instant was all smiles again. "Not so much. I'm already getting some of his 'sponsibility while he's away." He pointed to his chest. "I'm in charge of caring for all the saddles now, and I'm to be the General's driver while he's here."

"That is certainly a great increase in responsibility," I said. "You must be proud."

He nodded, grinning. "The master is giving me more money for what I did. I used to have eight pounds a year, but now I'm to have ten pounds a year." He held up all of his fingers for emphasis.

It was a considerable increase in income for the boy, a testament to Sidney's gratitude for his efforts.

"Very good," I said, praising him. "Now, can you tell me what happened in more detail?"

Unfortunately, Ike wasn't really able to tell me much, other than that everyone was calling him the hero of Herbert House. I pressed him further as to what he had heard or perhaps seen, but all he remembered was his own heroism. I was disappointed, but I supposed I couldn't blame him a whit for his boyish, immature recollection.

The cook, recognizable by not only an apron but a face permanently reddened from peering into boiling pots and fiery ovens, entered the kitchen. She winked at Ike. "You haven't touched my walnut cake, have you, boy?"

"No, Mrs. Flowers," he said, folding his hands on the table as if to prove he had been good.

"Well, then," she said, immediately getting out a knife and slicing an enormous hunk of it for him. "Good boys must be rewarded. Go on with you."

Ike loped out with a wave as I stood with the cook, watching him go with the cake already half devoured in his hand.

"He's a sweet boy, but already eighteen and not showing any signs of becoming a man. A little simple." With a knowing look, the cook tapped the side of her head. "But he's very obedient, and everyone from the master down to the parlor maid likes him, even if he blathers on too much."

Eighteen! The boy was only half again as big as eleven-year-old John Wesley, the Establishment's errand boy.

I stayed back to interview Mrs. Flowers, but she clearly spent all her days and most of her evenings toiling away in the kitchens and rarely left the house. I gleaned nothing of interest from her but proffered her a card identical to the one I had given Alice Nichols with a request that she let me know if she heard anything suspicious.

I took my leave and traveled back to the Establishment, where, upon walking through the door, I encountered complete bedlam.

CHAPTER 3

Most of my nurses were huddled together in the library, believing themselves to be whispering, but I heard them chattering the moment I came into the entry hall. Pausing only long enough to toss my bonnet onto a hook, I went to see for myself what was causing such a dither.

The Establishment's library was a glorious benefit of my position here as superintendent. It had rows of bookshelves filled with novels and travel books for the patients, as well as some rather impressive medical texts for me. The best part of the library was the pair of alcoves at one end of the spacious room, which had been a ballroom in the building's previous incarnation as some Georgian aristocrat's London home.

I loved to retreat here to read, study, and work on my statistical charts of disease, even though the library had once been the scene of a nurse's demise. Sidney had mentioned a cholera outbreak in Soho. If it were true, I would be preoccupied with gathering data on it. For the moment, though, I concerned myself with the present turmoil in the room.

I clapped my hands sharply together. "What is the source of

this babbling? What could be so important that all of you are neglecting your duties?"

As I surveyed the library, I realized that not only were my five nurses there, but so were Mrs. Webb, the cook; the hospital's manservant, Charlie Lewis; and even John Wesley was part of the fuss and clamor.

In fact, he hobbled over to me. "I'm glad you're not dead, maum," he said to me in great earnest.

John Wesley had been injured about a year ago, suffering a broken kneecap. He had been treated by a surgeon and had—thank the Almighty—survived without infection, but his ability to walk had never been the same. With a child's resilience, though, he had taken his infirmity in stride and had resumed his duties as soon as he could. I do confess that I continually worried about him.

John Wesley had simply shown up at the Establishment one day, offering to do anything for a penny. I had no idea if he had a home, had escaped a workhouse, or was simply a street urchin. We kept a trundle bed for him in the kitchens and let him be. He seemed to prefer his freedom.

"Now why would you be fearing that?" I asked, tousling his blond hair with great affection.

Clementina Harris, my most-trusted nurse, stepped away from the others and gravely announced, "King Cholera has arrived, Miss Nightingale."

So what Sidney had said was true. I now saw the fear and distress in everyone's eyes. I was unsettled myself. Cholera was notorious for starting in a neighborhood for no apparent reason, sweeping through, and claiming not only the young and old, but also the healthy and sick. Victims could die within mere hours of contracting the illness.

Then, after several weeks of devouring nearly everything in its path, cholera would disappear as quickly as it had arrived, leaving a trail of misery, grief, and putrid bodies in its wake.

"Where?" I inquired, dreading the answer.

"Soho. People are contracting it at least in Broad Street, Berwick Street, and King Street. Should we prepare to take in additional patients?" Harris had thick auburn hair, done in serious, precise loops around her head. Her coiffure matched her disposition.

"Does Dr. Killigrew know?" I asked. "Was it he who told you of it?"

Harris shook her head. "No, miss. That Constable Lyon stopped by, looking for you. When we told him you were out, he decided to tell us instead. So that we would know straightaway."

I was glad I had missed Constable Douglas Lyon. I had encountered him while working on a previous investigation. He possessed the curling hair, broad shoulders, and intelligent mind of Richard, and it pained me to be in the man's presence. I was thankful that he had thought to notify the Establishment, but seeing him always set my emotions on edge and seemed to dredge up my past.

I set my mind firmly to considering the potential trouble at hand. "If it's as far as King Street, we may run the risk of it reaching us here if it then goes into Regent Street and beyond. Our first responsibility will be to prevent our existing inmates from getting sick. They also must not be alarmed. All of you, return to your work and refrain from talking about this."

They all started to file out of the library when I heard one of them screech in the corridor.

"Now what is it?" I called out. I couldn't seem to keep the vexation from my voice. "There is nothing to be afraid of within the Establishment's walls."

Everyone ignored me in the commotion, and in a few moments I saw a streak of fur run past me and disappear somewhere within the shelves. "What was *that*?" I yelped, immediately irritated by my own loss of control.

Another of my nurses, Marian Hughes, returned to the room, breathless. "A squirrel, miss. We think he came in through an open window."

As if there wasn't enough to deal with, now I had a potentially vicious rodent in my hospital. It had to be dealt with immediately.

For the next hour, we all worked together, turning the library into a garbage heap, trying to find the animal.

In the end, John Wesley was the only one small enough to reach into the tiny space the creature had found between two bookcases. By the time he had successfully captured the quivering young creature, he had decided it was his pet.

So in contradiction to any rational sense I might have had in my head, I permitted John Wesley to cage and keep Dash the red squirrel in residence.

★　★　★

I was once more in the library with Mary the following day, sitting in my favorite alcove with her as we prepared some blank charts in which I would document any cases of cholera we might encounter when we traveled to Soho. I had not yet informed Mary that we would be taking this trip. It seemed to me that the next fitting thing to do would be to interview anyone who might have witnessed what happened in the carriage attack, and it wouldn't hurt to collect some information about how the cholera was spreading while we were there.

Poor Mary seemed very distraught. "What is it, Goose?" I asked, putting down my own pen. "You're jumpier than that ridiculous creature John Wesley is carrying around in the cage Mr. Lewis made for him. Is it the heat? Shall we open the window?"

"Sorry, Miss Florence. It's just—do you think we might see cholera arrive here? In the building?"

"I hope not. We will do all we can to prevent it. You're probably safer here than anywhere else in London." I tried to sound reassuring, but the truth was, nothing could stop King Cholera once he decided to knock on your door. It would take all our collective nursing skills to try to keep alive whomever he visited.

She swallowed and nodded, then returned to drawing lines to form an empty chart. She was going to be beside herself when I announced my plan to head directly into the outbreak area.

We had continued with our charts for about an hour when Charlie Lewis appeared in the doorway of the alcove, worrying his cap in his hands.

"M-m-m-miss?" he said. Charlie had an unfortunate stutter that only cleared up when he talked about his time in the Navy, a time that had been cut short because of his unrelenting seasickness. Nevertheless, he had been aboard ships long enough that his face was weathered and he possessed a stoop. He was around thirty years old but looked nearly twice that.

"Yes, Mr. Lewis?"

"Y-y-y-you will want to come quick l-l-l-like. There's a m-m-m-man down in the kitchens."

I didn't understand. "What do you mean? What does he want?"

Charlie shook his head. "He's h-h-h-hurt. He's a-a-a-asking for you."

My thoughts flew to the Herbert family and servants. I hoped it wasn't anyone from that household. I didn't waste time asking any further questions but jumped up and fled the room. Mary was close on my heels, as was Charlie. Nurse Hughes saw us racing down to the kitchens and instinctively joined us. I was glad for her clever intuition.

I did not recognize the man who had stumbled into the Establishment, but I did recognize his problem.

Cholera.

He was slumped in a chair, dried vomit making a large stain on his shirt. His clothing suggested a high-level servant to me. He looked up at me, bleary-eyed. "Water," he rasped.

"Mrs. Webb, go pump some water."

"Miss Nightingale," she protested. "This isn't the sort of illness we accept here at the Establishment, is it? Much less in the kitchen! We should send him away, back to his own home. This man's miasma will infect us all!" Mrs. Webb's eyes bulged in fear as her voice rose in alarm.

I did not want panic spreading through the hospital. If the inmates realized there was a cholera sufferer here, I could be facing a revolt, if not outright bedlam.

"Get a pitcher of water for me," I instructed calmly, "and you can be relieved of any other duties for the remainder of the day." My nurses were trained in how to prepare invalid food; they could certainly manage meals for themselves.

The woman happily scurried away from the scene of pestilence, and I returned my attention to the man. His breathing was now shallow and labored.

"Sir, what is your name?" I asked him.

He mumbled something indecipherable.

"I am Miss Nightingale," I said. He nodded his understanding even as he swayed unsteadily back and forth.

"Can you repeat your name for me?"

He seemed to be summoning great strength as he endeavored to sit up straight and look at me. "Fenton." The effort to say it seemed to exhaust him, and his chin lolled against his chest.

"Nurse Hughes, go fetch my stethoscope," I said.

She immediately ran to do my bidding.

While waiting, I sat next to him and took one of his arms into my hand. He didn't resist me. I could see that he must be a fairly young man, perhaps my age, yet his skin was shriveled and papery to the touch and his lips protruded noticeably from his face. I gently pinched some of his skin between a thumb and forefinger, lifted it, then let go. The skin dropped slowly back into place. This man was exceedingly dehydrated, most likely because he had violently and repeatedly evacuated his bowels and purged his stomach.

He certainly stank as if that were the case.

"Do you need to visit the closet?" I asked.

He shook his head no. His misery was palpable. "Nothing more," he rasped.

Which explained why his skin was so very dry. I was estimating that he had been infected for at least eight hours.

"Mr. Fenton, do you have family I can send for?" I asked.

He grunted as he looked in my direction, his eyes trying to bring me into focus. "My master . . ." he began.

"Who is your master?" I asked urgently.

We were interrupted by Nurse Hughes's arrival with my wood stethoscope. I put the narrow tip to my ear and the flared end to his chest. His heartbeat was wild and erratic, another sign of the dreaded disease.

There was no longer any doubt whatsoever. All I could do was make the poor man comfortable.

But it was too risky to move him into an inmate room. We needed to fill him with water, tea, and broth, then isolate him from the other inmates.

"Mr. Fenton," I said again, handing the stethoscope back to Hughes. "Who is your master? Where do you live?"

"Herrrrb," he slurred. "Devil's Dice."

Devil's Dice? "Where is that?"

The man named Fenton summoned enough energy to snap at me, "No, damn you, the murder. Tell Mr. Herbert . . ."

The man's dehydration was causing him to be delirious, but he gamely persevered. "Help . . . Mr. Maddox."

He raised his glassy gaze to my own, staring at me with those sunken, desperate eyes.

"Maddox?" I said. "Who is that? Where will I find him in order to help him?"

Fenton replied with a wracking cough and managed to grunt out, "Might be too late."

Before my eyes, and those of my nurses, Fenton slumped forward for the last time, no longer breathing.

CHAPTER 4

I was not unaccustomed to death within the walls of the Establishment. After all, it was a hospital. I had even had the dreadful opportunity to behold a murder inside the building last year. But somehow this felt different.

The room was as silent as an abandoned tomb, despite there being a gaggle of us in there. I couldn't even hear the roar of the stove fire, as if it, too, had extinguished itself out of respect for the dead man whose head lay on the kitchen table.

The quiet was shattered by Mrs. Webb returning with a pitcher of water drawn from the well. She instantly realized what had happened, and with a high-pitched squeak, she hurriedly shoved the pewter container—sloshing with freshly drawn water—into Nurse Hughes's arms. The cook then stumbled back to her own room at the rear of the kitchens, mumbling about how we would all be dead soon.

My mind was packed with questions, but first I had to prevent hysteria from spreading. I began issuing instructions to my staff, from having John Wesley fetch the undertaker so the body could be removed to having a nurse attend to the cook. I told Charlie Lewis to begin opening windows throughout the building so that we could release any miasma Mr. Fenton had brought into the building. I directed the remaining nurses to check all the inmates for any choleric symptoms, but to be discreet when doing so.

With everyone else having scuttled out of the kitchens to do as they'd been bidden, I turned to Mary. "It looks like a return trip to Sidney Herbert's house is in order, for I have to assume that's who he meant. First, though, I want to see if he bears any proof that he belongs to the Herbert household."

Mary nodded as she stepped back, almost bumping into the stove as she worried her hands together.

I went to Mr. Fenton's body, which was of course still very warm to the touch. In fact, he remained almost feverish. The poor man. I hated to do this, essentially ransack his person. But if he was a Herbert House servant, what had he been doing in Soho? How had he known to come to the Establishment to find me? I hoped that his words—as murky as they were—did not constitute some sort of confession.

After a few moments, I came across a pouch of calling cards. They were on fine-quality white paper and stated, "Compliments of Mr. Sidney Herbert, Belgravia."

So this was a high-ranking footman or other manservant of Sidney's, someone who might accompany Sidney on visitation and leave behind a card if the person was not at home to receive Sidney.

I also discovered a few items that any servant might be carrying—a candle stub, a key, and a few coins. I did not deem them to be of any importance.

It was my next find, though, that was much more curious. In the interior pocket on the other side of the man's jacket were three ivory dice. They were scuffed and obviously well used. I was no expert in gambling dice, but these were unlike the traditional cubes I knew were typically used.

In the place of concave pips denoting the value of each of the six sides of a die, there were carved symbols.

I turned one of them around in my palm. I saw a crown, quite elaborately done in such a small space; an anchor; and then the remaining four sides were the symbols of playing card suits: a heart, a spade, a club, and a diamond. The heart and the diamond carvings had been filled with red paint, whereas the others were painted black.

All three of the dice were identical to each other. I didn't think Sidney would be happy to hear that Mr. Fenton might have been frequenting seedy taverns to gamble in his spare time, but my friend had to know about this.

Was it a coincidence that Fenton had been in Soho at presumably the same time Liz had been attacked?

I was puzzling through this, jiggling the dice in my loosely closed fist, when Mary interrupted my preoccupied thoughts. "Miss Florence, have you completed your, er, task?"

"What?" I said with a start. "Oh, right. Yes, I think so."

As Mary and I rode together in a taxi to Herbert House, I showed her the dice. She glanced at them distastefully and refused to touch them. "My Milo always said that idle minds were the devil's playground, and that minds were never as idle as they were when gambling."

I sat up straight. "So Devil's Dice isn't some squalid part of London. Fenton was referring to the dice themselves."

Mary shrugged. "The sooner you are rid of them, the better, I say. I don't think Milo would approve of my being in the presence of such evil items. Why, I remember Milo once saying . . ."

I let Mary prattle on without paying much attention.

As we bounced our way to Belgravia, I examined the dice again against my tan leather–gloved palm, gently rolling them and admiring the carving work on them. Whoever had carved them was a talented artist, for certain. The anchors had a clearly defined rope entwined around each of them. All the diamonds were perfectly shaped with even sides. The crowns were—

That was odd. I turned all three dice so that the crown sides were facing up. At the top of each crown was a different number or letter. One was a "D," the second a "G," and the third a "5."

Strange. Perhaps they were the carver's initials and the "5" was a . . . what? Maybe these were part of a larger set containing other numbers that would make this more meaningful. Like a birth or death date.

Or perhaps there were more dice that, when placed alongside the "D" and "G," would form a word or phrase. Other than a simple word like *dog* though, I couldn't begin to imagine what it would be.

★   ★   ★

If I thought my hospital had been pandemonium, it was nothing compared to the state of the Herbert household.

Liz was no longer abed, and to my surprise, appeared to be fully recovered from her brush with death.

She was in one of the private family parlors, surrounded by her children. Three-month-old William Reginald lay in a cradle, kicking and gurgling happily to himself through the proceedings.

Four-year-old George and his younger brother Sidney were

oblivious to my presence, for they were completely entranced by a trembling, whimpering creature that had taken refuge beneath a deep settee that sat along one wall of the room.

The children were a two-man army, strategizing how to coax it out of its hiding place. As I watched, Sidney waved his hand under one end of the settee, and the animal crawled its way backward in the opposite direction, away from the waggling fingers, only to be unceremoniously grabbed by George.

The boy triumphantly dragged out and held up a thin, short-haired puppy with a dove-colored coat. Its legs were quite long for its skinny little body, but I suppose the young of all species have their ungainly stages.

"Isn't he sweet?" Liz declared, gazing adoringly at the dog, who was now being smothered in kisses, pats, and tugs by her two older children. "He's a toy greyhound. The Italians breed such beautiful beasts. We call him Alberto, for the Prince Consort."

I wasn't sure the queen's husband would much appreciate being immortalized in the body of an anxious, mousy dog like this—although the pup certainly had the makings of becoming a striking animal, if the Herbert children did not give it a canine apoplexy first.

However, I had far more dire issues on my mind than the Herbert dog.

I quickly introduced Mary, who'd had the good sense to grab her writing notebook—bulging with our newly made charts—and held it in both hands as she dropped a tiny curtsy to my friend. She seemed awestruck about being in the home of an important man like Sidney Herbert.

"Is Sidney here?" I asked, hoping I didn't sound as anxious as the greyhound. "I must speak with him."

Liz smiled. "Flo, dear, you know Sidney and my father spend most of their days at Westminster. Do you already know who attacked my carriage? That was certainly fast work on your part."

I hesitated. Should I tell Liz about their second dead servant before telling Sidney? "No, I don't have an answer yet, but I do have some news, and I was hoping to tell you both at the same time."

I should have known that she wouldn't accept such a flimsy statement. Tilting her head to one side and looking at me as though she could see straight through my soul to the wall beyond, Liz said, "They should be home anytime. Flo, whatever the news is, I'm ready to hear it. How much worse could it be than what has already happened?"

She shooed the two older children out of the room. Alberto attempted to run back under the settee, but George and Sidney weren't having it. Again they tricked him back into their arms, but he wriggled valiantly as they reached the door. He escaped the children with an inelegant thump to the floor and, much to my horror, dove under my dress.

George had enough sense at his age not to attempt to lift my skirts to retrieve his pup. Young Sidney, however, was willing to employ any means necessary, and he was immediately on the floor, attempting to crawl in after Alberto. I was in such a state of astonishment that I almost didn't hear Mary catch herself in a laugh behind me. I did see Liz hide a smile behind two fingers brought to her lips.

I lifted my skirts and stepped away from boy and dog as gracefully as I could. With Alberto thus revealed, both of Liz's sons attempted to snatch him again, but they flailed against air as the puppy scrabbled out of the room on his own. The boys followed him, screeching like a pair of barn owls in sight of a rabbit.

It was only then that I realized that Alberto had piddled on one of my boots. A dark stain ran across the top of the brown leather, although thankfully it hadn't been enough that it had reached through to my stockinged foot. I quickly arranged my skirts again before Liz could realize what the dog had done.

Alice Nichols entered the room at that moment. "Mrs. Herbert, did you wish for me to have your green silk laundered for next week's—oh." She stopped abruptly at the sight of me, and I could almost see her worrying that I was standing there to report upon her to her employer.

"Good afternoon, Mrs. Nichols," I said as warmly as I could. "I spoke with you when I was here yesterday."

"I remember," she said, her words a theatrical sigh.

I introduced Mary to her, and I hoped the informal, friendly gesture would put her mind at ease.

"Yes, Nichols, the green silk," Liz said. "And don't forget that I'm having tea with the ladies' committee for the South- wark Female Society soon, too. I think perhaps the mauve and black stripe for that. Check the hat I always wear with it. I recall last time I wore it that some of the flowers needed sprucing up."

"Of course, ma'am." Alice Nichols left the room. Or rather, she exited, stage left. She was not so talented an actress that she was able to disguise her apprehensive expression as she turned away.

Liz didn't seem to notice, or, more likely, she was too caught up in her family's troubles to be worried about it. "Flo, I must tell you about the Southwark Female Society, in which I believe you will be most interested. Its goal is not to supply the poor with money but to afford relief in cases of sickness or lying-in. We offer linens, clothing, coal, and groceries and deliver them straight to the indigent of Southwark. The benefits are not confined to any particular denomination, which I know is important to you."

I had had a major tussle with the Establishment's committee, which wanted to restrict inmates to those belonging to the Church of England, but I had insisted that we admit Catholics, Baptists, Methodists, and any other female of middling status who could afford to stay. I am a Unitarian myself and a firm believer that a good Christian demonstrates godly principles in charity without prejudging the condemned on God's behalf.

Right now, though, my hands were full between the Establishment and this task Sidney had given me. "May we speak of it when I—"

The doors to the room opened again. Sidney and the General had arrived home. Liz's husband went straight to her to plant a kiss on her cheek.

Liz held up a hand to stop him, then indicated my and Mary's presence. "Flo!" Sidney exclaimed in a cheerful greeting. I was about to change his happy mood, and my innards twisted at the thought.

"That was quick work," he commended me, practically parroting his wife. "What news do you have?"

I crossed the room and shut the door, hearing the brass lock click tightly shut before turning back to face the room. "I've brought my companion, Mary Clarke, with me," I said to clarify her presence. "She is of invaluable help to me when I work on a project, as she takes notes and helps me think through things."

I didn't need to glance in Mary's direction to know she was preening at the compliment.

Sidney, Liz, and the General nodded at me. They obviously didn't care who Mary was; they just wanted me to get on with it. So I did.

"It is my sad duty, dear friends, to inform you that a man by the name of Fenton, whom I believe to be in your employ, died at my hospital a short while ago."

My words hung in the air like the coal fog around a factory town. Liz silently raised her hand to her chest, the General gaped liked a netted fish, and Sidney—well, poor Sidney looked as though he'd been bashed by the swing of a fireplace poker. He was somewhere between maintaining a shocked, statuelike presence and simply crumpling to the floor. He reached out and grabbed the back of a nearby armchair.

"I—I hardly know where to begin," he faltered. "You're sure it was Fenton? He's my personal manservant. How . . . ?" There were hundreds of bewildered questions in Sidney's eyes.

I explained what had happened.

"Cholera!" Liz gasped, and I knew she was probably feeling great relief that he hadn't brought it back to Herbert House and that he hadn't been attacked as she and the General had.

"What was he doing in Soho?" the General demanded. "Did he not realize there is a madman on the loose there? Surely he knew what had happened to my daughter and me."

"And particularly to Mr. Pagg," I offered, probably more sarcastically than I should have, but no one would ever accuse me of being a tactful diplomat.

The General was still full of outrage and paid me no attention. "He's brought shame onto this house, Sidney! Your servants cannot be permitted to dash about wherever they like. Not only do they get themselves into trouble, they contract disease. They die, for God's sake."

Liz's father was working himself into a fearfully righteous rage.

"Papa," Liz said, seeming to forget her own distress in the moment and going to her father. She took one of his burly hands in both of hers, trying to placate him. "We don't know yet why Fenton was there. It may have been innocent. Perhaps he had family there."

"Well, I may have the answer to that." I pulled the set of dice from my dress pocket and held them out for the three of them to inspect.

"Dice!" the General roared, brushing his daughter aside. "Just as I said. Servants who are not on a tightly held leash get themselves into trouble. This is an appalling show of disrespect for you—for us—and I for one will not tolerate—"

"Sir," I interrupted him and his rant. At this rate, I would never finish my story, and I still intended to head into Soho myself this afternoon. "I beg of you, restrain your temper until I have departed."

My curt admonishment startled him into silence, which I knew was only temporary. With one hand, I tapped my open palm containing the dice. "They do not look like typical gambling dice to me."

Liz removed one from my hand. "Are they all the same?" she asked as she held it up to scrutinize it more closely.

"Yes, in that they all have the exact same designs for each of their six sides: an anchor, a crown, and the symbols for all four suits of a deck of cards."

Sidney and the General each picked up one of the remaining dice in my hand. Sidney tossed his into the air and caught it deftly. "I believe these are the type of dice sailors use, aren't they, Father?"

General à Court squinted at the die in his hand and grunted. "If you say so. Best thing to do is throw them into the fireplace and not let the others know he had been behaving so dishonorably toward you."

Mary sniffed in agreement. However, I was not about to callously incinerate what was not only a memento of a favored Herbert servant but might somehow be linked to Liz's attack. What if there was some sort of connection between Fenton, the dice, Liz, and a trip through Soho?

"Was Fenton ever in the Navy?" I asked.

Sidney shook his head. "He came from a family with a long history of domestic service. Impeccable character references."

"Did he have a male relative who might have worn the uniform? Or a friend?"

Sidney shrugged his uncertainty. "I confess I didn't know the man's personal background very well. Not my business to pry into a servant's life as long as it isn't impacting my household."

I braced for what I was sure would be another tirade from the General on how dreadfully this particular servant's behavior was affecting the household. Surprisingly, it didn't come.

"There's something else," I continued. "Look at the crown side of each die. See the engraving above it?"

"D," Sidney said, followed by the General reading off the "5" and Liz declaring the "G" on her own die. "What do they mean?" she asked.

"I cannot fathom what the significance is," I said. "I can

only imagine that these dice are missing from a larger set, and that perhaps the other dice help to spell out a longer word or phrase."

"Five Good Dice?" Sidney suggested.

Could it really be that simple? I wondered.

"Perhaps the '5,' which begins with an 'F,' really stands for Fenton," Liz speculated. "Fenton's Good Dice."

"Or Fenton's Gambling Dice," Sidney said, his face darkening. "Maybe it's just a monogram spread across the dice."

Mary sniffed again, but I could hear her pen dutifully scratching across paper.

I nodded. It was as good an explanation as any. "There's one more thing. Fenton referred to them as 'devil's dice.'"

Not surprisingly, the General thundered back to life. "Of course he did! His time-wasting with the dice led him into some unsavory den in a back alley in Soho where the fetid air of cholera blew over him. He was responsible for his own murder and he knew it. My boy, you must allow me to assist you in selecting your menservants in the future."

Sidney cleared his throat. "We won't worry about replacing Fenton too quickly. His loss is great." Sidney's voice cracked on the word *great*.

"Darling," Liz said to her husband. "Do you believe Fenton may have been expressing regret for his gambling habits? Could he have possibly been in debt?"

I hadn't thought of that. It was an interesting idea, although I wasn't sure whether I should pursue it. Even if Fenton had owed money to someone unsavory, surely it had nothing to do with the attack on Liz.

Sidney shrugged. "I couldn't possibly know. But Fenton was

competent and loyal, and I'll not have him buried with a slur against his name."

Hopefully I could bring him a small bit of comfort there. "Morgan Undertaking will be bringing him back here in a sealed coffin. I did not know where else to have him taken."

"Quite right," Sidney said, composed once more except for that small tic at the corner of his right eye. Surely the shock of losing two trusted servants in as many days was overwhelming.

However, the hairs on the back of my neck were prickling for another reason. Was it possible that what the General had said was true? That Fenton had merely been expressing remorse over possession of the dice? Still, it seemed to me that as a life-long military man, the General should have been able to identify the dice the moment he saw them.

I made a mental note to show the dice to Charlie Lewis. Perhaps he could explain to me what the dice meant. Maybe he could even tell me why a man of elevated rank would disavow any knowledge of them.

As I contemplated Fenton and his mysterious dice, Sidney sniffed at the air, his expression puzzled. Knowing exactly why he did so, I stepped backward as gracefully as I could, pretending I was consulting with Mary on what she was writing down in her notebook. Sidney frowned and shook his head, then examined the die in his hand again. "What of your brother, Liz? He's been known to spend an evening in his cups playing cards. Would he know what these mean?"

Liz bristled, and I knew she didn't like to hear her family member being insulted in front of guests, even if those guests were an old friend and the friend's companion. "Charles Henry is educated on a variety of topics. But he's in Wiltshire now with

Emily, and I'm sure he doesn't plan to return to London until next season. Surely you can find someone at the War Office who could identify the symbols."

"Good Lord, no," Sidney protested. "I don't want there to be a hint of unsavory rumors floating around Westminster started by asking around about my dead servant's dice. I would be heaped with questions and become the subject of great innuendo. Absolutely not. Florence, I'm afraid we must rely on you to discover what Fenton meant with the dice."

"At this point, I must agree," the General said, his voice the calmest I'd heard it since he had arrived. "Charles Henry can be of no help in the situation, and we must let him be with his new bride if we are to hope for more additions to the family name."

Liz's face registered surprise. "Why, Papa, that's the kindest thing you've said about Charles Henry since . . . well . . . in a very long time."

The General harrumphed, clearing his throat. It sounded very gurgly, and I wondered if he had a deep chest cold he was hiding. "Well, your old papa doesn't need to point out the boy's flaws too often. And certainly not when he isn't here to receive the benefit of my wisdom."

"Papa! He attended St. John's College at Cambridge as you'd hoped, he's an MP for Wilton, and now he has even married Emily Currie, also as you wished. No, no." Liz waggled a finger back and forth at her father. "Do not protest and do not think I don't know that she was *your* idea. You can hardly suppose that a milquetoast like Emily was Charles Henry's cup of tea. He's done everything to please you. You know where his passions lay."

The General rolled his eyes. "Yes, in those ridiculous tubes of paint. The boy is damnably lucky that I took him by the ear and guided him onto a proper life's path. You were never so recalcitrant, Elizabeth, and see how successful your life is."

Liz bit her lip. I knew she adored Sidney and her children and had a full society life. Thus, she had no proper argument against her father, but I would also have been willing to bet she sometimes tired of her expensively furnished cage. I was about to intervene to save Liz from this conversation when an interruption saved me the trouble.

The doors—which I was certain had clicked shut when I pulled them closed—burst open. It was George, breathless and red-faced. "Mama! Have you seen Alberto? He's after something, and we—" George stopped short at seeing his father in the room. His heavily lashed eyes opened impossibly wide, and then he threw himself at Sidney's legs. "Papa! You should come play with us. I'm training Alberto to be a great hunting dog."

I could see that the General thoroughly disapproved of George's outburst, but Sidney was not a typical father. He swept the boy up in his arms, probably grateful to have this bundle of life barging in to take his mind off all the death surrounding him. "Is that right? Have you taught him commands the way I showed you?"

"Mmm, I think so." George looked up in the air as if trying to remember what his father had told him as long ago as the previous day.

More commotion arrived in the form of a darting little mouse, with Alberto racing and yelping close behind it.

"Alberto!" George shrieked, pushing out of his father's arms to join the zigzagging trail of dog and mouse around the room. This awoke William, who began howling in outrage over his disturbed slumber.

The General muttered about "lack of discipline" and "not seen in my day," but both Sidney and Liz seemed bemused by the antics.

As for me, I just didn't want the puppy urinating on me again. I scooted close to Mary while the scene played itself out.

Now an experienced mother of three, Liz didn't react in panic to William's crying but simply went to his cradle. Settling herself in the chair next to it, she began rocking him while making soothing noises that were completely inaudible over the din of everything else.

Finally, the mouse managed to do what mice always do—discover a previously unknown hole between the floorboards and disappear. Alberto barked and stamped at the tiny slit through which the animal had escaped, but soon gave up when it was apparent that the chase was over and he was not the victor.

"We'll find another," George promised the dog in consolation, offering it a childish pat on the head. In response, probably fearing that the boy was going to grab him again, Alberto tore off again, nails scrabbling against the wood floor. This time, though, he banged straight into Sidney's legs. Although Sidney reacted with no more than a grunt, the poor dog must have been stunned. A dark stain began to spread beneath its hind legs.

Sidney sniffed the air again, and I knew that he was recognizing a familiar odor. It was time to depart this lively scene of family domesticity. I made a hurried departure with a promise to return as soon as I had information about the dice or anything else I might discover in Soho.

But reaching Soho was not going to be easy, for Mary chose the moment of leaving Herbert House to turn into a stubborn mule.

*   ★   *

"Miss Florence, it is folly to go to Soho. I'll not go, and your mother would cook me for breakfast if she knew I had allowed you to go there." Mary stood obstinately at the cab stand in Belgrave Square, while around us well-dressed nannies pushed prams in the late-August heat. Not even the treed park provided much relief from the sun.

Why had she picked this moment to suddenly discover her spine?

"Goose," I explained patiently. "Surely you realize that without going directly to the location where the attempt was made upon Mrs. Herbert's life, and where presumably Fenton contracted cholera, we cannot make any steps forward in discovering who may have wished Mrs. Herbert dead, and who may still be intent on seeing her put into a coffin. And, just as importantly, how cholera is spread."

Mary was shaking her head before I even finished my sentence. "It will be *us* put into coffins if we go there. Of what use are you to Mr. Herbert if you're *dead*?" She squeaked out that last word.

What was I to do? It probably wasn't safe for a woman to be alone there, particularly not a woman wearing a silk taffeta dress. I could return to the Establishment and ask Charlie Lewis to look at the dice and then return to Soho with me, but he would be of little help in note-taking. Mary understood instinctively how my mind worked and what I considered to be important information. I wasn't sure Charlie was even literate.

No, Mary must be convinced that she had a duty to go with me.

"Don't we have a responsibility to see what sort of services the Establishment can provide to the sick and dying there?" I asked.

She considered this for only a moment, then shook her head vigorously, a lock of hair tumbling out of its pin beneath her hat as she pushed up her falling eyeglasses. "There are plenty of London relief societies who can do it. Mrs. Herbert was just talking about the one in Southwark. We have no reason to willingly enter that den of disease. Not even to pursue a criminal," she added, stopping me before I could utter the words.

I tried another tactic, hoping my suggestion would ease her primary fear. "What if we were extra careful about avoiding any miasmas, and we left if we smelled anything foul?"

She stared at me, aghast. "The moment the odor comes to us, it will be too late. We will be covered in noxious air! It's bad enough that we don't know how much of it that Mr. Fenton brought in."

I was beginning to believe that Mary was far more clever than I had given her credit for. There must be a way to have her accompany me without complaint. Time was elapsing at a critical rate as we stood arguing in front of a bronze statue of someone who must have once been very important or heroic. I looked away from her so I could think and espied a young couple walking arm in arm. It gave me an idea.

I did not much enjoy manipulation as a rule but felt desperate enough to attempt anything. "What would Mr. Clarke say about this were he here with us? Would he wish to run back home, or would he bravely face whatever elements he might encounter in Soho?"

Milo Clarke had been shy, studious, and completely unable

to tether my juvenile self to his method of teaching, but he had been the sun, moon, and stars in Mary's life. I wasn't really sure what he would have done in the hypothetical situation I presented, but I knew Mary would be absolutely certain of her husband's mettle and fearlessness.

"Why, I suppose he would—well, my Milo was not one to run from trouble, I will say that," she declared, her consternation palpable.

I let her continue thinking it through. "He always said that problems were to be worked through, much like mathematical equations." Now she was frowning deeply and hugging her notebook to her.

"Oh, Miss Florence, Milo would want me to do whatever I could to help." Mary said this as an anguished cry, as though it was the worst realization of her life.

She finally agreed to enter a taxi with me, wearing the doomed expression of a criminal on her final ride to the hangman's noose. I couldn't say I didn't share her concerns, but justice had to be served.

CHAPTER 5

The cab driver was well aware of the Soho outbreak and refused to drive us any farther than the Royal Opera House in Covent Garden, leaving us to walk to Broad Street, where Liz's carriage had been attacked.

I was struck by how quickly our surroundings deteriorated. The buildings were small, cramped, and dilapidated, and some were so near to completely crumbling that I feared they might topple over into the street at any moment. They were blackened so deeply from coal soot that they appeared to have all been in a raging fire at some point, with only the charred brick remains still standing. Or leaning, as the case might be.

What a difference in scenery the two miles between Belgravia and Soho made.

I admit to having had a very comfortable youth and adulthood, although I had certainly visited some of the poorer cottages in my village of Wellow down in Hampshire. I had become known for my enthusiasm in nursing the sick, yet I confess I had never, ever experienced anything this vile.

Children and adults alike sat not only on poorly built stoops that were tilting and rotting, but inside windowsills as well, their dirty legs and feet dangling in the air. I assumed it was cooler and fresher in the August air than inside. The sorts of miasmas that must fill these places was beyond my imagination.

I noticed a boy seated in the corner formed by a stoop and a building. He had his arm around a younger girl—his sister, I assumed. One of his unshod feet had an enlarged toe that oozed pus. He seemed oblivious to it, and the two of them sat there, staring listlessly at me as though I were a fly on a piece of rotting fruit.

I felt something catch in the arch of my boot. I lifted my foot, and whatever it was ran squeaking off.

Not a blade of grass, nor a stump of tree, nor a shoot of plant, was visible anywhere. Perhaps all manner of flora had simply given up and withered away here. As a result, there was no color. Everything was dull shades of ebony and ash.

There was little horse traffic here, as well. Our taxi had refused to enter, so why would I have supposed anyone else would either? The street was crowded enough, but unlike in prosperous areas, the people did not have the busy air of those going about their business. Indeed, I almost had the sense that they were apathetically passing time until they could permanently lie down.

I now understood, deep within my soul, Mr. Dickens's complaints about slums and why he felt compelled to write about them. My mind swiftly flew to what sort of medical care was available for these poor creatures. I would have to ask Liz if the Southwark Female Society—or any of the other charities to which she belonged—had doctors numbered among them.

A small, painfully thin boy tentatively approached me, and I stopped, despite Mary's attempt to pull me along.

"Mama," he said, peering up at me from beneath a tattered cap.

Was he so malnourished that he was delirious and confused about his surroundings? "I am not your mother," I said gently.

He shook his head in frustration. "My mama," he said, and turned to point toward a narrow, two-story building whose roof had a large hole in it.

I was beginning to understand. "Is she hurt?"

He nodded.

"What is your name?"

"Lucky. Lucky Reeve." The ironically named child stared up at me with eyes that were enormous in his tiny face. I saw a louse crawling through his tousled hair and shuddered.

How could I walk away from this needy young lad? What if his mother was dying? Did he have any other family to care for him? I started following him toward the building, although I fervently hoped his mother was not on the second story, as I was seriously doubtful that it was structurally sound enough to hold Mary and me.

"No!" Mary hissed in displeasure, but I ignored her. She must have realized that I intended to enter the building, for she sighed loudly and dramatically enough for even Alice Nichols to envy her talent, then scurried to keep up with me.

The stench of the house was a jolt to my senses before I even crossed the threshold. It was bad enough that I actually took a step backward, then paused to gather my courage. In doing so, I glanced in the doorway of the building to the right of the place the boy called home.

Directly inside the doorway were several steps leading down to where a man, a woman, and two teenage boys appeared to be assembling leather shoes and boots. A heavy rain would surely flood their little shop. That's when I noticed the sign outside their door, almost completely faded from the weather, that read, "Sorrell Quality Shoes." I wondered what emporium was buying their sad goods.

I remembered my own urine-soaked foot covering. What had seemed so calamitous earlier was now hardly a thing of note.

I pulled aside the patched sheet hanging that passed for a door. It was so dark inside the boy's home as to be nearly murky. There wasn't even a candlestick burning in the cramped room, which had only a single chair and table, a bed with a lumpy mattress, plus a tiny fireplace.

Nestled inside the dying embers was a pot, containing what appeared to be an unappetizing, pasty gruel that had congealed.

As my eyes adjusted more to the darkness, I realized that there was a woman on the bed. She was as lifeless as everyone else I had encountered, her head lolling back against the wall and her eyes closed. She held a tiny, mewling babe to her breast. I doubted she was able to provide milk.

Mary gasped, and in that moment I saw what she saw.

Lying on the bed next to the mother was a small form, wrapped in a dirty sheet.

Good Lord, had cholera already visited this house? I turned as calmly as I could to the young boy. "Who is that?" I asked.

"Jenny," he said. "My sister."

"What happened to her?" I held my breath for his answer.

The boy shrugged. "Mama rolled over on her."

"Pardon me?" I was trying to comprehend what he was telling me. No wonder the woman was stupefied. "How many people sleep in this bed?"

He looked at me, puzzled. "All of us."

I blew out a breath. I had been worried he would reveal that cholera had come to the house. The truth was so much worse.

"Where is your father?" I hoped such a man existed, but had there really been four people and a baby sleeping in this bed?

"He's at Tyburn," the woman said, lifting her head and giving me a dull gaze. So the mother wasn't insensible after all. She looked at me, coughed, then turned her head and spat on the floor. "Public hanging today. He sings street ballads. Hangings draw crowds and people pay him good money for his songs." She began coughing again, this time more violently. When she spat again, I saw blood.

"You need a doctor," I said, my obvious words sounding foolish in my own ears.

She gave me one more bleak look, then tilted her head back against the wall again.

Her son tugged insistently on my skirt. "Help my mama," he pleaded.

"I—I—" I felt completely helpless. This household needed so much more than just a doctor, although certainly to lose his mother would put the boy—and the infant in his mother's arms—in a perilous position.

"Miss Florence," Mary said. "Do you think Dr. Killigrew would come?" Mary had performed a complete turnabout in the situation.

Dr. Killigrew was the physician to Lady Canning, who had been the driving force behind starting the Establishment. He mostly attended to society people and only made weekly visits to the hospital as a favor to his patroness. Would he be willing to make a trek to this depressing place? Should I wait until I could see about a doctor associated with the Southwark Female Society?

"I don't know," I replied. "I shall ask him, but I couldn't promise anything."

"You can convince him, Miss Florence," Mary said. "This poor mite . . ."

At that moment, the makeshift doorway curtain was pushed aside, providing a moment of light, enough to illuminate the man who now entered, whistling as he jangled coins in his pocket. The boy shrank back around me, while his mother turned her head in the direction of the brief light without opening her eyes.

He was tall, but as gaunt as everyone else in the hovel. I definitely saw the resemblance between him and Lucky. He narrowed his gaze at me as both whistling and jangling ceased. "Who are you two fancy ladies? You'd best not be soliciting my boy."

Mary gasped in indignation. "Why, I never! I'm a respectable matron. My husband—bless his soul—would be most angry to hear—"

The last thing we needed right now was Mary's death-induced righteousness. "My name is Florence Nightingale. This is my companion, Mary Clarke. We are in this neighborhood seeking information about an attempted murder upon a friend of mine. Your son asked for help for your wife, who I can see is very ill."

Lucky slowly stepped from around me to face his father.

Mr. Reeve's expression was skeptical. "And you just decided to twirl your parasol on down here to do a bobby's work, is that right? And then you nosed your way in here."

I couldn't blame him for being suspicious of us. "Not at all. It is as we say. In fact, I would like to seek out a physician for your wife, and you must realize that your daughter—"

"So then you're one of them Baptist charity women, come to preach fire and brimstone and then drag us off to the workhouse? I'll have you push off now. I can take care of my family myself."

I sighed. "Mr. Reeve, I mean no ill intent toward you or your family. Your son stopped me in the street for help for your wife, who is clearly unwell, and that's how we came to be here."

Reeve turned his ferocious gaze on Lucky. "I'll deal with you later, boy."

Lucky shrank around me again. I was becoming irritated. "We are neither from a church nor a workhouse, nor are we prostitutes. We are merely passersby."

Now he sneered at me. "Now I know who you are. You're one of the lawyers' wives, come to inspect and fine me for something."

What was he talking about? "What lawyers? For what would I fine you?"

He pulled a penny out of his pocket and threw it in my direction. "There you are. Have your husband tell the vampire who owns this place that you collected as much as whatever damage you dreamed up is worth."

I ignored the coin, which flew past me, hit the wall next to the fireplace, and landed on the worn floorboard with a tiny clink. The man had brought up an interesting point. "Who *does* own this place?"

"I'm sure you know it belongs to Reverend Whitehead at St. Luke's."

I kept thinking I'd heard the most outrageous thing possible, but then Mr. Reeve would surpass himself with yet another statement. "Reverend? Are you saying that a *churchman* owns this sorry place?"

"Don't act like it's of surprise to you. It's them and the fancy lords what own everything down here. They never visit themselves but have their bootlicker lawyers come down to complain about lead stripped from roofs or panes stolen from windows. Then they fine us whatever they want."

I hardly knew how to respond. I was outraged to think that a man of God would permit this filth and squalor. Reverend Whitehead would be receiving an unwelcome visit from me in short order. However, my present visit could be likened to a train run completely off the rails and into a cow pasture.

I took a deep breath. "Mr. Reeve, let us focus on the vital matter at hand. Not only is your wife gravely ill, but your daughter . . ." I indicated the shrouded lump on the bed, which he had ignored since arriving. Were we really arguing about rents and fines when his dead daughter had yet to be acknowledged?

Reeve grunted. "What'd you do, Amy?"

His wife made no response. Her shallow breathing was the only indication that she had not also departed the world.

I lowered my voice. "I believe she rolled onto your daughter during sleep. An accident, I'm sure."

The airless room was silent for several moments except for the breathing and the faint crackling of embers. When Reeve made no move to do anything whatsoever, I went forward and knelt on the floor at the side of the bed where the child lay. I clasped my hands together to pray for her poor anguished soul.

Mary also dropped down next to me, sniffling and digging into her pocket for a handkerchief.

As we did so, Reeve came alive again. He shouted at his wife that she was the Whore of Babylon, his son was a devil's imp, and I was Satan's bride. Then he turned on his heel and stomped out of the hovel he called home.

Whore of Babylon. Hadn't Liz told me her attacker had accused her of being the Babylonian Whore? I hoped it was merely a distasteful coincidence.

★　★　★

I gave young Lucky some coins before we left, and promised I would send an undertaker to them, reassuring the boy that I would pay for a shroud and a spot in a pauper's grave from my own purse.

We passed back into the street. Even without a cholera outbreak, this place reeked of despair and death, although the outside now seemed charming and welcoming compared to what we had experienced in the Reeve household.

Despite the warmth of the day, I was chilled, as if the specter of Death were hovering over my shoulder. I could not banish the images of the dead child, the dying mother, and the outraged father from my head.

"Miss Florence, I told you this was a horrid idea," Mary whispered, clutching the notebook to her chest with one hand as she grabbed my arm with her other. However, as daunting and disheartening as everything was here, its citizens seemed to be working hard to give us a wide berth.

We reached a small road junction that impossibly had seven different roads jutting out from it. In the center of the junction was a tall column topped by several sundials placed around its circumference.

As we stood there, I saw that nearly every visible building was a tavern or public house. They had names like "Dirty Dick's," "The Crooked Bobby," and "Hangman's Noose." Who could blame anyone living here for wanting to drown his misery in the bottom of a foul tankard of ale?

"This must be Seven Dials," Mary said, pointing up at the

column's multiple sundials. I felt her shiver next to me. Her earlier bravado had evaporated. "We are in a terrible part of London. Dear Lord, please rescue me from my foolishness in agreeing to come here. I know now that my Milo wouldn't have wanted me here and that I let my pluck get the better of me. Dear Lord, please send someone to rescue us. Dear Lord, please—"

"That's enough, Goose." I spoke more sharply than I intended. I was going to lose my own nerve if she didn't stop, and I was determined to see this through.

A new question was forming in my mind, though. Why ever had Liz chosen to come this way to the British Museum? Surely she could have circumvented it.

Unless her father had chosen the route, but he had no reason to do so either.

As if she'd read my thoughts, Mary said, "Miss Florence, I don't think Mrs. Herbert and the General would have come this far into Soho to get where they were going, do you?"

I didn't dare agree aloud for fear she would balk like a mule and refuse to go any farther.

"It's impossible to know right now. Let's not waste the trip," I said, selecting St. Andrew Street at the junction and continuing to walk. St. Andrew Street, indeed. What would this disciple of Christ's have to say about the squalor of his namesake road? Which reminded me that I needed to locate St. Luke's Church as well.

St. Andrew Street opened into Broad Street, and by now Mary was no longer a stubborn mule but a cat dancing on coals. She was so anxious about proceeding any farther that I thought I might have to find her some laudanum.

We now had a large building on our right, better built and

in better condition than most of the others on the block. In the street in front of us was a large, octagonal metal structure with perhaps a dozen men and women crowded around it while others entered through an opening along one side and still others departed it on the side opposite.

The stench wafting from it was the most disgusting that we had yet encountered here in Soho. Surely not all the area was like this. Public flushing toilets had started popping up in London over the past couple of years, ever since one had been displayed at the Great Exhibition in 1851.

A little farther past the toilets was a water pump, recognizable as a black, round metal column with a pipe jutting out from the middle of it and pointing downward. Water poured freely from the mouth of the pipe, and people—mostly women and children—collected water in buckets, bowls, or whatever implement they had that didn't leak. With containers full, they left the pump, presumably to return to their own dark, dank hovels.

I glanced up at the business sign painted above the fourth-story windows of the building next to us.

Lion Brewery
John and Edward Huggins, Proprietors
INDIA PALE and NO. 3 STRONG ALES
Bottlers of ALE and STOUT for Exportation

A trademark barrel drawing adorned the sign.

There were at least eight windows running across each of the upper stories of the building's front facade. Surprisingly, few of them had broken panes. Soaring over the roofline were at least as many smokestacks, gently but persistently puffing smoke into the air. On the ground level, the door was freshly painted scarlet, an incongruence in this place of drabness and despair. Above the door was a pub sign on a pole attached perpendicular to the brick building. It swung listlessly in the light breeze. It indicated that through the door was the Red Lion Inn, and the words were on a backdrop of, naturally, three languid lions, emulating those on the royal arms of England.

I was about to make the highly inappropriate suggestion that we enter the public house together to see who might be in there who could give us information. It might be a mere public house, but it was certainly the nicest building in the area, so I assumed we would be safe.

Before I could utter the words, though, a middle-aged man stumbled out of the building, groaning and clutching his head. He fell upon the roughly cobbled street, begging for someone to bring him death.

CHAPTER 6

Was it not possible to walk more than a couple of blocks through this part of Soho without encountering death and misery? And were we now facing another cholera victim? Perhaps we should have returned to the Establishment for some bone broth before coming here. This man could certainly use the nourishment, as could the Reeves.

Mary sighed in exasperation, too, but at least this time she didn't attempt to pull me away.

"Sir," I said, leaning over the man, who was now on his back, a hand clawing at his heart as though he were trying to remove it in some ancient ritual. "Can you speak to me?" I quickly assessed him as best I could, given that he was writhing and moaning.

Like most of the residents, he wore threadbare clothing. When he had first stumbled out of the building, I had guessed him to be around forty years of age, but up close I realized he was younger than that. Maybe thirty?

His teeth showed the initial signs of decay. They were spaced far apart, and the two front ones were twisted in toward each other. His pitted face suggested he had once had smallpox or some other disfiguring ailment. He was as tall and skeletal as Lucky Reeve's father.

He finally opened his eyes to look at me. "Bella?" he said, a cloud of confusion in his eyes. His words were carried to me on a cloud of liquor fumes.

"Who is Bella?" I asked softly. "Is she your wife? Your sister? Your sweetheart?"

The man was sweating profusely. Although I smelled a generous helping of whatever was being served inside the Red Lion Inn on him, I did not smell excrement, nor did he seem to have a fever. I did not think he had cholera. Mary and I had now been fortunate twice. Could this luck continue?

"Wife," the man said, panting but at least no longer thrashing. "Bella!" he cried out. Tears leaked from the corners of his eyes.

I stood up straight. A firm hand was needed here. "Sir, I cannot help you if you do not speak rationally to me. I'm going to help you to sit up. Do not resist me."

I signaled to Mary to help me and, to her credit, she did so willingly. She was blowing both hot and cold at me, but I couldn't really blame her. This had been a very peculiar day thus far. We had witnessed a man die at the Establishment, then spent time in a Belgravia mansion, and now here we were in a dreadful part of London, having already witnessed one tragic situation and likely about to be involved in another.

And, to the man's credit, he was also cooperative. Once he was in a seated position, I realized that many of the people who had been clustered around the urinal across the street were now far more interested in watching us—in a lethargic sort of way. I suspected that if the man were to die in an instant, the people in the street would turn their attentions back to their conversations at the urinal.

Speaking of which, I was concerned that the miasma from the public toilet would impact the man, particularly since I was not quite sure yet what ailed him.

Mary and I were crouched on either side of him. He was still breathing rapidly but was not sweating. "Sir, what is your name?" I asked.

"George," he said. "George Maddox."

Surely this was not the same man Fenton had begged me to care for with his dying breath? I hated to plague the suffering man with questions, but when might I have another opportunity to discover what I needed to know? "Sir, do you know a servant of the Herbert household named Fenton?"

He grimaced with the effort of considering my question. "Fenton, yes. Believe . . . he is . . . a frequenter of the Lion. Keeps to himself. Good dice player." Maddox seemed exhausted with the recollection.

A gambler Fenton might have been, but he certainly recognized pain and misery in others.

Maddox's pitiable condition made me feel even worse about continuing to interrogate him, but I had to proceed. I pulled Fenton's dice from my pocket. "Do you recognize what these are?"

The man squinted at the three cubes in my open palm, then looked at me in confusion. "They are dice. Don't you know that?"

I was being obtuse. "My apologies. I mean, do you recognize these as being Fenton's personal dice? And do you know what the symbols on them mean?"

"Ah." He squinted again and picked one up, examining it.

"'Fraid I don't know much about gambling. Not my particular vice," he added sheepishly before putting it back in my palm.

I refused to bother this tormented man any further. "Well, Mr. Maddox, I am a nurse, and I think you are sick and need rest. Where do you live?"

"No, no," he protested, shaking his head. "Not sick." He allowed himself to be pulled up to standing. "It's my wife, Isabel. She and my son, Arthur, are sick."

I was thoroughly confused. His wife and son were ailing and he was out imbibing spirits until he became senseless? "Are they at home?"

He nodded yes.

"Then we are going straight there," I said firmly, taking one of his arms while Mary took the other. He didn't resist and instead nodded again, this time in resignation.

Thus did we walk three abreast until we reached his meager quarters in Museum Street. I could see the British Museum looming in the distance, a beautiful, imposing building overlooking all the squalor and misery of Soho.

It still didn't seem possible that Liz would have chosen this route just a couple of days ago. I needed to remember to ask her what routing they had actually taken.

For now, though, I had some possible patients. I silently prayed that Mrs. Maddox and her son did not have cholera.

Unfortunately, they did.

★ ★ ★

I wouldn't have guessed it possible, but the Maddox quarters were only marginally better than those of the Reeves, primarily because although the space was twice as large, the entire front part of it was occupied by Maddox's upholstery shop. The waist-high table in the center of the shop was heaped with fabrics, brass tacks, springs, lengths of rough Hessian cloth, and cones of thread. Bags of feathers lay in a pile on the floor. A nearly finished armchair done in a garish shade of yellow sat in the window ledge, which was low to the ground and enabled pedestrians to peer in. I refrained from grimacing at the work.

The damask pattern of the fabric was completely askew. The piping where the fabric met the wood was crooked, as though it had been applied by a palsied hand.

George Maddox was a terrible upholsterer.

But perhaps he wasn't as efficient as he typically was because of his sick wife and child. Or perhaps it was the spirits he imbibed. Mary and I followed him through a narrow doorway behind the shop to his living quarters.

The stench was overpowering, particularly in the August heat. I swallowed against my impulse to gag from the suffocating air surrounding us. Mary coughed behind her gloved hand and did not remove her hand once her convulsing was over.

There were a couple of candles illuminating the room, and I almost wished I could blow them out to blot away the image before me.

Poor Isabel Maddox, dressed in an old, dirty chemise, sat in a chair with an overflowing slop bucket on the floor next to her. The woman was wild-eyed in her illness, and her hair was so tousled it was as if I were in the presence of a witch. This was no Amy Reeve, nearly unconscious in her misery. Mrs. Maddox seemed ready to do battle with the supernatural darkness. Actually, she would have made an interesting figure in Madame Tussaud's Chamber of Horrors.

Her son lay curled up, sleeping fitfully in a trundle bed pulled halfway out from under the parents' bed. He was tow-headed and reminded me of John Wesley. Our appearance in the room did not rouse the boy, so consumed did he seem to be from a nightmare or other disturbance.

I could not be sure which of the two was sicker. No wonder Fenton's dying words were a plea to help these poor souls.

"Bella?" Mr. Maddox inquired tentatively. "Here are some nurses come to see you." For his part, Maddox was beginning to recover from his fit in the street, which I now believed was less liquor-induced and more a reaction of grief and frustration.

She turned her head to one shoulder to peer at me through one eye, as if she were a hawk. "What do you want? Have you come about the murderer?"

I froze. Had Isabel Maddox witnessed the attack on the Herbert carriage? "What did you say? How do you know about that?"

She cackled. "I know more than most people do. I see more than most people, too. Including you, Barton." Her features changed instantaneously into a glare for her husband before transforming yet again into that of a wise sage to address Mary and me. "He'll be back again to take us all. All of us who *see*."

Her eyelids shut halfway, and I could see her pupils darting back and forth beneath them. Surely she was merely delusional. Who was this Barton of whom she spoke?

As if reading my mind, George Maddox murmured, "My dead brother. She has been fixated on his memory as of late. Was there actually a murder somewhere?"

I nodded quietly but did not elaborate. I saw no reason to upset the man any further.

"My wife has the gift of sight?" he gasped in wonder.

At this point, I wasn't ready to believe or disbelieve anything.

After a few moments, Isabel's eyes flew open again, and it was as if she were seeing me for the first time. Her gaze had an intensity to it that was almost unearthly. She pawed at her hair and cried, "George! Where is my mirror? You didn't tell me we had visitors."

"Mirror?" George said. "We don't have—"

I held out a hand to stop him. The mirror wasn't important. "Mrs. Maddox," I said calmly. "Tell me again about the murderer. How many of you are there who 'see'?"

The eyelids began to close again. "Doesn't matter. We will all die."

Bella Maddox was eerily mercurial, and my skin began to prickle. Was she this way because of choleric delirium, or was this simply the woman herself?

"Ah, oh," she moaned, clutching her stomach. "I'm afraid I'm not up to visitors. You must go now."

I wished to stay with her to at least figure out how to take care of the disgusting slop bucket, but George refused me, desiring to leave his wife in privacy. Mary and I followed him the few steps out into the shop.

I wanted to offer him some hope. "I should like to return with a couple of my nurses tomorrow. We will bring some nourishing broth and toast for all of you. That will help make your wife and son strong. And I would like to clear the air in here."

I saw a faint glimmer of optimism in his eyes. "Do you think that would save them?"

"I cannot promise anything, but I believe it will provide the best circumstances possible for them to get well."

However, I had already concluded one thing. While the boy

was far sicker with cholera, Isabel Maddox was far more ill in her mind.

★ ★ ★

I was exhausted by this point and wanted nothing more than to return to the Establishment for a steaming cup of tea before I had to assemble some of my nurses to make a plan for returning to Soho the next day. I suspected we would end up helping more than just the Maddox family. And I had still accomplished absolutely nothing with regard to Sidney's request.

Mary and I made our way back into Broad Street with the intent of seeking out a taxi once we got out of the immediate area. "Are you quite all right, Goose?" I asked her. Her expression was pensive as we dodged around a particularly foul carcass of what might once have been a cat.

"It's quite frightening, isn't it?" she said, wrapping her arms around her own substantial form as we walked, even though it was stiflingly warm out.

There was so much here that was disconcerting that I wasn't sure what she specifically meant. I was momentarily distracted by a haggard, toothless elderly woman sitting in an upper-story windowsill who was staring intently out at the sky as if expecting an owl or a hawk to swoop in for a visit. I lifted a hand in a wave, but the woman frowned suspiciously at me and disappeared inside her accommodations.

I returned to my friend's vexation. "What do you mean?" I asked.

A ball made of rags rolled clumsily into Mary's path. She held up her skirts and gently kicked it, but it gained a distance of only perhaps five feet. A boy darted out from nowhere to snatch it up and run away with it again. Mary gazed after the boy, and I saw her eyes fill with tears. "It's frightening how much sadness and tragedy exist in this place, really only steps from us, and they get their misery further compounded by cholera."

I nodded in solemn agreement. Her thought was truly sobering.

"Two very different households we encountered today, yet both seem to be steps away from total devastation. I can hardly imagine what your nurses can even do to improve the lot of the Maddoxes." She stopped in front of the Lion Brewery and frowned at me. "I confess I should be most angry with you, Miss Florence, for dragging me into this pestilent place. Yet all I wish for right now is a safe place for a cup of tea."

"My own thoughts exactly," I declared.

"Hmm," my companion said. "After I'm done with that, I am sure I shall return to chastising you for putting me in this awkward position with your parents. Imagine what your mother would say if she knew that you not only walked straight into Seven Dials, but that I personally accompanied you! She would bake me for supper, she most certainly would. And that you went into not one, but two, houses visited by cholera. Oh yes, she would serve me up with a glass of fine burgundy."

Poor Mary. Even though she had decided to throw in her lot with me and defy some of my mother's expectations, the specter of Fanny Nightingale still periodically rose up in her mind and terrified her. I couldn't help teasing her.

"Don't forget that you also permitted me to walk through town with dried urine on my boots."

"What?" Mary said, aghast. "What are you talking about? Did you step in it here in Soho?"

I explained what had happened with Alberto, the Herberts' puppy.

"Oh, that's fine, then. I cannot be held responsible for things that occur at the homes of my betters." The look of relief on Mary's face was amusing, and yet I had no heart to tease her further.

We proceeded farther down Broad Street, seeking the narrow intersection with St. Andrew Street that would lead us out of here.

I heard the commotion before I saw it, a riotous banging accompanied by screeches, laughter, whistling, and even some liberally sprinkled cheers.

Mary's relief was now ended. She stopped and clasped a hand to her heart. "What is that? It sounds like an invading foreign army. I hope we are not to die here today."

Although I thought Mary a little melodramatic, I was also concerned by the grand cacophony that pierced the muted despair of this neighborhood. Wishing to be cautious, I pulled Mary to one side of the street, so that we walked uncomfortably close to the bereft souls lounging on their crumbling stoops.

No one bothered us. In fact, they all seemed focused on the approaching noise as well.

Just as we reached St. Andrew Street, the source of the tumult came into view. Leading what could only be termed a small mob was a man dressed in a shabby suit. He was himself unremarkable except for his long, flowing beard, which he had tucked over one shoulder. Attached to his torso with over-the-shoulder leather straps was a brightly painted box. The man was working some sort of handle on the right side, and discordant music ground its way out of the box. On top of the box was a scrawny little monkey in a yellow vest, the source of the screeching we had heard.

Accompanying the man was a teenaged boy carrying a drum, which he beat with the enthusiasm of the blissfully untalented. The musical duo had a following of at least twenty people, presumably residents of the neighborhood, who yelled and shouted their appreciation of the music and danced with abandon behind them.

It was dreadful by any cultured standard.

Despite our efforts to blend into the background, it was impossible for a woman wearing clean, pressed silk to go unnoticed, and the organ grinder made straight for us as soon as he espied me.

His ragtag troupe of followers straggled behind him, continuing their gyrations. With his free hand, he held out a cup and shook it. I presume a few coins clinked together inside it, although it was impossible to know, given that the music did not cease for a moment but instead blared in our faces.

We were surrounded on three sides by the organ-grinder and his people, and behind us were the stoop-sitters, whom I could sense rustling restlessly behind me.

In distress, Mary clutched my elbow with a trembling hand.

I wasn't quite sure if we were in danger or not, and it was impossible to even speak over the din of pounding, singing, screeching, and organ sounds. Finally, I held up my hands in surrender, which cued the man to hold up his own hand to silence his group. Except for the monkey, of course, who jumped down from the organ box to more effectively lecture me for some unknown offense by chattering and hopping back and forth on spindly, furry legs.

The organ-grinder shook his cup at me with bold insistence, and I shook my own head in reply. "Sir, we are minding our own business and seek no trouble with you."

I started to leave, with Mary still attached to my side like a tumor, but the organ-grinder started up his blaring music again and made to follow us.

That's when I realized that the money was not just desired, but expected, and that he and his band would follow us relentlessly until I gave him some coins.

I reached down into my dress pocket and found my coin pouch. Hurriedly extracting a few without even looking at their value, I handed them to him. The music died down again, and this time the monkey did not fill the void with his insane chatter. "Thank you for the entertainment, sir," I told the man through clenched teeth.

"Pickle is my name, ma'am," he introduced himself, removing his hat and sweeping into as much of a bow as the organ strapped to his middle would allow. "I'm mighty grateful for a fine lady such as yourself 'preciating my music."

I nodded, not wishing for any further conversation but merely desiring to extract Mary and myself from our present predicament.

Pickle bowed once more and turned to continue up Broad Street from the direction in which Mary and I had come. The monkey jumped back on the box, and he and everyone else in the entourage began making a racket again.

Mary breathed in relief as we resumed our journey, but I found myself watching the backs of our tormentors in fascination. For it occurred to me that even though Pickle was extorting money from people in a most unsavory way, he was bringing joy to those who chose to follow him. There was surely little enough of that in this neighborhood. Perhaps not every single thing here was misery, and slivers of happiness could cut through the oppressive fog of hopelessness no matter whom it surrounded.

"Miss Florence, perhaps we shouldn't return tomorrow. Or ever. We were lucky today, but perhaps we will be murdered when we come back. Or worse, forced to join that band!" Mary shuddered next to me as we picked up our pace on St. Andrew Street.

I had recovered from my initial fear, though, and knew that between my investigation for Sidney Herbert and the welfare of the two families we'd just met, we would be back. Repeatedly. We would have to get used to death and calamity outside the walls of the Establishment.

"I think it far more likely that we would fall prey to a miasma of cholera, don't you?" I said as cheerfully as I could. I meant it as a joke, but the sound of Mary's strangled cough told me that I should leave the humor to Dr. Killigrew.

★　★　★

By the time we returned to the Establishment, the undertaker had removed Fenton's body, and the savory aroma of thyme filled the kitchens as Mrs. Webb prepared supper for the hospital's inmates.

The afternoon mail delivery was piled upon the entry table. I stayed behind to go through it while Mary went to her room to take a nap "after our harrowing adventure." I had hardly begun glancing at the *Times'* headlines when I noticed another, less pleasant, odor around me. I sniffed tentatively at the air and realized that, although a cup of tea followed by a nap would be most pleasant, I needed a change of clothing first. Or at least I needed to get out of these boots.

I knelt to inspect the damage that Alberto had wreaked on my feet when the heavy leopard's-jaw knocker on the front door clanged loudly, nearly causing me to start and tumble backward. With both my boots and the mail forgotten, I answered the door.

To my great surprise, in front of me stood Sidney Herbert.

"Flo," he greeted me. Was I mistaken, or did my friend look embarrassed?

I welcomed him into the Establishment and invited him to sit in the library, the scene of so much activity since I had been at this hospital. The loose squirrel had only been the latest commotion.

"May I offer you some tea?" I offered, once more hoping he didn't notice the smell of dog urine on me. The smell had faded some, hadn't it?

He declined, and as I couldn't very well request a tray be brought up just for me, my hot cup of tea would have to wait.

I sat in my favorite chair and indicated another nearby for him. The moment I sat down, I felt an overwhelming weariness seep into my bones. It had been the longest day I had had in recent memory. I stifled a yawn.

Sidney noticed it. "I shan't keep you long. I just needed to talk to you—privately, you see." He shifted uneasily in his seat and crossed one leg over the other. "I apologize that I didn't say this earlier, but I couldn't do so in front of Liz and her father."

I was instantly awake again. "What is wrong?"

He templed his fingers. "It's about Fenton. There's something important you need to know about him. It's my fault he's dead."

I gasped in a most unladylike fashion at him. "Pardon me? He died of cholera. How could it possibly be your fault that he's dead?"

Sidney sighed and passed a hand over his eyes, then put both hands on the chair's arms, as if doing so would prevent him from falling. "I sent the man into Soho to do some quiet investigating into Liz's attack. I figured he could more easily move about down there than you could."

Now I was positively irritated. "Then why did you bother me at all?" I snapped. "Why not just let your manservant do your bidding and figure out for yourself who attacked Liz's carriage? I do have a hospital to run, Sidney. And there are cholera cases arising that I may need to address. I do not sit around with needlework waiting for a waddling goose to wander by so I can set to chasing it." I heard my own voice rising an octave.

"Flo, Flo, please," he begged, obviously trying to soothe my riled spirits. "Let me explain."

I waited, my lips compressed so firmly I was certain they looked bloodless. Had I endured this entire day for *no reason*?

Of course, I reasoned with myself, it was no wrong thing that I had encountered two families who desperately needed help that I could provide to some small extent.

But still . . .

"Fenton was a valuable servant," Sidney began. "Very intelligent and willing to do most anything for the Herbert name. But he has—had—no clout. And I believe there may be some, shall we say, ancillary deeds occurring that will require investigation by someone who is not part of the household."

My anger evaporated in a mist of curiosity. "What do you mean?" I asked.

He paused as if carefully gathering his thoughts. "Everyone has at least one event in his past that he wishes he could erase, as a schoolboy might eradicate a bad work on his sums on a chalkboard, right?"

"Yes." Why did I have the sudden feeling I wouldn't like what I was about to hear?

"And so did Fenton appear to have a past with gambling, a past about which I did not know. No doubt if he were alive, he would like to wipe that part of his life clean."

"Yes," I said again, waiting for a salient point to be made.

"I imagine even you would like to erase something from your past, Flo," Sidney suggested, loosening his grip on the chair's arms and templing his fingers again, a sign that he was relaxing.

Naturally I would have erased many things. The memory of Richard, for starters. Which reminded me that I still needed to decide what to do with the letter he had written me. I mentally brushed that cobweb out of the way. Time spent thinking of him could ensnare me like no organ-grinder ever could.

"Are you accusing *me* of something, Sidney?" I asked.

"No, no, of course not. I'm just making a point. None too well, it would seem. What I am trying to say is that I think there are secrets of the past in my own household. And although I sent Fenton into the streets in an attempt to call out whatever miscreant actually fired the shots, he would have had no capacity for calling out whoever was *behind* the trigger-puller."

Sidney gazed at me steadily, and I sensed that he was trying to communicate something he could not say aloud.

For my part, I was stunned by what I believed him to be transmitting to me.

"Sidney, are you suggesting that either Liz or the General has a past so horrendous that someone paid our killer to attack the carriage?"

The moments ticked by. Finally, Sidney repeated adamantly, "Everyone has a past, Flo."

But Liz had had no past to speak of before marrying Sidney eight years ago at the age of twenty-four. General à Court undoubtedly had a murderous past in the Army, but he wouldn't be the instigator of a plot against his daughter. As gruff and unlikable as he was, he clearly adored his daughter.

"Sidney, can you cease being vague and mysterious for just a few moments and tell me whom you suspect to have this dangerous and illicit past?" Dealing with ailing women each day who perpetually lied to me about what they ate and drank while being transparently coy was bad enough. I had no patience for this same conduct with someone I called a friend.

He heaved another sigh. "I'm worried that it is me."

CHAPTER 7

"You?" I exclaimed, nearly barking with laughter. "To what dark deed could Sidney Herbert possibly lay claim?"

Sidney shifted uneasily in his seat again. "Well . . . before I met Liz, I had an, er, attachment to a woman, Lady Caroline Norton."

Liz had never mentioned this to me. Perhaps she didn't know.

"Were you victim to the time-worn tale of being unsuitable for someone of her status?" I asked.

Sidney smiled grimly. "If only it were that easily explained. No, the actual trouble was that she was married."

I blinked several times. Sidney was a devoted father and husband. It was impossible for me to think of him placing a cuckold's horns on another man.

"Obviously, nothing came of the relationship," I managed to say through my astonishment.

"No, but not for lack of trying. George Norton was—is—a brute in many ways. Is jealous to the point of insanity. About twenty years ago, Caroline began publishing romances and books of poetry, and the earnings were enough to enable her to leave him. Norton, though, claimed that he was entitled to the earnings. Not surprising, considering that he is a totally incompetent barrister, incapable of earning his own fees."

Had Caroline Norton had affairs prior to Sidney? Were they the cause of George Norton's mad jealousy, or had his jealousies driven her to commit that of which her husband had already declared her guilty?

As if reading my mind, Sidney continued, "A great scandal erupted in 1836 when Caroline developed a friendship with Lord Melbourne, who was then prime minister. Norton accused Melbourne of committing adultery with his wife, which was positively ridiculous. Melbourne was a fifty-seven-year-old man and Caroline was only twenty-eight. He was merely a father figure to her."

I said nothing, wondering if Sidney had swallowed an embellished narrative from his mistress.

"The case went to court and the newspapers gobbled it all up," he said. "Don't you remember?"

I had been sixteen years old at the time and living tucked away in Hampshire. It wasn't the sort of subject my parents would have discussed at the dinner table, no matter how much chattering was going on about it in town or in the papers. "I'm afraid I was too young to be aware of it."

Sidney nodded. He himself would have been twenty-six at the time, and had likely read all of the accounts himself. "The case was thrown out of court, but Norton used the situation to keep their three children and to block Caroline's attempt at a divorce. Poor girl, treated so shamefully and then prevented from having the comfort of her boys. Ultimately, I think Norton was furious not so much that Caroline might have had an affair, but that she was no longer using her beauty, wit, and political connections to further his otherwise nonexistent career."

Sidney was working himself into quite a righteous snit over Caroline Norton.

"Where did you figure into the situation?" I asked.

"I met her in 1840, at a party of some sort, I can't remember who hosted or where it was; all I remember from that evening was Caroline in a dress of the brightest pink you've ever seen. I was utterly besotted." He rose restlessly from his chair and feigned interest in the nearby bookshelf, running his finger along a series of titles. "We both were."

Now I understood where this was all going. "But her husband wasn't going to permit her a divorce based on the suspicion of a relationship with the prime minister, so it was certain that he wasn't going to relent because his wife was in love with a nobody like Sidney Herbert."

Sidney dropped the trailing finger and bristled. "Well, I wouldn't say I was *nobody*. I already had a seat in the Commons for a part of Wiltshire and had held some minor offices under Prime Minister Peel. My talents were recognized even then."

"Of course," I said soothingly. "But you could not maneuver a path to secure your inamorata's divorce?"

He sat down again. "No. I did try. But eventually I realized that with my brother off on an illicit dalliance in Paris, it would be up to me to take care of the Wilton estate. That meant I needed legitimate children to inherit it all. If she and I could not be married, then I would be forced to marry elsewhere. That was the hardest day of my life, leaving her." He amended that thought quickly. "Well, the hardest day save the terror of Liz's near miss with death."

I could empathize with Sidney on this. Leaving Richard was the hardest thing I had ever had to do. However, I wasn't sure what this story had to do with the attack on Liz. I took a stab at it. "And so you think it's possible that George Norton has held a grudge all these years and sent someone to attack your carriage, believing you would be in it? I've seen some strange behavior in my life, Sidney, but that strains credulity."

"Bad men frequently behave in a manner that strains the sensibilities of cultured women like yourself, Flo. I do think it's possible. Melbourne is lucky he's dead now, or perhaps he would be under attack. Anyway," he said, rising, "I thought you should know. Liz is aware of Caroline, although I haven't shared the extent of my previous feelings for the woman. It's all in the past, and I am completely devoted to Liz."

He laughed without mirth. "If only my forty-five-year-old self could have told my thirty-year-old self how foolish liaisons could impact the future, I might not be in this situation."

I rose as well. "If you believe George Norton to be behind the carriage attack—and I cannot possibly fathom that to be true— then why did you send Fenton into Soho? What did you think he could investigate?"

"As I said," Sidney said, his tone awash in measured patience. "Fenton could move about in Soho relatively easily. And if George Norton was behind the attack on Liz, he obviously wouldn't have done it himself but would have hired a ruffian in a dark corner to do the work for him. I had hoped Fenton could find that lout."

Sidney's theory about how Liz's carriage had been attacked still seemed largely ridiculous to me. Even more ridiculous was the fact that the theory was coming from the mouth of someone as intelligent and logical as the secretary at war. Why was he flogging his horse down this path?

I walked with him to the entry hall of the Establishment. Sidney's step was lighter now, like a penitent who had just offered up a confession behind closed doors and now felt the sweet relief of forgiveness. I had witnessed many people like this—running to the devil with hounds all week, then seeking the confessional on Sunday to make everything right. Yet I could hardly conceive of Sidney as someone who would be sneaking out the back door on his wife. Even if he were, he would be intelligent enough not to report it to her friend, no matter what the circumstances.

We stopped at the hall entry table, where Sidney picked up his hat and turned back to face me. "You understand why I couldn't speak of this in front of Liz and her father? It would only distress my darling wife needlessly. And the General . . ." He shrugged, as if attempting to explain his father-in-law's incorrigibility. "Even if Fenton was guilty of a gambling vice, he still deserves justice in the form of apprehending my wife's attacker. I hope I haven't unduly upset you, Flo, and that you will continue your work."

I had a surfeit of emotions about Sidney's behavior, both past and present, but I, too, had a passion for justice. That passion was understandably magnified given that it involved my dear friend Liz. "Of course," I said.

I opened the door to see him out, then thought of one more thing. "Where is Caroline Norton now?" I asked out of feminine curiosity.

Sidney shrugged and shook his head. "I don't know. Returned to her family home, for all I know. Or perhaps she's still in London. Or maybe even gone to the continent."

My heart sank, for I could tell by the subtle change of tone in Sidney Herbert's voice that he was lying. He knew exactly where Caroline Norton was.

I gave him a stern look, but he misinterpreted my disapproval. "At least we don't have to worry about her," he said, securing his hat on his head and disappearing into Harley Street.

I stared after his retreating figure for several moments as I replayed our unsettling conversation in my head. When I finally abandoned those thoughts, I retreated to my study for a light supper of salmagundi and tea.

While eating, I dashed off a note to Dr. Killigrew, asking him to visit the Reeve family in Seven Dials. I thought there were better than even odds that a gentleman doctor like Killigrew would read my request in complete horror and refuse, but I had to try.

With my meal finished, I checked on John Wesley and his ridiculous little squirrel, then stumbled off to bed. I needed an unfitful night of sleep, for I feared the next day would be at least as hard as this one had been.

★   ★   ★

The next morning, I dressed in my plainest work dress, given that I expected to end the day covered in filth. I then selected a different pair of shoes to wear and took my stained boots down to the kitchens to see to them with a vinegar-and-soap mixture.

The inmates were up and about, several reading in the library. Others were in the rear garden with a nurse, enjoying the outdoors before the heat of the day set in.

As I gazed out a library window at the rear garden—noting

that I needed to speak with Charlie Lewis about some vines that seemed to be eating a portion of the shrubbery along the rear wall—I saw that the sun was not to be tempered by clouds today. It had already risen blindingly in the sky.

I didn't look forward to the heat, but there was work to be done.

Before I could gather Mary and the nurses to explain what I wanted done in Soho that day, Mary herself appeared in the library. "Miss Florence, you have both a message and a visitor."

She handed me the loosely folded note—a couple of lines from Dr. Killigrew stating that he would be unable to attend to the Reeves. I sighed and handed it back to her. I admit I was disappointed, but not very surprised. Of more concern was who might be awaiting me.

"Is it Sidney Herbert?" I asked with dread. "Or anyone from the Herbert household?" I wasn't sure I was ready to face Liz and pretend as if I now knew nothing about Sidney's past.

"No, it's a messenger from Middlesex Hospital. Shall I attend you?" Mary held up her writing journal. How much I relied on her to make notations for me.

I nodded and followed her out to the entry hall. My visitor, however, was not exactly a messenger but more of a harbinger of doom.

The man was older than me, perhaps forty-five years of age, with a closely trimmed beard. He wore fine clothing and possessed an austere air about him. I immediately recognized him as a gentleman physician. Most had the aura of distant compassion, although our own Dr. Killigrew—with his silly joking and laughter—was much the exception to that archetype.

He nodded formally at me. "Miss Nightingale? I am

Dr. Stephen Goodfellow. I am an assistant physician to Middle-sex Hospital. We—the hospital—have come to the conclusion that we need a particular . . . expertise . . . that we believe you can provide for us."

My interest was stirred at once. "What is that, sir?"

"As you probably realize, King Cholera has reared his ugly crown in nearby Soho. We have few resources at the hospital for actually stopping the disease's spread, and what we mostly need now are people to care for the victims. Nurses, I mean. It is well known how you have improved this small hospital and that you rigorously train your nurses, so I am here to see if you and a few of your nurses would be willing to help us. For our part, we can recompense you for your time."

I shook my head. "I take no salary, Dr. Goodfellow, for I have a considerable allowance from my father. My nurses, though, are not so fortunate. You may offer them payment. First though, I need to see your hospital."

I was fairly certain it would be in the same stuffy condition the Establishment had been in when I had started here over a year ago and would require extensive airing out, at a minimum. However, the invitation to assist at a larger hospital was most flattering. "I can come shortly."

His expression was one of disappointment. "Can you not come now? I have a taxi waiting outside."

I had been derailed enough over the past twenty-four hours. "I must tend to other work this morning, sir," I said firmly. "I will be there in a couple of hours."

Goodfellow frowned. "My superiors believed that I would bring you back with me. You must realize that we have a bit of a difficult situation over there and need immediate help."

"Nevertheless, I must attend to my other duties first." I moved to show him out the door. He was clearly unhappy with the delay, but I could not be expected to leap every time someone wanted something of me. I was already taxed enough under Sidney's demands, and it had only been a day since meeting with him.

As he left, Mary scribbled notes in her journal, not that I was likely to forget an appointment with another hospital.

I called my nurses and Mary to join me down in the kitchens—the only place with a table large enough to accommodate all of us together—to explain why I needed a couple of them to come with me to Soho. Most of them blanched, but Clementina Harris and Louisa Lambert readily volunteered. I had expected it of Harris, but I was a bit surprised by Lambert.

"I can be ready to leave as soon as I visit Mrs. Parris again. She had a restless night of sleep." Lambert stood in respect as she addressed me, although she kept her head at a downward angle, not meeting my eyes.

I had hired Nurse Lambert last year after firing several other nurses on my staff. I had been glad to find a woman in her thirties, as younger applicants could sometimes be too flighty for the work of nursing. Lambert came from a modest background, and her unfortunate visage ensured she was not likely to attract a suitor. She had a purpled, lumpy birthmark running down the right side of her face, from the corner of her right eye to a sharp point below her chin. She attempted to distract attention from it with very strange hairstyles and even stranger hair caps.

The inmates didn't mind her, though. In fact, I think it made them feel better to be cared for by someone they saw as being in an even more pitiful state than they were themselves.

Lambert might be a bit pitiful, but she was dedicated to her work and I liked her immensely. I hoped to one day convince her that she could be as satisfied with nursing as she might have been in the marriage that would never materialize for her.

As it also wouldn't for me.

"Thank you both," I said, expressing my gratitude with a smile. I issued other instructions for the day, then left Harris and Lambert to check on their inmates and prepare some food and supplies for the two families while I spoke to Charlie Lewis about the ivy and visited John Wesley once more. He hardly acknowledged my presence, as he was completely enthralled with his little red squirrel, which he had eating berries from his open palm.

Satisfied that the Establishment was running smoothly for the day, I left for my visit at Middlesex Hospital. It was in Mortimer Street, a mere half-mile walk from the Establishment. I decided the exercise would be beneficial for me, and I made my way there with my head down, ignoring the noise and busyness of London as I considered what needed to happen after my visit.

After the nurses and I visited the Reeves and the Maddoxes, I wanted Mary to go with me to the Lion Brewery to talk with the owner of that establishment. And of course there was a list of hospital supplies that needed to be ordered, and I must ask Charlie Lewis to figure out what window Dash had come through to see if there was a nest of them outside. I was so absorbed in my thoughts that I almost didn't notice Middlesex Hospital in the near distance. It startled me that I could have been so lost in thought, for the hospital was a magnificent structure, with two wings on either end that gave it a U shape facing the road. Dominating each wing was an enormous Palladian window made up of dozens of panes. Elegant fringed draperies were swept back in an artful way to frame the windows.

What elegance these inmates must enjoy, I thought.

As I turned to go through the black iron gates, which surrounded the three-story property, I became instantly aware of a familiar stench. And then I saw it all.

Lining the lawn on either side of the walkway to the front door were dozens of people, some on good hospital linens and some on rags. All of them were pitifully weak as they attempted sleep, cried out in pain, or relieved themselves in overflowing slop buckets. A few orderlies walked helplessly from patient to patient, offering ladles of soup or water from pails.

Now I thoroughly understood why Dr. Goodfellow had wanted me immediately. Death had set up camp here and was not likely to leave anytime soon.

CHAPTER 8

I am not often speechless, but I was having difficulty gathering my thoughts as I waited for Dr. Goodfellow in the hospital's entry. As I stood in the company of a slovenly orderly, I was assailed by the disgusting combination of moldy lime-green paint peeling off the walls, dust and debris all over the floor, and the strong odor of urine in the hot, airless place.

A man came limping by in the care of a nurse. She held him roughly by the elbow as he clutched a bloodied bandage wrapped around his middle. The poor man grunted in pain as the nurse pulled him along to some unknown destination.

I tasted bilious anger in my mouth. Had these appalling conditions always existed not a half mile away from me?

"Ah, Miss Nightingale, good of you to come." Goodfellow greeted me with both warmth and relief. "I will escort you to our meeting room. The other physicians are waiting to meet you."

I had been to these sorts of "meetings" before with the Establishment's management. They were usually opportunities to attempt to bend me to someone else's will.

That was not going to occur today.

"I think not," I said decisively, folding my hands in front of me and raising my chin.

Goodfellow seemed genuinely taken aback. "Pardon me? Have you decided not to help us? Obviously, you must have seen how overwhelmed we are simply by the number of poor souls outside."

My temper flared with righteous indignation, and for once I didn't even mentally chastise myself for it. "Based on what I have seen so far, I suspect the poor people dying out on the lawn have it better than anyone imprisoned inside the walls of this place."

His response was both gentle and apologetic at the same time. "Yes, there is much that can be improved upon here. We do the best we can."

I was unsatisfied with his answer. "Sir, this is your best? Look at this atrocity." I pointed with a gloved hand at the wall. "Surely there was a moment in time when you could have hired workmen to redo these walls."

He seemed nonplussed by my outburst. "Surely *you* must realize that we operate with few funds, Miss Nightingale."

"Is it expensive to open windows? To sweep floors? Before I meet with anyone, I should like to visit the corridors of this hospital."

Goodfellow looked around as if noticing for the first time the conditions to which I was objecting. He shrugged. "It is perhaps not as clean as Buckingham Palace, but we are here to save lives, not to impress guests."

I followed him as he showed me several hospital wards. It was a much larger hospital than the Establishment and had both men's and women's wards on each floor, plus there was a special maternity ward. Each ward was a long, wide hallway. About twenty beds lined both sides of each ward, with headboards up against the walls—walls that were as moldy and peeling as those in the entryway. How long had it been since the walls were scrubbed?

However, the room's arrangement was efficient, as it allowed doctors, nurses, and orderlies to go from inmate to inmate quickly.

Unfortunately, the staff appeared to be moving as if gelatin were attached to the bottoms of their shoes.

Every bed I saw was filled, and some inmates lay on lumpy mattresses on the floor between beds. Everyone seemed to be either in pain, dehydrated, or seemingly unconscious. Many of them were obvious cholera victims. At least there were multiple tall windows in each room, yet they all remained tightly shut. The sunshine filtering through the dirty panes did nothing but illuminate the dust floating in the air. It was difficult to breathe in the hospital, so sealed off was it.

Dr. Goodfellow stopped to greet a young man in one of the men's wards. He was a boy, really, and I guessed he had been in some sort of factory accident that had mangled his right arm, which was wrapped in bandages and showed an obvious stump at the end.

While the doctor attended to him, I walked on, examining other areas. The supply cabinet was disorganized and did not contain an adequate provision of bandages, morphine, syringes, stethoscopes, or invalid drinking cups. I heaved a sigh in disgust as I shut the cabinet doors.

The water closets were too wretched to even describe. I stepped away from them as soon as the doors were opened for me; the vile smell told me all I needed to know.

I asked to see the kitchens, by which time Dr. Goodfellow had rejoined me. I was in too much of a rage to even speak as we went into the basement, where I found what I expected to find: dirty pans, rancid butter, spoiled wine, unwashed linens, and a host of other calamities that I would never tolerate at the Establishment.

"Who is in charge of this place?" I demanded of Goodfellow, whirling around on him so violently that he actually took several steps away from me.

"Why, Mr. Mitchell is our superintendent," he replied in a startled tone. "He is also waiting for you upstairs."

I nodded. "I certainly wish to meet with him."

Goodfellow recovered enough to make an impatient sound. "Yes, Miss Nightingale, as I had intended when you first arrived."

We went up two flights of stairs and ended up in a large room in one of the magnificent windowed wings of the building. Around a long oak table sat six of Goodfellow's colleagues, seated in tufted leather chairs. All of them were dressed in fine gentlemen's clothing.

Even as Goodfellow introduced each of them, I immediately forgot their names, so blindingly angry was I. They all gazed at me curiously, and I realized I was still wearing my plain work dress instead of something finer for meeting with gentleman physicians. But I believed us at this point to be far beyond concern for elegant attire.

"Miss Nightingale," began one of the physicians, leaning forward on the table, his fingers steepled together. "You probably saw the distressing condition of the creatures out on the lawn. We have asked you here to assist us with caring for these cholera victims, as we are certain there will be more and more cases, and we have no room for what we have."

They all looked at me expectantly. I did not give them what they anticipated. "You do indeed have a terrible situation here, and I know that I can personally bring at least two more cholera victims to this hospital. However, I would not permit a feral dog to live here, much less an ailing person. I have several conditions that must be met before I—or any of my nurses—can assist you."

Six pairs of jaws dropped in unison. Poor Dr. Goodfellow seemed particularly confused. No doubt I was coming across as a hysterical mental patient.

"Miss Nightingale, we are merely seeking assistance in nursing care for this unfortunate outbreak. It is well known that you are training nurses to be more than cold compress holders, and we would like to bring that expertise here," he explained.

The doctor did seem a kind man, so it stabbed my conscience to be so prickly with him, but the conditions in this hospital were *horrendous.*

"I appreciate your desire to care for the sick, but I believe the current conditions of this facility will lead people to perish more readily from a stay in one of your beds than from wasting away at home with cholera." I sat back against the leather.

Another man, who had to be reintroduced to me as Mr. Mitchell, Middlesex Hospital's superintendent, found his voice and challenged me. "Miss Nightingale, our hospital has been in existence in this location since 1757. Why, the foundation stone was laid by our first president, the Earl of Northumberland, and we were the first hospital in England to have lying-in beds. In fact, this location began as a sixty-four-bed hospital, caring solely for sick, lame, and lying-in women of Soho." Mitchell began ticking off his points on the fingers of one hand. "We opened a special ward for sick French clergy who had escaped their revolution back in '96. We had the first endowment for a cancer ward more than fifty years ago. Six years ago, we added a third floor and two wings, and we now have two hundred and forty beds. We have treated thousands upon thousands of the sick and lame. My point, dear lady, is that we are a highly respectable hospital, not some tawdry boarding house."

There was silence in the room, with the hospital's doctors and administrators nodding in agreement with Mitchell. Goodfellow spoke up again. "This is a bit exasperating, Miss Nightingale. After all, as Mr. Mitchell says, we are a highly regarded hospital. Nonetheless, we have recognized that we need a little help to overcome this temporary crisis. Your outburst seems most unnecessary."

I had no argument with Middlesex's past, nor with what it purported to have achieved. I objected to the condition of it today. However, there was no point in squabbling about it.

I rose from my chair and took a deep breath as I once again folded my hands together. "Gentlemen, I will return tomorrow to meet with your nurses and orderlies. Until then, I wish the following to be done." Now I was the one to tick things off. "First, all—and I do mean *all*—of the windows in each ward must be thrown open to air the place out."

Mitchell huffed his disagreement. "Preposterous. It is well established that the sick must be kept confined and not exposed to any outside air containing vapors."

I pressed my lips together. "Sir, you have called me here because of your respect for my ways, is that not correct?"

"Well, yes, but—"

"Then I am sharing with you the manner in which I have found it best to ensure that a hospital inmate recuperates fully.

Fresh air is better than stale air, even at the risk of miasmas." I began enumerating my demands once more. "Your orderlies must remove all the slops from the water closets and from any chamber pots next to beds. All bedding must be laundered, preferably by chloride of lime dissolved in water to ensure they are well bleached. The kitchen larder must be emptied of all its food, every bit of it, and new purchased in its place. I will provide you with a list of foodstuffs to procure, but be assured it will center upon eggs, meat, tea, and quality wines."

"Miss Nightingale!" Goodfellow exclaimed. His consternation was evident in his voice and on his face. "Have you no idea what that would cost? Many of our inmates cannot afford admission here whatsoever, and we have to rely on our generous donors for money. Imagine our having to go back to them to ask for additional donation because we chose to dispose of all of our food in the midst of a crisis!"

I ignored his plea. "Also, the supplies in this hospital are maintained in an utter jumble and there aren't enough basic necessities kept on hand. I will make a list—on second thought, my nurses and I will return to put things in proper order and we will purchase supplies ourselves. You may reimburse me for them."

The men around the table said nothing, but I saw one man pull a small leather journal from the pocket of his vest and begin taking notes. I had no idea if he would remember my instructions accurately—how much better it would have been if Mary had been with me—but his action meant he was at least taking me seriously.

I spent some time outside with the poor souls suffering on the lawn before leaving, doing my best to comfort them and assure them that they would receive the best care possible, even while knowing that cholera was a harsh jailer. I wasn't sure how much effect I could have upon this hospital.

The one thing I knew for sure was that Middlesex Hospital itself would have to be cured before it could be expected to treat the desperately sick.

★   ★   ★

Nurses Harris and Lambert, Mary Clarke, and I returned to Soho later via a hired wagon. We four sat on a bench running along one side of the interior of the wagon, surrounded by fresh linens, freshly pumped water in bottles, gallons of bone broth, and a plethora of rags and cleaning supplies.

I had to offer our driver a king's ransom not only to take us all the way to Seven Dials, but also to sit and wait for us. He was very tetchy about it, but I finally named a price that would have bought him a suit of clothes and fed his family for a month, and so he agreed.

As we made the jarring ride into Soho, I gave my nurses what I hoped was an inspiring speech: "I'm sure you have heard many things about this part of London. I admit some of it is true, and the residents there are not like the middling-class women you have been used to treating at the Establishment. Yet it is our great duty to help these unfortunates, to go where they are and offer them comfort. We shall be brave and fearless and will not count the cost to ourselves. Remember that the Lord says it is more blessed to give than to receive, and give we will."

Lambert nodded, the untied strings of her cap dancing as her head moved. Today she wore a pale-yellow head covering that reminded me of an old medieval wimple. It did effectively cover much of her birthmark and reminded me of the nuns I had met while training at Pastor Fliedner's deaconess training center. The nuns there were compassionate and ruthlessly efficient, and I planned that Nurse Lambert would one day resemble one of Fliedner's nuns not only physically, but in her abilities too.

"Miss Nightingale, we will do as you say, but do you think it possible that we will have cholera ourselves by the end of the day?" Lambert gazed at me steadily, her quivering lower lip the only sign that beneath her courage lay the fear of a young woman who had not yet done much in life and desperately wished to do so.

Thus far, Mary and I had shown no signs of it, but sometimes diseases had a habit of erupting when least expected. I wanted to encourage her but did not wish to be overly optimistic. "Whatever is to happen, we will face it together, nurse. And we have the added benefit of one another, and who knows how to care for the sick better than the nurses of the Establishment?"

Nurse Harris clasped Lambert's hand in her own in support and nodded once at me as if to let me know she understood and agreed. The woman was quiet and solid, standing like a piece of granite in a hurricane. I envisioned her one day running the Establishment or some other hospital herself.

By the time we reached the Reeves', tragedy had already struck, and the devil himself must have had a hand in it. We discovered from a neighbor lounging around outside, who spoke broken English with a heavy Italian accent, that the family was no longer there and for the worst reason imaginable: Mr. Reeve had returned home the previous evening and done in his poor wife for unintentionally killing their daughter. First had come a tempestuous, one-sided argument by the husband. Then, the neighbor said, the woman's screams could be heard up and down the street before he silenced her with a slam of her head against their crumbling fireplace.

The young boy, Lucky, had last been seen running down the street as though he had a demon on his heels, and I suppose in some ways he had. He hadn't been heard from since.

Mary sniffed and put a hand to her mouth. "Poor mite," she whispered.

Mr. Reeve had left the house in a rage, although not in the same direction his son had gone, and several nearby men had entered the lodgings. One of the men had instantly assessed what had happened when he saw poor Mrs. Reeve crumpled in a pool of blood and the long-dead girl on the bed. He had run after Reeve while some women had collected the dead bodies. He had found Reeve an hour later inside an alleyway latrine, already suffering the effects of cholera.

The woman I talked to assumed Reeve was dead, too. She smiled a mouthful of rotting teeth at the thought that Lucky's father had received his comeuppance in so short a time and expressed her pride that she was now caring for the poor orphaned infant.

We unloaded some of the food and offered it to the woman, who fell upon it in disbelief.

I worried that the scene at the Maddox residence would not be much better, and that the ravages of cholera might seem an improvement to what we had witnessed here.

CHAPTER 9

A<small>s</small> the wagon rumbled down the narrow, rutted street, my bones were jarred near to breaking. It was a relief when the driver had to slow down to maneuver around obstacles. As we entered Broad Street, Mary nudged me and pointed to a sign on a post freshly erected near the Lion Brewery. I had the driver stop so I could read it.

The GOVERNORS and DIRECTORS of the POOR

HEREBY GIVE NOTICE

That, with the view of affording prompt and Gratuitous assistance to Poor Persons resident in this Parish, affected with Bowel Complaints and

CHOLERA,

The following Medical Gentlemen are appointed, either of whom may be immediately applied to for Medicine and Attendance, on the occurrence of those Complaints.

Dr. John SNOW—Sackville Street
Dr. Stephen GOODFELLOW—Middlesex Hospital and Infirmary

SUGGESTIONS AS TO FOOD, CLOTHING, & c.

Regularity in the Hours of taking Meals, which should
  consist of any description of wholesome Food, with
  the moderate use of sound Beer.
Abstinence from Spirituous Liquors.
Warm Clothing and Cleanliness of Person.
The avoidance of unnecessary exposure to Cold and Wet,
  and the wearing of Damp Clothes, or Wet Shoes.
Regularity in obtaining sufficient Rest and Sleep.
Cleanliness of Rooms, which should be aired by opening
  the Windows in the middle of each day.

For Spiritual Comfort, the **Rev. Henry Whitehead** of
St. Luke's Church—OLD STREET has thrown open
the doors to all who seek solace and prayers.

By Order of the Board,
N. Newell
Clerk

I indicated to the driver that he could move on.

I was glad to see that the authorities had responded so quickly to this burgeoning crisis. I would have to act quickly myself to get Middlesex in order if they were going to be able to successfully treat more victims.

I would also have to perform some sort of miracle to discover who had made an attempt on Liz's life and ended up killing the Herberts' coachman instead. I needed it resolved so I could turn my attention to the more important matter of the cholera outbreak.

Perhaps it would be better for me to beg off or defer Sidney's task. Surely he would understand the gravity of the situation in Soho. There were potentially hundreds—if not thousands—of lives in great danger here. Liz would remain safe—both from madmen and cholera—as long as she stayed home.

But then I thought of Joss Pagg, who had died in Liz's stead. Didn't he deserve justice? And what of Fenton, a cholera victim simply because he had been doing his master's bidding? Should there not be a resolution so that his death, too, was not inconsequential?

I must have sighed aloud, for Mary silently handed me a handkerchief from her sleeve. I smiled and handed it back to her.

"I am quite fine, Goose. Just woolgathering. And here we are." The driver had stopped in front of the Maddox home, distinguishable from every other place in its tenement housing row by the faded blue paint on the door, the remnant of a more prosperous time for the neighborhood, a time long past.

George Maddox seemed surprised that we had actually returned to tend to his family. I introduced Harris and Lambert to him, and then we got to work on the tiny room occupied by Isabel and young Arthur Maddox.

The boy had weakened more overnight, and Isabel's mind was even more . . . suspicious.

"I don't know you," she said to Lambert, who was attempting to bathe the woman while Harris unfolded a sheet from the small pile of linens we had brought in. "Did he send you to kill me?"

Lambert stopped her ministrations to look up at Isabel. "Pardon me? No, madam, I am here to help you."

But Isabel Maddox was already recoiling, having gotten a glimpse of Nurse Lambert's birthmark.

"You are a witch!" the woman screeched, pointing at the nurse's face.

Lambert dropped her washing cloth and backed away herself. "I am no—what? Why am I so accused?" She blanched at what I imagined was the worst insult that had ever been hurled at her.

I inserted myself between the raving woman and my valued nurse.

"Mrs. Maddox!" I said sharply. "You are ill and not in your right mind."

I glanced to my right, where George Maddox stood in the room's entryway, his expression one of mortification. "Bella, please . . ." he said helplessly.

Isabel Maddox was obviously parched and in a delirium as a result of spattering her bowels' contents for two straight days. It was a wonder she had not yet died. Perhaps she was of a far stronger constitution than I had credited her with.

Whatever her condition, she was determined to find fault in others. With Lambert now forgotten, she pointed a brittle-nailed finger at her husband, the new object of her venom.

"It was Barton! Always the bad son! Always convinced of your own brilliance. But I know what you did. It will be eternal damnation for you, won't it?"

Isabel's hair seemed to be coming undone of its own will, and those piercing gray eyes of hers were burning a hole straight through me. Clearly Isabel Maddox was chastising her husband in the name of his brother.

Fortunately, she calmed down after this particular outburst, so Harris quickly moved to change the woman's bed linens. The nurse moved to toss the thin, torn, filthy sheet the woman had been lying on into the fireplace, but I stopped her.

"We must not show disrespect to anyone's belongings," I said quietly. "No matter how meager."

Harris nodded in understanding, and instead began folding it as if someone would eventually wish to reuse the ratty thing.

Lambert was going through our foodstuffs in an attempt to make a palatable tray of food. I decided in that instant that we would leave everything behind for this family. I had enough allowance from my father to replace it all.

I knelt down next to the Maddox boy. He stank of old sweat and new vomit. His breathing was shallow, and he did not respond to my gentle movement of his shoulder. He was so frail I thought he might break at my mere touch.

"Try to get some beef tea between his lips," I instructed Lambert. "He might respond to an enticing aroma."

I had little hope for the poor boy, but he would at least be as nourished as possible.

I left the nurses to complete their work, signaling to Mary to join me in the outer room with George Maddox, who had retreated there to idly do some work.

He looked at me hopefully from where he stood with a mallet in his hand as we joined him around his messy worktable.

"You did truly come for us," he said. "Thank you, Miss Nightingale. How do my wife and child fare?"

I hated to add to the ash heap of the man's woes, but I also did not wish to offer false hope. I had offered enough of *that* with Richard.

"Your son is not well, sir. Surely you know that," I said.

He silently passed a hand over his eyes.

"Your wife, however, seems to have an iron constitution. I believe vitriol may carry her back to good health."

"Forgive my wife," he said. "She is so sick. What am I to do if she dies? And I apologize for my earlier . . . condition, Miss Nightingale. You caught me at a very low point of weakness. I'm afraid I haven't been quite myself lately. Now with illness upon my household . . ." His expression was bleak.

The more he spoke, the more I realized he had an upper-middle-class sound to his voice. "How did you come to be in Soho?" I asked delicately. "I don't sense that you have lived here all your life."

"No, I haven't. Sometimes I can hardly believe this is what has come of my life. And to think that it is likely to become worse. You might not believe it, Miss Nightingale, but I come from a prosperous family."

I nodded. "Actually, I do believe that."

"My father was an upholsterer, and I inherited all his tools and supplies. But the demand for my work is not so great here as it was in my father's shop in Regent Street. He was quite well known and was hired quite regularly by the officers within the East India Company after he came up with some designs that blended Indian patterns and concepts into our own English style. Father even had a few pieces displayed at the Great Exhibition's Indian Court. He enjoyed some royal patronage when he was hired to make a special chair for Princess Vicky to sit in during her first birthday celebrations back in '41."

So the Maddox upholstering business had been profitable thirteen years ago, anyway.

George began absentmindedly playing with a stray tack on the table, twirling it about on its head as though it were a miniature spinning toy top. "We had a nice life, our family. My father had moved us into a new, three-story townhome with a forty-year lease on reasonable terms. But my father was unhappy."

I, too, had been born to comfort and had been vastly miserable.

George continued, "Neither my brother nor I wished to partake in the upholstery business. Barton was anxious to join the Army. He'd been enamored of the scarlet uniforms, the sashes, and the medals since he was a young boy. The thought of being imprisoned among bolts of fabric and crates of horsehair nearly drove him mad. I thought my father would also go insane the day my brother ran off in '39, leaving behind a note."

"This is the brother of whom your wife spoke?" I asked.

"Yes, but I have no idea what she's talking about. I suppose he was the bad son in my father's eyes for running off, but he never harmed anyone in his life. Or at least he didn't do anything to deserve damnation."

I could at least soothe George Maddox on this count. "Be of rest, sir. Many people who rave while ill have no recollection of it when they come to their senses. No doubt your wife won't even remember it and would be most penitent to know she had uttered such slander."

He sighed and nodded. "To my knowledge, she never even met him."

"What happened after your brother entered the Army?" I asked, more interested than was probably proper in the situation. I figured he would tell me that his father's madness had led to the fall of the business. But the truth was worse than that.

George winced, and I saw that he had accidentally stuck himself with the tack. A drop of blood appeared, and he wiped his finger against his trousers. "He turned all his attention to me, assuming I would be his grateful heir after Barton had been such an ingrate. But I, too, wished for a different future."

He then turned to a messy stack of small boxes along one

wall and selected one, managing to pull it out without the rest collapsing. He handed it to me. I pushed aside some of the debris on his worktable and lifted the lid. Inside were yellowing pages covered in a cramped, spidery scrawl, with many scratch-outs.

"I had—have—a love for the written word. I wrote my novel in secret for a long time, knowing my father would disapprove. Besides, it wasn't as though anyone was begging to publish my manuscript. But when my brother fled the household, I felt I must share my desires with my father so that he would understand I did not wish to carry on with the family business either."

I stood in this jumble of a room, pretending not to notice what was going on in the next room. Poor Bella Maddox groaned. There still wasn't the tiniest chirp out of Arthur, though. I hoped he still lived, even now.

With mild curiosity, I flipped through several pages of George Maddox's manuscript box as he continued his story. "Father reacted much as I expected, informing me of what a ridiculous specimen I had become and threatening to turn me out of the house for following my brother in ruination of the family's future. I argued with him daily until I was hoarse from it, and my mother took to shutting herself up inside her bedchamber."

Maddox's story appeared to be about an Arthurian knight on a quest to rescue a maiden. The writing was flowery and overwrought.

"Despite all of that, we three limped along together without Barton for nearly a year, until he was reported killed. He'd barely gotten his ears wet. My father was devastated, particularly since we never saw his body. We didn't even know where he was buried. As angry as my father had been that Barton had run off, now he had the realization that there was no hope whatsoever that his eldest son might come home one day and take up the reins of the business. My father was stuck with me, and here I was, crouched in a corner with ink all over my fingers. Meanwhile, my mother almost never came out of her chamber, partially because of my brother and partially because of me."

My own mother wouldn't have dreamt of allowing me to miss the benefit of a tirade by staying in her rooms upon the great occasion of my proving a great disappointment to her.

"Barton had always considered joining the Army to be his patriotic duty to England, and I attempted to write some odes to his service in order to cheer my father up, but they only made him morose. And angry at me."

"So terrible," Mary uttered, shaking her head sadly. I could see that she had deep empathy for this man, who was likely to lose his spouse, as she had also lost hers all those years ago.

"I met Bella at a stationer's shop one day when I was out buying writing paper. She was simply perfect. Sweet, kind, loving. And beautiful. Why was she interested in a wastrel like me? But she was, and I was not about to waste a stroke of blessing. She was so different then. She was interested in what I had to say, letting me talk on about my brother and about my father's disappointments."

Mary was still shaking her head in sympathy. "A loving spouse is so critical to one's happiness, isn't it? I was married to my Milo for nearly thirty years before God saw fit to take him from me. We were never apart, except for when he was tutoring his young pupils. In fact, we even—"

I surreptitiously elbowed Mary, and she had the grace to cease talking about the sainted Milo for the moment.

"Bella found it interesting that my father had a successful upholstery shop and wanted to know all about it, in addition to asking me about my writings. Knowing that my brother was gone, she was determined to reunite me with Father. She managed to charm both me and my father into it, and soon we were married and living with my parents. Bella had a good head for . . ." Maddox paused, as if deciding on the right term.

"A good head for motivating others to work." He nodded in satisfaction at his phrasing.

"So Mrs. Maddox was a very good wife to you," I prompted. "Until her recent illness, I presume?"

He frowned. "I'm not sure when things specifically happened to Bella. My father became withdrawn and isolated from the family, and I cannot say it was a surprise when he took a plunge from Westminster Bridge. However, it left me with a business I did not want and a mother to care for.

"Bella was magnificent. She cared for my mother night and day, even while heavy with our son, and used every opportunity to urge me along in the business. Despite Bella's care, though, Mother died about a year later."

Mary made sympathetic noises.

"Did she also . . . inflict her death upon herself?" I asked.

"No. She just sort of wasted away without warning. I always assumed it was too much for her to live without my father. Arthur's arrival eased that pain. But that didn't last, either."

There was yet more tragedy in this poor man's life? I wondered how many times this story had played out throughout this densely populated neighborhood.

"My father had left behind a large backlog of orders, plus more continued to pour in, so I decided to hire a manager to assist me in handling the customers and bills so I could focus on the upholstery work. Snead ended up stealing nearly everything my father had worked so hard to build."

I looked around. Perhaps George Maddox should have hired an upholsterer and managed the business himself.

"What happened with Mr. Snead?" I asked.

Maddox shrugged. "I confronted him over the thefts. He admitted readily to it and offered to make restitution, so I agreed that he could work off the amount he had stolen. Bella didn't like it much, thought I should drag him into court at the very least, but doesn't every man deserve forgiveness?"

Mary nodded her agreement solemnly at the man, and I followed suit.

"Before he could even begin paying me back, he disappeared," Maddox said.

"Disappeared?" I repeated. "Where did he go?"

Another shrug. "I don't know. He left one day to purchase a shirt to replace one that he accidentally tore in the shop, and didn't return. I never heard from him again."

The hairs on my neck prickled. I didn't like the sound of this at all. "So you never recovered your money, either?"

"No. I gave up the lease on our home and moved us into smaller quarters. But it wasn't enough. I just didn't seem to have the same ability to attract customers that my father had. I wasn't able to secure any additional work with the East India Company, and everything began tattering. Soon I wasn't able to afford the lease on my shop, so I sold much of my equipment, and then moved my wife and son here because it was all I could manage on my earnings." He swept a hand to demonstrate that all he could afford were these meager quarters.

That was when I noticed some wet plaster in a corner of the ceiling. It was sagging and black with mold. In fact, most of the ceiling was stained, peeling, and bulging downward.

"You have tried to establish your business here, then," I said, already understanding the rest of the story.

"Yes. As you can imagine, there isn't much use for my talent here. I've made a few pieces for the Lion Brewery. They maintain quarters for their shift managers, and I've picked up work that way. Tried to convince the British Museum to let me make some of their seating benches inside their corridors, but they were dismissive of me. No doubt they only want to use upholsterers who have the royal warrant."

I glanced over at the chair in the window. I didn't think that was the reason at all.

"What of your writing?" I asked, handing him back the manuscript box.

"In my spare time, I've worked on my novels, but have never found a publisher interested in them. Not even William Blackwood and Sons, who seem to be taking on so many authors. You don't happen to know any publishers, do you?" he asked hopefully as he took the box and laid it on top of a tottering stack along the wall. I held my breath, but the tower did not collapse.

It was my own great hope to be able to publish my own thoughts on nursing one day as an instruction for women who wished to learn proper techniques. How discouraging to think that getting a book published was so difficult.

He saw the expression on my face and said, "No, I wouldn't have thought so. Anyway, my life has rotted away like a gangrenous toe will eventually eat an entire leg. Bella became very unstable once we moved here, and who can blame the dear girl?

Nothing turned out the way she had planned, and she worked so hard to help me. Now this is how she will be repaid. The vagaries of life can mean such cruelty for those who don't deserve it."

"No one is promised an easy life," I said, recognizing my own grievous hypocrisy. After all, my own difficulties had never extended into miserable poverty, just multiple battles of will against others. "We can only manage with what we are given," I finished lamely.

He nodded in a thoroughly unconvinced way. "I suppose we must. I have been thinking lately . . ." He paused as if unsure whether to share his thought.

I waited calmly and without complaint for him to make his decision, much as I would with a hospital inmate who could not decide whether to take a cup of hot beef tea or a bowl of Turkish broth to accompany her buttered toast.

Finally, he decided he would include me in his ruminations. "I've been thinking of trying something completely new. The Lion Brewery is looking for a supervisor for its long overnight shift. Mr. Davies says he would consider me because of my business experience. I don't know much of anything about ales and stouts—well, other than sometimes overenjoying them, I suppose." He looked at me sheepishly.

"It would certainly be steadier income in your situation," I said.

Maddox nodded. "Oswyn Davies is the manager there and runs the public house part of the brewery. He was once in the Army and says he would like to show benevolence to the brother of a dead soldier. But either John Huggins or his brother, Edward, would have to approve me. They own the brewery. I'm just not sure if I should do it."

I couldn't believe the man's hesitance. "Why would you not do it?" I countered.

He hesitated again. "It's just . . . I think both my father and my brother would have been disappointed in me. My father for not carrying on the business, and my brother for not pursuing book publication. I wouldn't have much time to myself for writing if I worked at the brewery. Anyway, I suppose I have wasted too much of your time on my woes, Miss Nightingale. My apologies; I'm certain you have other people who need attending to."

"Actually, Mr. Maddox, I have learned a great deal by spending time here in Soho. I should have come sooner." I meant it.

He offered me a strange look that suggested I had taken leave of my senses. "Don't think I've ever heard anyone say they should spend *more* time in this wretched place."

I couldn't help but smile at the unintentional wit. "Nevertheless, I am glad we could be of service to your family. I suspect there are many more with illness behind their doors who require help. We shall return again tomorrow to check on you all again."

If Mrs. Maddox was better, I planned to question her regarding her comments about Barton Maddox and murder. Although I believed her statements to be the gibberish of an unwell mind, I had to be sure. I also wanted to alleviate the peculiar sensation I had that something was not quite right about the supposed death of Barton Maddox. After all, the family had never seen his body. Was I grasping at straws?

Maddox's eyes widened. "I would be grateful for your visit. And . . . I will let you know if I secure the position at the brewery."

Something important occurred to me. "This Mr. Davies you mentioned. How long has he run the brewery?"

"I'm not sure. No, wait, he told me he has been there for five years."

Five years was a long time in which to witness the goings-on of a neighborhood. I needed to chat with Mr. Davies.

Harris and Lambert entered the front room, indicating that they had done all they could. With assurances that we wouldn't forget the Maddoxes, we left to return to the wagon. I hoped that the driver hadn't gotten spooked enough to leave us there despite how much I had paid him for the job.

As I followed everyone out, I paused to look back at the Maddox residence. It was a shabby, sad hovel in the midst of so many others. Did George Maddox contemplate the downturn of his luck every time he walked up to his warped door? Had Isabel Maddox made the same reflection every time she pulled up the ratty coverlet on their lumpy bed? It was frightening how far one could fall in such a short space of time.

I shook my head and turned to follow my nurses once more. I would accompany them back to the Establishment, then return with Mary to visit the Lion Brewery.

The driver was indeed still waiting. We all climbed back onto our rough seats in the rear of the wagon. Mary was pensive as we rode off, and I thought that the second visit to the Maddox home had been even more distressing for her than the first. As we left Soho, the sky literally brightened and Mary spoke for the first time in nearly an hour.

"Miss Florence, it seems to me that Soho causes the death of anyone who lives there."

I thought of Sidney's servants, Fenton and Pagg. "Or of anyone who merely visits," I said grimly.

CHAPTER 10

With Harris and Lambert safely returned to the Establishment, I asked Mary to return to Soho with me.

"Again?" she asked, her expression stricken.

"Yes. Do you remember Mr. Maddox mentioning a Mr. Davies at the Lion Brewery? I believe it would be helpful to speak with him. He may have seen something the day Liz's carriage came through."

Mary shook her head but didn't protest.

We returned to Soho by way of taxi, but this driver refused to wait even a few minutes for us. The neighborhood was becoming familiar enough to me that I almost didn't mind.

"Have a care, ladies," the driver said gallantly, tipping his hat before hurrying off with his nickering horse. Even the mare seemed unhappy to have driven into Broad Street.

As if to emphasize its offended equine sensibilities, the horse deposited a great steaming pile of excrement onto the street as it trotted away. It was particularly malodorous in the late-August heat.

Mary wrinkled her nose in repugnance. "Let's hope the

inside of the brewery doesn't stink so badly," she said, holding a gloved finger beneath her nose.

We entered the Lion Brewery via its Red Lion Inn entrance. What better way to introduce your wares to the surrounding neighborhood than with what was essentially a shop full of samples?

I had never actually entered such a socially inferior establishment before. My mother would have been clawing at the draperies if she'd had any idea her daughter was frequenting a public house.

"Miss Florence, what is so amusing?" Mary asked as she removed her gloves while we stood in the entryway and stuffed them inside her dress pocket. She was already opening her notebook to a blank page.

"Nothing at all, Goose," I said putting away my own gloves. They were slick with perspiration, and it was a relief to be rid of them.

I was surprised to find that the interior of the Lion's public house wasn't nearly as seedy as I had expected it to be.

To the left were an assortment of mismatched tables and chairs, some with occupants who glanced at us curiously but soon returned to their games. The air was filled with the clicking of dice, slapping of cards, and jingling of coins on the tabletops as the men bantered jovially with one another.

An enormous brick fireplace dominated a rear wall, and a large, square bin stood to one side of it. The bin was heaped with coal in preparation for cooler weather, and I suspected it was more coal than could be found in total in the rest of the neighborhood.

I had rather expected the ceiling to be low, made even lower by old, scarred wood beams, as if the building had been some old medieval manor, but I was pleased to find that this was not so.

The ceiling was in fact at least ten feet high, well plastered and painted, and several gasoliers hung from it. Candle lanterns on most of the tables assisted the gasoliers in illuminating the spacious room.

Certainly there was the odor of spilled ale permeating the space, with an underlay of old vomit not quite scrubbed out of the planked floors, but all in all, I thought Middlesex Hospital was far more frightful a place.

To our right was a long bar of polished oak. Occupying half the wall around the bar were about a dozen barrels that lay stacked on their sides. The rest of the wall contained shelves filled with glasses, tankards, and a variety of mismatched dishes.

At the left end of the bar was a doorway, with a sign over it reading, "Worker Entrance to Brewery."

It was a place for men, to be certain, but compared to everything outside of it, the Red Lion Inn was really quite innocuous.

The only disturbing part of the public house was the man who stood behind the bar, wiping out glasses with a rag that was old and stained. He was staring straight at Mary and me.

"Yes?" he said impatiently, as we were clearly dawdling in the entryway. "Where you two ladies intended to go, are you sure?" Your husbands wander out of your home to sneak some peace and quiet here? Have a look about to see if they're here."

He said this as if it were a regular occurrence.

Mary huffed in indignation. "Certainly not! My Milo would never have gone off to drown himself in spirits. He was a devoted husband who would never have avoided me by—"

I reached out a hand to stop her. "I don't think he means

anything by it, Goose," I said quietly. "He just doesn't think we belong in this neighborhood."

I approached the bar with Mary on my heels. The man standing behind it tossed the rag onto the counter and, spreading his hands out, leaned forward against the wood. It felt almost aggressive in nature, and if we weren't two defenseless women, I would have thought he was anticipating a fight.

"Are you Mr. Davies?" I asked. "I am Florence Nightingale, and this is my companion, Mary Clarke. We've come to ask you about a customer you may have had recently."

The man only grunted in response and returned to glass polishing.

Up close, he was quite terrifying. He reminded me of a cadaver, tall and gaunt and seemingly uncomfortable in his ill-fitting clothes. It was surely difficult for him to find trousers and shirts that fit properly, as evidenced by the bony wrists that protruded far out from his sleeves. His face was adorned with a very long chin beard, of chestnut brown flecked with gray and remarkably well groomed, an incongruity against his rumpled clothing.

The beard's shape was an unfortunate choice for him, as it did nothing to conceal his prominent cheekbones, which rose up like mountain ridges on the sides of his face. His hair straggled around his temples and over his ears. Overall, his hair growth gave the effect of a halo around his head.

He held up a glass with his left hand, examining it in the light from the gasoliers. I noticed that two of his fingers were mostly gone, and the nubs showed gnarled skin on them, as if some blind butcher from a previous century had clipped his fingers and then sewn up the skin while wearing thick winter gloves.

The man continued to work as though we were not standing across the bar from him. Thus far, he hadn't been at all inquisitive about our presence.

"Mr. Davies, please, if I may speak with you a moment about an incident that occurred here about a week ago."

He looked down at me through hooded lids and said nothing.

"Sir, I must assure you that neither of us has an errant husband. I wish to ask you about the attack that happened about a week ago. It was upon the Herbert carriage, and their coachman was inadvertently killed."

His only reaction was increased color on his cheekbones.

"Did you witness what happened?" I asked.

Davies grunted again.

This was going to prove very frustrating. "Mr. Davies, it is of utmost importance that I talk to you. My friend, Sidney Herbert, is the secretary at war, and his wife was almost murdered. The culprit must be found."

"Secretary at war, eh?" Davies said. His voice suggested that he wasn't impressed at all. He turned around to put the glass on a shelf behind the bar, then turned back to me. "And care what the secretary at war thinks, why should I?" He gazed steadily at me, and I saw anger brimming in his muddy brown eyes.

I was taken aback. "Because he is . . . responsible for this nation's defense. He is the queen's trusted servant. He will—"

"Pretty words." Davies said, practically sneering at me. "I'm sure Reverend Whitehead could use them in his next sermon. He's as devoted to Her Majesty as Mr. Herbert seems to be." Another glass went on the shelf.

Whitehead. Why did I know that name?

I pulled Fenton's dice from my pocket. "Have you seen these before?" I asked, holding them out in my flat palm.

Davies gave them a cursory glance. "Sure. Hundreds of times I've seen them before. Have a look around." He waved a hand out over the rest of the public house. "Every soul in here has a pair just like them."

I thrust the dice at him again. "But look at the engraved markings atop each crown side. Aren't they unusual?"

He made an impatient noise, and I realized that, in my own frustration, I was being less than endearing. He took one of the dice from me and squinted at it, then dropped it back into my palm. "Men mark up game pieces in all sorts of manners to ensure their valuables don't find their way into someone else's pockets. Sometimes it be initials, sometimes it be an important date, and sometimes it just be pure nonsense."

I was disappointed that Mr. Davies could offer no more help than that. I also didn't believe that the dice in Fenton's pocket were inscribed with nonsense. I put them back in my pocket.

Davies leaned against the wood counter once more. "Get back to my work, I must. The middle shift will end soon, and I must take care of the lads."

"Sir . . ." I began, unsure what would pierce his suspicions of me.

Mary accomplished the task by interrupting me with five simple words. "Might we try an ale?"

He raised a skeptical eyebrow at Mary, a woman of deepening middle age and stout, schoolmarmish looks. "Sample the wares here, you wish?"

Mary nodded. "We both do."

He shrugged, took a glass from the shelf, and went to the

stack of barrels behind the counter, each of which had a tap on the end and a different marking above it. He turned to look over his shoulder. "India ale you want? It would probably be the easiest on your female constitutions."

He twisted the tap, and a pale golden liquid flowed into the glass. He set the glass down in front of Mary and retrieved another to fill.

"Why is it called India ale?" Mary asked. "You brew it here, do you not? It doesn't come from India, does it?"

Davies shook his head as he placed a second glass of warm liquid in front of me. "No, woman, from India it doesn't come. The original India ale was brewed by a company located near the East India Docks. Quite fond of it the East India Company traders became, hence the name. We brew our own version of it."

I picked up the glass and sniffed the contents. The aroma transported me back to my childhood at Lea Hurst. Monday was baking day, and our cook would line tables and sills with rising loaves of yeasty bread, each waiting its turn in the oven. The smell of those loaves always triggered something primal in my youthful soul, and I could hardly wait to sample the first one out of the oven, which I always slathered with Cook's freshly made butter.

I took a tentative sip. It didn't taste like my beloved bread. It had a fuller, stronger tang. It reminded me of summer grass, or perhaps freshly baled hay. It was a strange sensation on my tongue, but not unpleasant.

Mary's puckered expression suggested that she was not impressed at all with the ale, and I worried that she might spit it out. She eventually swallowed her mouthful down. I drank down a bit of my own, and as soon as Mr. Davies turned around again to tend to something, I poured part of her glass into my own so that he would not think she had rejected the beer.

He faced us again, once more spreading his hands across the counter. I was surprised it didn't have grooves shaped to fit his hands on it, given that he seemed to pose in the exact same spot each time. "What would you ladies say about the Lion's India ale?"

Mary pursed her lips, and this time I jumped in to answer for us both. "It is quite unusual. And tasty," I added, taking another swallow for his benefit.

Davies nodded in satisfaction. "Good ales we have here. Some brewers hop it too heavily for a pleasing drink, but the extra hops do make it able to survive the six-month journeys the East Indiamen make."

It was then that I noticed something I could not believe I hadn't seen in the several minutes Mary and I had been sitting before the man. "What happened to your ear?" I asked.

Davies instinctively reached up and pushed hair over his right ear to cover it, but not before I got a full view in the gas-light to see that the upper part was mangled. The top of the ear had just split open and was now bleeding.

"Come!" I commanded, setting down my glass and walking to an empty table. I turned back to him and pointed at a chair. "Sit," I further instructed.

He obeyed me immediately, probably in shock at my transformation from pleading female to imposing nurse.

I reached down into one of my voluminous dress pockets, where I carried an emergency supply of everything. My fingers found a roll of bandage and a soft leather case that held a pair of tiny scissors. I swiftly cut a piece of the linen and folded it multiple times, using it to staunch the flow of blood from his ear.

Discarding that, I cut and folded another piece, which I asked Mary to hold against his ear while I wrapped the remaining length of the bandage around his chin and head to secure the pad in place.

His shirt had some blood spatters on it and he now resembled a partially wrapped mummy, but we had stopped the bleeding before it became a serious problem.

I pulled a chair around to face him, while Mary sat across the table. "That is a very nasty injury, sir. Was it damaged here at the brewery? Did your fingers also suffer an ordeal here?"

"No," he said, the good fingers of his right hand reaching up to touch his bandaged ear, as if to assure himself it was still there. He winced in pain as he rubbed over the spot, and a tiny prick of blood stained through the bandage.

"I have a good liniment I can bring you," I offered. "It will ease both the bleeding and the pain."

He nodded, and I sensed him softening toward me.

"Has it ever been infected before?" I asked.

He nodded again.

"We shall have to keep an eye on it. I don't want you falling ill from it."

He gazed at me, and I knew he was coming to a decision. Finally, he spoke. "My position here I like. Don't want to be fired."

"Of course not," I said soothingly, wondering why talking to me about a thwarted murder attempt would see him terminated from employment at a brewery.

Now Davies's gaze shifted off to a distant point on the ceiling. "Lost my fingers to a rifle and my ear to a yataghan knife, all inside an hour. That was the one moment I regretted leaving my home in Aberdare, in Wales."

Wales. That certainly explained his odd speech patterns.

"But with Ma already dead and Da gone in a mine collapse, what choice did I have but make my way into Her Majesty's army? No other prospects."

I had the feeling we were about to hear another sad story about a resident of Soho, although Mr. Davies appeared to have decent employment and did not bear the aura of hopeless despair that seemed to consume everyone else in these parts.

"Where did you receive your injuries, Mr. Davies?" I asked.

He grimaced. "I was in the war with no purpose. No purpose, no glory, no benefit, no victories. Just a putrid, bloody mess."

The pain of whatever he had experienced was palpable.

"Were you in the opium war?" I asked. "Or in India fighting the Sikhs?"

He laughed joylessly. "If only it had been that pleasant. No, in Afghanistan I was."

As well read and studied as I was, I couldn't for the life of me remember what that conflict had been about. I vaguely recalled that the trouble had started in the late thirties when I had not quite reached my majority.

Wasn't Afghanistan just an arid desert with no particular resources to speak of? Why had Great Britain even cared about it?

"Sir, I confess I know very little about that war except that it was called the 'Calamity in Afghanistan.'"

He rolled his eyes. "It is known as the 'Disaster in Afghanistan,'" he corrected me. "And for good reason."

I saw that this was another way to make inroads with Mr. Davies. "Could you remind me of what happened there?"

Another laugh without a hint of mirth in it. "Women never understand war. And well they don't. It is an unspeakable horror."

I stiffened. "Sir, I can assure you that I have witnessed my share of blood, pus, and misery."

That elicited a genuine laugh from Davies. "You've seen nothing, and I wouldn't wish it upon the worst criminal, much less a lady such as yourself. But if you wish to know it so badly, I'll tell you, though how the knowledge can be of any use other than to give you night terrors, I know not."

I braced myself, and Mary sat poised over the notebook that lay open on the table.

"I was still in Wales when the agitation began in '37. Nearly twenty years ago, if you can believe it. To put it as simply as possible, the result of gamesmanship between Great Britain and Russia was the war."

That sounded unsettlingly familiar.

"A special mission in the East is what Russia considers herself to have, to conquer much of Asia; mostly Central Asia and China. Great Britain interprets this as including British interests in India.

"Don't misunderstand. The Russians don't like Great Britain and its liberal democracy, but only to the extent that they find us strange, not that they seek an invasion of British colonies."

I stopped his story. "You seem well versed in the Russian mind-set. How is this so? Were you an officer in the Army? Have you political experience?"

"Shush your noise," he said drily. "I was one of countless, nameless privates whose meager pay could let me live like royalty

in a place like Afghanistan. So even if I was interested in studying war strategies and tactics, it was in my own best interest to
keep my learning to myself.

"Now, I'm sure you are well aware of Great Britain's far-
reaching influence across the world."

"Of course," I said. Every schoolchild knew the British
Empire was the most impressive the world had ever seen, encom-
passing such far-flung places as Australia, Canada, and India; and
she continued spreading her influence.

America had been a terrible loss in the previous century, but
perhaps we were better off as friends with them. They were now
struggling violently with the ugly issue of slavery, and why
should Great Britain have to spend treasure to help them untan-
gle themselves from it?

"And the East India Company manages the jewel in the
crown—India," he said. "With the encouragement of the half-
wits in Parliament, the Company concluded that Russia was
attempting an incursion into the Crimea, and that Afghanistan's
emir was welcoming Russian influence.

"The Company tried to replace him with an old ruler that
had been deposed because he was so terrible. Sit well with the
Afghans it did not. Imagine if someone wanted to replace our
queen with, I don't know, Napoleon Bonaparte. There was
rebellion, but we crushed them, and the emir was sent into exile.
They set up the old ruler in his place, but believe me when I say
the Afghan tribes are wild and vicious and were not about to put
up with an imposed leader. Particularly one who took orders
from a foreign power."

Davies rose and returned to his spot behind the bar. Mary
and I dutifully followed. Davies continued his story. "Constant

insurrections there were. A spark here, a little flame there, and soon we were trying to put out multiple conflagrations of pure hatred and defiance. The Company seemed helpless to stop it. We were eventually contained in a swampy garrison northeast of Kabul. Apparently Major-General Elphinstone could find no better quarters for over sixteen thousand people, which included twelve thousand camp followers. And he compounded the problem by positioning supplies in a fort over three hundred yards away. A *scrut*, the man was.

"Living in a swamp is fine for soldiers, but for women and children? But what was to be expected by a tired old man who was bedridden with gout and rheumatism?"

Davies removed a box from behind the counter. He opened it to reveal a small treasure trove of coins. He began counting them as he spoke. "By late 1841, the Company realized that the tribesmen had grown very powerful and determined. Time for us to leave the capital city it was, and Elphinstone decided to lead us out en masse. The Afghan tribes had promised safe passage."

Davies finished the count. He appeared to be writing it down on something and did not speak for several moments, as if stalling while he decided what to say next.

"Surely they did not attempt to stop you from leaving since they wanted you gone so badly?" I asked.

"Stop us? That sounds so . . . mild . . . compared to what happened. No, no, *stopping* was not what happened. In January 1842 did we begin our march and had to help women and youngsters make their way through snowbound mountain passes. We didn't have enough tents, or blankets, or food for the trip, and frequently had to scrape a place in the snow and lie down hungry in the intense wind and cold."

Davies shook his head at the abominable memory. "No more than a few miles per day could we make, and the constant ambushes by the Afghans we had to repel, despite the promise of safe conduct. In one instance we were in such close contact with our attackers that there was no time to load weapons and we fought solely with bayonets. That's how this happened." He touched his bandaged ear.

"We eventually came to the Khurd–Kabul Pass. It was five miles long and so narrow and shut in on either side that the sun could barely penetrate through the gloomy cavern through which we traipsed. It was there that . . ."

He stopped, and I realized that my heart was pounding so erratically I could feel it in my throat, dreading what he was to say next.

Finally, Davies resumed in a resigned tone. "Once we were essentially trapped in the pass, the real attack occurred. They spared almost no one. Any breathing British or Indian man, woman, or child was worth murdering to them. Many were injured and left to freeze to death in the pass. A few of the women and children were scooped up to be made part of the tribal families. Some of the Indians managed to escape by offering to be sold into slavery. At least there was a blizzard that night to cover up the mangled bodies that we had been unable to protect.

"About a hundred of us made it through the pass and then through the thirty miles of treacherous gorges and passes lying along the Kabul River afterward. Down to about twenty working muskets, a little bit of ammunition, and some bayonet knives we were. Ironically, with most of the women and children gone, we were free to more effectively fight, but we hadn't eaten properly in weeks and had very little constitution to fight with."

Mary's pencil scratched along the pages of her notebook on top of the bar counter. I suspected she was as riveted by his story as I was. So many people killed in such a fruitless effort.

But was this not a story played out year after year for millennia? Even the ancients were known to have gone marching across deserts and mountains to engage in bloody battle, with no more reward than a mass grave full of rotting corpses.

"Some of us had also lost limbs to frostbite at this point and were unable to wield a gun properly anyway." He held up his left hand and waggled his remaining fingers. "A rumor started that we were to be captured as hostages, as the goat herders figured the East India Company would pay good ransoms for our freedom. Addled as he was, Elphinstone was ready to believe that after all that slaughter, they had changed their minds and now just wanted a tribute payment." Davies shook his head.

"So you dropped your weapons?" I guessed. "And they attacked you anyway?"

"Not hardly," Davies replied. "A scrut Elphinstone may have been, but the rest of us were not. Those who could still manage weapons held on to them tightly. I was at least able to swing mine around by the barrel and use it as a club. They attempted to slaughter the remainder of us, but we held strong. There was a Captain Shelton who was so fierce a fighter, who personally cut down so many Afghans, that by the end of the day they refused to fight him anymore. But it didn't change the outcome of his bravery. Those of us not killed were taken captive. A few of us managed a later escape and endured the entire experience of fleeing again, except this time warm at least the weather was. We made it back to India and from there got transport home."

That was surely a tale in itself. "How did you come to employment at Lion Brewery?"

Davies shrugged indifferently. "Wandered about the Hampshire countryside for a while, then spent several months in Andover workhouse doing bone crushing. Fled that the minute the warden wasn't paying attention, and I came to London. Mr. Huggins put up a notice in the streets around here that he wanted some clean, responsible workers. None too clean was I at the time, but I knew how to be responsible. Started in the back, breaking hops and barley; now I manage the brewery for them."

His truly was a remarkable story. Very few people escaped workhouses. To have escaped both a workhouse and certain death in war suggested that he was either very lucky or very determined.

"Was everyone else as fortunate as you were?" I asked.

Another shrug. "Not sure about most others. Elphinstone died as a captive and as far as I know was buried in an unmarked grave. He was elderly, indecisive, weak, sick, and utterly incompetent. Deserved his fate, he did."

I was silent, for I had no retort to such a statement. But I did wonder, "Was that the end of it all?"

Davies grunted. "No. That was not an insult to be tolerated. Once the weather warmed, more troops went into Afghanistan and inflicted a crushing defeat at Kabul. The remaining prisoners were rescued, and the city's bazaar was demolished. It is sadly amusing to me that a vast and flourishing empire such as ours would so greatly desire to wield power against a barren land of desert and mountains that offered no reward for the trouble."

Mary had stopped writing and was instead gaping at Davies in naked sympathy.

"You have suffered greatly," I said, unsure what else there was to say.

"No more than any other man there. The worst moment

was sitting on the iced-over ground in Khurd-Kabul Pass after one of their attacks, trying to recover myself, and having another man's head land in my lap. Damn, but those goat herders fight nasty. We should have never been there, should have understood the enemy in the first place. The Afghans were never going to be subdued the way the Indians were. They had no army, no real government, no leadership . . . but they had fire in their bellies. And a good reason to hate us."

"Because of our imposition of a leader, you mean?" I asked.

"No, because we were guilty of—" Davies seemed to draw the line on his confession there. He compressed his lips, and what was exposed of his cheeks reddened again. "Kabul is a graveyard for our soldiers that no one can visit," he said cryptically. "And that, Miss Nightingale, is all you need to know."

It was all a fascinating story, one I'm sure Sidney would have never revealed, but I had the feeling that I needed to know much more, as several interesting possibilities were swirling around in my head.

I recalled my main theory that Liz had not been the intended victim at all, but that perhaps it was her father, General à Court, who had been targeted. I needed to know what part he might have had in the Disaster in Afghanistan. Were there more men out there like Davies, who had seen indescribable horrors and who now needed some sort of atonement? Or revenge?

I tried in various ways to encourage him to tell me more, but he became as stony and immovable as a castle wall.

I thought it was time to offer the man a service for all the revealing he had done to me. "You have been very gracious in telling us all of this, Mr. Davies. I'm sorry you weren't able to shed any light on the dice I presented to you. As a nurse, I am also most concerned about the cholera outbreak here in Soho. May I ask, have any of your men experienced choleric symptoms that require attention?"

He shook his head. "Not yet. All of my men here are fine."

That surprised me. "How many workers are in the building?"

He glanced upward, thinking. "Maybe seventy."

"They all live nearby?"

"Sure, most of them," he said, his expression puzzled.

"And *none* of them has contracted cholera?" I pressed.

"Not thus far, although if King Cholera comes here, ruined will the Huggins brothers' business be. Plus, there's more than one ex-soldier hired here, and it would be a right sorry state for them to have survived war and imprisonment only to end up dead in a few hours from cholera."

I could hardly believe that not a single man in the brewery had yet been touched by the disease. Cholera tended to dash about a neighborhood from door to door like a juicy tidbit of gossip, taking down anyone who showed the least interest in it until finally everyone was exhausted from it. The disease flared up and died down with amazing rapidity.

"Well, sir," I said, withdrawing one of my calling cards from my pocket. "Should you experience any cases here, please send someone for me. Also, Middlesex Hospital is taking on cases."

Davies took the card and slipped it into his vest pocket without so much as glancing at it.

As we stepped back out into the street, a wagon full of stacked beer barrels with a Lion Brewery sign emblazoned on the side of it clattered by. I presumed that each shift meant that finished barrels would soon find their way to points across London and the rest of the country.

Once the wagon had cleared our vision, another posting of the cholera warning sign was revealed to us across the street. I hurried Mary over to look at it. At the bottom was the repeated announcement that Reverend Henry Whitehead of St. Luke's Church was offering spiritual comfort to the afflicted.

I pointed to the line containing Whitehead's name. "That name again. Goose, we must meet this Reverend Whitehead, because he may have witnessed something that Mr. Davies did not. We are headed to St. Luke's."

CHAPTER 11

Oswyn Davies's talk about the horrors of Afghanistan had left me both unsettled and yet determined to ensure that no more horror visited the Herbert family.

I was also interested to meet this supposed man of God, Reverend Whitehead, to see what he could tell me about where the outbreaks were concentrated. Surely his interaction with those suffering both spiritually and physically would have provided him with that knowledge.

With that information, my nurses could be better equipped to help, as could Middlesex Hospital.

I also wondered how well he knew the residents of the area, given that he presumably owned some of the tenement buildings. He might also have information on the assailant.

It was a two-mile walk to St. Luke's, whose unique obelisk spire served as a tall beacon to guide us as we neared Old Street. St. Luke's had its own small churchyard, overflowing with dilapidated headstones. However, this open space to one side and the rear of the church offered a little relief against the barren despair of all the buildings jumbled together around it.

It was as if one might find hope here, even for a brief moment, before returning to one's daily squalor.

The grounds themselves were very damp, despite there having been no rain for at least five days. I felt as though I were walking upon the seashore. We climbed the three steps up to the church's stoop and encountered a woman and child sitting on the ground in a recess next to the church's doors. The child, a girl, stood up and mutely held out her hand to us, staring at me with round, vacant eyes. In that ageless custom of alms, I completed our silent transaction by placing a coin in her dirty palm. I did not ask about her circumstances; she did not thank me for the money.

I was disturbed by the encounter. Were we each so afraid of the other?

Mary and I stepped inside the stone church, our eyes adjusting slowly to the dimness. No candles or gas lamps burned in the interior. The tall, multipaned windows that ran down each side of the sanctuary were grimy with dirt. The only light was from a stained-glass rendering of the Last Supper at the far end of the building. The panel of Judas had been ironically shattered and left gaping, marring the sacred picture but offering a little more light into the room.

As my eyes became accustomed to the murkiness inside the church, I became aware of just how many people were currently here.

Beneath the stained-glass scene, an old robed priest with a flowing dark beard that reached midway down his chest was offering communion to a line of parishioners.

I squinted my eyes. No, he was ladling out bowls of soup.

On the other side of the church, another priest, this one so young and clean-shaven that I had to assume he was fresh out of seminary, was offering prayers over a group of women in ill-fitting mourning wear.

What most dominated the interior, however, were the numbers of people sprawled out on pews, motionless and silent.

At first, I thought they might all be cholera victims, but I soon realized that they were suffering not from illness but from a deep-rooted ennui.

The stale, unpleasant odor of long-unwashed bodies hung in the air, in no way masked by the acrid remnants of recently burned incense wafting ineffectively around us.

I wondered how much succor one lonely little church could offer the members of a parish with so many needs.

The priest doling out soup bowls noticed us. Handing off the work to a helper standing nearby, he threaded his way down the center aisle to where we still stood at the rear of the church.

"May I help you?" he asked. Even in the dusky light, I saw that his eyes twinkled with good humor, as though confident that the misery around him would be overcome soon enough and thus that there was plenty of reason for joy.

I introduced myself and Mary. "I am seeking the Reverend Henry Whitehead."

He smiled broadly. The lack of any lines in his face made me realize that this was a fairly young man, probably no older than me. The beard aged him considerably.

"You address him now. Are you from the Benevolent Friend Society? I can show you the room where we are storing the blankets for—"

"No," I said, interrupting him. "I am—" I paused in hesitation. Was I here as Nightingale the nurse or Nightingale the detective?

I supposed I would be both.

"I am the superintendent of the Establishment for Gentle-women During Temporary Illness, in Marylebone."

He raised an eyebrow at me. "You are a distance from your hospital, madam."

"Yes. Some of my nurses will be assisting in the work of caring for cholera inmates at Middlesex Hospital, and I—"

Now it was his turn to interrupt me. "Ah, why didn't you say so? You'll want to see my charts, then." Whitehead stepped between Mary and me toward a door to one side of the church, beckoning us to follow.

"He has charts?" Mary whispered, sounding worried. "I will never get you out of here."

I waved her off, for I was intrigued to know what sort of charts the good reverend had. I was a complete devotee to the idea that charts and statistics could be effectively used to track illness and disease. Had I perhaps just found a kindred spirit?

Whitehead led us into a cramped room with a single window in it overlooking a sad tree in the churchyard. A thick vine climbed upward, strangling the tree and smothering its life. It seemed an apt depiction of existence in this dismal part of London.

The priest's office might have been tiny, but it was immaculate. A bookcase on one wall contained various theological tomes, all methodically arranged. A neatly made camp bed had been placed in front of the bookcase. His desk contained nothing but an inkwell and pen, plus a stack of stationery emblazoned with St. Luke's return address. It was all in total contradiction to what was outside the door in the main part of the sanctuary.

Whitehead must have noticed my surprised countenance, for he explained, "This is my oasis from the troubled world beyond.

I must have order in my private space so that I can pray and meditate in peace before giving of myself to those poor tortured souls out there."

He pulled two boxes out from inside his desk—a long wood box and a shorter metal one. He slid back the lid on the wood box to reveal a large cache of candles, from which he removed two, and returning to another desk drawer, he retrieved two iron holders and placed the candles in them. The metal box contained matches, and the garlicky odor of phosphorous filled the air as he struck one and lit both candles.

We now had decent light in the room, but the obvious question begged to be asked. "Reverend, why do you not use some of your candles to illuminate the sanctuary?"

Whitehead slid back the lid onto the candle box and put it back inside the desk drawer. "You must understand, my parishioners can eat, weep, and pray in the darkness. However, I cannot write letters begging for money in the dark. Thus, I must reserve them for the critical work that benefits them." His expression reflected the despair in his words. "Alas, my pleas frequently fall on ears deafened by years of callowness and disregard."

He placed the box of matches next to the candle box, firmly pushed the drawer in, and said, "Now on top of it all, I am begging for help with this hellish disease. I'm afraid our government doesn't care as much about this epidemic as it should. Posting signs about where to get help is all well and good, but that isn't much assistance to those of us providing the help, is it? I've tried in every way possible to get their attention, from letters"—he touched his pile of stationery—"to haunting the doors of any official I can think of. There is little concern for it, because everyone knows that cholera eventually burns itself out as quickly as it arrives. Thus, why bother to help a few hundred, or thousand, slum-dwelling unfortunates who will otherwise simply end up in a workhouse or existing on charity?"

The reverend's gentle, cheerful manner was quickly being replaced with indignation. "Nothing I've done has even raised an eyebrow, neither at Whitehall nor at Buckingham Palace. The devil take them all."

Whitehead took a deep breath and smiled once again, although it seemed forced this time. He pushed aside his desk chair and changed the subject. "I apologize that my meager quarters do not permit for comfortable accommodation of guests. If either of you would like to sit here—" He tapped the old wood corner chair. At one time it must have been beautiful, but now the needlepoint seat done in tiny black-and-cream chickadees against a solid salmon-colored background was faded. It was as shabby as the rest of the church.

Now a genuine smile reached his eyes, the corners of which crinkled as he said, "You are doubtless wondering how I came into possession of such a fine piece in my limited priestly circumstances. One of my parishioners found it next to a rubbish bin. Some wealthy matron tossing out her antiques made popular in George the Third's time and now replacing it with what our good queen finds fashionable, eh?"

My mother was very conscious of maintaining current styles, no matter how far in the country we lived. Our own circumstances, while far from poverty, would not have permitted her to randomly toss away perfectly good furniture. Mother would have handled it all by recovering, rewallpapering, and redraping. However, whoever had disposed of this chair had unwittingly done a good deed.

Mary gratefully accepted use of the chair, and Whitehead

brought it around for her. "Now, you are interested in my cholera charts, correct?"

He returned to the other side of the desk and once more dove into another drawer. He retrieved several sheets of paper without a single crinkle or curled edge to them and separated them out on the tabletop. They were full of notes taken in a careful hand, plus street map sketches and lists of names of infected people, along with data such as sex, age, address, and whether the person had died or survived. His approach was a little rough, but I immediately saw the value in it.

I picked up the list of names, wondering if I could quickly assess any links among the shared characteristics of the victims Whitehead had thus far been able to track. Unfortunately, the information wasn't arranged in logical tables, so it was difficult to draw conclusions just at a glance.

I pointed to the map. "What do the red circles represent?"

"Locations where I have seen or heard of at least three cases in a single household. I'm trying to track the direction in which the miasmas might be traveling. Thus far, I believe it to be lingering along Broad Street, and there are also quite a few cases slightly to the northeast on St. Anne's Court."

I nodded. "That makes sense."

"Do you think so?" he asked, perking up at me. "Dr. Snow thinks I am chasing my tail on this."

Dr. Snow's name was listed on the cholera sign as one of the doctors who was treating cholera victims. "Why is that?"

"He believes it has nothing to do with naturally occurring miasmas. I'm hoping my research here in the thick of things, so to speak, will prove him wrong."

I was fascinated by his work. Mary sighed loudly from her chair, but I ignored her.

"As I said, I am offering help to Middlesex Hospital beginning tomorrow. How can I be of help to you?" My mind was already whirling with the sort of analysis I might perform on Reverend Whitehead's existing data, if he would let me take it with me overnight.

"Well, I should like to know where any new cases come from and who they are. I can provide you with a sample of how I record data—"

I shook my head. "You may rely upon me to give you detailed information, sir. In fact, I should probably return here daily with whatever I learn, so that facts can be quickly compiled."

I ignored another pointedly long sigh from Mary's direction.

"Excellent. Your assistance will enable me to continue my work with the downtrodden here in the parish without making constant trips out. You would be surprised to learn how dispirited and demoralized even the healthy become during times when Death surveys his dominion and begins plucking people out with cruel swiftness. It is even worse in an area like this, which is already disheartened by the scanty living conditions."

I smiled grimly in the candlelight. His hypocrisy did not surprise me at all. "I have heard that you are one of the men responsible for such scanty living conditions," I said in challenge to him.

"Me?" he said in some surprise.

"Do you not own one or more of the squalid buildings in Soho?" I demanded.

He stared at me for several long moments. "What a strange thought. Of course this is not true. I live almost as meagerly as anyone down here, as you can see." He spread a hand to indicate his surroundings.

Now I was indeed confused. Hadn't Mr. Reeve insisted that Whitehead was part of the tenement problem?

"I have it on good authority that this is true," I protested.

Whitehead shook his head. "There are other men who take advantage of the poor in such an ungodly way. I assure you it is not my own manner of behavior. In fact, there is a man of the cloth at St. Helen's by the name of Whitewood. Perhaps I have been confused with him."

That was certainly possible, given Reeves's state of mind when I met him. Well, for the moment it didn't have anything to do with the cholera problem. I let it drop.

Whitehead seemed to take no offense.

"Now that I'm thinking about it," he started, pulling a piece of stationery from his stack, then flipping open the inkwell and dipping his pen in. "It would greatly interest Dr. Snow to realize that you are assisting me with quickly gathering information from Middlesex." He wrote slowly on the page in a precise script. "Would you be so kind as to meet with him and explain? I am writing a note of introduction now."

Ah, good fortune had provided me a bargaining chip. "I can certainly do that. It might be helpful for my preparation to assist you if I could take your papers with me—just overnight—to examine them."

Whitehead silently signed the letter and folded it, and I could see he was debating whether he trusted me enough to do it. Finally, he conceded, "Overnight, then."

As I gathered up his papers and the folded letter, I realized that I had been so carried away by the thought of helping out in this dangerous outbreak that I hadn't even brought up anything to do with the Herbert carriage attack.

"With regard to cholera sufferers you have met," I began, "I am wondering about someone specific whom you may have encountered."

"A friend of yours?" Whitehead's expression suggested he didn't believe I would associate with anyone who frequented St. Luke's.

"Not exactly. Someone who was in the employ of a friend of mine. His name was Fenton."

Whitehead slowly crossed his arms in front of him. The crinkles around his eyes had become furrows in his brow. "And you believe he contracted cholera?" His tone was cautious.

"He most certainly did contract cholera," I stated. "In fact, I witnessed his unfortunate demise. He had recently spent some time here in Soho, so I thought perhaps he had passed through the doors of your church."

Whitehead remained still, his arms still crossed and his face still pensive. "Not everyone who lives here deigns to set foot in God's house, madam. What makes you think this Fenton did?"

"Fenton was the manservant to Sidney Herbert."

Whitehead blinked. "Herbert?" was all he said.

"Yes, the secretary at war."

Whitehead's jaw dropped, sending his beard a little further down his chest. "And why would Mr. Herbert's manservant, who presumably had snug quarters inside his master's home, be roaming about in Old Street?"

"He was investigating the recent attack on Mrs. Herbert's carriage. Perhaps you heard about it?"

He shut his mouth and stroked the upper part of his beard with his right hand. "I do recall something about that," he said cautiously. "She was traveling through on her way to a charity dinner or some such thing?"

"She and her father were on their way to the British Museum and she was attacked by a madman. In the chaos that followed, her coachman was killed."

"I am very sorry to hear that," the priest said quietly. "It is always distressing to hear of a soul being lost. I presume the madman was found?"

"Actually, no, not yet. I am—"

"Do you suspect this Fenton of having done it?" Whitehead asked. "It wouldn't be the first time a servant turned on his master."

His answer stopped me short. "Well, no. He was investigating the attack on his master's behalf."

"Ah." Whitehead said. "So you have no suspects for the attack, then?"

"Not yet," I replied. Was it my imagination, or did the priest's shoulders sag in relief? "I was wondering if he might have come here, seeing as this is a focal point for the Soho community. He may have asked you questions, or, more importantly, told you something. He was in his late twenties, tall with a thin chest but already carrying a bit of a paunch."

Whitehead shook his head. "Those features could describe any number of men."

"He also had very thick lips. He was well groomed and attired, of course, as Mr. Herbert's manservant." I slipped my hand into my dress pocket to make sure I still had possession of the dice, which were the object of a dying man's last words.

Whitehead slowly shook his head once more. "I cannot specifically recall meeting someone named Fenton. However, you must understand, Miss Nightingale, that even had I met with such a man, I could not break the seal of the confession."

I jumped upon this. "He confessed something to you?" Was

this why the priest had asked me if Fenton had turned on his master?

Whatever sense of reticence I had perceived in this man was gone now. He smiled and shook his head at me in a chiding manner. "Miss Nightingale, you are clever, but assuredly there have been craftier men and women who have tried to smuggle an admission out of me. But let me set your mind at rest. I have taken no confession from anyone who presented himself to me as Fenton."

Was that genuine or merely a contrived answer?

"Thank you. But perhaps you might know something about these?" I withdrew the dice from my pocket and held out my closed fist.

Whitehead naturally opened his own palm, and I dropped the three cubes into it. He then picked up a candlestick to illuminate them more clearly. He rolled them in his palm with his fingers to look at all the sides. "The vice of dice," he said. "Did these belong to your Mr. Fenton?"

"Yes. Have you seen a set such as these before?"

"Certainly. Many a man down on his luck has reached his nadir through the use of them. Typically, I see old sailors with them."

To my great surprise, he set down two of the dice, then held one of them over the candle flame.

"Sir, what are you *doing*?" I demanded.

"Shhh," he whispered, brushing my entreaty aside. After a few moments, he put down the candle, then picked up his pen and touched the metal nib to the die. Nothing happened.

"They're real ivory," he pronounced. "If they were bone, the metal would have left a scorch mark. I'd say the owner of the dice is a sailor who has probably spent time in ports like China, India, and the like, in order to obtain the ivory. Or at least learned how to carve from someone else who gave him the ivory. I'm guessing they are made from walrus tusks, which I understand is what is most commonly used for small objects."

That was actually helpful. "How do you know this?" I asked.

He shrugged. "You would be surprised the sorts of things people share with a priest." He put down his pen, picked up the other two dice, and made to hand them back to me, but I held up a hand to stop him.

"But you are certain you haven't seen this *particular* set of dice? Note the tiny engravings above the crown on each die."

Whitehead once more held the candlestick over the dice in his other hand, rolling them around with his thumb until they were all crown side up. "G. Five. D. Well, they aren't the initials of the carver, are they?"

"No. I've been told that the personalizations on dice can sometimes be nonsensical." I hoped he could confirm whether that was true.

He shook his head. "I do not fashion myself an expert in gambling dice, Miss Nightingale, despite the little I know about how they're made. However, any symbolic carving of numbers, letters, and the like would most certainly have meaning to the carver."

He continued to move the dice around with his thumb, putting them in different orders. Finally, he reared back in discovery. "Oh! It is so simple."

He held the dice back out for my own inspection. He had put them in the order of "5," "D," and "G." "I believe these to be some sort of military unit description," he said. "The fifth something or other." Having felt that he had divined all that was possible from the dice, he held them out to give back to me.

I was dumbstruck as I took the dice back and put them back in my pocket, thanking him for his assistance.

Both Oswyn Davies and General à Court were military men, and neither one could identify them as such? Or had they simply refused to do so? Regardless, which man should I confront first?

That answer came to me easily. Davies had no vested interest in the carriage attacker being found. À Court, however, should have been most stimulated to see justice done. If what Reverend Whitehead had suggested was true, the General should have immediately recognized the dice for what they were and offered the information to me as a clue. Why had he pretended otherwise?

Moreover, why would Fenton have these dice on his person? He had never been in the Navy, so unless he had won them somehow, there seemed no logical explanation for why he would have had them.

I heard Mary in her chair busily scratching out notes, for which I was glad. There would be much to puzzle out later.

CHAPTER 12

As we departed the church, I saw that the beggar woman and her child were still sitting in the recess of the building. I decided that this time I would not merely press a coin into the young girl's hand. She and I would help each other.

I knelt down next to the woman. "How long have you been here?" I asked, for lack of any other discussion point.

She looked at me suspiciously. "Two months. I'll not go ta Cleveland Street," she said resolutely.

"Cleveland Street?" I asked, perplexed. "What is in Cleveland Street?"

Her eyes narrowed. "Don't say pretty words ta me. I won't go ta live inside Strand Union. Myself and Betty here are just fine."

The young girl who had earlier held out her palm to me gazed at me with her dull, vacant eyes.

I realized now what the woman was refusing. "I'm sure you are doing just fine, and I would never suggest that you go to a workhouse," I immediately said to placate her understandable fears. "My name is Florence."

At first, she said nothing and just stared at me, as if weighing my sincerity. Finally, she said grudgingly, "Berenice. Berenice Porter."

"Truly?" I said. "How regal. Why, you share a name with a queen of Egypt."

Clearly, she had never heard this before, and the implied compliment cracked the frosty reserve around her by an inch.

"Didn'ta know that," she said. "Betty here is named for my mama, Elizabeth."

"Another great queen," I assured her. "I only ask how long you have been here because you may have seen a young man in a servant's uniform come through here."

"Your beau?" she asked. "Left you, did he?" Her presumption of my troubles melted her just a little more.

"No, no, nothing like that. He worked as a manservant for Sid—for someone I know. He may have been here to . . . I don't know . . . talk to a priest about his gambling. Or he may have been asking questions about an attack that occurred over on Broad Street. Did you hear about that?"

She poked a tongue into one cheek, contemplating. "You mean that high-and-mighty who was attacked? Sure, we all heard about it."

If only I could find someone who had actually witnessed it. "One of Mr. Herb—one of the high-and-mighty's servants was in Soho to investigate it. His name was Fenton." I described him for her.

Betty tugged at her mother's dirty sleeve and leaned over to whisper in her ear. Berenice nodded. "That'a be right, sweetheart." She looked back at me. "Betty remembers that we saw him over at the flush toilet on Great Chapel Street."

"How far away is that?" I asked.

"Maybe a few blocks that way." Berenice pointed back in the general direction from which Mary and I had come. "I remember him now because his clothes were fine, like yours. And he had them lips like it was hard for him to talk. He was asking about a woman—no, a man."

"You're sure he was asking about a man, then?" I asked.

She bit her lip for a moment. "Yes'm. I'm sure it was a man. I think."

"And did Fenton say why he was looking for this man?"

She shook her head. "'Twern't none of my business," she explained. "I wouldn't ask you why if you asked me about someone, neither, miss."

"And had you seen the man?"

Another shake of the head. "No."

"Do you remember how he described the man?"

Berenice looked up again, remembering, then shook her head once more. "Don't remember that it was an unusual-like description."

I rose unsteadily, feeling a little stiff from having knelt for so long. "You've been very helpful." I started to pull more coins from my pocket, but an idea popped into my mind fully formed.

I wasn't sure it could work, but it was worth a try. "Mrs. Porter, do you have any employment?"

"I'm not so special for you ta call me that. It's just Berenice. And no, not since Mrs. Burington fired me for Betty tippin' over a potted fern. The girl was just clumsy was all. Mrs. Burington wouldn't give me no character, either."

Without a character reference, it was difficult for household servants to find employment elsewhere, and some employers wielded the threat of no reference like a medieval battle-ax. "You were a maid, then?"

She nodded. "Went into service after my husband was lost

three years ago helpin' ta lay the telegraph cable across the Channel."

"If I could find you a position where your employer will not be too particular about a character, would you be interested?"

Berenice was suspicious again. "What'll you expect of me in return?"

I smiled. "You have already paid me in full by talking to me. I'll visit this gentlemen tomorrow to ask him about hiring a maid; then I'll be back to fetch you."

"That'll be all right, then," she said, but there was no confidence at all in her voice.

Now I did press a couple of coins in her hand, a silent deposit on a promise I hoped I could keep.

★　★　★

We returned to a minor scene of chaos at the Establishment. One of the inmates, a Mrs. Foliot, had been vomiting regularly for the past two hours, and most of the staff were convinced she had cholera. The woman had been moved into a room far from the other inmates so that they would not be disturbed by the sounds of her violent heaving.

Leaving Mary in the library, I went to check on Mrs. Foliot myself. The woman was exhausted and glassy-eyed. I gently pinched the skin on her arm. It bounced back reasonably well, but she felt overly warm.

"Have you been evacuating your bowels?" I asked.

Mrs. Foliot blushed to the extent that her ashy skin would allow. "Such an intrusive question," she said.

"Yes, and a vital one for you to answer," I said. "If we are to make you well again."

She nodded. "Yes, I have been . . . evacuating."

"Is it runny?"

Another nod.

"Is it milky? As though it's water that rice has been rinsed in?"

Now she frowned. "No, not at all."

"Have you eaten any supper?" I asked.

"No, but I shall tell you a secret," she said in a conspiratorial whisper. "I didn't like the luncheon tray that Nurse Lambert brought me earlier, so I went down to the kitchens and found some leftover mutton and potatoes. It was cold, but still very tasty."

I sighed and left Mrs. Foliot's room, seeking out Nurse Lambert. "Mrs. Foliot is suffering from nothing more than food poisoning," I said when I found her. "I think she went rummaging in Cook's scraps for her supper. I'll need to see to it that she wraps them more tightly before discarding them."

Lambert exhaled in relief. I gave her instructions to have the woman drink as much broth as she could tolerate and then slowly introduce some bland foods like rice seasoned with a little butter and nutmeg, plus perhaps some restorative jelly. Dr. Killigrew could check on Mrs. Foliot on his next visit.

My nurse nodded her understanding, then said, "I'm glad you've returned, Miss Nightingale. Might I have a private word with you?"

I hoped she wasn't planning to terminate her employment with me. "Of course. Take care of Mrs. Foliot, then meet me in my private study."

Mary was waiting for me in the library, as I had assumed she would be. Now that I was assured no one in the hospital appeared to have contracted cholera, I let her know that I would return shortly and retreated up to my study. There was a single piece of folded paper on my desk, with my name scrawled across the front.

I unfolded the letter and read:

Dear Miss Nightingale,

I regret that I missed seeing you upon my visit this afternoon. Please be assured that all has been done according to your wishes, and everyone at the Hospital anxiously awaits the arrival of you and your nurses tomorrow. Can you send word as to what time this will be?

Your Servant,
Stephen Goodfellow

I wondered how much had really been accomplished at Middlesex Hospital in a mere day. Poor Mary would have to wait, for after I was done with Nurse Lambert, I would have to gather up the nurses I wished to take with me to the other hospital tomorrow and tell them what was planned.

For the moment, though, I was in peaceful solitude. From a drawer, I slid out Richard's letter again.

My dearest Flo,

I hope that you will be happy to hear from an Old Friend, who continues to hold you in the highest regard.

I recently saw your dear Sister and Mother, both on holiday in Brighton, where Annabel and I were also on a month's stay. Parthenope gave me a most favorable report on your activities, although I did sense that she misses you terribly.

*Over the past couple of years, I have been trying my hand
with poetry. I include here one of my favorites. Might I impose
on our bonds of friendship to have you read and critique it before
I make a decision about publishing a small volume of my work?
I believe this poem will strike a chord in your heart.*

*I trust I will have your thoughts and opinions in my hand
at the soonest convenient time.*

Yours Always,
Richard

I also reread his poem, a flight of fancy about sailing along
the Nile, a place I myself had once visited.

> *I had a dream of waters: I was borne*
> *Fast down the slimy tide*
> *Of eldest Nile, and endless flats forlorn*
> *Stretched out on either side,—*
> *Save where from time to time arose*
> *Red pyramids, like flames in forced repose,*
> *And Sphinxes gazed, vast countenances bland,*
> *Athwart that river-sea and sea of sand.*

Was Richard trying to torture my heart in repayment for all
the vacillating I had done when I held his own heart in my
hand? Why else would he reinsert himself into my life like this?

Unless he was trying to truly extend the olive branch of
friendship to me. That thought pained me almost as much because
it suggested that he was genuinely over any romantic feelings for
me. As for myself, I could not say that I had completely buried
him in my mind.

I also found it curious that he was sending me poetry to critique. Our verbal sparring had always been over weighty matters such as church doctrine. I knew he delighted in poetry, ballads, and other rhythmic works, but our discussions together had tended to be much more like intellectual battles.

Perhaps he was letting me know that he didn't care for the effort of engaging in such battle with me anymore. Or he was taking a soft, deferential approach to disarm me.

Or perhaps I was overthinking this. I shook my head in exasperation. Soon I would need to create a chart to analyze the sum total of possible motives Richard Monckton Milnes might have had in contacting me in order to decide the most likely answer.

I folded up his letter once more, promising myself that I would make a decision on how to respond in the next few days.

I sat and made notes to myself for several minutes, including a reply to Dr. Goodfellow at Middlesex. I was truly enjoying the quiet of my room and was particularly pleased with the bright light emitting from my gas lamp after so much time at St. Luke's today.

Nurse Lambert tapped lightly at the door, and I beckoned her in. She sat down, looking around almost furtively. Or maybe it just seemed that way because she was in yet another odd cap. This one had a comb attached to the crown of her head, with a long length of cream-colored lace sewn to it. The lace covered much of her hair and dangled down both sides of her face. It reminded me of a Spanish mantilla veil. Or a tablecloth. Perhaps she was preparing her head to accommodate a tea service.

But the head covering did disguise most of her birthmark.

"What can I do for you, nurse?" I asked, putting aside my papers.

Louisa Lambert sat down across from me, fidgeting with the wide lace ends of her cap.

I knew I really should insist that she wear a plain white head covering, but I didn't want to discourage her. There would be time enough to work on her appearance once she was more confident in her work.

"Miss Nightingale, I haven't breathed a word of this to anyone, because I know you would not want gossipy rumors spread."

I kept my features neutral, but already my insides were churning. What now?

Lambert tied the long lace ends of her cap together under her chin. She looked even more like a Spanish matron, but at least she was no longer fidgeting.

"But you will want to know this. It regards Mrs. Maddox, the woman we cared for in Soho."

It was on the tip of my tongue to chastise my nurse for not reporting on a patient's condition immediately upon noticing it, but then I realized that this probably had nothing to do with the woman's cholera.

"Did she do something to you? Or to Nurse Harris?" I asked.

Lambert shook her head inside her lace tent. "No, miss. She *said* something to me. It made me think that perhaps she is not addled in her mind at all, but that something has made her very, very cross."

I hadn't overhead anything while we were there, although admittedly I had been paying most of my attention to George Maddox, not his wife. Still, their quarters consisted of two tiny rooms. How could I have missed hearing something of importance at the ranting volume level Isabel Maddox employed?

"What did she say?"

Lambert leaned forward, cupping her hands together in her lap. "She—she grabbed my chin, pulled me to her, and whispered in my ear. I was most upset, miss, thinking that any vapors in her mouth would poison me with her illness. Well, and it was quite disgusting up close." Lambert wrinkled her nose at the memory.

"And what she whispered upset you?" I hoped to move her along.

"Not for my own self, but perhaps for someone else. I think that although she seems to be sick in her mind . . . I'm not sure she is. In fact, I believe she knows something—or has done something—for which she feels guilty. Or at least angry."

"Nurse, please simply tell me what she said." My impatience always simmered just below the surface of my skin, although in my defense, it was these sorts of verbal expeditions I had to go on that tended to stoke the fires.

"She said that her revenge was complete, that she had accomplished what she needed to before dying."

That sounded completely like a deranged rant to me. "What made you think it wasn't the act of a sick woman?"

"There was more. She also muttered something about having invested greatly in something and not receiving the return she had expected. Her whispering was rather wild, so it was hard to follow her, but I took her meaning to be that someone had disappointed her."

"Financially? Romantically? In another way?" I still wasn't convinced.

"I don't know." Lambert shook her head in frustration.

My nurse meant well, but a sick woman's defeats or failures were none of our business.

"Even if what you suppose is accurate, what do you propose that this means for the Establishment?" I asked.

Lambert frowned and bit her lip. "Nothing directly, miss. I'm just worried for that man and his son."

"I appreciate your concern for them, but our job is to tend to the sick, not to sort out domestic disputes."

Nurse Lambert took a deep breath and nodded, shifting her glance away from me as she returned to fidgeting with the ends of her lace cap.

"Is there something else?" I probed gently. "Was there more that she said?"

She shook her head no, her gaze still cast downward.

"Nurse, what is it?" I asked.

Lambert finally raised her anguished gaze to mine. "I worry, miss, that I might turn out like Mrs. Maddox."

"Whatever do you mean?"

"I could end up sick. Alone. Alone because I have never married—and aren't my prospects dimming now that I'm in my third decade?—or alone because I have a husband as helpless as Mr. Maddox. At first, I didn't find it odd that he wouldn't approach his wife's sickbed. After all, we see many sick women whose husbands just stand in the doorway until the doctor gives them a diagnosis, something upon which the husband feels he can then *act*. But Mr. Maddox, he . . . he . . . well, don't you think he seems a bit *afraid* of his wife?"

I paused to consider what she had said. True, the man had not entered that back room on the two occasions we had been there, and he had expressed himself weakly against her tirades, but did that mean anything?

"First, I believe you can have a very fulfilling life here in the hospital, Nurse Lambert. I, too, have dimming prospects, but you will find that the work here can consume all your thoughts and attentions. It can help to drain the well of loneliness on a continual basis, I assure you." My statement had proved mostly true in my own life, even if I had a letter in my desk that might suggest otherwise.

"Second, what you must learn as a nurse is not to allow your patients' personal lives to permeate your soul, else you will become as tumorous and fevered as they are. You must keep a clear mind and eyes. It is good for both yourself and your patients."

Lambert nodded, her expression a mixture of disbelief and hope.

★   ★   ★

I resisted the urge to completely collapse in the chair next to Mary's in the library, instead mustering the energy to sit down as sedately as possible.

Mary wasn't fooled for an instant. "Miss Florence, you need tea and biscuits." She jumped up before I could protest and ran off to the kitchens, leaving me alone with my thoughts once more. I must have instantly dozed off, for I found myself coming to as she reentered the room, managing a tray with two cups, a teapot, and a variety of breads and cakes on it. Two slices of rabbit pie had also been added to the tray, the rich, aromatic gravy spilling out on the plates and causing my stomach to rumble.

I dove in with more gusto than that with which I normally approached food. How long had it been since I'd last eaten?

My companion and I devoured most of what was on the tray, and I felt thoroughly revived. Once Mary had returned from delivering the remainder to the cook, we sat down to talk.

I began by relating to Mary all that had occurred outside her presence—from Sidney Herbert's visit to my time at Middlesex Hospital. Setting up Middlesex properly had no bearing on Sidney's case, but I had become accustomed to telling Mary everything. Plus, she would probably end up there with me the next day anyway.

For her part, Mary read to me her notes from our visits with Oswyn Davies and Henry Whitehead. She looked up at me when she was done. "And you told Berenice that you would help her find employment."

I nodded. "I have a plan. Overall, it seems we have a jumble of information, about both helping to care for the cholera outbreak and trying to assist Sidney in uncovering his wife's attacker. Other than Fenton dying of cholera, the two seem unrelated, so we must devise a way of keeping them separate."

Mary nodded and flipped to a blank page farther in her notebook, folding it in half vertically. "I shall confine notes about cholera to the pages before this one, and notes about Mr. Herbert's investigation to the pages after it."

It was as good a system as any. "And you can make notes for future nursing instructions inside the cholera pages," I said.

"Oh no, Miss Florence," Mary objected, shaking her head. "I keep those in a separate notebook."

Even better.

We finished up by redrawing all of Reverend Whitehead's notes, putting his gathered information into tables and trying to assess any patterns with regard to *whom* was being struck by cholera in conjunction with his map of *where* the concentrations seemed to be. All I could ascertain was that, with few exceptions, entire households were being swallowed up once King Cholera knocked on a door. There seemed to be little reprieve for the young and hale, nor any relief for those who worked outdoors versus inside a factory.

I studied Whitehead's map until my eyes were bleary. In

frustration, I turned the map this way and that, upside down and right side up. It was then that I had an inspiration. "Goose, do you think you could redraw the reverend's map without the circles?" I asked excitedly.

She looked at it. "Certainly. It won't be as fancy, but—"

In my eagerness, I interrupted her. "That's fine. We just need lines showing the various streets."

While she worked on that, I devised a coding system for myself. A circle would indicate a location where one person had died and then the disease had gone away. A square would mean two to three people had died in a location, a triangle would mean four to six people had been taken, and so on.

With my coded legend complete, I went through my recharted information of Whitehead's, dredging out information about the numbers of people who had died in specific locations. I felt a flush of excitement creeping up my neck, for I was certain I was on the verge of a discovery.

When Mary had finished her crude map, I applied circles, squares, and triangles to the map according to what knowledge I had gleaned through the better organization of Whitehead's compilations.

I held up the newly marked map for Mary to see.

She pointed to the center of it. "It's obvious. Most outbreaks are along Broad Street."

I nodded my assent to her astute declaration. "Yes, but why? What is so tragically special about that area? Is it somehow seeping up from the ground?"

Mary gave me a shocked look. "Miss Florence, I think we should be more concerned about how much time we are spending down there, and whether we are risking our very lives. Why, we might exhibit symptoms at any moment!" She laid her open notebook in her lap and rubbed her arms with her hands, as if warding off a chill inside the warm building.

I was far too animated by my findings to worry about contracting cholera. I needed to visit Reverend Whitehead again to show him my conclusions. I needed to make meeting Dr. Snow a priority as well. I could travel to see both men after I concluded my work at Middlesex Hospital tomorrow.

Sidney would be furious at my delays, but it would only be one more day. Besides, what hope did I truly have of determining who it was that had attacked Liz?

I turned my attentions back to the cholera outbreak, thinking about the people we had witnessed in Soho, both in the streets and in their meager quarters. Cholera was striking some down within hours, causing others to linger for days in agony—such as Isabel Maddox—and in some instances people recovered completely. How pernicious yet capricious this illness was.

But as I examined my newly marked map, it occurred to me that some residents of the area were obviously not afflicted at all. Take, for example, George Maddox. Was it curious that he had not contracted the disease, or just one of those unexplained coincidences of life?

I was about to open my mouth to discuss this when Mary brought up the carriage attack. "I think it wise to concentrate more upon Mr. Herbert's situation, don't you? To catch a murderer rather than miring yourself in the foulness of cholera. You should probably spend tomorrow interviewing General à Court, and maybe even seek out this Caroline Norton of Mr. Herbert's."

I smiled. "You are concerned solely about justice, are you, Goose?"

She reddened. "I am concerned for your health and well-being, of course," she said primly. "But I also have a theory about the carriage attack."

That immediately caught my attention. "A theory about who the attacker was?"

Mary nodded, self-satisfied. "Isn't it obvious? That Mrs. Norton was responsible. She is jealous of Mrs. Herbert and wants to see her rival eliminated."

I had to protest, even though my heart wasn't in it. "But Sidney said he doesn't know where she is, that she may have returned to her parents in the country or even gone to the continent."

Mary gave me a wry look. "Men can be so foolish sometimes, even great men like Mr. Herbert. You mark my words, that woman is here and trying to get rid of poor Elizabeth Herbert. It's obvious just from the method employed."

"You mean a deranged man rushing the carriage and then possibly someone else shooting wide and accidentally killing the coachman? That is a society lady's method of attempting murder?"

Mary raised her chin. "What I mean, Miss Florence, is that clearly this man was hired to do the work. However, he was also a bumbling fool. Most men of any class would have enough reach into the lower classes to find an expert assassin to do the job. A woman might be stuck with a lesser sort because she wouldn't know the proper people to accomplish the task."

"So you are saying"—I raised a speculative eyebrow—"that Caroline Norton—whose satin slipper has probably never touched the ground outside of Mayfair—managed to find someone in Soho who was willing to undertake a crime for her?"

Mary nodded. "Through a friend. Or maybe through a

well-worded advertisement in the paper. She probably hired the first man that came along, because you can't exactly check references on these sorts of things, now, can you?"

I was trying to give credence to what Mary was saying. "And what was Mrs. Norton going to do once Liz was dead?"

"She would plan to comfort Mr. Herbert in his grief, and thus make her way back into his life. With his affections secured, she could move into Herbert House."

"But she hasn't been able to secure a divorce!" I exclaimed in order to pop her hypothetical bubble.

Mary put a finger to the side of her nose. "Since Eve in the garden, women have been willing to perform acts way outside the bounds of decency and rule to accomplish their desires. If her marriage was that abusive, she might risk societal disdain to have an escape to Mr. Herbert's house. Even if he does have that awful dog." She shuddered. "Of course, most women are not in Mrs. Norton's position. My Milo was not capable of doing anything that could even cause me to raise my voice, much less cause me to act in a manner—"

I let Mary ramble on about her sainted dead husband while I contemplated her theory, ridiculous as it sounded. If Caroline Norton was somehow responsible, would Sidney really want this investigated? I couldn't imagine he would want to see his ex-lover committed to the gallows.

Yet since Sidney had come to confess his affair with her to me, it was reasonable to assume he did not think her guilty of anything, else he would have kept it buried. I would never have known otherwise.

I interrupted Mary, who was in the middle of a story about Milo once rescuing a fawn who had gotten stuck on an ice-covered pond, to share my thoughts. Afterward I added, "It can't be Mrs. Norton, because it would almost imply that Sidney was involved."

Her immediate reaction surprised me. "Then how would the attacker know when the carriage was coming through unless Mr. Herbert told him? Or *her*."

That stopped me. It did point in Caroline Norton's direction, but worse, it also pointed in the direction of the General, or even Liz herself. And half the servants of the Herbert household would have known when the carriage was departing, including Fenton. Any of them could have innocently or purposely told someone about the routing to the British Museum.

"You accused a jealous wife once before, and you were wrong," I reminded her.

"But was I really?" Mary countered defensively. "I perhaps guessed the wrong culprit, but I did understand the motive."

I thought back on my Nurse Bellamy, who had been murdered last year inside this very room because of jealousies. I couldn't very well argue Mary's point.

When Mary and I had exhausted ourselves talking, I decided to shoo her off to her own quarters before it got too late for her to be in the streets. Her lodgings had previously been mine, but I hated to live outside the premises of my hospital and had taken rooms on an upper floor not long after first arriving. I had given my old rooms over to Mary not only so that she would have her own private space but so that I could have time alone, too. The lodgings were a short distance on foot, but I still worried for Mary's safety. Even the best streets of London had the occasional robber or murderer skulking about on them.

With Mary gone, I gathered up the two nurses I had decided

would help at Middlesex Hospital: Lambert and Hughes. I had weighed having Harris go, because I knew how quietly efficient she would be, but now, with much of my time taken up by cholera and the Herbert problem, I needed someone who could oversee things at the Establishment in my absence. Harris was just the one for that. And Lambert had already dealt with cholera at the Maddox household, while Hughes had the right temperament for what I knew would be backbreaking work.

Yes, I was satisfied that I had selected the correct nurses, and both of them expressed gladness for the assignment. I spent an hour going over what our anticipated duties would be at the other, larger hospital and told them to be ready early the following morning.

I then checked on all the inmates, feeling a warm glow spread inside my chest as I saw that I had no complaint whatsoever with any of their conditions. All bedcoverings were clean, rooms were aired out, and no half-eaten trays of food lingered at any inmate's elbow. My nurses were learning well.

As I climbed the staircase up to my bedchamber, I caught a glimpse of Charlie Lewis with little John Wesley. They were sitting together inside a closet, the door opened wide and the glow of a lantern on the floor beside them illuminating their activity. They had Dash between them, and Charlie appeared to be trying to entice the young red squirrel to do tricks using bits of boiled eggs as reward.

John Wesley was completely entranced by what the hospital's manservant was doing, and I smiled to see the boy so happy.

Which immediately reminded me of young Arthur Maddox, whom I expected was probably gone by now. How cursed and unfair the world could seem.

CHAPTER 13

What a sight the four of us—Nurse Lambert, Nurse Hughes, Mary, and I—must have made, marching determinedly down New Cavendish Street to Middlesex Hospital. The nurses wore the apron-topped uniforms that I had designed and Hughes had created last year. Mary was in her usual plain, solid-color dress—today a muddy brown. For myself, I wore a day dress in the silk taffeta of which I was so fond, this time a naval-blue jacket over a corresponding blue skirt with two horizontal ebony stripes encircling the lower part of the skirt. I, too, wore an apron over my dress, unsure of what spills and mess the day might bring.

Behind us was Charlie Lewis, dragging a small cart loaded up with hospital supplies, such as clean sheets, pillows, feeding cups, and the like.

I had sent John Wesley off to the grocer's to order the food supplies we needed and to request that the grocer deliver it all to the hospital as soon as possible. There had not been time to send a list to Middlesex to have them do it.

Despite Dr. Goodfellow's assurances otherwise, I was not going to assume that all had been done according to my wishes and figured my nurses and I would likely have to make things right once we arrived.

There were still victims sprawled about on the lawn—thank goodness it was late summer and not one of our country's damp winters—although I noticed that most of them were now females. How curious. I was glad Mary carried her notebook with her, stuffed full of Reverend Whitehead's and my own charts. I would have to make note of all Middlesex's inmates.

Dr. Goodfellow greeted us in the hospital's entry and had an orderly assist Charlie with bringing in everything on the cart. Along with the hospital's nursing staff, we went straight to work. I quickly walked through the hospital again with Mary and my nurses, showing them the deficiencies I had noticed the previous day. Unfortunately, the slop buckets and water closets still overflowed, the kitchens hadn't been touched, and not a single inmate's bed had been freshened.

In fact, of all the instructions I had left with the hospital's leadership, the only task accomplished had been to open the windows. Even that had been executed poorly, with someone having lifted just a single window in large rooms containing six or eight of them.

I was mentally furious, but it would do no good to upset the inmates nor the nurses or orderlies, who all looked at me expectantly once I returned to the hospital's lobby with Lambert, Hughes, and Mary. Also awaiting me were the physicians I had met with the previous day. It seemed as though an eternity had passed since my first visit.

Goodfellow introduced the hospital staff members I hadn't met before. There were too many names to remember, but I did take note that most of them looked as bedraggled as the members of my own staff had a year ago. I worried how many thieves, drunks, and swindlers dwelt among this group, but there was nothing to be done about that now.

I instructed my own nurses to inspect each inmate in every ward, with a priority on bathing them and changing the linens as they saw fit. "If we run out, Mr. Lewis can return to the Establishment for more, or we will have him scour London for them, or as a last resort buy six-foot lengths of cotton and wool from a draper and we will hem them ourselves."

Once every bed and its occupant were clean, I wanted them to make note of symptoms, sores, and the verbal complaints of each inmate, which would be compiled into a report for the hospital's doctors. "You won't get to all of the inmates in a day, but we will keep returning until they have all been reviewed."

I made full use of the orderlies, telling them to burn any bedcoverings the nurses deemed unfit for human use and to ensure that linens in decent condition were sent out to a laundress. After that, I wanted all water closets thoroughly cleaned out. "And," I ordered sternly. "I do mean thoroughly. You should go through many cakes of carbolic soap. After that, the kitchens will need a meticulous scrubbing, particularly the stoves." They had been coated in so much grease it was a wonder all the filled cook pots didn't slide right down to the floor. "Keep a special eye out for the beetles and crickets that have found the place to be fertile breeding grounds."

They eyed me with disdain, and one man protested, "We are orderlies, not housemaids."

I maintained my temper and shot back, "You are strong, muscled men, and this work requires the stamina and brawn of oxen. Do you suggest that women attempt such exertion?"

The man who had spoken out lowered his gaze.

As for the Middlesex nurses, well, I could hardly trust them to deal with the freshly bathed inmates. I contemplated them for a few moments and said, "Dispose of all the food from the larder and cold pantry so that the orderlies can clean them. Then I want all the floors scrubbed, both in and out of wards. The orderlies will, of course, take care of the kitchen floors. Once you are done with that work, you may retire to bathe yourselves. By then the replacement groceries should be here, and I will show you how to properly feed the bed-ridden and weak."

With everyone having received their instructions, and Dr. Goodfellow having offered a very short speech in which he stated that I was to be obeyed without question, I had Mary accompany me to the medicinal supply cabinet in one of the wards. Some of the boxes of hospital goods that Charlie had toted here were stacked up in front of the cabinet. With Mary's help, I pushed them aside so that we could clean out the cabinet itself.

I attempted to be thoughtful in reorganizing the cabinet, but everything was so brittle, moldy, or cracked that I decided to do a clean sweep of it all, much as I hoped the Middlesex nurses were doing down in the kitchens. Then I brushed out all the dead insects from inside the cabinet. It seemed as though I was covered in dust from head to toe in mere minutes, and already there were streaks of dirt across the front of my apron.

Mary grimaced as she watched me working. "Miss Florence, how do you suppose this many flying and crawling creatures have gotten in here, given that the first time in the hospital's history that a window was opened was probably yesterday?"

I couldn't help it; I laughed aloud at her comment. "Goose, that is an excellent question." From the corner of my eye I saw a desiccated spider corpse on my sleeve, which I brushed away. "But we are going to set everything to rights for these poor inmates."

I then had Mary help me unlatch the crates of supplies, and together we organized the shelves with ointments, syringes, bandages, invalid drinking cups, and other items.

When we were finished, I clapped my hands together and said, "That's the first one."

We then proceeded to work on the other cabinets within the hospital, going through the same routine of jettisoning everything existing in each cabinet, cleaning out the insect remains, and reloading it in an orderly manner. Our only interruption was from Dr. Goodfellow, who stood and observed us for several minutes before walking away, shaking his head and muttering about the increased admission cost.

After several hours of working, Mary began to plead exhaustion. I reluctantly stopped so that we could track down Lambert and Hughes for a break outside. We four stood out on the expansive hospital stoop, which put all the outdoor sufferers directly in my line of vision.

"We have to make room for them inside," I declared.

Lambert and Hughes nodded their heads, and we began discussing how to rearrange wards to accommodate everyone on the lawn.

In the midst of this, a large wagon arrived, with the grocer's name emblazoned on a sign in red and gold against a cream-colored background. Foodstuffs were brimming over the top of the wagon, and I oversaw their delivery into the freshly scrubbed kitchens, asking Mary to keep inventory of every single box, tin, bottle, and paper-wrapped package coming through the door.

The four of us, along with the grumbling and suspicious existing staff of Middlesex, must have seemed like whirling

dervishes with skirts, aprons, and coattails flying. As we proceeded through this work, I found it exhilarating; so much so
that my heart pounded and my pulse raced from the sheer joy
of seeing the hospital slowly take on the form of a clean and
decent environment for patient recovery. It would take days, if
not weeks, for my nurses to finish it all, but for now at least it
wasn't appalling.

Understandably, Mary did not share in my exultation. She
was eventually limping from pain in her knees and found herself
a chair in a corridor outside the lying-in ward. As I walked by
her repeatedly in the execution of some errand, her nose was
buried in her notes and she was writing away furiously.

In all the tumult of cleaning and reorganizing, I found my
own mind leaping from topic to topic related to both the cholera
outbreak and the Herbert attack. I was a nurse, and so my attentions desired to be fully on the epidemic. How was I going to
manage Sidney's request at the same time?

Make a chart in your mind, I thought.

As I ordered tins of meat on shelves, I made a mental image
of the list of people I needed to see—whether for Sidney or for
cholera—down the left side of the page, and where they were
located across the top. Now, if I could just imagine what people
intersected each other geographically, I might be able to—

Nurse Hughes entered the pantry, out of breath and flustered.
"Miss Nightingale, we have counted and assessed the women
lying outside."

I frowned. "Do some of them belong in the lying-in ward?
If so, we must take care of those inmates first."

Hughes bit her lip in consternation. "Well, one or two
belong there, but the, er, problem is that they all seem to belong
to a . . . lower . . . sort of class."

"Lower than Seven Dials?" I asked.

"No, miss. They are largely prostitutes," Hughes said nervously. "Should we still bring them in?"

"Ah," I said. This was a delicate matter. I couldn't have it known among the male inmates that prostitutes had moved in en masse and were anywhere nearby, lest they think the hospital was providing some sort of illicit service for them. Yet the poor souls had to be brought in from the elements.

I at least understood now why Goodfellow and the other physicians had sequestered the women from everyone else. However, they could not remain outdoors.

I decided upon a course of action. "The lying-in ward is not full. Move those women to the left wall, then have the orderlies figure out a way to fix some sheets together to fashion a drape along the ends of their beds. This will separate them from the other side of the ward. Bring the outside women into the beds along the right wall as quickly as possible. I'll be up to help as soon as I'm done here."

Hughes scurried off to do my bidding while I took a deep breath, determined to finish my current task and my mental charting before heading up to the lying-in ward.

I began humming as I worked, and I found that the rhythm of it made me think more clearly. In fact, by the time I dusted off my hands from organizing the foods according to what ailments they were suitable for, I had decided upon my next steps.

I would drop in on the Maddox family, as I had promised to do, and then on my way out of Soho I would visit Oswyn Davies to see about employment for Berenice.

With good news for her hopefully in hand, I would find this Dr. Snow that Reverend Whitehead had mentioned, then return to St. Luke's to see Berenice and to drop off my revised charts and maps for the priest.

If I had not dropped from exhaustion at that point, I would go to Herbert House. The General and I were going to have an extensive conversation about Fenton's dice.

I also needed to check in on Liz. I realized it had been a couple of days since I'd seen her. She must think me a dreadful friend by now.

Thus resolved, I retreated back upstairs to assist with moving the prostitutes into the lying-in ward.

The expectant mothers, whose view was now restricted by white sheets strung together that permitted them to see shadows beyond them but no actual activity, were anxious.

I stepped behind the sheets to speak with them, raising my voice so they could hear me over the moans of the sick and the creaking of iron bedsteads occurring on the other side as the prostitutes were settled into the ward.

"I am sorry for the disturbance in these final hours of your confinement," I began.

The woman in the bed next to where I stood reached out and clutched a fistful of my skirt. "Who are they? Have you moved *men* in here?"

The others nodded and vocalized their anxieties.

I patted her hand in comfort. "No, no, they are women also. But they have cholera and must be kept separate from you. That's why we have erected this curtain." I estimated that the choleric women were at least fifteen feet away from these women about to give birth. As long as we kept the cholera side thoroughly aired out, all would be well.

I hoped.

The women before me, some swollen to an extent that they were probably unrecognizable from their normal states, nodded, willing to trust me in their distress.

"How long has it been since a doctor has been through here?" I asked brightly.

The woman who had grabbed my skirt released it. "Yesterday afternoon," she answered.

"Yesterday!" I exclaimed. "All of you need close attention. I will seek out a doctor immediately."

As I stepped out from behind the makeshift drape, I nearly collided with a well-dressed man I didn't know.

"Forgive my eavesdropping," he said. "Perhaps I can be of assistance. I am a physician. My name is John Snow."

Standing before me was a man at least in his forties. He had thinning hair swept to one side and a bulbous nose planted squarely on top of a flat face. His lips were thin and his eyebrows thick. Those eyebrows were quite expressive over his dark, intense gaze. He wore the clothing of a professional man.

"Dr. Snow? The same one who is the physician treating cholera victims in Soho?"

He laughed gently. "Most people these days ask if I am the same physician who administered chloroform to the queen while she gave birth to Leopold back in April, but yes, I am also working to help these unfortunate souls."

I knew that Queen Victoria had started a rage among women to have chloroform render them insensible while birthing their children. I was interested in having a future discussion with him about it, but there were so many other more pressing topics for now.

"I know of you, not only from the signs posted, but I have met with Reverend Henry Whitehead." I held out my hand, which he clasped, bowing over it in a courtly manner. In that moment I saw that he was every bit a gentleman accustomed to working with members of society.

"I live on the outskirts of Soho myself," he said. "So it is convenient to treat those who have come down with it. You said you needed a doctor?"

I couldn't believe that the man himself had come to me. "I—actually, I need to speak to you specifically, sir."

I stopped one of Middlesex's nurses, who was inexplicably walking past me with a vase of snowy white delphinium stalks in it. Were they for one of the doctor's offices?

"Nurse, can you find Dr. Goodfellow or one of the other physicians and ask him to come round to visit the lying-in women?"

The woman, whose complexion was as pale as the flowers in her arms, gazed at me in disbelief. "Tell a doctor what to do?" she asked dumbly.

"No, of course not," I said. I did not believe nurses should assert themselves over doctors, although I supposed I did not always follow my own rule. "*Ask* if one would mind attending on the women. Say I have requested it."

Snow interjected, "Would you like me to—"

I quickly shook my head. "No, it is imperative that I speak with you privately."

I led Snow outside the lying-in ward, where Mary still sat, scribbling away, and asked her to join us with her notebook stuffed with papers.

I then sought out the room where I had met with the physicians the previous day. Fortunately, it was not in use, and the three of us sat down at one end of the table.

"I am Florence Nightingale, sir. I am the superintendent of

the Establishment for Gentlewomen During Temporary Illness. I have been asked to assist here at Middlesex with the care of cholera inmates." I also introduced Mary to him.

"You seem to have brought violent winds of change with you," he observed. "I've never seen the staff here move so quickly before. It's almost as if they are in terror of something." He smiled at me.

"Yes, well, I am simply employing some techniques for hospital organization that I devised when I entered service at the Establishment. Presumably the physicians here will not toss me out before I am done."

Snow nodded. "I, too, am assisting here in my own way. I am working on theories about how the disease is spreading through Soho, and since many of the sufferers end up here, I have offered my services while gathering data on each victim."

We were quite possibly duplicating work. "I happened to meet Reverend Whitehead at St. Luke's, and he presented me with his research on how the epidemic was spreading. You see, I have a great penchant for charts and statistics, too, and the priest thought I could be of some use in analyzing his work thus far."

Snow gazed at me curiously. "How unusual for a woman of your station to be interested in such matters."

Despite my dusty, bedraggled appearance after so much hard work, I was glad that I had chosen a nice day dress to wear to the hospital, for it enabled me to speak with Snow as an equal. "My mother wouldn't have described my interest as unusual, but unseemly. However, I appreciate your courteous description, sir."

He nodded. "Did you wish for me to review your analysis, or did you have some other reason for speaking to me?" he inquired.

Without my asking, Mary handed me all the new charts and

diagrams she and I had developed together, and I spread them out for Snow to see. He pulled a pair of brass spectacles from the inside of his vest pocket and put them on, then glanced through my papers quickly. "You have also seen that the concentration is in Broad Street," he said.

"Yes," I agreed. "I wonder if something is emanating from the street there that is causing it."

He removed the spectacles and placed them on top of my map. Looking at me with great seriousness, he said, "I have another theory, but Reverend Whitehead disagrees with me."

Given that Whitehead and I were in general agreement, I wondered what Snow's theory was.

"The cholera victims all suffer the same symptoms, do they not? Severe, milky diarrhea; vomiting; and the related dehydration, irritability, and lethargy. If all the symptoms are occurring within the digestive system, does it not make sense that the disease is a digestive affliction rather than a miasmatic one?"

This made no sense to me. "But can't we see that the disease spreads from house to house and street to street? If it is digestive, that implies that it is something one is eating. Unless everyone is sharing the same meal—quite an impossibility—then it cannot be digestive."

"Ah." Snow put his spectacles on again and put his finger on my map, pushing it across the table to me. "But what sorts of things do you know are located in Broad Street?"

I thought on this. "Many dilapidated houses. The water pump. Street performers. A public toilet."

"And animal carcasses," Mary offered.

But also nearby was the Lion Brewery, where almost no one had been infected. Why was that?

A strange thought came to me. Was it possible that there was something within the brewery itself that was causing the spread of the disease? Were the plentiful smokestacks carrying the disease away from the building itself to deposit cholera elsewhere?

Snow had his own opinion, though. "I think it might be a disease contained within the water pump. People gather water from the pump and take it home to drink. Then the household is infected."

I tried to give credence to what he was saying, even though my mind was preoccupied with thoughts of the Lion Brewery. "But doesn't the water to the pump come from the Thames? If what you are saying is true, then the entire Thames is contaminated, which would mean cholera should be everywhere in London."

He seemed impressed with my argument. "You make a point. However, I am convinced that this is what is true. I not only studied the '49 outbreak in Lambeth, but also had the unfortunate experience of growing up in York along the River Ouse, in a neighborhood which flooded every so often. Each time, there would be disease."

I was doubtful. "It seems to me that disease would spread much more effectively through the air than through brackish water," I insisted, even though I was formulating another theory.

To his credit, Snow took no offense, but simply said, "In my medical research, I have learned that it is frequently that which we cannot possibly suspect is true which is very often the deadly culprit."

I felt my stomach flutter as my mind turned to the Herberts. The doctor had just said something very profound; I was sure of it.

★　★　★

I gathered up the papers and thanked Dr. Snow for his time. Mary and I then sought out Dr. Goodfellow to tell him I would ensure my nurses returned each day for at least a week, and that I myself would be making visits as often as I could.

Goodfellow acted uncomfortable. Had I insulted him? I always seemed to cause the most offense when I was the most passionate and sure about a topic. "If this meets with your approval, of course," I added.

He cleared his throat. "Ahem, yes, yes, that would be fine. Er . . . Miss Nightingale, I must express appreciation on behalf of us all, but, it will be . . . difficult, to say the least . . . to dredge up the funds necessary to pay you and your nurses. Particularly since we, well, since we already need to find money to pay for all of the new supplies you've brought in. It's as though a new hospital has been erected in a single day."

I didn't have the heart to tell him that there was much more to be done—scrubbing walls, repainting, and creating outdoor gardens where inmates could get fresh air, among other things—but I wanted to reassure him.

"Sir, as I said once before, I do not require payment. I am a volunteer. Mary here is paid out of my own purse. I believe we can work out an arrangement for you to pay for only part of my nurses' time." I could probably ask my father for additional allowance to cover their time at Middlesex Hospital, but I wouldn't commit to that until writing Papa a letter. "For now, I think we must concentrate on curing the inmates."

He offered a word of thanks but still seemed nervous. I waited patiently until he said, "I believe there is a way to recompense you. I have a great interest in treating nervous and hysterical disorders. I would like to offer my services at the Establishment in return for your time spent here. Truthfully, it would help my own research efforts, and perhaps I can be of assistance to you."

I wanted to take umbrage at the idea that he thought most of my inmates had problems of the mind, but it was certainly true that some of them did have illnesses with no apparent physical basis to them. Moreover, Dr. Killigrew came only on Tuesdays, and we could use a physician on the premises with more regularity. I struck the bargain with Dr. Goodfellow.

The Establishment's oversight committee might disapprove greatly of my independent decision in this, but it would not be the first time I'd had to do battle with them.

I went searching for my two nurses, gathering them together to give them final instructions before they, too, left for the day. Next, I sought out Middlesex's existing nursing staff, demonstrating for them how to properly use feeding cups with their patients.

I then hurried away from Middlesex with Mary on my heels, puffing and wheezing. "Miss Florence, why are we in such a rush?"

I stopped and looked back at her, lagging ten feet behind me. She limped, favoring one leg over the other, and I realized that she was in pain from the day's work. "I want to make some visits down near Broad Street before dark. But I am very inconsiderate; we should ride down there. Unless you prefer to go home now?"

Mary shook her head resolutely, so we walked to the nearest cab stand. I was fortunate enough to find a driver who would take us all the way into Soho.

As we rode, Mary shared with me what she had been so furiously working on whilst writing in the hospital corridor. It was her list of proofs that the attack on Liz had been the result of a jealous lover. Mary had settled her reasoning essentially as thus:

> The killer had to have purpose. It was unlikely to have been
>   a random attack.
> The attacker called Elizabeth Herbert a prostitute.
> Mrs. Herbert is no such thing.
> The attacker must have been sending her a jealous message
>   before ostensibly attempting to kill her.

"Goose, you have very romantic notions," I said, handing her back her notebook.

However, Mary had remembered what I had forgotten: that the carriage attacker—who might or might not have been the same man who later shot at Liz—had indeed called her such a disturbing name. "But perhaps you are right that I should at least consider Caroline Norton as a possibility."

A flush of pleasure crept up Mary's neck as she smiled happily.

The driver deposited us at the corner nearest the Maddox home. He was either polite enough or uncaring enough not to issue us any admonishment about staying there too late.

I was not prepared for what awaited us inside the Maddoxes' dilapidated rooms.

As if she were a demon in the last throes of panic before being cast into the eternal pit, Isabel Maddox was shrieking at her husband, oblivious to the presence of two women and a man—who presumably lived in the upstairs portion of the house—who had come down and were watching in petrified silence. It was quickly apparent that this group consisted of a husband, wife, and the wife's sister. The two women looked very much alike.

There was little time to worry about these housemates witnessing Isabel's total breakdown. Maddox was inadequately defending himself, with his arms thrown up, as his wife assaulted him using both words and hands.

"How could you have so ruined us? We could have had a good life, a rich life, but every single thing you've done has been to destroy me. Your father, your brother, *you*."

Those gray eyes glittered at her husband. Despite the heat of the day, I shivered at the sheer malevolence in them. Perhaps Isabel Maddox suffered from more than just cholera.

We all watched in frozen horror as she pummeled at her husband's chest in frustration, but the effort was great, and it became too laborious for her to continue. She exhausted herself into a rasping cough.

"Bella, sweetheart, you cannot think—" George Maddox began, but his wife held out a hand to stop him. She was bent over now in her heaving, and her foul breath threatened to consume us all.

Isabel sank to the ground and I rushed to catch her. I dropped awkwardly to my knees to prevent her from hitting her head on the ground and found myself cradling her shoulders and head in my lap.

One of the two upstairs women gasped, but none of them moved toward the woman I held. Even George Maddox was paralyzed.

Astoundingly, Arthur had recovered to such a degree that he was sitting upright on a lumpy pallet in a corner of their tiny back room. He watched his mother cautiously through dark locks of hair that fell over his face. The boy was painfully thin and his face hollowed out and pale, but it would seem that he was going to live after all. I never could have predicted that he was strong enough to survive his illness.

Isabel looked at me piteously, all the fire gone from those once piercing gray eyes. One last time, she reached out one of those spectral hands to me, but she had no strength to do any more than graze the skin. My face was hot where she touched me. "I hated to do it," she confessed in a ragged whisper.

"Mrs. Maddox," I said desperately. "You must get well. For your son and your husband."

Her eyes were closed now, and she shook her head. "Too much disappointment with him."

I crouched on the dirty, crumbling floor, willing this dying woman to live.

She refused my urging, and with just a few final rattles of breath, Isabel Maddox died with a shuddering sigh.

With her head still cradled in my arms, I looked up at George Maddox. His face was twisted in grief and he stumbled past his neighbors into the front room. The neighbors followed him out, and I heard them assure Maddox that they would lay Isabel out, build her a coffin, and make her ready for burial the next day. Sobs exploded from the man as they made their condolences and offered their help.

I realized in that moment that Death, in his chaotic and turbulent manner, does not always conduct his business in the way that one expects.

CHAPTER 14

I was deeply shaken by Isabel Maddox's death, not only because I had expected her to survive but because of the frightful manner of her demise as well. I confess I was also at a loss because I had wanted to question the woman further about what it was she had "accomplished" in her ostensible revenge action against persons unknown.

Mary must have sensed my disquiet, for she stopped me before we reached the Lion Brewery and took one of my hands in hers.

"Miss Florence, there was nothing you or anyone else could have done for that poor woman. Do you know what I think? I think she wanted to die, and cholera gave her a perfect excuse." She turned to continue walking, still clasping my hand, but I shook her off and stopped again.

"Why do you say this?" I said sharply.

Mary's expression was one of bewilderment. "Is it not as clear as the ink on a page? She despised her husband, took no notice of her son, and seemed to loathe the other members of her husband's family. There was something deeply troubled in that woman." She knowingly tapped the side of her head with one finger.

I resumed walking with her. How unsettling to think that a woman's life might reach a state of collapse and death because of real or imagined slights, disrespect, or failures. How could her husband—or anyone—have even prevented what had happened?

I made a conscious decision to put the Maddox family woes behind me. I didn't have the capacity to nurse anyone back to a sound mind, and there were many other duties at hand for me. Thus resolved, I entered the Lion Brewery once more.

Oswyn Davies was not overjoyed to see us, yet neither did he treat us with the same suspicion as before. He even poured us complimentary cups of India ale and invited us to sit at a private table removed from most of the rest of the tables in the brewery's public house.

"Presume to see me is why you're here?" he said as he sat down with us.

"I have been working at Middlesex Hospital to improve conditions for the cholera sufferers here. You mentioned Reverend Henry Whitehead on my previous visit. I visited him, and we are joining forces to try and determine how the cholera is spreading."

"Two good occupations for a nurse, I suppose," he said, bored.

I continued on brightly. "What of you, Mr. Davies? Have you had any recent developments here?"

"Developments? We sent out a hundred and eighty barrels of beer last week, about twenty-five more from the previous week. Is that the sort of 'development' you mean?"

I was fairly certain he was beginning to think me a lunatic. I pressed on. "Have you made any recent hires?"

"I brought on a new supervisor for the night shift," he said.

"Oh!" I said in delight. "Would that be George Maddox?"

"How would you know that?" He was regarding me with interest for the first time.

"Mary and I had occasion to care for his family. His wife has just died of cholera."

Davies's eyes flickered briefly. "Sad for any man to lose his wife. But happens around here every day as of late."

Satisfied that Mr. Maddox and his child would at least have some reliable wages to help them through their grief, I said, "Speaking of which, both Mr. Maddox's wife and child contracted cholera, but he has not, and he is a frequent patron of the Lion, isn't he? You said last time that none of your men has fallen ill to the disease."

Davies looked at me strangely. "Are you saying that power over cholera the brewery must have? Imagine that posted sign: 'Enter here for your magical cholera prevention elixir.' Ha! Right out of business we'd put the laudanum men." He shook his head.

"Oh, that reminds me," I said, remembering another reason for my visit to Davies. "I brought you the salve I promised." I reached into my pocket and brought out the tin for him. "Apply it to your ear twice a day. It should help immensely."

He nodded his thanks at me.

I changed the subject. "Speaking of helping immensely, I thought you might be willing to take on another employee," I suggested.

"Didn't you hear me say I hired Maddox as night shift supervisor? That was the only opening I had."

I waved a hand around the public house. "Do you not think you could use some help cleaning and serving? It would give you much more time to manage your brewery operations."

His gaze followed my waving hand, and then he turned back

to me. "You mean like an old tavern wench?" He shrugged. "Plenty clean in here it is. Besides, why would you want a job like that? Or is it for you?" He looked at Mary, who put a hand to her chest.

"No, I mean for a woman I've met, who used to be in service until she fell on hard times. She lives nearby"—I didn't really even know that that was true of Berenice—"and she is very eager for work."

Davies shook his head. "Don't need a woman around here distracting my workers."

I pretended I hadn't heard him. "She has a daughter, too, who can sweep and polish."

"No," he said curtly.

"The two of them will work for a single wage, and you will have twice the work accomplished."

"No," he repeated, more firmly this time.

"Her name is Berenice. She is very particular in her cooking, too. She makes the freshest loaves of herbed bread you've ever had." I was lying rashly now, pulling from my memory of my family's old cook.

"Again, a maid I don't need," he said, starting to rise.

"I will personally vouch for her," I finished desperately. "If you are unhappy with her after a fortnight, I will pay her back wages from my own purse." I had nothing else left with which to convince him.

He stared at me for several moments, then sat back down. "Fine. If she is unsatisfactory, *you* will pay for her."

"I agree to your terms, sir," I said.

"*My* terms?" Davies rolled his eyes. "In this little negotiation did I play any part? That was an expensive pot of salve, Miss

Nightingale. I'm best served if you leave me to suffer unto death next time."

"You survived the retreat in Afghanistan; I'm sure you find little threat in a tiny woman such as myself," I said, biting back a smile over my accomplishment.

To my surprise, my flippant comment registered deeply with Davies. "The women of Afghanistan are much simpler and less difficult, Miss Nightingale," he said, his tone more serious than I had ever heard it.

I wasn't sure what that meant. "I meant no offense, sir. I was only—"

"Of the Afghan women I do not like to be reminded. They were the source of all the problems there." His expression hardened.

"I thought it was the tribal rebellions that caused the problems leading to the retreat," I reminded him.

Davies grunted. "It was what led to the rebellions that caused us to be slaughtered."

I frowned and glanced at Mary, who shrugged in ignorance as she closed her notebook, as if she sensed that this conversation was not something to record.

Hadn't he already said that the Afghans had risen up in order to remove the Britons from their country? Perhaps Davies didn't remember. "You mentioned that the Afghans did not like having a government imposed upon them."

Another grunt, accompanied with a shake of the head. "What they ultimately did not like was our pride. Make no mistake, they are a wild, ungovernable people. If they aren't cutting down members of the British Empire, they are bludgeoning one another for minor insults. But what I saw . . ."

We three were silent for several moments, and then Mary

said quietly, "Would you care to unburden yourself, Mr. Davies? What did you see?"

Mary was at her matronly best on occasions like this. I probably could have learned a bit of diplomacy from her, given that my tongue ran a hundred feet ahead of my self-control on most days.

Davies pressed the fingertips of his good hand to his forehead as though pushing away a headache. Finally, he dropped his hand and looked up at us both. "Will you not only heal my ear, but my soul as well?"

Mary reached out a hand and squeezed Davies's arm. "If it is confession you seek, we will take you to Reverend Whitehead. If it is untroubling yourself, we would gladly serve you now."

How I admired Mary at this moment, for Davies looked at Mary as though she were a cool drink of water waiting for him to soothe his parched spirit.

He began to talk. "It was an immense caravan of us that went into Afghanistan in 1839. The Army of the Indus, we were called. Not just twenty-one thousand British and Indian troops, but nearly forty thousand camp followers—victualers, washer women, wives, children, and so on. Thirty thousand camels it required to carry all the goods put on parade through the country. Never had much myself in life, but it was far more than the goat herders had, and even I was put out of sorts by the conceit of it all.

"I remember a pack of foxhounds one regiment took along. Another required two camels to carry all their cigarettes. One senior officer used sixty camels to carry his own personal effects into the field. Even junior officers were accompanied by dozens of servants. Turned into a royal palace it was as though the country was to be our kingdom."

Mary, who had never removed her hand from his arm, gently squeezed again. "But this was not your doing," she said softly.

"No, it wasn't," he agreed.

"And it was certainly no reason for them to cut you down so terribly," she continued.

"That is a singular opinion shared only by a few, Mrs. Clarke. But the living excesses—the staged hunts, the lavish parties, the extravagant pleasure gardens—paled in comparison to what happened with some of the people. And it was what was done to the *people* that led to our devastation."

I felt a sudden nervous prickling. "Surely you aren't saying that we dragged the Afghans into slavery or anything," I said.

I remembered my journey to Egypt, where men were essentially enslaved to work on temporary national building projects, such as roads, bridges, and palaces. We had eliminated slavery in Great Britain, but were we secretly employing it elsewhere, in countries where a blind eye might be turned?

"Not exactly," Davies said. "You see, very beautiful the Afghan women were. Large, almond eyes with lithe bodies— begging your pardon for the frankness. But they were so very poor, and a British private could keep an Afghan woman in luxury even on his meager wages. Many of the women found this a temptation they could not withstand and were willing to visit the quarters of the Christian strangers in order to become rich. The British officers in particular were open about these relationships, even in full view of the Afghan tribal leaders."

As much as I was in open admiration of Mary's wise approach to Davies, I also feared his most recent statement would prompt her into an endless prattle about Milo's virtues. I shot her a warning look as she opened her mouth. She snapped it closed and let him continue.

For his part, Davies was lost in his own reverie and not

paying attention to Mary or me. "But just shameless was some of what went on, and it was prevalent among the British officers—those very men who represented the rest of us. The East India Company's second officer, Sir Alexander Burnes, was noted for being particularly . . . insatiable. He would bathe with his Afghan mistress, and even invite two of his other lovers—both married to men within his command—to join in with them. Needless to say, many men followed suit and engaged in these sorts of wanton practices. After all, the camels had brought along plenty of wine, cigarettes, and opium to deaden any sense of wrongdoing.

"The Afghan menfolk became furious at the scandalous way the British were treating their women. Not only was this worthy of revenge in Afghan eyes; it is to be remembered that women are subject to honor killings for intimate relations outside of properly arranged marriages. Disappeared from British homes, some of the women did as a result of a brother, father, or uncle stealing her back, but it was of no matter to our officers. Another would soon arrive in her place." Davies heaved a sigh.

I was spellbound by this story, horrific as it was. As much as I considered myself well traveled, having been to Germany, Egypt, Greece, and Italy, I had never heard of such oppressive treatment—and I had been spat upon by local men while in Egypt simply for being in public without a husband.

"But we British argued that we were not using them as poorly as the Afghan men were, as they held even their supposedly free women in virtual slavery," Davies said. "Even married their con-cubines, some of our men did. Of course, to the Afghans, that was a double insult. First we used the women, then we kept them. In their humiliation, the Afghan men complained to one another that the women of Kabul would soon give birth to half-caste monkeys, bringing even more disgrace to their menfolk.

"Of all the aspects of British occupation that infuriated the Afghans, it was this wanton use of their women that blind with rage it made them. It was how they finally decided to plan their savage attack on us." Davies compressed his lips into a thin line.

"Mr. Davies," I said. "It sounds as though the treachery ran in both directions. Each side expressed cruelties."

He ignored my assertion. "The Afghan women who married into the British ranks were not saved from the butchery, either. They were among those who attempted to flee Kabul, and because of their perceived treachery, they were cut down just as readily as any British citizen. Hanged for it all, those scruts Burnes and Elphinstone should have been," Davies said, banging his fist on the table and wincing. The impact must have caused great pain to his already-damaged hand. "Those two, among others."

"Your anger is deep," I observed.

"Be blamed, can I?" Davies snapped. "And now our good and gracious government is sending men into another bloodbath in Crimea. The secretary at war is spilling good British blood to chase down filmy Russian specters. He should expect that someone will eventually be able to stop him."

My blood chilled in my veins. "Are you—have you attempted to stop him?"

He did not directly answer me, but instead began another story. "There was an Afghan slave girl who belonged to a Pashtun chief. No doubt she was badly mistreated, and she ran away to a particular lieutenant-general's quarters to put herself under his protection. He, of course, took her immediately to his bed and had one of the chief's men beaten. A secret council of the

Pashtun chiefs was held to discuss this violation of *Pashtunwali*, their unwritten code of law."

"Oh dear," Mary said. "I sense this is a tale of vengeance."

Davies nodded. "They did not care about the slave girl herself, but about the contempt the British showed for their country, even going so far as to carelessly offend tribal leaders. The Pashtun chiefs decided then and there that they were justified in throwing off the English yoke, lest they lose all their customs and codes. They were ready for *jihad*. I tell you, that slave girl situation was a match struck to dry, aged tinder, and burned us all did the resulting fire."

Mary no longer had her hand on his arm but was sitting back, that same hand to her chest as she breathed rapidly. "What happened to the poor slave girl?"

Davies snorted. "The general tossed her back to the Pashtuns, knowing they would kill her, did he. He considered it a worthwhile trade to keep the peace. But he underestimated their anger. In giving the girl back to them in a showy ceremony so that all could witness his supposed diplomacy skills, the officer told the Afghans—in front of many of us—'I've given you this, now you owe it to us to come to heel.' That was, of course, the moment that our doom was secured."

Davies's retelling of the horrors of Afghanistan was disturbing in many ways. However, I was beginning to see an association here that seemed ominous. Despite my fear of the answer, I had to pose a single question. "Who was this general?"

He looked at me curiously. "What does it matter? But if you must know, his name was Charles à Court."

I blinked several times, finding myself unable to form a response. Did the General have more enemies than I realized?

★ ★ ★

Mary and I left the Lion. I no longer had need to find Dr. Snow, so we headed straight over on foot to St. Luke's. I was so disconcerted and agitated that I hardly noticed the day's heat, nor that heavy-hanging clouds were threatening imminent rain.

As we walked, I realized I needed to sort out my feelings on what Oswyn Davies had just told us. First, though, I had to offer credit where it was due.

"Mary, I had no idea you had such persuasion skills," I said with warmth. "I'm sure a mob with pitchforks couldn't have pulled out of Mr. Davies what you just did, and it was very valuable—if unexpected—information."

"Thank you, Miss Florence," Mary said, blushing but trying to pretend nonchalance at the compliment. "But you aren't going to turn Mr. Davies into a suspect, are you?"

Not just *a* suspect; he was looming in my mind as *the* suspect.

"How could I not consider him such?" I asked.

She shook her head decisively. "He doesn't have a motive," she insisted firmly.

I sputtered in a most unladylike fashion. "No motive? I can think of several." I began to tally them on one hand. "Maybe this is purely a case of revenge against a superior officer. After all, Davies has permanent injuries from the flight from Kabul, injuries he might blame on the General.

"Or perchance Davies hasn't told us everything about the General. Given the General's proclivities for the local women, perhaps there was an Afghan woman of whom Davies was fond and the General destroyed the relationship.

"Maybe"—another thought came to me—"maybe he is worried that the General will go to the Crimea and wreak havoc there, and he wants to prevent that." I was just warming up.

"But Miss Florence," Mary protested. "It was Mrs. Herbert who was attacked in the carriage, not the General."

That stopped me, but only for a moment. "Isn't it possible that the attacker wanted to murder Liz right in front of the General to make him experience maximum suffering? Or that the General was the real target and the attacker missed his intended victim?" There were so many possibilities and motives to assign to Oswyn Davies.

The strange spire of St. Luke's loomed before us, a couple of blocks away. I hoped Berenice would be there.

Mary stopped me before we reached the church. "But revenge is not as great a motivator as jealousy, especially the jealousy of a woman, Miss Florence. I do believe you need to look into this Mrs. Norton. She is part of it all, I am certain."

I promised that I would do so, but after I paid a visit to the General. Mary's expression was one of disapproval, but she remained silent.

Fortunately, Berenice was at the church. Today she was inside the dimly lit structure, lined up with her daughter for soup. Once they had secured their bowls, I went to where they sat together on top of a bronze grave marker located in the floor in one of the side aisles.

I gave Berenice the news that I had secured work for her, omitting my commitment to pay her wages if Davies was displeased with her performance. At this point, I was beginning to wonder if I was placing her in the employ of an evildoer. I suspected, though, that the poor woman would accept employment as Lucifer's parlor maid, sweeping the ashes of the damned, as long as it would provide her with a living that didn't cause her to resort to the profession of fallen women.

She gaped at me when I told her that she and her daughter could report to the Lion Brewery the following morning, then silently reached out, took my hand, and kissed it in open gratitude.

We then met with Reverend Whitehead in his office. He once again lit candles as I spread out my charts for him. He mumbled and nodded as he looked over what I had done.

"This is a definite improvement on my own work, Miss Nightingale," he admitted, finally looking up at me. "Well done. The disease seems to be hovering over this part of Broad Street." He pointed down to my map.

"Yes. However, I did meet with Dr. Snow earlier today at Middlesex Hospital."

Whitehead sat back in his chair, no longer touching the papers. "Did you? How did you find him?"

"Very intelligent. He told me he believes the cholera problem to be a digestive one, possibly relating to the Broad Street water pump."

Whitehead laughed. "He does indeed. This is why I am so anxious to provide findings to eliminate the likelihood of his supposition as quickly as possible. However, he has asked me to go round and personally interview people along Broad Street to see if there is commonality in what they have ingested. Because I am one of the parish priests, they are more likely to talk to me than some hired clerk. We shall see what they say."

I was also interested in this. I thought Snow's thesis to be far-fetched, but I had also considered old Mrs. Drayton drinking urine to cure her thrush during her stay at the Establishment last year to be far-fetched as well, and certainly that had worked.

"I might be able to assist you," I offered. "I am gathering information on the inmates at Middlesex. I will compile it and bring that to you for study as well."

He expressed his thanks, and then Mary and I took our leave. It was very late in the day and I wished to return to the Establishment before dark. As we left St. Luke's, the sky had opened up to perform that irritating method of spitting down rain that was too forceful for us to avoid getting wet but too light and intermittent for pedestrians to be bothered with umbrellas.

Mary and I walked to the outskirts of the area until we found a cab stand, then rode in relative comfort back to the Establishment.

Tomorrow I planned to return to Soho to attend Isabel Maddox's funeral. It would seem I was already abandoning my resolve not to be involved with the poor wretches of Soho. Following the funeral, I would then finally return to Herbert House. The General and I needed to have an extensive conversation.

CHAPTER 15

The light drizzle had continued overnight into the following morning and had become full-fledged rain when I went alone to Isabel Maddox's meager funeral. A cascade of heavenly tears, as the saying goes.

She was buried in St. Luke's churchyard. Only George Maddox, his son, a few neighbors—including those from upstairs—and I were in attendance to pay respects, with the clean-shaven priest officiating. No doubt he and Reverend Whitehead were trading funereal duties like this on a daily basis.

I felt guilty that I was the only one there who actually possessed an umbrella to protect myself from the rain. However, the others didn't even seem to notice that the weather was any different than on any other day.

The neighbors drifted off as the priest concluded his reading from his Book of Common Prayer. I remained behind to express condolences to Mr. Maddox, but the man seemed to be almost in a trance as he let the rain sluice over him.

Arthur Maddox stood unsteadily a few feet away from his father. The lad shivered as his long, uncut hair became plastered to his face and across his eyes. He needed to be put back to bed;

he wasn't entirely well yet, and now he had endured his mother's funeral in a saturating rain.

"Mr. Maddox," I said, holding my umbrella up to cover us both.

"Miss Nightingale, good of you to come to see Bella off." He murmured this politely, with no emotion.

I offered him my condolences, which he accepted with no more than a nod. It was as if I could see the light fading from his eyes. I hoped he would not soon join his wife.

Despite my desire to be sensitive to his grief, I felt compelled to ask him about the circumstances surrounding his wife's death. "Sir, pardon my rudeness, but I would like to ask you about yesterday's . . . incident."

Another vague nod. "Yes?"

"As Mrs. Maddox lay in my arms, she said, 'I hated to do it.' Did she do something to you?"

He shrugged in apathy. "It doesn't matter. She's gone now."

"Of course," I said. I felt instant contrition for having intruded on his grief. I couldn't bear to ask him another question about his wife, who was not yet cold in her grave. I turned to take my leave, but Maddox stopped me by offering an explanation.

"I—I told her that I had gotten a job as a supervisor at the brewery. I thought she'd be happy. Instead, she—she—turned on me. I don't understand why it was wrong. It was steady work." He gazed at me miserably, as though somehow I might explain it for him.

I couldn't explain it, but I had to offer him some sort of hope and comfort. "Sir, your wife was simply exhausted from her illness. Think of how we say frightful things when we are in the heat of anger. How much worse is it when someone is in pain and failing health?"

He nodded but appeared thoroughly unconvinced. "I had even stopped talking about my novel, too. She was still bitter with me. I suppose I was never very satisfactory as a husband. Maybe she was expressing regret at her anger. Now it's just me and the boy, except . . ." He trailed off and looked away.

"Except what, sir?" I prodded him.

"Mr. Davies offered me free lodgings in the brewery's attic, so I can leave my other place behind. But I never told Mr. Davies about Arthur, so there's no job there for him. Don't think I can ask about it now; I'll look like a charity case. Arthur's a small boy. I could probably get him placed as a chimney sweep somewhere."

I thought the man's pride was preventing him from understanding that he did require a little charity in his situation. However, Mr. Davies had not been very accommodating about my idea of Berenice and her daughter coming to work at the Lion, even without lodgings. I could understand Mr. Maddox's reticence to ask that the man accommodate Arthur, too.

However, Maddox had essentially lost every single thing in his life except his son. I might not be able to help every poor soul down here, but I could at least help one.

I had an idea.

"Mr. Maddox, might I propose that you permit Arthur to come and stay at the Establishment for a while? Until you feel steady and secure again? Your son also needs more recovery time."

My suggestion broke him out of his languor. "What? You want my son to be bedded down in a women's hospital?"

"No, no, nothing like that. You see, we have another boy who lives there. He runs errands and does other odd jobs. He has his own quarters, and Arthur could share them. He would have nourishing food to eat, and there are many people to watch out for him. Our manservant, Charlie Lewis, could teach Arthur valuable skills as well."

Maddox frowned with indecision. "I don't know . . ." He glanced over at his son. "Arthur, come here. Miss Nightingale would like to ask you something."

The drenched boy trudged over to us in abject weariness and looked up at me, blinking. "Yes ma'am?" His voice was so low and ragged I could hardly hear him.

I bent to one knee. It was immediately soaked through and I knew my dress would require cleaning. "I know you believe you have met me only once. But some of my other nurses and I tended to you and your mother while you were sick. We would like to tend to you a while longer, while your father gets settled into his new job. He will eventually have enough money to move you somewhere better."

"Where do you live?" he asked. I wondered if he had ever been more than a half mile from his lodgings.

"Actually, I live inside a women's hospital," I said.

Arthur looked at me doubtfully. "A hospital? Don't people go there to die?"

The boy's pallid countenance somehow tugged at an emotion deep inside me. I smiled gently at him. "Arthur, you have bravely survived a difficult illness all by yourself. I don't think you have anything to worry about at the hospital. Besides, there is another boy there you can meet. His name is John Wesley, and he has a pet squirrel named Dash."

The Maddox boy tilted his head in curiosity. "A squirrel? Is that like a dog? I never had a pet before."

"Not quite. But John Welsey's squirrel knows tricks, and I imagine he would let you take Dash through his set of them."

Arthur's interest was clearly piqued by now. He turned to his father. "Papa?"

Maddox exhaled a breath full of pain and anxiety. "Do you want to do it? I'll come for you as soon as I can."

Arthur considered me for several moments, staring intently at me through his plastered locks. "Yes, I'll go."

The first thing I would do was ensure the boy had a bath and a good meal, and then he could disappear into John Wesley's world. I suspected it would do him an abundance of good. Of course, John Wesley might teach Arthur a little too much, but that could be dealt with later.

★　★　★

I took Arthur back to the Establishment with me, where the nurses immediately began doting on the little waif, much to the boy's astonishment. He soon found himself wrapped in a cocoon of hugs, soup, and soap down in the kitchens.

Nurse Hughes offered to sew him some clothes, while Nurse Harris took a comb and pair of scissors to Arthur's hair. He submitted to the haircut in stunned silence. Or perhaps the boy's full stomach made him pliant.

Charlie Lewis found John Wesley down the street rolling hoops with some other boys and brought him back to meet Arthur. John Wesley's intelligent gaze took in everything—the freshly scrubbed and smiling Arthur, the cooing nurses, the aroma of freshly baked cake—and immediately recognized that he had a rival in the building.

John Wesley bristled visibly, but Nurse Harris bent over and spoke quietly in his ear. He nodded several times and then just as visibly relaxed.

Lewis gazed longingly at Nurse Harris as she calmed and cajoled John Wesley. Lewis had held a long-standing affection for her, an affection that she did not return, largely because she was still a married woman. Harris had escaped a terrible marriage and had effectively gone into hiding at the Establishment, and in a beneficial turn of events had proved herself to be a competent nurse.

"Mr. Lewis, might I talk with you for a moment?" I said.

He reluctantly gave up his adoration and followed me up to my study. I drew out Fenton's dice to show him. "Do you know what these are?"

He bent down over my hand, careful not to touch me. "Sure, M-M-Miss Nightingale. They are gambling dice."

I had him hold out his hand, and I dropped the three cubes into it. "Look at the carving above the crown on each one. What would you say they represent?"

Mr. Lewis picked each die up individually and looked at it. "I don't know, m-m-m-miss."

Why was it that every military man I talked to claimed to have no knowledge of what the carvings meant, but a priest working in a church in a poor section of London did?

"Is it possible that they refer to a military unit inscription?" I asked.

"Well, s-s-s-sure." He looked at me blankly.

I bit back my impatience. "And do you have a guess what that might be? Or how I might figure it out?"

He frowned at them again. "I think these m-m-m-might be for an army unit. But I was a tar; I wouldn't know what this refers to, m-m-m-miss."

"I see." This made me doubly angry; clearly, then, the General would have known what the symbols on the dice meant but had pretended total ignorance of them. Why? It seemed an extraordinary idea, but could they have anything to do with Afghanistan? If so, this meant that Oswyn Davies had likely also lied to me when he looked at the dice.

I thanked Mr. Lewis for his time, and fortunately he did not question why I was asking about the dice.

By the time I had changed my dirty dress and left for Herbert House, Arthur and John Wesley were already fast friends, bound together by a mutual affection for Dash. The two boys were plying the young squirrel with vegetable scraps from the kitchen. The animal gently took a carrot top in its teeth from John Wesley, then sat on its haunches and nibbled away in enjoyment, the carrot scrap now held securely in its front paws.

The simple joy of it momentarily stole my breath, and I was glad for it.

★   ★   ★

I slipped out of the Establishment quietly, again without taking Mary with me. She would be hurt by my apparent abandonment of her, but at this point she was so wedded to the idea that the completely unknown Caroline Norton must be responsible for the carriage attack that I wasn't certain I could have a dispassionate interview at Herbert House in her presence.

The rain had stopped but the heat had not, leaving the city in a state of oppressive clamminess. The taxi dropped me off at the Belgrave Square cab stand. As I walked down the block toward the Herbert residence, I noticed there was a quality, highly polished landau sitting about a block beyond Herbert House. It stood out to me because the carriage's coachman was sitting on the driver's box, as if waiting for his passengers, yet there was a glamorous woman sitting in the open carriage, patiently watching the house.

The carriage was neither pulled completely off to one side of Grosvenor Crescent nor attempting to pull into traffic.

I found myself slowing my own pace. Was I mistaken to think that the woman was observing my friends' home?

It was then that the woman raised a pair of opera glasses to her eyes, pointing them directly at an upper window of the Herbert home.

I was outraged that someone thought she could spy on the secretary at war in such a brazen manner. I picked up my walking pace, intent on confronting the woman, especially when I considered that this might be the infamous Caroline Norton.

I neared the landau, not bothering to hide or be discreet, for I wished to catch this spy off guard. "Pardon me," I said loudly, feeling disadvantaged for being so far below her.

The woman yelped in surprised and, keeping the glasses raised to her face, lowered them briefly to peer down at me.

"Sorry, ma'am," her coachman said to his passenger, having also just taken note of me. "I didn't see her." Now he addressed me. "Madam, if I could ask you to move—"

"Who are you?" I demanded angrily, ignoring the man and not taking my eyes from the woman's face, which was once again masked by the pearl-handled glasses.

With long, tapered fingers, she slowly lowered the glasses to her lap. An unusual, tight-fitting gold bracelet adorned her wrist.

I now stared up at a woman who was quite beautiful, with flawless skin, dewy sapphire eyes, and an erect, almost noble, bearing. Her dark hair was carefully sculpted beneath a large, feather-trimmed, sky-blue hat, which showcased her luminous eyes. She seemed neither flustered nor dismayed by the heat.

Yet, on closer inspection, I could see that despite her exquisiteness, she was clearly older than me and had pale shadows beneath those eyes. She reminded me of a rose discovered on a vine late in the season: so very beautiful compared to the withered-up blooms around it, but a little desiccated when plucked and viewed in one's palm.

The woman blinked twice languidly. "I believe the appropriate question is who *you* are, madam," she said, without the least hint of offense at my presence.

"I am Florence Nightingale, a friend of the Herberts. You appear to be studying their home."

She smiled, those rosebud lips parting to show perfectly even white teeth. "You are mistaken. I am not studying their home, only their occupants. I don't recall Sidney mentioning you."

"But I have heard of you," I said flatly. "I presume you are Caroline Norton."

She tilted her head to one side. Naturally, she had a swanlike neck with not even a freckle interrupting its graceful line. "Does he speak of me?" Despite her languorous tone, I sensed an eagerness to her question.

"Only in a manner that makes me concerned for his good health and happiness. What do you wish to achieve, Mrs. Norton, perched out here like a peregrine falcon, waiting for your unsuspecting prey?"

Caroline was quiet for several moments, but even from the ground looking up, I could see her mind whirling behind her gaze. "It is impossible for me to wait, Mrs. Nightingale," she said cryptically.

"I am unmarried," I replied. "I do not understand what you—"

"Of course you are unmarried," she said. Her voice dripped with the insult, and I confess it was not an insult to which I responded well.

"But I am no snake in a garden, either, plotting and deceiving against another woman." I was in a righteous snit, but I realized it was going to lead me nowhere. I took a deep breath as Caroline Norton arched a delicate eyebrow at me.

"My apologies," I said, tasting bile. How had this woman so irritated me in the space of seconds? "I am, as I'm sure you understand, concerned for my friend, Liz, who is extremely *innocent*." I hoped she understood the implication.

"Innocent?" Caroline Norton's laughter tinkled both mockingly and charmingly at the same time. "There is very little innocence in that family. If you are such a good friend, you should know that."

Did the woman speak only in cloaked statements? I wished to say so sarcastically, but instead attempted conciliation. "Is there a way I can offer you assistance?"

"A friend of Elizabeth Herbert, helping me? I hardly think so." Again that tinkling laugh, like bells on a breeze. "No, I am just waiting for . . . for certain events to unravel."

I wished I could climb up into the carriage to face her evenly. But I couldn't climb in without an invitation from her and some assistance from the coachman in pulling out the steps and helping me up. Mrs. Norton was showing no inclination to share her seat with me.

"Events?" I asked. "Do you mean those occurring in the Crimea that the secretary is handling?"

"War." She wrinkled her nose. "I experience that on a daily

basis, Miss Nightingale. No, I don't concern myself with men's affairs among themselves. I am more interested in domestic matters."

"Sidney will not leave his wife for you, Mrs. Norton," I said. "He is devoted to her."

Her lips curled in secretive delight. "He just needs a little time. And society will need a little time to adjust."

I had completely lost control of this conversation. "The Herbert family has enough worries right now, madam, what with the attack by a madman on Mrs. Herbert's carriage a few days ago. Is this perhaps something you know about? Someone shot at her but missed the mark and ended up killing their coachman."

I had clearly given her a valuable piece of information, for she smiled at me in gratification, then spoke so sharply and quickly to her own coachman to move on that I was barely able to jump out of the way in time to prevent the rear carriage wheel from running over my foot.

I stood there helplessly as her carriage moved into traffic and disappeared. Caroline Norton still sat erect and regal in her seat, the only movement coming from the feathers adorning her hat.

All in all, it had not been my finest Christian moment. I had been agitated, outraged, and blunt. Moreover, Caroline Norton had presented herself as someone who had some sort of secret knowledge critical to my investigation, and I had let her simply roll away.

Mary was going to be very smug when I told her about all that had transpired.

CHAPTER 16

I was still shaking as I was shown into the same parlor at Herbert House as on my previous visit. I waited for Liz near the brightly burning fireplace, holding myself steady on the mantel as I replayed my encounter with Caroline Norton in my head. As I did so, I gazed up at the Madonna-and-child painting of Liz and little George on the wall above me. My nerves were entirely too taut, for I could have sworn Liz was frowning in disapproval from above me.

I forgot about the painting as I heard a strange, erratic thumping that drowned out the rhythmic ticking of the mantel clock.

What was that?

That was when I noticed Alberto curled up on a settee, rhythmically wagging his tail against the back of it. He wore some sort of miniature wool jacket, and the dog was shivering from the outdoor dampness that seeped into every home after a good soaking. Apparently not even the fireplace heat could remedy the chills for him.

He also had a damask pillow under his paws, and a clutch of feathers in his mouth. I shook my head at him, and he lowered his jaw to the torn pillow, looking at me pitifully with worried brown, doelike eyes.

"You'll not get forgiveness from me," I told Alberto. He whined and thumped his tail faster.

To my surprise, it wasn't Liz who greeted me, but Sidney. He carried a folded newspaper in one hand.

"Flo!" he exclaimed, grabbing me and kissing both cheeks, as was his custom.

I don't know whether Alberto was as pleased to see Sidney as Sidney was to see me, or if the pup was just a little jealous, but the little greyhound whined, jumped down from the settee, and excitedly bounced up against Sidney's leg several times.

Sidney bent down to chuck the dog under the chin, then pointed back to the settee. "Off with you now. I have business to conduct."

As Alberto slunk back to his resting place, Sidney noticed the destroyed pillow lying on the seat. "Not long ago, that would have been cause for great concern on Liz's part. Now it appears we are subject to every manner of canine terror and destruction."

Sidney's expression belied his stern words. He was obviously as besotted with Alberto as everyone else in the family.

He sat down next to the dog, who immediately nosed his way into his master's lap.

Sidney tucked the newspaper at his side as he invited me to sit in a chair across from him. "Have you information for me?" he asked as he scratched behind Alberto's ears.

"Some." I briefly outlined for Sidney most of what I knew thus far, including what Davies had told me about Afghanistan.

"So you believe my father-in-law should have known what the dice inscriptions are, and purposely hid that knowledge for some devious reason?" Sidney's disbelief was palpable.

I hesitated. "I would say he did so for an as yet unknown reason. Truthfully, my primary purpose in coming here today was to talk to the General, not you. But there's something else . . ."

Sidney gave Alberto a final pat on the head and shifted the dog from his lap. Alberto whined once, then slithered to the floor and went bounding out of the room.

Sidney leaned back, an arm across the back of the settee. "What is this 'something else'?" he asked.

I willed myself to display more decorum than I had outside Herbert House. "Are you aware that Caroline Norton has been loitering outside in her ostentatious landau, observing your home—no, excuse me, observing the occupants of your home?" Was I being too harsh?

Sidney sat still for several moments as he registered what I had said. He cleared his throat. "I had no idea. I shall immediately see to it. I cannot have Liz upset."

I huffed disapproval. "I hardly think that a visit from you will convince Mrs. Norton that you are *not* interested in her. Moreover, you said you do not know where she is."

"Yes, quite right, I did say that. What I meant is that I can make some inquiries as to where she might be. I saw no reason to do this before, but this is quite a different situation."

Why was I suspicious that he was lying about her whereabouts? Had my inopportune confrontation with Caroline Norton finally convinced me that Mary's theory was correct?

"Sidney, given your past attachment to the woman, might it not hurt Liz more if you were to meet with Mrs. Norton? Perhaps I should meet with her again."

I had quite enough to do and did not want to be dragged into correcting Sidney's mistakes. But I also did not wish for Liz to be hurt emotionally in addition to the trauma she had experienced in the attack.

He rubbed his chin with his free hand. "Yes, I suppose that would work. I'll write down her address for you."

I nodded as he retrieved writing materials, disappointed to learn that he knew exactly where Caroline was and had lied previously when we had spoken about her. "It is my hope that Mrs. Norton is not responsible for anything," I said.

Sidney made no comment to this as he handed me the slip of paper with Caroline's address on it, but instead changed the subject entirely. "You may wonder why I met you instead of Liz. She's in the nursery with the children and will be down shortly. I told her I needed to speak with you first."

He pulled the *Times* from the settee and unfolded it, holding it up so I could see the blazing headline.

Her Majesty's Army in TATTERS before hardly engaging the ENEMY

He extended the paper to me and I read the article, which described the appalling conditions the British Army was encountering in their initial days in the Crimea.

Roughly a hundred men a day were dying of starvation and disease due to the swamp of filth in which they were living. Ponies and camels were joining their owners in swampy graves.

A woodcut drawing accompanied the article. Its being a mere drawing did not diminish the horror it portrayed.

It depicted part of a brick building. In front of the structure were soldiers, some sitting on the ground, some seeming to hobble around, and others apparently making sleeping spots on the dirt.

I pulled the newspaper closer. "Sidney, these men lying prone on the ground—I believe they are *dead*. Is this real?"

Sidney nodded and looked away, spots of color on his cheeks. "Yes, I had no idea. But now with the new photographic processes that exist, artists can now accurately sketch out the disaster occurring from the photographs that are sent back. Even worse, the general public sees it all before we do."

I finished reading the article. "This suggests that the Army is poorly equipped and that there is a shortage of nearly everything—food, clothing, and bandages. More men are dying in the hospital than in the field." I handed the newspaper back to him. "What have you permitted to happen, Sidney? Are you letting our poor boys needlessly suffer?"

The color on his cheeks heightened, even as he bristled in indignation. "Of course not! Our generals here simply didn't know the extent of the squalor. Our bureaucracy means that photographs like this are arriving long before filed reports."

If the British public were only half as outraged as I was at the moment, the entire War Department might soon find itself being whipped out of London.

"Why do you show me this? It is an abomination on our country," I declared.

"Yes." Sidney rose and went to a wide flat table, done in intricate marquetry, and opened the top, flipping through papers until he found what he wanted before closing the table.

"Join me," he said, spreading out several drawings.

They were pencil sketches of both the interior and exterior of an enormously long brick building, with seven-story towers at each corner. It looked almost like a prison, except it was large enough to have held the entire criminal population of England. "What is this?"

"This is our hospital in Scutari, Turkey, a ferry ride away from Istanbul."

Sidney pronounced it "Skoo-tuh-ree." What an odd name.

"They were previously barracks for the Turkish army," he explained to me. "The Turks allocated it to us to house troops on their way to the front, but we have quickly turned it into a hospital. What we didn't realize when we moved into it was that the building had been long in disuse and disrepair. Not to mention that all we really did was tear down some walls to create long wards, as you can see in this drawing." Sidney pointed to a sketch showing two long wings attached to one another by two shorter wings, which formed the perimeter of the building's vast rectangle. "It's roughly six hundred by eight hundred feet. There are three floors on three wings, and only two floors on the eastern wing because of the inclined terrain."

I frowned. These were extraordinarily long wings. How could doctors and nurses walk along them without suffering pure exhaustion?

But Sidney made me realize the problems there went much deeper. "Ironically, cholera has erupted inside the hospital as well as here in London, and it is already devastating our troops. Not only does it hamper our ability to quell Russian ambitions, but the dreadful publicity being generated by these photographs is going to turn the public against what we are trying to accomplish."

"It is also a problem for the soldiers themselves," I added drily.

He gave me a wounded look. "Flo, I am not insensitive to their suffering. But in my position, my first responsibility is to the effective prosecution of the war."

As usual, I was being overly harsh. "I apologize. I know you would not purposely see good men sent senselessly to their graves. Please forgive me."

"It's nothing," he murmured. "But I wish to seek your good counsel."

Sidney picked up one of the interior drawings and offered it to me. "Can you advise me on what should be done to improve the hospital?"

I waved my hand in refusal. "It would be difficult for me to do such a thing."

"Didn't you just advise the doctors at Middlesex Hospital how to make improvements? In fact, you completely overhauled the Establishment, remember?" He thrust the drawing at me again.

I shook my head, ignoring it. "I walked through those properties myself. This is merely a drawing. It tells me nothing about the interior conditions of it—how medicines are stocked, the cleanliness of it, the food inmates receive. I know nothing other than what you've just told me."

"This is all I have. The field reports don't give me any information, because the officers do not ask the doctors their opinion on anything. After all, troop movements are not dependent upon the hospital's struggle with cholera." The sketch continued to hang between us.

I wavered. How could I tell Sidney that I was interested— beyond measure—in what he was asking me, but my mind was nearly overcome with other concerns? That those concerns included working for Sidney, and I had made very little progress in that area? I contemplated his pleading expression for what seemed an eternity.

I sighed and held out my hand for the paper. I spent several minutes studying the drawing and finally pointed to one long wing. "There seem to be a great number of windows here. Can they open? Fresh air is very helpful to recovery."

He shrugged. "I don't know." He opened a drawer further down in the desk and removed pencil and paper. He scratched out a note. "I shall recommend that Dr. Hall there consider opening the windows if possible."

"Also, I believe the men should be separated according to the severity of their injuries. Put the injured on one floor and those with disease on another."

He continued writing as I spoke. "The wards must be smaller with nurses assigned to each one, so that the women don't have to traverse miles of corridors visiting patients."

Sidney's expression stopped me. "What's wrong?" I demanded.

"I'm afraid there are no nurses at Scutari."

"None? At all?" I said, aghast. "What about doctors and orderlies? How many are there?"

"Actually, Flo, there are only three doctors and a scattering of orderlies."

I stared at him until I thought my eyes would pop out of my head. "Pardon me? Surely you are joking. Sidney, that must be rectified immediately. How can hundreds—or even thousands— of men be adequately treated by a handful of men? That is the worst atrocity of all. You need nurses there, lots of them."

Sidney looked at me thoughtfully. "I see." He abruptly changed the subject. "Why don't I take you to Liz?"

★   ★   ★

"Flo!" Liz exclaimed as brightly as her husband had upon seeing me. She removed William from her lap and placed him in a bassinet. The other children were clumsily playing marbles together. "I'm so glad you came to visit. What news have you?"

She proffered her cheek for Sidney to kiss. He nodded to me with a warning look as he left the room.

"Not much, I'm afraid." I sat down on a chair across from her that was probably meant for an older child. It actually wasn't that uncomfortable. I told Liz the same story I had told Sidney, although I softened my thoughts on the General and made no mention of Caroline Norton.

She looked crestfallen. "I had so hoped we might know who attacked me by now. But to think someone might have been after Papa is even more heartbreaking. It distresses me to think this evil man is gallivanting about London, completely unscathed."

"I am trying. There's just so much in the way, particularly with this cholera outbreak."

Liz clucked her tongue. "I've read about it. No doubt you will banish cholera from the city by giving it a stern lecture followed by your caring ministrations to its sufferers."

"You flatter me, Liz, but I will try to live up to your adulation. Meanwhile, I just wanted to see how you're feeling. You seem to be getting on well." My friend looked much better. Her coloring was rosy, and she was back to her usual self.

"I am, as long as I don't think too much about what happened. Sidney has been so concerned, and of course Papa has been like a prowling Bengal tiger over it all. He says he is waiting for an opportunity to hang the guilty party himself. To be truthful"—Liz dropped her voice to a conspiratorial whisper—"I am worried about Papa. I've caught him muttering to himself on more than one occasion. He is so very troubled by the attack, I think because he feels as though he did not adequately protect me. Now that you believe he may have been the target, my fear is that—"

I could readily finish her train her thought. "That the longer this goes on, the more disturbed the General will become, and you are worried that he might lash out foolishly before I have a chance to discover the perpetrator. Yes?"

Liz laughed nervously. "I didn't realize you knew my father so well."

"I suppose I have become well acquainted with human nature. Any loving father would react as the General has." I couldn't express my doubts about Liz's father to her. There would be time enough for her to be shattered if and when I was actually able to accuse him of something.

I noticed that Alberto had somehow made his way into the room. He sat at Liz's feet, still wearing his little wool coat, and offered her a delicate whine. Liz reacted as though the dog were one of her children running to her over a stubbed toe. "Poor little dear, are you unhappy?"

She picked up the greyhound, and he curled up in her lap. From a table at her elbow, which was also covered in children's drawings, she plucked a tiny nugget of some sort from a covered dish. "Does handsome little Alberto sweetboy want some pressed duck?" she cooed, holding it just above the dog's nose. He licked at Liz's hand, which made her laugh in delight. She dropped the treat into his mouth and Alberto turned to look at me. I could have sworn the dog gave me a self-satisfied smirk.

I presume he needed me to understand my lowly place in the family compared to his own exalted one. I'd had no idea dogs could be so competitive.

Alberto's triumph lasted mere seconds, though, for George

and Sidney caught sight of the dog from across the room, and with squeals and shouts went after it. Alberto scrabbled out of Liz's lap and went tearing out of the nursery, a young boy and his toddler brother on his heels.

Liz looked after her children's retreating backs with undisguised affection, even as she mildly protested their noisy departure.

Liz's maid, Alice Nichols, entered the nursery carrying a tea tray, casting me a furtive glance before addressing her mistress. "Mrs. Herbert, the kitchen maid was on her way up with a spot of refreshment, and I told her I'd bring it the rest of the way." Nichols pushed aside the box containing Alberto's treats to make room for the tray.

Nichols bobbed quickly at Liz and turned to leave, again eyeing me questioningly as she left the room, pulling the door closed behind her.

Liz poured out cups for us, then offered me a warm slab of Eve's pudding. I eagerly accepted, so she poured rich golden custard around the sponge cake–topped base of sugared, cooked apple slices before handing me the plate. For a moment I forgot about all the anxieties and burdens in my life as I gave myself over to the luscious sweetness. It was not often that I was so enamored of food. I suspect in this case it was simply a diversion from the overwhelming list of tasks that lay before me.

By the blissful expression on Liz's face, it would appear that she, too, enjoyed the culinary diversion. When she had dredged the final bite of cake through the custard and finished it off with an unladylike smack, she said, "Oh, I should tell you that my brother is coming today for a monthlong visit. I haven't seen him since his wedding back in March. You've never met Charles

Henry, have you? I was hoping he was coming with his bride, Emily, since they've only been married a few short months. But he wrote to me that one of Emily's cousins is getting married up north in York, and Emily wishes to go stay a while and help with the planning. Charles Henry had no desire to be part of that, so he decided it was a good time to make a visit to his favorite sister." Liz laughed at her own joke.

I laughed politely, too, but my mind was reaching back to what Alice Nichols had told me of her love affair with Liz's brother, spoiled by his engagement to Miss Emily Currie. Nichols surely knew that Charles Henry was scheduled to arrive here—alone. Perhaps that was the source of her covert glances at me. Did she wonder if I remembered what she had told me and if I was to be trusted not to mention it to Liz once I discovered that Charles Henry à Court was going to be staying under the same roof with her?

I considered this silently as Liz chattered on happily about how much the children loved their Uncle Charles Henry and how much she looked forward to riding out to see the reconstructed Crystal Palace at Sydenham Hill with her brother. "They say it's an entirely new experience from the Great Exhibition, with various courts showcasing important historical eras—there's an Egyptian court, a Grecian court, a medieval court. I'm looking most forward to the Renaissance one. Flo, is anything the matter? Did the pudding upset you?"

She was making me realize that I had an important question for her. "Liz, I would like to talk about the carriage attack."

"Again?" she said, shuddering.

"Yes, please. When you decided to travel to the British Museum, did you know that cholera had broken out in Soho?"

She frowned, considering this for the first time. "I suppose I had some awareness of it."

I reached over to put my cup and saucer on the table next to Liz, then sat back down, leaning forward earnestly in my little seat. "Then why did you go to the museum that way? Why not go up through Mayfair and Marylebone to get there?"

"I didn't choose the routing."

"Who did?" I asked.

The furrow in her brow was deeper. "I hardly thought about it at the time. I supposed our coachman simply went in a manner he considered most direct. No, wait." She looked upward in thought. "Didn't Papa want to drive through St. James's Park? That would have meant it only made sense to go to the museum the way we did. Why is it important to know that?"

"I—" Now the pudding really *was* souring in my stomach. "I'm just glad you and the General didn't contract cholera on top of everything else."

"Yes, that would have been terrible, wouldn't it? I would have especially been devastated if my father had taken ill. Papa is still a very vigorous man, but he is getting up in years."

My friend's father was not just a vigorous old man, but an old man with secrets, of this I was certain.

CHAPTER 17

I found the General in Sidney's study. George must have tired of chasing Alberto, for he and his grandfather were now positioned across a table from one another, moving tin soldiers around on an enormous paper map. Clearly the boy adored the General, who spoke to his grandson as an adult as he instructed him on battle tactics and troop movements. It appeared that they were recreating the Battle of Waterloo.

I cleared my throat from the doorway. The General turned to see who was interrupting his lecture on the unsurpassed swordsmanship of the Household Brigade cavalry troops and the heroic fearlessness of one of Major-General Ponsonby's regiments of heavy dragoons after Ponsonby was captured.

"Miss Nightingale," he said gruffly.

"May I speak with you privately, sir?" I said.

He nodded and sent George away, promising that later they would work on the Battle of Hastings. The eldest Herbert child bounced out of the room, and the General raised himself to full height. "My son will be here for a visit soon," he said curtly. "What can I do for you?"

Apparently, I would not be welcome once Charles Henry arrived. "I wish to speak with you regarding the carriage attack."

"I've told you all I know."

I shook my head in open dispute. "I do not think this is true. Can you tell me why you specifically routed your carriage through Soho, which you must have known was not only experiencing a cholera outbreak, but is also not as—pleasant—a path for your open carriage as say, Mayfair, would have been?"

His expression was incredulous. "What bearing can that possibly have on the lunatic who shot at my dear Elizabeth? Are you suggesting that whoever wished to harm her would have been thoroughly unable to do so in Mayfair? Does a pistol only fire in downtrodden neighborhoods?" The General's face was flushing red as he vented his anger on me.

But I noticed that he had not directly answered my question, and it did not appear that he intended to do so. However, I tried once more.

"You do know that Sidney has asked me to assist in this investigation. I would think you would be eager to share anything you know or think." I nearly put my hands on my hips like an angry governess dealing with an incorrigible pupil but caught myself before doing so.

The General grunted. "I have no bone with you personally. I just don't think that a nurse, no matter how polite and privileged she may be, has the qualifications for the surveillance and foraging required to find out who the culprit is."

"Your son-in-law does not agree," I maintained.

"My son-in-law has many foolish thoughts and has done many foolish things, particularly as of late. I worry that he has lost his head as I have so done in the past. But he has become an important man, even more so than I have been, so I must weigh my options carefully when deciding what to do to protect my daughter. Currently I am in a tactical withdrawal, given that I am on disadvantageous ground."

I knew Sidney too well to ever think him a fool. I reached into my pocket and withdrew Fenton's dice yet again. "Is it that withdrawal that caused you to lie to me about these?"

The General looked at me blandly. "And why would you think to so accuse me?"

I held the three cubes out to him and he reflexively accepted them. "You know what the markings above each crown side mean," I asserted.

He picked one die up out of his hand and hefted it in the other. He replaced it in his palm and picked up another die, also scrutinizing it heavily.

"If you think I know what they mean, then you have probably already figured it out for yourself," he said, once more fending me off.

"I believe so," I said. "I met a man who was present for the retreat at Kabul in 1842," I said.

The General's eyes narrowed. "Did you? What of it?"

"He did not have kind words for you, sir. He implied— actually, he directly stated—that you were in part responsible for the tribal chiefs launching the attacks that resulted in the withdrawal from Kabul, which I do not believe was *tactical* in the least."

He continued to watch me carefully. His next words were those of an overbearing military commander. "Who was this disloyal turncoat? I will see him strung from the highest gibbet I can find."

Now it was my turn to be incredulous. "I should hand over to you one of the only sources of information I seem to have at the moment, given that you seem to be concealing yourself behind a figurative battlement? Not likely, sir. Moreover, I learned from a man of the cloth that those symbols, the "5," the "G," and the "D," must refer to some sort of military unit. The fifth something or other. If a mere minister could decipher it, how was it possible that you couldn't?"

The General rolled the dice in his palm, as if buying time before responding. His fingers were leathery from years in the sun. "Never said I didn't know it."

"What? I showed them to you, Sidney, and Liz almost as soon as they came into my possession. You told me you didn't know what they meant."

He shook his head and smiled coolly. "You remember our conversation incorrectly. I said no such thing. I merely said that it was unconscionable that one of Sidney's servants was off gambling. But since you have trapped me like a honey badger corners a wood mouse, I will say that I had my suspicions of what the dice engravings meant, but I could not be certain. And it would not have done me any favors for them to be symbols for a military unit."

I was becoming confused. "Why is that?"

He rolled his eyes. "The mere fact that you have to ask me such a question is proof of your being unfit for this task. Sidney's servant had not done any service in the Army nor the Navy, as far as we know. These sorts of carved dice are usually carried by jack-tars, but these symbols are of an Army unit. I believe they stand for the Fifth Dragoon Guards."

"Fifth Dragoon Guards," I repeated. "What does that mean?"

"They are a cavalry regiment. Been around since the late seventeenth century. Raised by the Duke of Shrewsbury and they've seen plenty of action."

"Were the Fifth Dragoon Guards in Afghanistan?" I asked, and I could see that my arrow had flown true.

"Yes," he said, his expression pained. "But Sidney's manservant had never been there, I'm sure of it. I would have remembered him, and he would have addressed me properly as his commanding officer rather than just acting as an obsequious servant."

The man before me bore all the hallmarks of a military leader: proud, decisive, and accustomed to having his way. Yet I had no idea what troops he had actually led. I did recall Liz once telling me that her father had been made a companion of the Order of the Bath on the occasion of old King William IV's coronation. But that had to have been nearly a quarter century ago.

"Who is under your command?" I asked.

He drew himself up and stated what I already knew. "I have the colonelcy of the 41st Welsh Regiment of Foot."

"I presume this is not cavalry." I really had no idea what the myriad British force groupings were.

"No, my boys are brave infantrymen. The Duke of Wellington joined the 41st as a young lieutenant, back in '88." The General swelled with pride. Military geniuses like Wellington didn't come along that often, so it was probably justifiable for him to boast about the duke having once been in the regiment's ranks.

Now that I understood a little about the General's authority, I asked, "Why do you say it wouldn't have done you any favors for the dice to have a military inscription?"

"Do you truly not understand? How simple would it be for

even a half-witted journalist to put together a trail of crumbs leading from those dice to their owner to Afghanistan to *me*?"

I still didn't comprehend the man's thoughts. "But you *did* want this investigated by the police."

"Yes, I had demanded that before you showed up with the dice. I couldn't very well have changed my mind in that instant, could I? If I ever find the man that attacked my girl, I will hold his windpipe until the light leaves his eyes, but I do not wish any bad publicity upon this family."

"But the truth must be found out, no matter what it is, sir."

"Why is that, Miss Nightingale? Is it your intent to destroy my reputation? How does that serve you? How would it look for Sidney Herbert to have a disgraced general as a father-in-law? Have a care, for I do not believe he would appreciate a *friend* creating an embarrassing stir for him. Imagine if he were to be forced from his position because of *your* indelicate and careless meddling." He brought his fist down heavily on the table, and several of the soldiers fell over as if wounded in battle. I started involuntarily, not expecting the noise.

Seeming pleased by my reaction, he continued, "I believe you can be most helpful by forgetting about the damned dice and finding some known derelict who would soon be picked up for another crime anyway and let him carry the blame for this crime as well."

I had regained my composure and was determined not to be cowed. "That would be grossly unfair and immoral, General; not to mention that it would mean a murderer still remained free."

"Good Lord," he said, sweeping a hand across the table and knocking over most of the remaining upright soldiers, reminding me now of a boy no more than George's age having a tantrum. "What must I do to make you disregard issues that do not concern you?"

But I was deeply concerned. I thought the General was hiding a great deal behind his bluster.

The General went to the wall and tugged on a bell pull that lay against floral wallpaper next to a stormy shipwreck painting. Within moments, Alice Nichols appeared, breathless. Was she the only servant on duty today?

"Nichols, fetch my box of Havanas, would you? As well as my Indian silk jacket and slippers. I'm of a mind to smoke." the General said.

The look she shot him was pure venom, no doubt because she considered the work beneath her position, but she dutifully replied, "Right away, sir."

Once the maid was gone, the General calmed down considerably for some reason and began gathering up the fallen toy soldiers.

"Here now, Miss Nightingale, there's no need for all this fuss and bother. We are both reasonable people. I'm sure you can conduct your little investigation without dragging my good name into it." He lined up all the pieces in a round wood box whose lid was marked "Warwick's Tin Soldiers, Swords, and Shields."

I said nothing, not willing to commit to his request and also not desiring to continue our verbal combat.

Nichols returned with the requested cigar box in one hand, and in the other a knee-length floral-patterned coat in garish shades of red and yellow, with quilted black cuffs and lapel and frog closures. In that same hand she also carried matching slippers. She placed the cigar box on the table atop the recently concluded

Battle of Waterloo, handed the clothing to the General, and escaped with undisguised haste.

He waited until the maid was gone, then said, "And so, if you will excuse me now, Miss Nightingale, I should like to enjoy a puff. In private."

Irritation burbled in my throat and I was on the verge of asking him whether he thought his daughter would approve of his dismissive tone with me, but I swallowed my indignation and took my leave. I still did not want to upset Liz before it was necessary. Having a spat with her father—when surely things were already tense between the General and Sidney—would accomplish nothing.

Besides, I was already turning over one of the General's comments in my mind. What foolish thoughts and actions had he considered Sidney to have taken lately?

★   ★   ★

I had no time to dwell upon the matter, for as I left the General and made my way down the corridor to the staircase, bemused by the fact that I was apparently family enough that no servant was summoned to escort me out of the home, I overheard hushed, angry voices coming from the other end of the corridor. One of those voices unmistakably belonged to Alice Nichols.

I looked around and saw no servants or family members nearby. I even looked over the balcony at the top of the staircase to ensure there was no one about to come up the stairs.

I felt both ridiculous and devious for wanting to hear what the Herbert maid was saying. I crept farther down the corridor, careful to stay on the Turkish carpet running down the center of the floor to avoid stepping on a bare floorboard that might creak.

I gently pushed on a door hanging ajar, from behind which the voices were coming. As I slowly opened it, I realized that the door opened into a small anteroom, and the speakers were in a large bedchamber beyond it. The bedchamber was done in masculine tones of burgundy and forest green. Trunks and leather-handled bags were stacked up on the floor to one side of the bed, indicating the arrival of a visitor to this room.

Standing in the middle of that room were Alice Nichols and a man I could only presume to be Charles Henry à Court, given his resemblance to the General himself; except this man was more cultivated and finespun in appearance. His clothes were elegantly tailored, and he was so darkly handsome that it was immediately apparent why Nichols had lost her senses over him.

Right now, though, the two were in a heated argument.

"I have to go," Charles Henry hissed. "My sister will wonder what's taking me so long. I told her I had forgotten to pack my favorite dining jacket and was having her new coachman drive me to Henry Poole's to purchase a new one. What happened to Pagg?"

"You mean the dead Joss Pagg? He was murdered. Last week." Nichols sounded almost spiteful.

"Is that right? Lizzie didn't mention it," Charles Henry replied, seemingly unperturbed by the news. They shifted to speaking in tones so low that I couldn't hear anything, and then Charles Henry raised his voice as he said, "I've told you. I cannot do this. I'll not be caught out again."

"After all I have done for you. To help you. Why would you cast me aside?" Nichols's tone was now plaintive. She threw her arms around his neck, and he took a step backward from the force of the maid pressing herself seductively against him.

"You know what my father will do. I cannot afford to disappoint him any more than I have. Besides, the help has not been one-sided." He took both of her hands in his and removed them from around his neck, gently pushing her away.

Glittering tears sprang into Nichols's eyes. "You are evil, Charles Henry Wyndham à Court. I should tell—"

"Do not even suggest it," Charles Henry warned, cutting off her threat by putting a finger to her lips.

She grabbed that finger and kissed it. "You cannot possibly intend to—"

He pulled his hand away from her, his expression showing regret at having touched her in such an intimate way.

The tears dried. "Perhaps Mrs. Herbert should know who her brother *really* is." Nichols was angry and snide again.

"Be quiet, you little fool, or I will silence you myself." Charles Henry tore himself completely away from her, and I realized that Liz's brother meant to leave the room.

I fled the house before he could see me and headed back toward the Establishment.

CHAPTER 18

By the next morning, I had calmed down from both my encounter with the General and the scene I had witnessed between his son and Alice Nichols. I knew I shouldn't be concerned with intimate family affairs, but I couldn't help but think that there was something very problematic in the household, not the least of which were the irregular levels of concern shown for the deceased coachman. Neither the General nor his son seemed to find it troublesome at all, whereas Sidney and Liz were very naturally distressed by it. Servants did become part of the family, after all.

I wondered what Charles Henry's reaction would have been to hear of Fenton's death, another casualty for which the General had no compassion.

After breakfast, I asked Mary to join me in the library. I decided I wanted to completely clear my mind by working on pulling together some of my thoughts on nursing. My idea was to one day publish a volume of these thoughts and use any proceeds to fund the work I was doing to improve the profession. I didn't want to be indebted to committees, investors, or charities for my work. I wished to do it all my way, unfettered by a patron.

If I could secure money in a way that was entirely my own doing, I could avoid that obligation.

Promising Mary that we would discuss what I had encountered at the Herberts' once we were done, we sat down to develop topic areas for my advice on good nursing practices, which I thought was a good way to begin organizing my thoughts.

"I don't think this should be aimed just at nurses, Goose," I mused. "Ordinary women should understand how to properly care for the sick, much as I have done my entire life. They should know that their homes must be as well ventilated and well lit, as clean and comfortable, as stocked with nourishing food as any hospital."

Mary nodded as she opened her notebook, and we began to work. I soon became immersed in addressing how someone nursing the sick should make inspections of her patient: asking questions that were neither leading nor misleading, asking about the proper symptoms, and cultivating proper observations about what the patient not only said but did not say. Soon I was downright pontificating on the subject and Mary was having a difficult time keeping her pen moving at the same pace as my speech.

This exercise was distracting enough that I soon felt as if I had put a sufficient distance between myself and earlier events, providing a fresh opportunity to look at the facts in a new light. After an hour or so of note-making, we were both tired, so I shifted to telling her about my visit to Herbert House. My recounting included Sidney's consultation with me about hospital design in the Crimea, Liz's inability to remember much about the carriage routing, the General's combative exchange with me, and the conversation I had overheard between Charles Henry à Court and Alice Nichols.

I saved the worst of it all for last, steeling myself for Mary's reaction to the news that Caroline Norton had been roosting outside Herbert House. My friend did not disappoint.

"I told you that woman was not to be trusted. I didn't even need to meet her to know that. Human nature is what it is, Miss Florence," Mary said primly, folding her ink-stained hands on the open notebook in her lap. "She intends to destroy that home in any way she can, and her status will enable her to get away with it."

"Perhaps," I replied noncommittally. It was an unthinkable idea, but I had seen something similar happen before, so I couldn't completely discredit it.

"Of course it is what happened," Mary insisted, her head bobbing up and down. "Women cannot tolerate rivals for their affections."

She wouldn't be budged from the idea.

John Wesley came limping into the room with Arthur Maddox on his heels. "Now watch me," John Wesley said to Arthur, who clearly already worshiped his new friend.

"I will," Arthur said.

John Wesley bowed his head and held out his palms to me. Spread across his hands was an envelope with a Penny Red stamp on it. It was addressed in a tidy, feminine script.

"Why the formality, John Wesley?" I asked.

He inclined his head over to Arthur. "He needs to know the ways of the world, maum. Money has to be earned properly now, don't it?"

"You little scamp," I said fondly, still pulling two pennies out of my pocket and giving one to each of the boys. As was his custom, John Wesley kissed the coin and tucked it into his shoe, and Arthur imitated him perfectly. I really shouldn't have paid him for walking less than a hundred feet to bring me a message, but John Wesley was difficult to resist. I wondered what slate of terrible lessons he had in store for the other boy.

He and Arthur departed the library, and I opened the missive.

If only I could have had my pennies back; better yet, if only the boys had just accidentally dropped the letter into a fire grate. It was a note from Caroline Norton, asking me to meet her at her home as soon as I could do so, as she had something of vital importance to discuss.

I showed it to Mary. "I guess I can dash off a note to Sidney that I've already found her."

"I told you," she said in triumph, but then in a motherly tone advised, "I'd put on my best day dress if I were you."

★   ★   ★

An hour later I sat across from Caroline Norton in her spacious lodgings. Dominating her place was her study, which was packed floor-to-ceiling on every wall with bookcases, stuffed full of books on every topic imaginable. Thomas Carlyle's lending library in St. James's Square would be envious of her collection, although I believed one would have found that library more neatly arranged. Caroline's study was that of someone who was in perpetual motion and could not be bothered to organize and neaten her belongings, so important were her tasks.

It was in direct contradiction to the beautifully groomed and arranged woman who sat at her desk before me. It made me glad I had followed Mary's advice to put on my favorite burgundy dress edged in black piping, even if the weather was a little warm for it.

Caroline was in the middle of writing a letter. Actually, it seemed to be several letters simultaneously, based on the pages that lay across her desk.

"Miss Nightingale, thank you for coming," Caroline said, rising from her work. She bumped against her desk, and a jar of ink sloshed but did not spill over the rim. We both exhaled held breath at the same moment. "No doubt you hesitated to see me," she resumed. "I assure you that my intentions are noble."

She came around the desk, practically gliding in a well-practiced movement. She offered me her hand to shake, and then we both sat down together on a long settee in front of one set of bookcases. The settee was done in alternating ultramarine, crimson, and mustard stripes.

"I wished to apologize to you in person," she began. "But I didn't think I should disturb you at the hospital."

"How did you know that is where I reside?"

She shrugged. "Such things are not difficult to discover. However, I was quite rude to you, and for that I am sorry. I wished for you not to think poorly of me and wanted to explain my situation to you."

I held up a hand. I didn't want to be drawn into a web of sympathy for her. "It's hardly necessary to—"

"But I must," she interrupted me. "First, where are my manners? Would you like some tea?"

I declined, knowing that this would draw out the visit and serve to make us too familiar with one another.

"You have an impressive library here, Mrs. Norton," I remarked, not just to be polite but because it was the absolute truth.

She smiled, genuinely proud of her collection. "This is

actually my uncle's home, although this room is my domain. He has graciously allowed me to live here under his protection. He travels a great deal, so it is almost as if I am mistress of my own home, except without the vicious threats, the burning of my papers, and the punching of holes into walls and doors."

I had no idea how to respond to this, so I only sat silently with my hands folded in my lap.

She sighed. "Very well, I don't know what Sidney may have told you about me, but please allow me to clear the air. I suppose I should start by telling you how I have reached the wretched state I am currently in.

"My grandpapa died in poverty when I was but seven years old, and my father died the following year, putting my family in dire financial straits. The Duke of Albany was an old family friend, and he managed to secure my mother and I a grace-and-favor apartment at Hampton Court.

"When I was sixteen, George Norton—at the time a Tory member for Guildford—spotted me during some sort of Christmas festivities at the palace and asked for my hand in marriage. I had no dowry, but he didn't care, so besotted was he with me."

I remembered that Sidney had used that exact term, besotted, to describe the mutual feelings between him and Caroline.

"I didn't want to marry George, for I sensed something dark in him, but my mother was in full support of the match, since it would rescue us from poverty."

I was already feeling far more empathy for Caroline than I wished. It was causing me to lose my objective grip on the situation.

"The early years of our marriage were surprisingly successful. We managed to have three children. I used my beauty and wit to develop political connections, and I became a society hostess. My connections could have helped to advance George's legal career, but he wasn't particularly good at the law. He also wasn't particularly good at managing our finances, so we began to fight bitterly.

"George eventually proved himself to be as stupid a brute as I had anticipated. He was not only unfaithful, but he banged about from one raging torment to the next. It was as though the devil himself rode around in his coat pocket, and the minute George reached in, he would be bitten by both conceit and despair. That would lead to several bottles of whiskey, which fueled outbursts against me. Sometimes he used his fists against the furniture and occasionally against me."

"Good Lord," I said in dismay, allowing myself to feel even more compassion for her. "Had you nowhere to run?"

Caroline shook her head sadly. "It is not so simple for prominent people to hide, as I had made us quite conspicuous in London society."

She resumed her narrative in a matter-of-fact way. "I discovered I had an affinity for writing and used that as a solace from my miserable life. I wrote poems and novels, mostly, which found publication. Then I was appointed the editor of a small magazine. With this I tasted a bit of financial freedom, and eighteen years ago I left my husband. Oh, the scandal."

Nearly two decades ago, but Caroline spoke of it as if it had been but yesterday. "I can only imagine society's reaction," I said.

"I could have taken society's reaction to my departure. After all, George's passions were common knowledge. But he twisted that frenzied fervor against me in unbelievable ways. He falsely accused me of adultery with a high-ranking member of Parliament. He laid claim to the earnings from my writings. Then, worst of all, he refused me access to our children."

I frowned. "But you were their mother."

"Perhaps, but he held all the power, given that the law stated that children were the legal property of their father. My reputation was ripped to tatters over his accusations of unfaithfulness—despite his own straying like a mangy, flea-bitten tomcat—especially when he hauled into court the man he falsely claimed was cuckolding him. George lost the court case, but I lost everything else. All the while, George claimed that he loved me 'to madness.' It was madness, but it was hardly affection. I did achieve one small victory though." She smiled at the recollection from her past.

Her smile piqued my own curiosity. "In what way?"

"I used our laws to my advantage. I went to various shops and ran up extravagant bills. Then when the shopkeepers came to collect, I told them to sue my husband for collection, since all the purse strings belonged to him. George was so furious he merely sputtered in impotent rage. It was worth the broken vases that day."

Despite her bout of spite, I didn't view Caroline Norton as anything but careful and calculating in her actions. "Surely you did not continue with that?" I said.

"No, I took to writing with fury, campaigning Parliament to have a care to ensure that women were supported properly after divorce, even though I had not yet secured my own. I had not completely lost my connections and influence, for the Infant Custody Act was passed in '39, which granted legally separated or divorced women the right to custody of their children up to the age of seven and guaranteed periodic access thereafter."

Caroline snorted in an unladylike fashion, and I knew she was unimpressed by her own accomplishment.

"Were you not able to get your children back, then?" I asked, fascinated despite myself.

"No. First because only my youngest son, William, was then under the age limit; and also because the law only applied to England, Ireland, and Wales. My husband took the boys over the border into Scotland to hide them with distant relatives I didn't know. I suppose the devil in his pocket made the recommendation."

Why did it feel so traitorous to feel softhearted at what Caroline Norton had endured? "Have you not seen your children since he took them away?"

I was surprised at the reaction my words engendered, for tears immediately sprang into the eyes of this woman who appeared to have an iron spine. "William had a spill from a horse in '42. His injuries were minor, but my *husband*"—she spat the word—"did not have him properly attended to and blood poisoning set in. Realizing the child was near death, George sent for me, but the dear boy died before I could arrive in Scotland."

Caroline pulled a handkerchief from her sleeve and dabbed at her eyes with it. "I have so few female friends with whom to have such conversations. Most of my discussions are on paper or in courtrooms. I actually find it refreshing to discuss my terrible story this way."

Hardly the way I felt about the conversation, as I was still anxious about her intentions behind the tale.

She patted once more at her tears. "Where was I? Oh yes, after William's death, George was generous enough to allow me to visit my other two sons, but he retained full custody, and all my visits were supervised. Not that it was practical for me to take regular jaunts to Scotland, anyway."

I performed a quick mental calculation. "Your sons are well into adulthood now."

She nodded. "Yes, Thomas married a woman in Naples last year. Fletcher is studying art in Paris. So still I never see them."

A shadow passed over her countenance, then cleared. "Right now, I am campaigning for more equitable divorce laws. I believe I am very close"—Caroline swept an elegant hand at the unfinished letters on her desk—"and will secure my own divorce from that barbarous creature soon. When I think of the days and nights of tears and anguish, days and nights that became months and years—well, even now the hot agony of resentment and grief rises in my mind. I suffered needless tyranny from this man, who possessed a power over me that nothing could control. If only he could have been tender toward me, or barring that, have been willing to release me from my cage . . ."

Caroline went to the bookshelf nearest to her desk and plucked a thin volume from the shelf. "I just had this published," she said, handing it to me.

I read the gilt lettering on the deep-green cover: *Caroline Norton's Defense: English Laws for Women in the Nineteenth Century.*

"In it, I discuss the dreadful marriage laws of our country, which make the marriage ceremony a civil bond for him and an indissoluble sacrament for her. The rights of mutual property are made absolute for men and null for women. This must be changed if we are going to be a proper civilized nation."

Caroline was clearly passionate in her depiction of the state of matrimonial affairs.

I tucked the small book into my dress pocket. This was just

what I had feared in a marriage with Richard Monckton Milnes. That, much as he claimed that I would be as free as a sparrow to pursue whatever was my passion or pleasure, I would end up trapped in a prison of my own making.

However, I didn't want to shift any of the focus of the conversation onto me. My path was settled and straight, other than that poem he had sent for my comment.

"What you have experienced can certainly only be termed a tragedy," I said in sincere empathy. "But somewhere along the way you met Sidney."

That brought the first genuine light to her face that I had seen. "Yes. A few years after I had separated from George, a mummy-unrolling party was held to which both Sidney and I were invited. Totally ghoulish to watch the men removing the layers to get down to a desiccated old husk, but there was a dinner and dancing afterward. Sidney and I were partners at a game of whist. He flattered me incessantly on my gown—which was in the most fabulous punch color; no one else had anything like it—and on my skill at cards. And he was unspeakably handsome. I was never sure if I was the sun and he was the planet, or the other way around."

She was making me feel even more unwanted sympathy for her even as she talked about her infatuation with a man who was not only my friend's husband but a friend of mine in his own right.

"But today he is the loving husband to his wife and father to—"

But Caroline was caught up in her own fanciful delusions. "Sidney was mine long before Elizabeth à Court came along, and he was pressured into marriage with her."

"But they are quite happy together. They have three children, and no doubt there will be more."

"Children are not always a sign of happiness, Miss Nightingale. I had three children of my own, who were used as pawns by my husband. Besides, I know that Sidney still loves me, for his expressions of empathy are so . . . sincere. And intense."

"Sidney is certainly a kind man, but he is far from an adulterer. Mrs. Norton, you must abandon this notion." Suddenly I wished I had a hot cup of tea in my hand to occupy me.

"You don't understand. If I can see our marital laws changed so that I can secure a divorce from George, then so would Sidney be able to more easily sue his wife for divorce as well, since he could offer assurances that she would not only have her children but that he would be legally bound to support her. My work serves us both. In fact, I have been working on several political treatises on marriage and family."

"Mrs. Norton, I don't—"

She interrupted me genially. "Please, you must call me Caroline. We are friends now, are we not?"

"Caroline," I said, trying to keep my patience. "I don't think you understand. Sidney is not likely to leave Liz even if you were to—"

She interrupted me yet again, sitting back and contemplating me seriously. "Miss Nightingale, you are an unmarried woman, so I must be very direct with you. Do *you* have designs on Sidney?"

Now the purpose of the requested visit started to come into focus. "Pardon me? How dare you suggest such a thing." I was glad I didn't have the cup of proffered tea, for it may have ended up splattered upon her head.

She bit her lip. Even at her age, it was a graceful, alluring gesture. "I imagine you think me a monster, Miss Nightingale, but assuredly I am naught but a lonely woman. Please forgive me. In fact, I should like to offer you a gift." Caroline rose, and I followed suit.

"It's not necessary. Besides, you have already given me your treatise on English law," I said, patting my dress pocket.

Caroline ignored me, heading over to one of the bookcases and pulling out a much thicker volume than the previous one. "Here," she said, bringing it to me and placing it in my hands. This cover was burgundy leather.

"*Stuart of Dunleath* by Caroline Sheridan Norton," I read aloud.

She nodded happily. "I published this novel three years ago. Please, take it. It will help you to better understand me."

I left Caroline Norton's residence deeply conflicted. Clearly the woman had suffered greatly and had channeled that suffering into trying to improve the lot of other people. Did that mean she was more or less likely to make someone suffer if she perceived the person as a threat?

That evening, when all was quiet in the Establishment, I curled up in bed with *Stuart of Dunleath*. After only a couple of hours of reading, I was more disturbed than ever by what was an exceedingly melodramatic story.

It was set in Scotland, the very place of Caroline's misery, given that her son had died there. It followed the story of a woman named Eleanor who was of angelic purity. Her beloved was assumed to have drowned, and she married a brutally bad, but wealthy, baronet, Sir Stephen. Eleanor suffered under this violent man, and her twin sons, her sole source of comfort, drowned as well. But her beloved, Stuart, reappeared on the scene, alive and well and having gone to America to make his fortune.

Eleanor attempted to obtain a divorce but gave up because of her overwhelming guilt for the passion she had for Stuart. Finally, Sir Stephen let her go, but she died of a broken heart because Stuart had already married a friend of hers.

I closed the book thoughtfully and turned onto my back. I held the novel to my chest with both arms as I contemplated what I had read. Had Caroline penned a thinly veiled autobiography? Was it an artful message to Sidney? I fell asleep without reaching an answer.

CHAPTER 19

I awoke early the next morning with my lamp still burning and the book having tumbled to the floor.

My first order of business was to dress and prepare myself for the day, then to go quietly to my study to spend time some thinking before anyone became aware that I was awake.

With my mind still troubled by Caroline Norton's sad but sordid story, I sat at my desk and pulled a fresh sheet of hospital stationery from my desk, flipping it over so that the return address did not show.

Normally I would have asked Mary to assist me with organizing information, but this morning I had a great desire to simply erupt upon paper by myself, to make sense of what little I knew about so many different concerns pulling at me.

I had achieved nearly nothing on the Herberts' great matter, but making myself a list of other achievements made me feel as though I was not a total failure.

Organized Middlesex Hospital for cholera inmates.
Adjusted Reverend Whitehead's cholera statistics.
Found position for Berenice.

Fulfilled Fenton's dying wish for Maddox family to be helped.
Assisted Mr. Davies with his war wound.
Advised Sidney on improvements to Scutari Hospital.

My great failures included the tragedy at the Reeve household and the death of Isabel Maddox. I knew logically that neither of these events was truly my fault, but death—whether by disease, accident, or intent—tended to make one want to abandon logic and reason.

I put those deaths from my mind so that I could more fully concentrate on the attack on Liz's carriage, which had resulted in the murder of Joss Pagg.

I made a chart in an attempt to establish relationships among everyone involved. The General, Caroline Norton, Sidney and Liz, Charles Henry à Court, Alice Nichols, Joss Pagg, George Maddox and his wife, Fenton, and Oswyn Davies.

I was completely dissatisfied. All of these people were either related to one another or servants of the Herbert household, with the exception of Mr. Davies and the Maddoxes.

That wasn't helpful at all. There must be some unknown person out there who had actually pulled the pistol trigger. Or had paid the attacker.

I made another chart to relate people to their possible motivations.

The General—?
Caroline Norton—elimination of rival for Sidney's affections.
Alice Nichols—revenge against the General for forcing Charles
    Henry to marry Miss Currie.
Charles Henry à Court—an unknown grudge against his father?

Oswyn Davies—an attack on the General as revenge for the Disaster in Afghanistan?

I would not, and could not, countenance the idea that Sidney had wanted an attempt made on Liz's life, nor that Liz was faking something. Both ideas were too ridiculous to be borne.

I made a note at the bottom of this page:

Gambling dice—Fenton, Oswyn Davies, the General.

I drew a heavy box around this. What did those dice mean? Was it possible that they meant nothing? That Fenton was mistaken in whatever he was tracking down? Perhaps Fenton had purchased them from someone for his own use, and in the throes of death was delirious in his rants about the "devil's dice," and I was burrowing into an empty rabbit hole with them.

As for delirious rants, I recalled many of the odd statements Isabel Maddox had made. It seemed as though she had perpetually confused her husband with his brother. And as she had died in my arms, she had claimed that she had "not meant to do it." Do what? But surely she had just been raving in her illness. Could Mrs. Maddox have possibly been involved in anything that had transpired, or was I being fanciful?

As I stared at my charts, though, what was becoming as clear as a Cumbrian lake was that it was quite possibly Liz's father who had actually been the one meant for a bloody, public death.

Perhaps it was time for another visit to Herbert House, and this time I intended to talk to every single resident of the household.

After making the rounds to check in on the patients, that was exactly what I did.

★   ★   ★

I was ushered into Herbert House by a crying servant who quickly showed me through the house and into the rear gardens, where the entire family and most of the servants stood around, looking for all the world like war casualties. None were bleeding, but they wandered aimlessly with expressions of shock blighting their faces. Even the Herbert boys were subdued and quiet.

The only exception to this was Liz, who was crying piteously with no regard for the servants, who were either watching helplessly or avoiding her.

Sidney and the General surrounded Liz. Their mutual distrust of each other prevented them from effectively offering comfort over whatever had Liz and the rest of the household so troubled. Charles Henry stood off to one side near the servants, his skin ashy and his stare blank. I'm not sure he even noticed my presence.

I picked up my skirts and hurried down the wide, curved steps that emptied into the carefully manicured gardens. Cluster-petaled dahlia blossoms, deliciously fragrant freesias, and dramatic, trumpet-shaped amaryllis were all blooming in fall splendor.

"What has happened, my dear?" I asked as I reached Liz. Sidney and the General obligingly parted to permit me access to my friend.

Liz was not hysterical—I couldn't imagine her being so even if her house were on fire while a flood raged through Belgravia.

She accepted my hug gratefully, clutching me for all she was worth.

"Flo, I can hardly believe it," she uttered sadly as she stood back from my clasp. "Look."

She pointed to a nearby bed of dahlias, which exploded in

a profusion of lavender, bronze, flame, and snowy white. So spectacular were the colors of the gorgeous stalks that I almost missed it.

Lying among the flowers was the body of Alice Nichols.

I could hardly understand what my eyes beheld. I stepped through a mass of crushed stalks and knelt next to the poor woman's body. Her limbs were splayed out as though she had been tossed there like an unwanted sack of rotten potatoes.

She wore a different dress than the one I recalled her wearing the day before. This one was a little fancier. Had she been preparing for an assignation, perhaps?

Her eyes stared up at me glassily, and I gently closed them. It required little observation to realize that she had been strangled, with the buttons popped off from around the neck of her dress and the mottled bruising on her skin that had no doubt appeared as her life had been choked from her.

I rose heavily. "Who found her?" I asked.

"'Twas me, miss." I was approached by Ike Bent, the young coachman I had interviewed. The day of Liz's attack now seemed like an eternity ago. Unlike everyone else, Ike seemed energized by Nichols's death, as though his having discovered the body had made him very important.

I supposed that at the moment, it did.

"When did you find Mrs. Nichols?" I asked.

"Just a short while ago, miss. I came out to cut some flowers for the mistress's carriage. I thought she might like a bit of cheering up, so I was going to wrap up some blooms and put them in her seat for when she went out riding later in the day. That's when I saw her." He pointed down toward Nichols's body without looking at her. "Nobody else noticed 'cept me."

"Did you notice anything else?" I couldn't quite ask precise questions out here in front of others. It didn't matter anyway, for Ike had no answers.

"No, miss. Just her, when I came to cut the flowers. I made sure to tell the master straightaway. I'm not in trouble, am I?" He had gone from excited to alarmed in mere seconds.

"Of course not," I assured him quickly. "I just want to help Mr. and Mrs. Herbert figure out who may have wanted to hurt Mrs. Herbert's maid."

He nodded. "That's all right then."

The boy was utterly without guile, and I rather envied him for it. However, perhaps I needed to talk to the rest of the staff, separately and in private, then move on to what I was sure would be dreadful conversations with Charles Henry and the General.

"Miss Nichols reminds me of Mr. Pagg, doesn't she?" Ike added.

This stopped me. "Why do you say that?" I asked more sharply than I intended.

The coachman frowned. "Because I found them both. And they was kilt in service to Mr. and Mrs. Herbert. Plus, you showed up right away afterward when they both died."

These were strange observations. Were they meaningful, or just the ramblings of an innocent? Hadn't Mary commented on its being *my* friend who had been attacked when the news first came?

Of course, Joss Pagg had effectively been an innocent bystander, while it seemed to me that Nichols had been intentionally murdered.

A troubling thought in the back of my mind was whether the murderer had mistaken Nichols for Elizabeth Herbert. The maid was clad in nicer clothing, no doubt one of Liz's castoffs, so it was certainly possible. I chose to keep that idea to myself, especially given how fragile my friend might be right now.

Liz and her family had edged away from where Nichols lay. I walked to where they stood and suggested that I interview the remainder of the household staff.

"Don't you see what is happening here?" Sidney demanded, his eyes filled with worry. "Whoever it is was unable to get to Liz, and so he attacked her maid. If he cannot murder my wife, he will at least drive her out of her mind! And I wasn't here when it happened to protect her."

Sidney's outburst had the unexpected effect of calming Liz. Her eyes immediately cleared, and she reached out to take his arm. "Darling, I'm safe. I have Charles Henry and my father here to look after me when you aren't here."

Her husband was not mollified. "I have no doubt they have your best interests in mind, but we still have yet another dead servant."

Charles Henry was moved from his stupor enough to bristle at Sidney's comment, though he did not reply.

The General attempted a rough consolation. "There, there, my dear," he said, patting Liz clumsily on the shoulder. "It's no great loss. You'll find another maid."

For the first time, Liz gazed at her father with something other than admiration. "But I won't find *Nichols* again, Papa. She was a good and faithful friend."

The General harrumphed and removed his hand from his daughter's shoulder.

I extricated myself from the family's exchange and set up further interviews with the servants inside the house. None of them claimed to have seen anything unusual prior to Alice Nichols's death. According to the housekeeper, the only strangers to the house had been deliverymen, one of whom had been sweet on Alice, but the maid was indifferent to him.

I could have let my imagination run wild in thinking that, despite the housekeeper's comments, Nichols had been involved with one of these deliverymen, but it made no sense whatsoever. She had had her sights set far higher, and furthermore, why would someone delivering wrapped packages of beef or butter desire to murder a maid? Or even think he could get away with it?

I sighed, willing myself to go into the lion's den with the General and finding him once again in Sidney's study. He surprised me by being more subdued than I expected.

"I assumed you'd be by to see me about the girl. Care for a glass of sherry?" Liz's father walked to a credenza and held up a bottle for me to inspect.

I shook my head. I wanted a clear head for this discussion. The General put the bottle down, then shook another decanter full of a cloudy, flaxen-colored liquid. He unstoppered that bottle and splashed a good measure of it into a glass. A light froth formed on the top of the drink. A strangely sharp and fruity aroma wafted over to me. It was mostly coconut, but there were nutty overtones, too.

The General must have seen my look of curiosity, for he held up the glass and stated, "Feni. I have it imported from Goa, on the western coast of India. Would you like to try it?"

I was far more emphatic in declining this time. I was becoming lightheaded just from the odor of it.

The General saluted me with his glass and took a deep

swallow. "Again you wish to accuse me of something, Miss Nightingale?"

"I see I do not need to inquire as to whether you have lost your sense of contempt, sir." Once more I regretted my unfortunate choice of heedless words.

The General seemed to take no offense and instead took a smaller sip from his glass. As I took my own seat, he sat on the edge of the table still containing the battle map.

I started without preamble. "Had you gotten to know Alice Nichols in your time here?" I asked.

He shrugged. "She was Elizabeth's maid. How well should I have known her?"

A reply without an answer. Very well, then. I decided to be exceedingly direct. "Were you aware that she was in love with your son and had hoped to marry him until you pressured him into marrying Emily Currie?"

The General took another deliberate swallow and put his glass down slowly, gazing at me steadily for several moments as he seemed to compose his thoughts. "Until yesterday, I had had no idea whatsoever."

"Yesterday? Did Charles Henry tell you about her?"

"No, she came to me herself. Told me that she and my son were in love and a bunch of other claptrap." He moved the glass in circles on the table so that the feni again formed a foamy upper layer.

"You didn't believe her."

He rolled his eyes. "Oh, I believed her. I just thought she was an idiot for telling me."

Quite frankly, so did I. "Why *did* she tell you?"

"Why do you think? She and Charles Henry had renewed an old affair, but Charles Henry came to his senses and cut it off. Realizing she wasn't going to have him, she decided that she would seek money as her consolation prize." He finished off the glass and returned to the credenza to pour another measure.

"Are you saying that Alice Nichols attempted to blackmail you?"

He turned back to me with another foam-topped glass. "It was more like she was attempting to embarrass me. She wanted enough money to leave service permanently and set herself up as an actress in Covent Garden. What a perfectly preposterous notion. As if I would do such a thing."

I couldn't help but agree with him. Even knowing the General as little as I did, I was fully aware of how stern and unyielding he was.

"Why wouldn't she blackmail Charles Henry directly? Why you?" I persisted in my line of questioning.

"My son has no money of his own to control, nor does he have any influence with me. She understood that. At least, that's what I assume." The feni was creating an almost overpowering miasma in the room. I would soon have to take my leave.

Perhaps that had been the General's intent in opening the bottle.

"I recall Nichols telling me that you had many visitors at all hours," I said.

"Of course I do," the General said, agreeing without hesitation. "I have certain deliveries made privately so that Elizabeth isn't aware of how many crates of cigars and spirits I am bringing into the house."

Another seeming dead end. I asked what I thought would be a final question. "Alice Nichols had the audacity to speak blackmail to you here, at Herbert House?"

"No, the girl was at least clever enough to ask me to meet her elsewhere."

"And where was that?"

For the first time in our conversation, the General betrayed a look of uneasiness. "The British Museum."

I tilted my head. "Why do you think she would wish to meet you there?"

He shrugged but did not look me in the eye. "It's a public place. You can find yourself a bench for a conversation that can be both private yet socially acceptable."

I didn't make the obvious comment about the significance of the location. Did Nichols have a distorted sense of humor, or was it simply as the General had said—that the space was both public yet private?

My skin prickled as I considered what might have happened. Had Charles Henry perhaps followed Nichols there and witnessed the conversation, thus causing him to act impulsively on his threat to silence her? Or had the General taken care of it on behalf of his son?

With that, I decided to seek Charles Henry out. I hadn't even been formally introduced to him yet.

I found him in his room where I had previously witnessed him arguing with the now-dead Alice Nichols. His profile was toward me as he tossed folded papers into the crackling flames of the room's fireplace.

Supposing I knew exactly what he was doing, I stated without preamble, "Destroying Nichols's love letters to you, sir?"

Charles Henry started and looked over at me. He quickly regained his composure and replied coolly, "Miss Nightingale. My sister has spoken often of you over the years. I find it curious that my family seeks out your assistance for such serious matters."

Like father, like son.

"You haven't answered my question," I said, determined not to be put off by him.

"Answer a question for me first. Why would you accuse me of such a thing? Nichols was merely my sister's maid. I am a married man."

I couldn't very well confess that I had eavesdropped on his argument with Nichols, nor did I wish to betray her confidence.

"I saw the expression on your face outside," I said, glad that I had so quickly come up with something. "It was the countenance of a man in torment. It wasn't difficult to conclude you might have had tender feelings toward the woman." I nodded at the stack of papers in his hand. "It is also not difficult to conclude that those are pieces of correspondence you are destroying, immediately following the discovery of Nichols's body."

He laughed without mirth. "Very clever, Miss Nightingale. Please leave me out of your amateur theatrics." Another letter landed in the flames and quickly curled up into a wisp.

"Do you deny that you were involved with Nichols?" I asked.

He shrugged. "You'll forgive me if I refuse to be interrogated by a mere nurse, no matter what her friendship is with my sister. You may simply rest assured that I put an end to what never should have been."

With that, he turned his back to me and heaved the remainder of the papers into the fire in one toss. They landed in an intact pile, but I knew he would remain there while the flames consumed the pages and I would never know what they truly were.

I also knew that my brief appearance was over, but as I turned to leave, I noticed that the street scene painting from Nichols's room was propped up against one of his trunks, as if he planned to take it with him. Charles Henry was certainly working quickly to ensure that no trace of his involvement with her remained. Were these the actions of an innocent man?

I left my encounter with Liz's brother feeling very unsettled. Surely he was just a lover unable to publicly grieve his dead mistress and there was nothing more to it. I worked hard to convince myself of that, for I didn't want to think that I was dealing with two potential murderers working against the Herbert household. Particularly if they were members of the Herbert family.

Regardless, there was something very sinister occurring inside the Herbert household, and I was no longer sure what to do next. Perhaps I needed to resolve once and for all whether the dice were significant and, if so, to whom in the family they were linked. Other than that, I had nothing to go on.

CHAPTER 20

I was becoming so accustomed to visiting Soho that I now hardly noticed the sad ruin and desolation of the area. Or perhaps I was so determined in my mission that I paid little attention to my surroundings.

I had Mary with me, and together we once again entered the Lion. It was much more crowded than we had witnessed before, and the air was heavy with laughter, smoke, and the sweet, tangy odor of ale. Men played cards and threw dice. They also shared clay pipes, cutting portions of tobacco from plugs and stuffing them into the bowls.

I did not immediately see Mr. Davies, so we stayed huddled close to the front door so as not to draw undue attention to ourselves. Most of the patrons were intent on their own play and companionship and thankfully didn't notice us.

As we waited for Mr. Davies to make what we knew would be an eventual appearance, I broke enough out of my huddle with Mary to observe the table nearest us. Four men were tossing dice just like the ones Fenton had had in his pocket—six sided, with each side having either a crown, an anchor, a spade, a heart, a diamond, or a club on it. On the table was a rough wood board, and it, too, contained one each of these same symbols. One of the men would place a bet atop one of the symbols on the board, then roll the dice. His payout would depend upon how many of the three dice rolled matched the symbol upon which he had bet.

It was simple enough for even a child to play, yet it provided fast-paced enjoyment for the men involved. Copper pennies were tossed onto the board to cover a particular symbol, followed by the clacking roll of the dice, and then the banker immediately distributed the proceeds.

One particular player was receiving the most coins. In fact, he was winning so often that one of the other men eventually banged his fist on the table. "You cheat!" he bellowed, rising out of his chair.

All camaraderie in the room stilled.

Just as suddenly, the accused man yelled back, "Can't take the poor luck, can you?"

Mary clutched my arm as the disagreement escalated on both sides. The other men watched with interest, as if waiting to see whether blows would come.

I could only imagine that they would be betting on that, too.

"Miss Florence, we should leave. No good will come of this." Mary tugged on my arm in urgent appeal, but I didn't budge. We might have to step out of the way while these men conducted their pugilistic business, but I hadn't come all the way down here not to obtain some answers.

Fortunately, at that moment Oswyn Davies came stalking out of the brewery door. "What is this now?" he said sternly, approaching the two arguing men.

Davies flicked an irritated glance in our direction but didn't stop to address me.

"Jemmy Hargraves, what trouble are you creating this time?" Davies demanded of the accused player.

"Nothing! I just want to enjoy my ale and maybe win a little money." The man was belligerent, probably half due to alcohol and half to embarrassment.

Davies held out his good hand. "To me you will give them."

"What d'you mean?" the player asked. "I'm minding my own business."

Davies looked as though he were ready to ignite, but his tone was still even as he said, "In my palm."

The player grumbled but handed over his dice.

Davies proceeded to roll them repeatedly on the table, scooping them up and tossing them down again. The room was now silent except for this clattering noise.

After at least thirty rolls, during which even I could see that the dice were noticeably coming up anchors more often than not, Davies picked up each die and scrutinized it, rubbing his thumb over each flat surface.

Finally, the brewery manager glared at the player. "Get out. Not be coming back, you will."

"Now, now," the man protested. "I'm just having a bit of fun and—"

"I run a respectable place. There will be no cheating dice used here," Davies said, now towering over the man. He really could be quite terrifying when he put his mind to it.

"Those aren't my regular dice," the man said, stalling his ejection from the Lion. "Those are my brother's. He asked me to keep 'em safe for him. He had to ship out to Crimea, and he was going to carve up some others while aboard his transport ship, and—"

"Enough of your lies!" Davies thundered.

In a move that startled me—and everyone else in the room,

based on the collective gasp—Davies reached over to the player and yanked him out of his chair by his collar.

The man yelped at being mishandled. Realizing that Davies was about to toss the man outside, I quickly threaded my way to the bar to get out of the way. Mary was still clutching my arm and came right along with me.

In a swift motion, Davies dragged the protesting man over to where we had just been standing. He kicked open the public house door and literally shoved the man outside. "Back to the earl's household with you!"

The man stumbled and fell to the ground, his limbs awkwardly splayed out.

I returned my attention to the inside of the room, where the other men began arguing among themselves as to who else might also be carrying cheating dice.

The din became loud enough that someone else came banging in through the brewery door—George Maddox.

How he had improved in such a short time. The widower was now clean-shaven and neatly dressed. He still had the dark shadows of grief under his eyes, but his gaze was alert and concerned.

Maddox joined Mr. Davies in ordering those present to settle down and go back to their glasses and games. Within a few minutes, all had settled down, and Davies signaled Maddox to join him as he walked to where Mary and I still patiently stood.

Maddox's grin upon seeing us was genuine and faded the shadows under his eyes just a little. "Miss Nightingale, Mrs. Clarke, have you come to bear witness to my new fortunes?"

"This job seems to agree with you, sir, and I am glad for it," I said, shaking his hand.

"Indeed. I am quickly learning. You cannot imagine how

many steps there are to making quality ales and how easily the flavors can be changed. Mr. Davies is a patient teacher. I've offered to write a manual containing descriptions of each man's job that can be used when new men are brought onto the line. How is Arthur? I have a day off next Thursday and would like to come by and take him to visit Bella's grave."

I smiled. "Whenever you like, Mr. Maddox. I must warn you that he has made a friend in our boy servant, John Wesley, who is tutoring him in all means of flattery toward his elders."

Maddox laughed. "Then he will be much more successful in life than his father has been thus far. I look forward to seeing what the boy has learned."

"I presume you are not here to bring Maddox current on his son's activities?" Davies inquired. "To his duties he needs to head back."

Berenice appeared from a doorway beyond the room's large fireplace. "Mr. Davies, I've finished wiping down the windows in the—" She stopped when she saw Mary and me standing with Davies and Maddox. "Miss Nightingale! Have you come to see me?"

"Berenice, you look well," I replied, adroitly sidestepping her question. "How is your daughter?"

The Lion's new maid slipped a covert glance at Mr. Davies. "She's a good girl, Miss Nightingale. She's learning how ta clean proper."

Davies nodded. "She is."

"So you are happy with her," I said to him.

"Well." Davies shifted uncomfortably. I could tell that he didn't want to have to admit to too much. "I'll say that taking your money I won't be."

"I'm glad to hear it, sir." I refrained from smiling at his obvious discomfiture. I was glad to have helped both Mr. Maddox and Berenice. At least two people in the area could be lifted out of their misery. And if the changes at Middlesex Hospital would result in more lives saved, I would be doubly happy.

"Just wondering what you'd like me ta do next, sir," Berenice said. "Perhaps flip mattresses in the sleeping quarters? Or if you need me ta do any shopping for you? I could also—"

George Maddox stopped her. "Can you see to the floor in the cask storage room? We tapped one to sample and it cracked, creating a small flood in there. I'm afraid that's a skill I haven't quite mastered."

"Of course, Mr. Maddox. Right away. Is there anything else you need? Don't forget I'm good with a needle and not a half-bad cook." Was I mistaken, or was Berenice positively glowing before George Maddox?

Maddox didn't seem to notice, nodding absently at Berenice as he headed back into the brewery. Berenice looked dejected as she, too, headed back to her duties.

Now Davies was free to fully concentrate on me. "I presume you are not here for a glass of ale, Miss Nightingale?"

"You are correct, sir. I actually came about something else, but first—you told that man who was playing dishonestly to get back to the earl's household," I said. "Surely he wasn't a member of the peerage?"

"No, he's a minor servant of the Earl of Albemarle's household in Portman Square. You wouldn't believe the number of them that will come to the Lion on their days off. None of their masters would bother looking for them here. All of them would be surprised by some of the mischief their servants get up to when out of their uniforms."

My mind was whirling furiously. Sidney said that Fenton must have been in Soho on behalf of the investigation, but the dice in his pocket suggested otherwise. Perhaps I needed to return to my initial assumption that Fenton was a gambler?

"How were you able to tell that he had cheating dice?"

"Difficult it's not. You roll them enough times to see if a symbol is coming too frequently. Once I saw that the anchor was rolled more often than not on all three of the dice after a few dozen rolls, it was evident to everyone that the dice were no good. I ran my fingers carefully over them to see if there were any subtle protrusions on any of the sides that would cause a die to keep rolling when hitting a particular side. The only flat sides to those dice were the ones opposite the anchor. Not all cheaters are particularly good at it."

Once more, I pulled the dice from my pocket and presented them to the brewery manager.

"This again? What is it now?" he said in exasperation.

"Are these cheating dice?" I asked bluntly.

Davies refused to take them from me. Now he looked even more uncomfortable than when I had pinned him down on Berenice's performance.

Finally, he ran a hand over his damaged ear, scratching at the skin above it. "I knew they were bad dice when I first saw them, but I couldn't say who they belonged to. Sometimes men leave 'em behind when I catch them out. I toss them into the rubbish bin, but I don't know who goes and digs them out. Burning them maybe I should be."

Had Fenton dug that set of dice out of the Lion's rubbish bin, or had he been the original owner?

"Did you ever have a patron by the name of Fenton?" I described what I remembered of Sidney's manservant.

Davies was still perturbed. "That sounds like every drunk-ard who walks in here. Missing an eye, was he? Did he limp? Give me something distinguishing to describe him."

But other than his rather large lips, I couldn't remember anything remarkable about him. I looked at Mary, but she shook her head. However, recalling Fenton's condition reminded me of something else.

"Have you still experienced no cases of cholera here at the Lion?" I asked.

"Not a one, at least nothing serious. Neither my workers nor my customers. The owners are happy, because it means no down time in the brewery."

I thanked Davies for his time.

It was as if the Lion had a blanket of divine protection around it. Why was cholera seemingly unable to penetrate the brewery building? Reverend Whitehead or Dr. Snow needed to know this. Reverend Whitehead was closer, so I would see him next.

But even as I considered making another visit to the priest, a story was forming in my mind. It was a tale full of anger and hatred and was so malicious as to be unfathomable. If my theory was correct, Liz might not ever feel safe again. However, she most certainly was not the Babylonian Whore.

The killer's face loomed large in my mind and I shuddered. But I was still missing one important piece of the puzzle.

"Goose, I believe I know what happened," I said quietly to her as we made our way back to St. Luke's.

Mary gave me an expectant look. "So I was correct in think-ing that Caroline Norton would do anything possible to destroy the Herberts' domestic bliss? That she would not only attack Mrs. Herbert herself but murder her servants?"

I sighed. "The reality is much more sordid than that. There's just one connection I cannot seem to make, and I'm not sure how to do so."

"How can I help?" she asked.

"Right now, you can stay at my side. Strength in numbers, right?" I laughed weakly, but I was becoming deeply concerned that the killer might know by now that I was figuring things out.

I took a deep breath. The sooner I finished my investigation, the sooner a murderer could be brought to justice.

I refused to say anything more for the moment, lest Mary make an accidental slip of the tongue in front of others.

Reverend Whitehead was bubbling with excitement when we arrived. "Welcome, welcome," he said, quickly ushering us back into his office and lighting candles for illumination. "I was hoping you might come by again. I have extraordinary news. I have become a convert."

"A convert?" I repeated, confused. "You are leaving the Anglican Church?"

Whitehead laughed, even as he practically danced behind his desk. "No, no, I am now a believer in Dr. Snow's theory that the cholera outbreak is spreading through the ingestion of contaminated water. I used your improved charting as a basis for determining where to conduct my interviews of residents in homes where cholera had come through, and they nearly all confirmed that they had drawn water at the Broad Street pump. Look."

He showed me his newly created tables that did indeed demonstrate that nearly all the people he had interviewed in infected homes had obtained their water at that one specific pump.

"But the Lion Brewery is practically next to this water pump, and none of the workers or patrons there have been affected," I protested.

Whitehead's expression was one of surprise. "You have been frequenting the brewery?"

"Not exactly. I have been there because of my search for the movements of the Herberts' servant, Fenton."

He nodded. "I do remember that you were seeking someone. Dr. Snow called upon Mr. Huggins, the proprietor of the Lion Brewery. There are seventy workmen employed in the brewery, and Huggins confirmed that none of them have suffered in the outbreak, other than one or two being mildly indisposed. They do not take water from the pump, as they mostly drink ale, plus there is a deep well in the brewery and water from the New River nearby that they use.

"From this point forward, I think we will see the numbers of new cases greatly reduced. The doctor is going to the authorities to see about having the pump shut down while the reason for its becoming infected is discovered. There must be a *source* for it."

I was greatly disturbed. Was I so wrong about miasmatic theory? How could that be? My techniques of keeping rooms aired out and clean in defense against miasmas certainly seemed to work. Yet I couldn't deny that Whitehead's work supported Snow's theory of the illness being ingested through water.

At least I could be assured that some of the unintentional deaths could be halted. It was now up to me to stop the purposeful ones.

This reminded me of something else I needed to know.

"If I may say so, Reverend, the conditions in much of this area are completely appalling. The rats in the streets enjoy a better standard of living than most of the residents. In the short time I have spent in Soho, I have seen crumbling homes, half-naked children, stifling odors, glassy stares, and violent outbursts."

Whitehead nodded. "That is probably as succinct a description as I have ever heard."

"I suppose what I don't understand is why it is like this. Why does everything crumble as soon as you cross a particular street?"

"Think about what is around you, Miss Nightingale. What neighborhoods surround Soho?"

"I suppose Mayfair and Marylebone to the west, Fitzrovia to the north, and Belgravia and Westminster to the south."

"Precisely. All fashionable areas full of fashionable homes and aristocratic names. Many of those peers of the realm—in addition to some churchmen who have discovered an easy way to enrich themselves—own most of the properties here and have done so for a long time."

"And you have said you do not count yourself among their number."

He smiled. "I own little other than the clothes upon my back and a few candlesticks. I believe that if any of the landlords ventured down here and saw the results of their disregard, they would immediately drop to their knees in abject repentance. You are one of few ladies of quality I have ever seen down here."

"Assuredly my family owns no properties here. In fact, we only have our family home, Embley Park, in Hampshire, and a summer home in Derbyshire. I confess they both encompass far more pleasant vistas than what I see here."

"Just the two estates, eh, Miss Nightingale?" Whitehead's teasing was gentle before he became serious again. "I'm sure your family has taken care to ensure your home is well maintained. But there is little profit to be made from improving things in this neighborhood. We call the owners the 'vampires of the poor,' as they sit on top of extremely valuable land that enables them to charge exorbitant rents on housing that never sees a single slate roof tile replaced. The landlords keep themselves hidden from their tenants by conducting all the leasing work through lawyers—themselves shadowy figures—so that the tenants have little recourse for complaint."

So many problems in London, and I was but one person, hardly able to do much other than provide some relief to the sick. "What can be done about it?" I asked helplessly.

Whitehead shook his head. "They will never permit this state of affairs to change. Some politicians have finally noticed the plight of these people and have several times initiated efforts to have the slums demolished and the residents rehoused, but the corrupt, ungodly governing council blocks it each time. You see, the council is made up largely of vestrymen who hold some of the properties. I just try to help whatever poor unfortunates down here that I can, knowing that the situation is a polluted morass of greed that shames and befouls landlords and residents alike. Much as I see you have done, what with helping Berenice Porter in obtaining a service position."

I was quiet for several moments as I contemplated what he had said, particularly about how the landlords lived largely in the wealthy areas surrounding Soho. Finally, I asked, "Do you ever fear for your person while serving here, Reverend?"

"No. Some people believe that poverty leads the residents of places like Soho—particularly Seven Dials—to commit more criminal activity. I fancy myself a quiet observer of human nature, Miss Nightingale, and I can state with certainty that the well-to-do have their own reasons for committing crimes as well."

CHAPTER 21

"Those poor creatures," Mary sighed in sorrow and sympathy as we left the church. "Not a chance in the world for them, is there?" She seemed to steel herself as she asked, "And where are we headed now?"

"I'm afraid we must see Mr. Davies one more time," I said.

"Oh," Mary replied, her final word on the matter during the remainder of our journey back to the Lion.

We waited again at the inside entrance. The room was not as crowded as it had been earlier. Perhaps the player being literally thrown out on his ear had dampened enthusiasm for games and drinking.

It soon became apparent that Mr. Davies was not going to show himself anytime soon, but I was not going to permit him to avoid what I had to say. "Let's go back there," I said to Mary, inclining my head toward the brewery entrance.

"Should we? Why don't we continue waiting here? I'm sure he will be out soon enough, and you said yourself there's strength in numbers. Look at all the witnesses there are out here."

I took her hand, worried that she was going to flee the building altogether at any moment. "Goose, we are going into a factory, which will also have plenty of witnesses," I assured her, already on the move.

She followed me most unwillingly, muttering about what Milo would have had to say about it all.

I pushed open the door, and we entered a long, wide passageway. Lining either side of the corridor were barrels, each marked with the Lion name and the type of ale it contained. I could only assume these were barrels for use in the public room itself.

Although there was no activity at all in the corridor, the noise coming from the factory floor was thunderous. We finally reached the entry to the factory, and I was amazed by how overwhelming it was.

Before us was an enormous and cavernous space of varying floor and ceiling heights, almost as if it had been built in different stages by a variety of men who all had a different idea of what it should look like. It was a cacophony of whistling steam, men shouting to one another, and the thumping and clattering of barrels being rolled against wooden ramps. The air was thick with a pungent odor that reminded me of bread baking, except much stronger. It was also heavy with a clammy heat. I instantly felt sweat forming at the nape of my neck where my hair was rolled and pinned. A glance at Mary told me that she, too, felt the heat in her flushed cheeks and the drops of moisture beading on her top lip.

To our left, the ceiling was low over a large, square pool made of stone. The pool's sides were perhaps three feet high. Inside it were men with long wooden rakes and spades, stirring and turning over a lumpy mixture. Extra spades rested against the side of the pool's wall nearest to us, as if waiting for even more men to jump in and move the thick concoction around.

Directly across from the pool, a steam engine was driving an assembly of gears that was in turn causing a large revolving device to spray steaming hot liquid into yet another enormous vat.

Other departments were hard at work all over the place. At first glance it was chaotic, but as I took it all in, I realized that there was an order to it, even if I didn't understand what was going on.

All the work on this level seemed to be in support of what I saw on a wide catwalk off to one side reached by a long, sloping wood ramp. Lining the wall of the catwalk were the most colossal barrels I had ever seen, reaching at least twenty feet up into the highest point of the building. They were so large they looked as though they were sized for a giant in a children's story.

I assumed the ale, once made, ended up floating in these vats for some sort of aging process before being placed in small barrels for distribution to customers.

Near one of these immense containers stood Oswyn Davies and George Maddox. From my vantage point, it appeared as though Davies was lecturing his new shift supervisor on something, but it was impossible to hear anything from my distance across the floor.

I held up a hand and waved, which caught Maddox's attention. He held up a hand in return and spoke to Davies, who then also turned to catch sight of us. Davies said something else to Maddox, and then the two men came down the ramp to join us.

Davies held a hand to one side of his mouth to concentrate his voice. "Miss Nightingale, what are you doing back here? This is a dangerous place for women."

I, too, cupped my hands around my mouth. "I wish to speak with you, sir. I know about—"

At that moment, a worker in a brightly colored vest came through, lustily blowing on a whistle. It clearly communicated a welcome command, for as a group, all the workers ceased what they were doing, shut down much of the machinery, which slowly screeched to a halt, and began filing out through a rear exit. Even the men inside the pool climbed out, dropped their spades, and dripped their way out the door.

A nearly blissful silence followed. "Why have they left?" I asked, my ears still ringing from the noise.

"This is their thirty-minute supper break," Maddox said. "It is my time to quickly check the equipment to make sure all is working well."

"Yes," Davies added. "It is far easier to keep operations smooth if we temporarily shut down once each day, rather than waiting until a breakage occurs."

"It is an extensive amount of equipment to check," I observed.

"Isn't it?" Maddox seemed joyful at the prospect. "Let me show you around."

As we walked, Maddox spoke avidly of malting, mashing, boiling wort, fermenting, and racking. I was thoroughly confused by the end of his explanation, although by the way he pointed to the machinery in turn, it did seem to be a logical method for taking barley and processing it with water and yeast to eventually create barrels of the beverage the English had cherished for centuries.

We ended up back next to the pool, which I now knew was a mash tun and was intended to mix malt with water to create a clean, amber liquid called wort that would be ready for brewing. It was an early stage of the complicated process.

"You are enjoying this work," I said.

"Yes, I am actually surprised by the similarities to upholstery work. You see, I have to constantly ensure that everything is affixed tightly together, lest it come apart. But doing it for brewery equipment is so much more satisfying."

I hoped he had proved better at working machinery than fabric, or the men might be in imminent danger.

"Mr. Davies here has given me quite a chance, letting me have run of the place so quickly," Maddox continued. "I'm even thinking of tossing out my silly little manuscripts and letting my future be here."

Davies laughed. "In less than a week, Maddox here has proved himself to be the best shift supervisor I've ever had. He's made it easy for me to disappear without Mr. Huggins realizing it." He turned serious again. "But for a tour I presume you are not here?"

"Actually, no," I said, deciding to be as direct and forthright as possible. "I now know who murdered Joss Pagg and Alice Nichols," I stated baldly.

Davies reacted with the merest eye twitch. "Who those two people are I have no idea."

George Maddox glanced back and forth anxiously between Davies and me. "Is there a problem?"

I didn't remove my gaze from Oswyn Davies. "Not just yet. Mr. Davies, you have long been lying to me, have you not?"

The tip of his injured ear grew red. "Lying about what? You are a woman who has disturbed the peace of this brewery on several occasions, and even caused me to reveal myself too much. Now you invade this place with accusations of lying and murder."

For the final time, I pulled Fenton's dice from my pocket and could see that Davies was physically repelled by them.

"You cannot seem to stop talking about these insignificant dice, miss."

I closed my fist around them. "But they are not insignificant. They are everything, aren't they? You knew who they belonged to, didn't you?"

Davies was sullen.

"What I've learned about you over the past few days, Mr. Davies, is that you are a brewer, a public house keeper, and a professional soldier. Quite an array of talents for someone living inconspicuously in Soho. But you are also a *liar*."

Mary inhaled sharply next to me as Davies's expression became fierce. "I recommend that you have proof of that, Miss Nightingale."

I tucked the dice back into my pocket. "You finally admitted to me that they were cheating dice, but said you had no idea whose they were. That isn't true. The owner of them was a frequent visitor of the Lion, is that not so?"

Davies's only response was to glower at me.

"When I witnessed you tossing that player out on his ear, it occurred to me that you would likely know many secrets of the men who frequent the Lion. Their marital struggles. Their employment problems. But most important of all—their gambling debts. Yet I am sure you took pride in keeping all these secrets to yourself. After all, if men could trust you, they would be more likely to spend money in your establishment. The more they spend, the happier the owner is, and the happier Mr. Huggins is, the more secure your position is."

Davies crossed his arms, his expression full of threatening storm clouds. "Of a crime being committed I have yet to hear."

"This is true. But you will. I first came to you to inquire about an attack on the secretary at war's carriage. You said you knew nothing about it. I showed you the dice I had, and you were very careful in your response to me. But that was because you realized the truth would be very injurious to you."

"Injury caused to me by some cheating dice? I wasn't gambling with them, and they meant noth—"

"I hate to interrupt," Maddox said. "But Mr. Davies, the men will be back shortly, and I need to make my rounds." He glanced nervously again at his boss.

Before Davies could open his mouth to respond to his employee, I said, "Please wait a moment more, Mr. Maddox."

My overstepping was not improving Davies's temper, but I plowed resolutely ahead. "Mr. Herbert's coachman, Joss Pagg, who drove the carriage that day, was a regular here, wasn't he? When you told me that many servants of society families hide out here, I realized that Pagg might well have been one of those servants. It would explain why he routed the carriage through Soho, being familiar with the place. And Fenton, Mr. Herbert's manservant, at least knew about this place, even if he was not a regular. And he most likely obtained the dice from whoever plucked them off Pagg. And Pagg died nearly right in front of your door."

"A crime I have committed I still haven't heard about."

I ignored this. "I confess I am grateful to you on many counts, sir. I learned the sordid history of the Disaster in Afghanistan, which was very helpful. You explained how cheating dice work. You even provided assistance to people in need. However, you knew that those dice had belonged to Pagg, didn't you, Mr. Davies? But you refused to tell me so. When I first determined that you were lying to me, I was angry, but I soon realized that you were in the habit of protecting your customers as long as they weren't cheaters. And you had never witnessed Pagg cheating inside your establishment."

"You have already established that I am able to keep my patrons' secrets," Davies said. "Now if you don't mind—"

"Yes," I replied dismissively, cutting off whatever he was about to say. "You've been helpful to me, and your discretion was very helpful to the men who frequented the Lion. But it was you, Mr. Maddox, who was ultimately the most helpful." I turned to the widower.

"Me? How so? Miss Nightingale, I'm running out of time before the men return." Maddox was practically hopping back and forth on both feet.

"You are running out of time in more ways than you know, sir. You are the most callous sort of murderer: a killer who starts with one ostensibly noble goal in mind but ends up disposing of others who displease you or get in the way of your goal. In total, you have murdered three people: Joss Pagg, Alice Nichols, and your own wife. All of that blood just to serve your initial objective of avenging your brother's death by killing General à Court. A feat which you were never able to accomplish and never will." I shook my head in disgust.

Mary, Davies, and Maddox stared at me, mouths agape. "Miss Florence, are you sure?" Mary said, nervously tugging on one of her loose bonnet strings.

I nodded resolutely. "When Mr. Davies threw out the cheating player, I not only realized that he knew many men's secrets, but I also realized he had done it before—when we found you outside the Lion. You apologized for being in your cups, but in reality, the worse problem was that you had been thrown out, hadn't you? You had—"

Davies interrupted me. "Miss Nightingale, I have forgiven Maddox for cheating, as sympathetic I was to his plight of having lost a brother and then a wife."

"Yes, except that his wife's death was no accident, was it, Mr. Maddox?"

"She had cholera!" Maddox exclaimed in insistent defense.

He was no longer antsy, but a wariness and subtle hostility had begun to overshadow his hitherto cheery countenance.

"She did, but she clearly understood something about you despite all her confusion. She talked about having the ability to see, and also referenced your brother Barton, who went off to war and perished. She told one of my nurses that she had accomplished what she needed to before dying. That accomplishment was to tell someone about her deranged husband. Isabel also told this nurse, in a very muddled way, that someone had disappointed her. That was *you*, Mr. Maddox, for being an evil man she couldn't escape.

"Her dying words in my arms were that she 'hated to do it.' I had assumed this was all feverish ranting, but it wasn't. She was trying to tell me that she had figured out that you were avenging Barton and had evil on your mind. I suspect what she hated to do was to accuse you of murder. She must have realized she was dying, and to accuse her husband of such a heinous crime would make her boy an orphan."

Maddox's eyes narrowed at me coldly. "Our lot wasn't my fault. And she was getting far too babble-mouthed once she got sick. You showed up, and I couldn't have her spewing out my private dealings to you. I cannot be blamed for her death."

Was Maddox implying that it was my fault his wife had died?

I was getting ahead of myself in the story, though. "The piece I had been missing is how you knew Joss Pagg," I said. "I imagine now you merely met him at the Lion."

Maddox rolled his eyes in scorn. "Pagg was a simpleton. He fancied himself moving up in the world. He wanted to find some wealthy widow whose home he could charm his way into. I tried to tell him he'd never manage it, no matter how handsome a fellow he might be. He thought the only problem with his plan was his gambling debt."

Next to Maddox, Davies's expression was a blend of incredulity and bubbling fury.

I continued, "That's when you offered to help him with the dice you had in your possession. 'Five-D-G' refers to Fifth Dragoon Guards. If I'm not mistaken, that would have been your brother's regiment, correct? A regiment that saw action in Afghanistan? I am guessing your brother was lost in the withdrawal from Kabul."

Maddox's confirmation was a mere grunt.

"You had possession of them—probably the only items of his that came back from Afghanistan—and you offered to give Pagg your brother's dice to use in winning enough games to recoup all his losses and pay off his debts. In return, though—oh, what you asked for in return."

"Why are you surprised? Nothing in this world is free. In fact, nearly everything comes at a very dear price." Maddox was waxing righteous now.

Davies raised a fist to him. "A dear price, you wish to see? I'll—"

I held up a hand to stop the Lion's manager. I needed a full confession before Davies began administering his own justice.

I continued, "You wished to bring harm to the General and perhaps his entire family as a means of retribution. Hence why Pagg routed the family carriage on such an unusual path to reach the museum. You would be waiting for the carriage to come through and strike at the right moment, killing either the General or Mrs. Herbert. Or both, if you were particularly lucky. But for some reason, Pagg had a change of heart."

Maddox grunted again. "You cannot go back on a promise. Fool told me he intended to use the dice to earn additional money, so he could pay me extra rather than carry out the task I had given him. Next thing you know, he would have been jabbering about it all over London. Couldn't have it. And anyway, even killing a Herbert servant would have been enough to get it all rolling. The family could come next."

I was chilled by the callousness of the man.

I resumed unraveling what I knew—or what I believed I knew. "I remembered what Mrs. Herbert had told me, that the attacker had called her the Babylonian Whore. A clever Biblical phrasing, it was, one that I coincidentally heard again on another visit to Soho. But I finally realized that she had misunderstood what had been shouted at her. It was 'Afghanistan war,' wasn't it?"

"And what would you know of war and loss, Miss Nightingale? My brother was smart, brave, and loyal. And he was sent in as nothing more than paltry fodder for the Afghans. Someone had to be made to pay for it, and obviously the Army wasn't going to do it. And the secretary at war had to be prevented from sending more good men into the Crimea—another muck pit. Is anyone surprised that he's the butcher's son-in-law? Of course these animals live and work together. I shouldn't be accused of committing a crime; I should be given a hero's medal for trying to rid the world of their villainy. I told Pagg as much, just as I'm telling you. He didn't understand how vital the task was."

Maddox's hardened responses were clearly affecting Davies, who was now reduced to growling next to the man.

"And so Pagg brought the carriage down Broad Street as planned, but in his change of heart, he fought you when you approached the carriage. You melted away, then shot him from a distance for his perfidy. In the aftermath, you managed to slip back into the crowd and retrieve the dice from Pagg while ostensibly helping the dying man, didn't you?"

Maddox gave me a prideful shrug as his answer.

"Sidney Herbert's manservant, Fenton, came down here to investigate on his own. His detecting work must have brought him to the Lion, where no doubt everyone was still talking about what had happened. You were unable to refrain from telling him *something*, right, Mr. Maddox?"

"Don't be absurd. I know how to keep a secret as well as your dear friend, Mr. Davies, here. I merely gave him the dice and extended roughly the same offer I gave Pagg. 'Use the dice to make yourself some easy money,' I told him. 'But you'll need to help me a little with your employer.' He looked a little queasy when I met him. Wasn't completely sure he could do it, but he was the only other way in to the Herberts that I had. Then all of a sudden he quit showing up at the Lion."

"Because he had died of cholera. But in fact, after Fenton disappeared with your dice, you saw all your plans being destroyed. You must have made some other attempt at teaching someone how to cheat at gambling in order to draw him into your web, but Mr. Davies caught you out and tossed you into the street. Where Mary and I found you."

Another dispassionate shrug. "A minor setback. Even with Fenton gone, I had plenty of plans and ideas. After all, a writer can always come up with a way for his characters to achieve their goals or get out of prickly situations. Got Mr. Davies here to forgive me and give me a job, didn't I, so I think we can say that I am far more clever than you credit me, Miss Nightingale."

He was deceitful, for certain.

Maddox continued. "My plan was to discard the idea of a helper and just take care of the family myself, as painfully as possible. I started with Sidney Herbert, but he was always with someone. And there was some fancy lady following him in her carriage. Too risky. So I moved on to General à Court."

"You began following him instead of Mr. Herbert."

"Yes, I was trailing him in my off hours, waiting for my opportunity to strike. When I saw him at the museum with that woman, I figured she was his strumpet and that he would be upset at her loss. It was easy enough to make a personal cask delivery to Herbert House, and once I was inside, it was even simpler to convince the housekeeper that the woman was my own ladylove and that I wished to speak privately with her."

Mary spoke up. "You are a fiend, sir," she pronounced in her quiet way.

Davies nodded in agreement, the flush of anger reaching from his neck to his eyebrows.

Maddox flicked an irritated glance at Mary as if suddenly noticing her for the first time. "It's not as though I shot her. I thought a gunshot would have been much more noticeable in Belgravia and it would have been difficult to get myself out. Strangling was much less messy for her, and just more polite. Just as helping Bella along a little bit with rat poison made it so she didn't have to endure any messiness."

The absolute shamelessness of the man who had so success-fully pretended to be not only a grieving husband, but also a grateful recipient of assistance! "I wonder whether I would have ever found you had Mary and I not stumbled upon you crum-pled upon the ground outside the Lion and helped you home."

"Yes, that was a damnable bit of bad luck for me."

"As for bad luck, I have no doubt that you will finish your life at the end of a rope, sir," I predicted. "You will not—"

Maddox moved so swiftly that I hardly registered at first what he was doing. In what seemed a mere instant in time, he had grabbed Mary—who stood closest to him—and dragged her the few steps to the edge of the mash tun. Before either Davies or I could react—or even Mary, for that matter—Maddox had swept her up in his arms and dropped her over the low wall. Mary made a sickening splash into the mash tun.

At this point, Maddox was more fevered than his dying wife had ever been. He followed Mary into the pool of liquid. She was starting to flounder and attempted to stand up, but her quickly soddening skirts were making it difficult. "Miss Florence!" she gasped. Her voice trembled with utter panic and horror.

"Would you like to know what it feels like to lose someone you love, Miss Nightingale?" Maddox sneered. His rabid hatred was now fully revealed for all to see. "Let me show you." He grabbed Mary by the hair and brutally yanked her upright with her head back. Mary stood restrained in his cruel grasp, but I could see her quaking uncontrollably. Only the whites of her eyes showed as she rolled them back in abject fear.

"Insane, he is," Davies muttered to me. Then aloud he cried, "Good God, man, I hired you when you were down on your luck. How could you betray me like this?"

Maddox's eyes were now bright with a deranged light that surely reflected the depravity within his soul. "It's men like General à Court who betray, not me. I seem to be the only one interested in justice for the thousands of men and women who were killed needlessly in Afghanistan, especially my poor brother." He shook Mary's head like he was a ravening wolf and she the helpless prey.

She yelped loudly in pain and fright, and I echoed her noise in my own anguish over what was happening to her.

"I was there myself, boy. Yes, it was grisly, but we don't go around murdering innocent women over it." Davies took a small step forward toward the edge of the mash tun.

"What's innocent about a woman who is part of preventing justice? Nothing!" With a forceful jerk, Maddox yanked Mary backward down into the mash. Another splash of the thick liquid, and I could see only her poor arms flailing above the surface as Maddox heartlessly held her down.

How could I ever explain Mary's untimely demise to my mother? Moreover, how could I live with myself if she died because of what now appeared to be my own reckless move in accusing Maddox here at the brewery?

Even as my heart sat lodged in my throat, Davies sprang into action, running and leaping into the mash tun with more grace that I would ever have given him credit for. He ferociously grabbed the collar of the man who was now attempting his fourth murder. I realized that he was trying to treat Maddox as an errant drunken gambler, as he had done before. But Maddox was far too strong and furious in his current state.

Davies continued to tug at Maddox's collar, neck, and hair, trying to extricate the man from the pool of mash. I attempted to remain calm, but it was obvious to me that Mary was about to be murdered. I had to do something.

I glanced around wildly. Was there a loose brick in the wall I could use as a projectile? A tool? A lantern? It took everything within my soul not to succumb to panic at the sickening sounds of Mary thrashing about in the mash.

That's when my gaze caught the stack of wood spades on the floor. Surely they would work.

I rushed to the pile and picked up the largest one I could find. I lifted it, surprised by how heavy it actually was. I shifted the spade so that I held it by the middle of the shaft with both hands. I actually took a few steps backward to gain momentum as I tore forward, slamming myself against the low wall and swinging the spade's head so that it connected with George Maddox's temple with the most satisfying crack I had ever heard in my life.

Maddox dropped like a bag of barley as Davies shouted at me, "Lord, woman, killed me you could have!"

Nevertheless, he reached down and grabbed Mary, bringing my soaked, sputtering, and wild-eyed friend up from where George Maddox had intended her to die.

As soon as she saw me standing before her, just a foot of stone separating us, she broke into a cascade of tears and threw her arms around my neck. I tossed the spade to the floor behind me.

The yeasty smell of mash was overpowering in my nose as it dripped like gruel from my beloved friend.

"Now, Goose," I comforted her, more relieved than I was willing to admit. I had no care for my own clothing as I wrapped my arms tightly around her trembling, sodden person. "Imagine how proud of you Milo would be right now. Why, you survived a very deadly attack."

I released Mary and she stood back, nodding and snuffling. I couldn't blame her for her reaction. Her eyeglasses were gone; they would no doubt be fished out by a brewery worker later.

Davies now held a swaying George Maddox firmly under one arm. Blood flowed freely down the side of his head near an enormous lump that had already formed, but he was conscious.

A strange, random thought occurred to me. "Berenice Porter will be devastated to hear about this, I suspect."

Mr. Davies frowned at me. "Not nearly as devastated as I was to have you call me a liar, Miss Nightingale. Accuse me of murder, I thought you were about to do."

"There was a time when I might have thought it, sir. But I'm glad we have the right culprit. And you didn't know you were harboring a murderer under your smokestacks." Another unbidden realization came to mind. I would also now have a second young boy residing at the Establishment. Soon it would no longer be a hospital, but an orphanage.

"Hold him under myself, I should do," Davies said in disgust. "But I suppose the correct thing is to turn him over to the authorities."

I agreed, and left Davies to see to Maddox while I hurried a soaked Mary out of the mash tun and as far away from the brewery as possible. As we passed through the doors into the public house, I heard the distant blow of a whistle.

CHAPTER 22

I stood inside Herbert House once more with four adults sitting and staring at me, agape.

Charles Henry à Court was the first one to speak. "Are you saying that Alice was murdered simply because this Maddox fellow caught her talking to my father and assumed they were involved with one another, and thus he believed himself to be creating a way to make Father miserable?"

I nodded sadly.

"Dear God!" he exclaimed. "This is all . . . beyond comprehension." I could see that he was attempting to control his emotions. No doubt all memory of his irritation with Alice Nichols had been erased on the occasion of her death. I had no comfort to offer him other than the knowledge that George Maddox was likely headed to the gallows.

"You're saying this had nothing to do with Liz or me but that Pagg was the intended target that day?" Sidney said, shaking his head. "I was so certain it had to do with—" He let the words drop. "And I lost my manservant Fenton because my coachman loved gambling. Fenton would never have contracted cholera if he had not gone into that pestilent part of town."

"Fenton must have had water from the pump, which he could have obtained in any number of ways while he was down there. If only he had confined himself to ale from the Lion, he might not have gotten sick." As the words left my mouth, I knew they were of no comfort at all.

The General cleared his throat. "But this whole affair did have everything to do with me. Should have listened to the nurse. I knew they were cheating dice the first time I held them, but it was important for me to conceal that they had belonged to someone who had seen action in Afghanistan. I knew that one day there would be a payment extracted from me for my crime."

Liz tilted her head in perplexity to one side. "What do you mean, Papa?"

"You heard Miss Nightingale. This Maddox fellow was ultimately after me, for what happened to his brother in Afghanistan. Am I never to shake this dog from nipping at my heels? I caused this mayhem."

Was the General about to confess to something? All our gazes were riveted to the General's face.

"No one ever knew that I actually loved that woman." The General passed a hand over his eyes. "But I let her go, knowing that those chiefs would murder her even before their miserable, tattered camel train was out of sight.

"Ah, don't look at me like that, my girl," he said, addressing Liz. "You think I don't know that your mother would have been pained to know of it? Anyway, I knew it would come to nothing. I wasn't about to abandon your mother and bring home a woman half her age. It was all just . . . we lived in a different world while we were in Afghanistan. It was intoxicating to have your money stretch out limitlessly, to buy anything your heart might desire.

"When it came to the men, though, there was no question that I had to make a sacrifice. Others thought that I just tossed Najiba to the wolves, but it wasn't so easy for me. I knew what would happen to her. Everyone knew. But I had to do whatever was necessary to save my troops. Of course, they weren't saved, and it was all for naught. Slaughtered. Just like Najiba was." The General's voice broke gruffly on the second mention of her name.

The room went silent. What was there to say?

Charles Henry finally spoke up, dispelling the gloom in the air. "Father, what say we go up to York together. We can buy some good Irish whiskey and play some terrible sets of lawn tennis while Emily and her gaggle of friends do all that wedding planning. We could even rescue the groom from it all."

Charles Henry made it sound like a very lighthearted affair, but the General did not agree to his son's suggestion. "No, I'm needed here with Sidney, for war strategy."

Sidney held up a hand. "Sir, I would not object to you spending time with your son."

The General was insistent. "Frittering away my days staring at the bottom of a whiskey glass and bounding about on the grass? I think not. I need to be *useful*. It is the best way for me to both atone for and forget about the past."

No one had an argument for that.

With the deaths of Joss Pagg and Alice Nichols now solved, Sidney ushered everyone out in order to speak privately with me. Closing the paneled doors, he turned to where I still sat and addressed me more seriously than I had ever seen him do.

"I must thank you for your discretion where Mrs. Norton is concerned. I presume you spoke with her?"

"Yes. She has clearly led a troubled life, but Sidney, I believe she thinks it possible to be reunited with you."

"What?" His shocked expression assured me he had never even contemplated such a thing. "What can she possibly mean?"

"She is a determined woman who is wielding her pen energetically to attempt to change divorce laws. She believes that she is close to doing so, and that once she secures her own from Mr. Norton, you can also do so from Liz."

He was aghast. "But I have absolutely no wish to do so. I love my wife and children and our domestic life together."

"I don't think Mrs. Norton understands that. She is very much clinging to the deranged hope that her past relationship with you will be revived in the future." I did not wish to share any of Caroline Norton's revelations with Sidney and hoped that he understood my warning.

Fortunately, he did. "I will see to this and let her know in no uncertain terms that this will never, ever happen. I cannot permit her to harm herself with false hopes, nor can I allow her to harm Liz. My wife has been through quite enough as it is."

I nodded. "Despite everything that has happened, I am relieved that Mrs. Norton was not involved in this sordid affair, which would have brought an even greater grief to your family."

Sidney finally sat down across from me. "Let us speak on other topics. I understand that Dr. Snow has discovered that the source of the cholera outbreak is centered upon a water pump in Broad Street."

"Yes," I said, not ready to admit that the doctor had been completely correct in his assessment about the spread of the disease while I had been very wrong. "He was able to trace it to a nearby cesspool into which someone had tossed a fouled, infected baby diaper. The disease leached from the cesspool into the pump water."

"Remarkable," Sidney replied. "I wonder if that means we can control any future outbreaks by simply seeking out from where the initial victim has drawn water. Imagine London without constant visitations by King Cholera."

I nodded. "Dr. Snow intends to publish his findings on it, which he hopes will not only inform public opinion but affect public policy. He has done a good turn for the city."

Sidney was quiet, as if gathering his thoughts. Finally I spoke. "Sidney?"

"Yes. Speaking of good turns, Flo, I've transmitted your hospital recommendations to Dr. Hall at Scutari. But even as the dispatch left my hands, I knew that the war effort would need more help than that. I have received an answer to an inquiry I made as to what the state of affairs truly is in the Crimea. I have learned that the whole ambulance service is comprised of two four-wheeled wagons, and that they were sent there without horses or harnesses. Each regiment has a mere ten stretchers for moving the wounded, and the stretcher bearers come from the Hospital Conveyance Corps."

I shook my head. "What is that?"

"They are men too old or too decrepit to be soldiers, and so they are assigned duties as stretcher bearers. But they often cannot perform even that task. Moreover, Dr. Hall—who was given the task of readying the medical service—prepared for a ten-thousand-man force. We will end up sending three times that many. Our soldiers have been deployed without shelter tents, without winter uniforms, and certainly without adequate food. There is only one surgeon for every two hundred troops. I stand on the precipice of complete disaster, Flo." Sidney's haggard expression relayed that fear well.

"I need someone to go to the Crimea, to take a firm hand in organizing medical care into something humane and competent. I want you to go there yourself."

I sat still, full of conflicted emotions. I was flattered, to be sure, but . . . why me? Surely there were competent doctors to do this? I had been working inside a hospital myself for only a year. Of course, I had made improvements there and then to Middlesex and had already received a glowing letter of appreciation from Dr. Goodfellow, but still . . .

Sidney must have seen the indecision on my face. "I am prepared to name you the Superintendent of the Female Nursing Establishment in the English Military General Hospitals in Turkey. You may choose whatever nurses you wish to go with you, but it needs to be done quickly."

I still hesitated.

Sidney smiled broadly in encouragement. "You will fix it all right up, Flo. You must do this for God and Queen, and the good of England."

I swallowed my uncertainty and slowly nodded my head. Yes, I would go, as a fulfillment of duty to both England and my divine calling. And in thanks that Alberto had not shown up again to relieve himself upon my boots.

CHAPTER 23

I finally sat down to respond to Richard's letter.

No. 1 Harley Street, Marylebone

My dearest Richard,

I send you happy felicitations from London where, as you know, I have been working as superintendent of a hospital for governesses. It has been the fulfillment of all the dreams which I shared with you on many occasions. It has not replaced Old Dreams of mine, but I am well content.

I am in receipt of your verses, for which I thank you. I regret to inform you that I shall be unable to correspond with you on it for some time to come, as I have agreed to raise a contingent of nurses to go to the Crimea at the earliest possible date. I anticipate that to be in the next two weeks.

I trust you are also well content, and do not think too harshly of your old friend for any past Unhappiness or Distress I may have caused.

As for me, I will always harbor the most tender respect for your Person.

I remain humbly and ever—

Your Flo

I was glad that Sidney had created an excuse for me, as, even after all this time, I found my willpower where Richard was concerned to be wavering. If enough time had passed without something to divert me, I might have written to him and suggested that we run away to the continent together.

Thank goodness a war had come along to save me.

Mary tapped at the door, interrupting my thoughts. "Miss Florence, would you like a luncheon tray?"

I flicked my glance to the clock on my desk. It was nearly half past one. "Perhaps later. Why don't you eat quickly and then gather your notes so you can make a visit with me?"

"A visit?"

"Yes. We're going to visit Father Bradshaw at St. Patrick's to see about gathering up some nuns to go to the Crimea."

"Nuns! The Crimea! Whatever are you talking about, Miss Florence?" In everything we had been through together, I had never seen Mary look so shocked. "What will your mother think?"

I put down my pen and carefully blotted my letter. "I am much more concerned about what *you* think, Goose, as I'd like you to go with me."

"To the Crimea?" Her voice squeaked so sharply I was surprised I didn't hear dogs howling outside.

Perhaps I had been too blunt with her. "Think on it, Goose.

I won't be leaving for a few weeks. I'd love to have you with me to continue working on the notes for my book."

"Notes?" she squeaked again. "Shall I take dictation while men with bayonets stab at us?"

Her melodramatic imagery made me smile. "We will be at the hospital, far away from actual fighting. But there will be more blood than you are used to seeing."

"Oh dear. Dear me. Haven't we been through enough? What would Milo say if he heard this?" Mary was fretting in earnest now.

"I believe he would say you were very brave."

She still looked uncertain. No, she was almost panicked.

"Do not think it a stay in purgatory, Goose. After all, Sidney is certain the war will only last a couple more months, so we couldn't possibly be there very long."

Mary continued to stare at me, her expression an amusing blend of dismay and astonishment. I rose from my desk to head downstairs to seek out a Penny Black stamp. "Coming?" I prodded her gently.

I left my study without looking back to see whether she was following me. My mind was already whirling with new plans for training an entirely new set of nurses for work in a war setting.

I knew I would face numerous hardships—none of my usual luxuries of food and clothing, little contact with the outside world, and encounters with surgeons who would no doubt disapprove of my presence—yet I felt a creeping excitement I had never felt before.

I would handpick nuns to become my cadre of nurses, using

the criteria that Pastor Fliedner had used in managing Kaiser-swerth. As a group, we would air out hospitals, bring nourishing food to the poor wounded soldiers, and prove that nursing was critical to their recovery.

I laughed in delight and joy for the first time in weeks.

Author's Note

In the first book of this series, I presented the reader with the Establishment for Gentlewomen During Temporary Illness, or as I call it, the Establishment. Although **Florence Nightingale (1820–1910)** was viewed with suspicion by many people for running a small hospital—what gently born woman would do such a thing?—she was generally permitted free rein to run it as she pleased. Thus was it made over into a very successful hospital in the short time that she ran it, until she was asked to go to the Crimean War in late 1854, after the cholera outbreak in Soho.

The astute reader will notice that I have overlapped the events surrounding the cholera outbreak of 1854 and the initiation of the Crimean War. Cholera arrived in Soho on August 31 of that year and was largely gone by the middle of September. Troops did not begin arriving in the Crimea until September 13th. I moved up the timeline for the war to better suit my fictional timeline.

By the middle of the nineteenth century, much of Soho was a decaying mess of slaughterhouses, sewers, and cesspits. Combined with the unsanitary overcrowding of many homes, the area was a powder keg of pestilence ready to be lit. The flame came in the form of cholera in September 1854. Cholera was already a fairly common occurrence in London, with outbreaks occurring periodically over the decades. The Thames was also heavily polluted with untreated sewage, a problem that would not be significantly addressed until after the "Great Stink" of 1858.

In fact, outbreaks occurred in many places across the world in the nineteenth century: Hungary, Egypt, Paris, New York, and Mexico, to name a few.

Almost as if the great plague had come back from the seventeenth century, few families in Soho were spared the loss of at least one family member in 1854. "King Cholera" did not discriminate between rich and poor, nor young and old. It was thoroughly devastating for the month that it lasted, killing more than 600 people. It killed as quickly as the plague, too, sometimes overnight. It should be noted, though, that the worst cholera outbreak in London's history was in 1849, claiming more than 14,000 lives.

Researchers would later discover that the Broad Street well had been dug only three feet from an old cesspit that had been lost when the city widened the street. The cesspit had begun to leak fecal bacteria from the cloth diaper of a baby who had contracted cholera from another source and whose diaper had been washed into this cesspit.

The Soho outbreak, however, which would become known as the Broad Street Outbreak because of its concentration at the water pump in that location, would prove to be a pivotal event in the science of epidemiology.

John Snow (1813–1858) was a physician who traced the source of the cholera outbreak to the water pump at Broad

Street. He was the first to propose what is now the accepted mechanism for transmission of cholera—that victims swallow something infected and it multiplies in the intestines. Snow had a difficult time convincing authorities that the pump was the source of the problem, since many people—including Florence Nightingale—believed that diseases were spread by noxious odors, or miasmas. It simply wasn't deemed possible that cholera could be passed through a contaminated water supply. Once Snow made his case thoroughly enough to have the Broad Street well pump handle removed as an experiment, the outbreak stopped almost immediately.

Although the leaking cesspit was identified as the primary problem, very little was done at the time to correct the numerous sewage problems in Soho, and it would continue to be a dangerous place until 1858, when the "Great Stink" finally resulted in the creation of a sewer network for Central London.

Snow is most famous for his work in epidemiology but also made major contributions to anesthesia. He was one of the first physicians to study dosages for ether and chloroform as surgical anesthetics, and in fact personally administered chloroform to Queen Victoria when she gave birth to the last two of her nine children.

Interestingly, Snow lived for about a decade in the 1830s as a vegetarian and completely abstinent from alcohol. When his health deteriorated in the 1840s, he returned to meat-eating and drinking wine, although he always boiled water before drinking it. He never married. He suffered a stroke at the relatively young age of forty-five and died less than a week later on June 16, 1858.

Another great influence on the study of disease outbreaks was an unusual one, **Henry Whitehead (1825–1896).** Whitehead was the twenty-nine-year-old assistant curate of St. Luke's Church in Soho during the Broad Street Outbreak. Following his ordination in 1851, he took up residence in the crowded slums of the Berwick Street area and became a welcome guest in the homes of his parishioners. His social acceptance proved of great value when he later became actively involved in proving John Snow wrong—only to prove him right.

Whitehead was very troubled by the cholera outbreak, primarily because he thought news reports of panic and wholesale demoralization of the area were exaggerated. He wrote his own account of the epidemic in 1854 but made no mention of the Broad Street pump. Like Florence, Whitehead was a believer in miasma theory.

However, a medical committee was carrying out its own investigations and invited both Snow and Whitehead to become members. Snow introduced Whitehead to his ideas, which Whitehead rejected outright. He looked forward to conducting the inquiry into the outbreak, which he believed would firmly demonstrate Snow's theory to be incorrect.

For the first half of 1855, Whitehead's acceptance among the poor of Soho enabled him to interview residents in great detail about their sanitary arrangements, water consumption from the Broad Street pump, and other valuable demographic data. At the conclusion of his interviews, Whitehead could no longer ignore Snow's theory and became a believer that cholera was spread through water contaminated by human waste.

In 1866, when cholera again came to London, Whitehead was considered the main authority on the Broad Street Outbreak, since Snow had died seven years earlier. Whitehead's efforts to caution the city on the public health lessons of the past went unheeded, and the disease raced through thousands of homes in the crowded slums of East London.

In addition to his work with cholera, Whitehead developed a special interest and expertise in juvenile delinquency during his life.

Whitehead worked in several other London parishes before moving to the small town of Brampton, in Cumbria, in 1874, and later to Newlands in Cumberland in 1884, finally becoming vicar at Lanercost for five years before his death on March 5, 1896. He left behind a widow and two daughters.

Although there were indeed churchmen who owned—and profited greatly from—properties in areas like Soho, there is no evidence that Whitehead ever did.

Stephen Jennings Goodfellow (1809–1895) was appointed as assistant physician at Middlesex Hospital in 1849 and was later made full physician in 1858. He was not only the hospital's lecturer on medicine, but he was also widely known in both England and America as an expert in the diagnosis and treatment of nervous and hysterical disorders.

Middlesex Hospital itself was a teaching hospital in Fitzrovia. Founded by twenty benefactors in 1745, the original location was in Windmill Street. It was moved to Mortimer Street in 1757 and opened with 64 beds. The hospital was expanded several times and by 1854 had 240 beds. The hospital remained in its Mortimer Street location until it was permanently closed in 2005.

It was indeed the first hospital in England to have a maternity ward, or "lying-in beds." It did also open up a special ward for sick French clergy who had escaped the French Revolution.

Even more fascinating was that it had the first endowment for a cancer ward—dating back to 1791.

During the cholera outbreak of 1854, Middlesex Hospital was overwhelmed with the sick and dying. Florence volunteered her services there.

Reappearing in Florence's story are Secretary at War **Sidney Herbert (1810–1861)** and his wife—and Florence's friend—**Elizabeth "Liz" à Court (1822–1911)**. Sidney Herbert was responsible for Florence going to the Crimea.

Elizabeth's father, **General Charles à Court-Repington (1785–1861)**, was a senior British Army command and politician. He joined the Army as an ensign in 1801 and progressed through the ranks to lieutenant-general in 1851. He was promoted to full general in 1856.

Born the third son of Sir William Ashe à Court, 1st Baronet of Heytesbury, he added "Repington" to his name by royal license in 1855 to comply with the will instructions of a cousin.

For a short time, Charles à Court served in Parliament representing Heytesbury, but gave up the seat.

While serving as a major in the 1st Greek Light Infantry, À Court was made a Companion of the Order of the Bath on the occasion of King William IV's coronation in 1830.

He was given the colonelcy of the 41st (Welsh) Regiment of Foot in 1848, which he held for the rest of his life. Formed in 1719, this regiment counted a young Arthur Wellesley, the future Duke of Wellington, as one of the men who passed through its ranks.

The regiment was sent to the First Anglo-Afghan War, seeing action in Kandahar and Ghazni. It would later be sent to the Crimea.

The 5th Dragoon Guards was a cavalry regiment raised by the Duke of Shrewsbury in 1685 as the Duke of Shrewsbury's Regiment of Horse. It was renamed the 5th Regiment of

Dragoon Guards in 1788, and then as the 5th (Princess Charlotte of Wales's) Regiment of Dragoon Guards in 1804. It saw service in major battles such as Blenheim, Salamanca, Balaklava, Sevastopol, and at least two dozen battles during the Great War. They were consolidated with the Inniskillings (6th Dragoons) to form the 5th/6th Dragoons in 1922. The regiment was *not* present for the Disaster in Afghanistan.

The complicated Anglo-Afghan Wars were fought in three conflicts: 1839–1842, 1878–1880, and a final clash in 1919. Great Britain fought from its base in India, seeking to oppose Russian influence in Afghanistan. Although much of the cause of this series of wars was ongoing competition for control in Asia between Britain's East India Company and Russia, there were also misunderstandings regarding motive and ambitions between the two countries.

Control of the area was also the primary cause of the Crimean War, which had already started by the time of this story.

The First Anglo-Afghan War, also known as the Disaster in Afghanistan, was destined to occur from the moment that Dōst Mohammad Khan (1793–1863) ascended the throne of Afghanistan in 1826.

Dōst Mohammad realized that both Great Britain and Russia were posturing for influence in Afghanistan, and he was concerned for the independence of his nation. His actions to preserve his nation's identity caused the British to believe he was hostile to them, or at least unable to resist Russian invasion. Great Britain decided to take control of Afghan affairs, first through an unsatisfactory negotiation with Dōst Mohammad, then by attempting to place a previously deposed—and despised—leader, Shah Shojā, on the throne in Mohammad's place.

The British were wildly unpopular with the Afghans. The country was so poor that even a private could live very well there on his meager salary. The British became known for extravagances beyond the Afghans' wildest dreams—installing enormous pleasure gardens, building ice-skating rinks, furnishing mansions with elaborate crystal chandeliers, staging horse races, playing cricket, and hosting lavish dinners. Many in the British leadership were viewed as imperious and arrogant.

But their greatest offense was in the treatment of Afghan women. Because the British could easily live like kings, many poverty-stricken Afghan women—who were considered great beauties by the British—were willing to enter into romantic relationships with the men. Some were paid for their services, but other relationships resulted in marriages. In fact, Dōst Mohammad's own niece married a Captain Robert Warburton, and a Lieutenant Lynch married the sister of a tribal chief. The Afghan men considered it humiliating to see their women fall in love with "infidels."

For their part, the British found the Afghans to be a wild, undisciplined, uneducated, and heathen people, whose greatest shortcoming lay in their moral code of *Pashtunwali* ("the way of the Pashtuns"). This strict set of rules for the men of the Pashtun tribe (the dominant ethnic group) contained a command that a man had to avenge any insult, real or imagined, with violence, in order to be considered a man. The British also reviled the Afghan practice of honor killings against the women who had taken up with members of the Army. Moreover, these tribesmen had no military training, but were ferociously warlike and forever fighting one another, much to British disdain.

In the military incursion that followed, Mohammad surrendered to British forces following the capture of his family in

1840, and he was deported to India. However, Shah Shojā and the East India Company forces would not long maintain the upper hand. The Afghans would tolerate neither a foreign occupation nor a king imposed upon them by a foreign power, and constant insurrections broke out. The British strongly pressured Shah Shojā to implement a standing army, but knowing that this would do away with the power of the individual tribal chiefs, the Shah Shojā rejected the idea on the grounds that Afghanistan lacked the financial ability to fund a standing army.

Shah Shojā was killed in an 1842 rebellion, and as the British (around 4,500 British and Indian troops and 12,000 camp followers) attempted a retreat from the capital of Kabul, they were massacred by bands of Afghan fighters.

Mohammad returned to the throne, and Great Britain continued to be unhappy with growing Russian influence. Parliament took control of India in 1858, and the East India Company completely dissolved in 1874. In 1875, the newly appointed governor-general of India, Lord Lytton, announced that he was sending a "mission" to Kabul. On the Afghan throne now was Shīr ʿAlī Khan, the third son of Dōst Mohammad. Shīr ʿAlī refused the British permission to enter Afghanistan, but in 1878 admitted Russia's General Stolyetov to Kabul.

Viceroy Lytton decided to crush Afghanistan over the insult and launched a second invasion in November 1878. Shīr ʿAlī fled Kabul, and the British government recognized his son, Yaʿqūb Khan, as emir of the country. In return, Yaʿqūb Khan agreed not only to hosting a permanent British embassy but to conducting foreign relations according to the wishes of the British government.

Once more, the victory was short-lived. In 1879, the British envoy was murdered in Kabul, and British military forces were once more dispatched to occupy the capital city. Yaʿqūb Khan abdicated, and his nephew, ʿAbd al-Raḥmān, became emir in 1880. During his reign, the modern boundaries of Afghanistan were drawn up in an effort between the British and the Russians. The lines effectively became a buffer between Russia and British India.

The third Anglo-Afghan War was a short, month-long conflict in 1919. When the existing ruler of the time was assassinated at the conclusion of World War I, his son Amānullāh Khan took possession of the throne and declared total independence from Great Britain. Although Afghanistan was now nominally self-governed, Great Britain still exercised great influence on the country's affairs. Thus began yet another conflict. This time, however, the British Indian Army was exhausted from the demands of fighting the world war, and a peace treaty was quickly signed that recognized Afghanistan's independence.

At the same time, the Afghans concluded a treaty of friendship with the new Bolshevik regime in the Soviet Union and became one of the first nations to recognize the Soviet government.

Many British voices, from Lord Aberdeen to Benjamin Disraeli, would criticize the war as rash and nonsensical, as the "threat" from Russia was overexaggerated given logistical problems she would have to solve to scale impassable mountain barriers in order to invade that country given resources available at the time.

In 1979, during the Cold War, the Soviets entered Afghanistan to prop up the communist government there against a growing insurgency against Soviet influence. However, the Afghan resistance proved too much, and Kabul returned to Afghan control in 1992.

The United States led an invasion of Afghanistan in 2001 to overthrow the Taliban. Russia did not participate, although she did permit supplies to pass through Russian territory.

Major-General William George Keith Elphinstone (1782–1842) was the British officer in command of the British Garrison in Kabul. He was elderly, unwell, indecisive, and utterly unfit for his post. He is buried in an unmarked grave in Afghanistan.

Captain Sir Alexander Burnes (1805–1841) was a Scottish explorer and diplomat. He traveled in disguise through Afghanistan in 1831, thus providing the first detailed accounts of Afghan politics. He later became a regular political agent at Kabul.

Because of Burnes's reputation for womanizing and the Afghan agitation against British occupation, a mob gathered outside the captain's residence in Kabul in 1841, killing both Burnes and his brother.

It was actually Burnes who kept an Afghan slave girl belonging to a Pashtun chief. However, it suited my story better to have it be true of General Charles Ashe à Court.

General à Court's son, **Charles Henry Wyndham à Court (1810–1903)**, was fairly unremarkable. In 1852, he was elected MP for Wilton in Wiltshire. Like his father, he resigned his seat, but to become a special commissioner of property and income tax in Ireland. There is no speech of his noted for the entire three years of his term in that position.

He did marry Emily Currie in 1854, and more notably produced a son, Lieutenant-Colonel Charles à Court Repington, who became a leading *Times* military correspondent. The son is believed to be the first person to use the term "First World War" in September 1918, hoping that the title would serve as a reminder that a second world war was a possibility in the future.

Caroline Elizabeth Sarah Sheridan Norton (1808–1877) led an unexpected life of social reform. The granddaughter of playwright Richard Sheridan, she was in near poverty after both he and her father died a year apart.

Salvation seemed to come in the form of marriage to **George Norton (1800–1875)** in 1827. However, despite three children, the marriage was a public nightmare of violent tantrums and lawsuits. Their relationship devolved much as I have described it in the story.

However, despite her sufferings, Caroline's intense campaigning would lead to the passing of the Custody of Infants Act of 1839, the Matrimonial Causes Act of 1857, and the Married Women's Property Act of 1870.

A younger Sidney Herbert was involved with Caroline for a few years in the early 1840s, but when it became apparent that she was not going to be able to procure a divorce for herself, he looked elsewhere and married the vivacious Elizabeth à Court. The two would go on to have seven children together and were both avid proponents of Florence's work.

Caroline was a prolific author of political pamphlets, poetry, novels, and plays. *Stuart of Dunleath* is a thinly veiled autobiographical novel Caroline wrote in 1851. Was it a paean to Sidney Herbert? I shall let the reader decide.

Acknowledgments

When I first sat down to begin writing this series, I had no idea how enjoyable it would be to inhabit Florence's skin. However, I've come to feel as though I know her at a deep and profound level.

Of course, I have the pleasant task of making up Florence's adventures, while there are others who willingly take on the effort of supporting all the fun I have.

First, I am grateful to my friend, Petra Utara, who pushes, cajoles, and threatens me as needed to ensure that this procrastinating writer meets her deadlines.

As always, my family pitches in to review my books to ensure my manuscripts are as "clean" as possible before I turn them in. I would be lost without my husband, Jon; my brother, Tony Papadakis; and my sister-in-law, Marian Wheeler.

Because of reader Raven Ackerman and her husband, Chris, I have been graciously welcomed into the Gettysburg, Pennsylvania, reenactor community. I love every opportunity I have been given to be involved in talks and presentations on Victorian life. I also love our dinners with the Ackermans at Dobbin House.

Expert seamstresses Donna Huffman and Dana Dement are responsible for accurately transforming me into Florence based upon historical photographs of the Lady with the Lamp. It gives me great joy to portray Florence at book signings and other events.

Florence would not be brought to life within these pages without the dedicated efforts of my publisher, Crooked Lane Books. I'm appreciative of senior editor Faith Black Ross's attention to detail, as well as for the enthusiastic responsiveness of editorial assistant Jenny Chen and marketing associate Sarah Poppe. Melanie Sun's cover designs have completely surpassed all my expectations. I'm lucky to be part of the Crooked Lane family.

Dei gratia.